"I have heard talk that the fire at the Cloister was not accidental."

Mariel's eyes in the candlelight revealed her shock. Inanely, she said, "That is always said after a fire."

"But?" Ian prompted.

"I don't know." Tears of sorrow at the loss of her beloved home glittered brightly as she flung out her hands. "Why would anyone want to destroy the Cloister?"

"Do you have any enemies?"

She laughed coldly. "You were at the town meeting tonight!"

"Those are adversaries, not enemies. There is a difference." He refused to let her escape from his hands as they grasped her shoulders. "Mariel, if the fire was intentionally set, you must contact the constable. There may be a madman in the Cloister. Who knows what such a person would do next?"

Terror wiped all other emotions from her face. Ian stared at her in disbelief. He had seen Mariel sparkling with happiness and fiery eyed with rage, but not totally incapacitated by fear. Not knowing what else to do, he drew her into his arms.

This was one situation he intended to remedy soon. He never wanted to view such naked terror on her face again.

The Foxbridge Legacy
by Jo Ann Ferguson

SYBILL
REBECCA
MARIEL

MARIEL

Jo Ann Ferguson

TUDOR PUBLISHING COMPANY
NEW YORK AND LOS ANGELES

Tudor Publishing Company

ISBN: 0-944276-43-1

Printed in the United States of America

First Tudor printing — March, 1989

For Dad and Mom

Who taught me to nurture my dreams,
and gave me the impetus to find them,
and who, from my earliest memories,
were an example of true and lasting love.
With thanks and love, this book is especially for you.

Prologue

Screams ruptured the night. A child's screams, exquisitely poignant in their helpless desperation. Even the everpresent pulse of the waves on the beach beyond the house was obliterated by the sound.

Footsteps. Running feet and the impact of a fist on a thick oak door.

"Georgie! Georgie, open the door!"

No response but an escalation of the terror in the child's voice. The man in the corridor ignored the sobbing of the child's nurse and the curses of two huge attendants holding massive cudgels. He pulled a handkerchief from the pocket of his silk nightrobe. Flinging it in the weeping woman's direction, he made one final attempt at reason.

"Georgie! Open the—" The innocent child's shriek of agony halted him.

He could not afford to delay. Sorrowfully, he turned to the burly men and nodded. As they raised the clubs, the dark-haired man turned his head to see the nurse wiping her eyes and wringing the handkerchief into shreds. His lean face remained shadowed in the uneven candlelight.

Each crash against the door brought more screams from within. The dark-haired man breathed a fervent prayer that they could save one. It was too late for the other.

Exultant shouts from the attendants announced the forced opening of the door. They swarmed into the storage room on the top floor of the house.

As the two strong men wrestled a raving man from his terrified victim, the dark-haired man watched silently. His flesh and blood, the child conceived of his loins. He shivered as the demented face turned toward him.

"How could you do this to them?" he demanded uselessly. He knew there would be no answer.

The madman's mouth, slack with insanity and soaked with spittle, moved, but no coherent words came from it. His glazed eyes followed the passage of his freed captive as she was assisted across the room by the hysterical nurse. With a growl, he broke free of his guards. His sudden surge of strength caught them by surprise.

In the doorway, the child heard the warning shouts. She turned to see the horror advancing on her. The child's blue eyes widened in unutterable fear. As the madman reached for her, she vindictively cried out a childish rhyme.

"Georgie Porgie, Pudding and Pie,
Kissed the girls and made them cry.
When the boys came out to play,
Georgie Porgie ran away."

The deranged man stopped and gazed at her with his own terror. He dropped to his knees. Covering his tear-streaked face with slender bone-ridged hands, he wept in infantile abandon.

Everyone in the room froze. The little girl wiped the blood from her face onto her nightgown sleeve. Regarding the sobbing man with unadulterated contempt too mature for her young features, she was pulled from the room by her nurse.

"No!" she cried. "Don't let them hurt Georgie." The nurse halted before she added to the child's injuries by dragging the youngster down the third-floor staircase.

With the tattered handkerchief, she wiped the stream of blood along the child's pale face.

"He hurt you. He—he—" The nurse could not continue through her sobs.

Patting her nurse on the shoulder, the child murmured compassionate words she meant with all her heart.

"That could be me. His madness could be mine."

The woman moaned and embraced her. The youngster pretended to be comforted while she listened to what was taking place in the attic room.

The silence broke when finally the man in the silk nightrobe ordered in a tired voice, "Take him to his room. Make sure he doesn't escape again. I will have the parson brought."

"And the sheriff?" She recognized the voice of the larger attendant.

"Yes, I will send for the constable as well. He must be satisfied with his own investigation." His voice strengthened as he stated, "When he arrives, tell him he cannot speak to the child. She is too upset by what she has seen."

"She must answer his questions."

"No!" he shouted with uncharacteristic rage. "What she has seen tonight could make her as insane as that fool. I will not allow that to happen. She is the only one left. She must be protected from the curse inflicting that one."

He could not bring himself to call Georgie by his given name. After tonight, the child wondered if he would want to think of her cousin Georgie as his son again.

The child watched as her uncle sent the gathering of curious servants scurrying away. His shoulders sagged in defeat as he descended the narrow stairs. The little girl followed, her nurse in tow. Bent by her own burden of the truth, she knew a death at the huge house would not be unexpected. Too much had happened here to have such a heinous crime be any cause of wonder.

Chapter One

"Lady Mariel! Lady Mariel! The reverend is here to see you."

Sparks of blue fury snapped in her narrowed eyes as the woman turned to see the maid coming toward her. She stood and clapped her ash-coated hands together. A sooty cloud rose to dim the raven lights of her hair. She tugged irritably at the fashionable silk gown now marred by fingerprints and a rip on the left side of the pink skirt.

"The reverend? Why in the blazes would I want to talk to Reverend Tanner now?" She glanced around in disbelief. A fire-weakened beam creaked ominously overhead, and she stepped quickly out of what once had been the cell of a fourteenth-century monk. "Tell him I'm too busy investigating the extent of the damage to the Cloister."

"But, Lady Mariel—"

"For God's sake, Grace, just tell Reverend Tanner I'm too busy today. I'll see him next Tuesday about the society fundraiser."

"But, Lady Mariel—" She paused when she saw that Lady Mariel Wythe had turned back to her grim task. Grace shivered as she glanced at the destruction around her. The once-magnificent original section of Foxbridge Cloister had been reduced to smoking ruins. Her nose wrinkled in distaste. The place stank of damp, scorched

1

wood. Even the strong breezes from the sea could not cleanse it.

She wondered why Lady Mariel had come out here. Lord Foxbridge would not be pleased to learn his niece had done something so dangerous. He would not want her poking about among the shattered glass and unstable stone walls. Even though he delighted in queer explorations, he wanted Lady Mariel to have, as he said so often, "a normal life."

Knowing it would be futile to argue with the chatelaine of the Cloister, she picked her way back to the "new" section. Built in the sixteenth century, it postdated the original monastery by nearly four hundred years. Fortunately, it had suffered little damage in the fire.

Mariel swore under her breath as she tripped on a fallen timber and scraped her shin on a stone bench in the center of the narrow hallway. Why the wide seat had been moved to obstruct the corridor, she could not guess.

With a sigh, she sat on it and gazed sadly around her. Sorrow pulsed stronger than anger within her. She had been born at the Cloister twenty-six years before. Memories of her childhood brought to mind scenes of playing games in these passageways and attending special family services in the now-decimated chapel at the end farthest from the "new" Cloister.

The fire had been an accident. How and where it had started, no one knew. Nothing could change it. Still, she longed to steal the gentle images from her heart and make them reality. No other children would play among the empty cells and dare the ancient spirits to awaken. All they would see was the empty-eyed stare of the glassless windows in the sections of wall still standing.

Tears burned her eyes as she gazed at the sky. The lead roof, which had survived King Henry VIII's dissolution of the monasteries, the religious rage of the Civil War, and the Restoration, lay melted in great, cannon-ball-sized blobs on the stone floor. Her right forefinger still smarted from foolishly touching one of the hot masses.

A crunch made her whirl on the bench. Silk protested with a sharp rip, but she ignored it. If Phipps had not made her so furious, she would have changed before coming here. She had liked this tea gown. Now it probably was ruined beyond repair.

Her suddenly clear eyes met those of a stranger. She noted with minimal interest his sea-green eyes and dark hair. As he stepped closer, a flash of auburn blared as the sun struck his hair. His perfectly tailored morning suit was littered with ash.

"Lady Mariel?" His voice resonated richly through the remains of the long corridor. As he moved toward her, she saw he depended on a cane to walk.

Irritation overcame her instinctively courteous reaction. She had not slept since the fire started two nights ago. Fatigue lowered her barriers to release her true feelings.

"Who are you?" she demanded sharply. "What are you doing tramping through here? You could get hurt."

His professionally serene smile dimmed as he kept himself from retorting as curtly. He viewed her tattered gown and the streaks of dirt crisscrossing her face in the dried paths of tears. Her defensive stance reminded him of a medieval lady standing in the ashes of her ancestral home. It urged him to speak gently.

"My lady, I am Ian Beckwith-Carter, the new pastor at the church in Foxbridge."

"New pastor?" She scowled as she sought in her mind for an elusive memory. A cold smile settled on her lips. "Oh, yes, I remember hearing Reverend Tanner was retiring."

"Remember hearing? I assume you are not a regular churchgoer, Lady Mariel?"

Her hands settled on the bench as she struggled to remain calm. She grimaced as the coarse soot ingrained in her palms cut into her skin. Ignoring the aggravating pain, she stood.

"Reverend, if you have come to Foxbridge Cloister to lecture me on my laxness in attending church, you chose the wrong day. You are new here. When you've been in Foxbridge a while, you'll learn, as everyone else has, that it is too late to save the souls of those crazy Wythes." She brushed off her hand and extended it to him. "Good day, Reverend."

He refused to accept her dismissal. "My lady, I make it a practice to call on all my parishioners, and—"

"Consider that obligation fulfilled." She turned to walk away. When he called after her, she paused. With a sigh worthy of a martyr, she said, "Very well, Reverend. I see you are less easy to dispense with than that old fool Tanner. I will meet you in fifteen minutes in the front parlor. We shall chat as you wish." Her eyes swept the littered hallway. "There's nothing more I can do here now."

He watched as the fierce martinet transformed into a pretty woman whose heart was shattered by the destruction of her home. That image lasted only a second before her stern expression reasserted itself. He stepped back hastily as she brushed past him to return to the undamaged section of the Cloister.

"Fifteen minutes," she called over her shoulder.

With a smile, he wondered if that was also the amount of time she would grant him for this reluctant interview. He did not move until she was out of sight amid the rubble. His eyes twinkled as he imagined the confrontation to come. He had been warned, but that made him only more anxious to meet the fiery, opinionated Lady Mariel Wythe.

Picking his way back the way he had come to find her, Reverend Beckwith-Carter anticipated their meeting in the fabulous house. From his small home in the village, he had seen Foxbridge Cloister perched majestically near the sea cliffs. It overlooked the land it once had controlled. Although most of the land was owned by the families of the onetime tenant farmers, he guessed the Wythes had lost none of their imperious attitude. He suspected he would be sure of that when this meeting was completed.

By the time Mariel reached her rooms on the second floor of the Cloister, she was livid. Reverend Tanner had been bad enough, with his bigoted ideas of where women fit into the scheme of the world. His continual, far from subtle hints that she should find a husband and raise a brood of children to repopulate the Cloister irritated her. She was sure he wanted only to stop her interference in village affairs. More than once he had denounced from the pulpit the law that allowed women to vote in local elections.

His retirement should have come as a relief, but instead she would be saddled with this new, more irritating minister. That she had backed down during this first encounter must not have any bearing on their future meetings. She was so exhausted and was burdened with the task of writing to her uncle to inform him of the damage to his home. Otherwise her usually sharp wits would have found a way to send the new parson back to town after ordering him to leave her in peace.

She stormed into her room. It was situated across the hall from the master suite where her uncle slept when he resided in the Cloister. Her rooms were almost as grand, for she had had all the suites of the massive house to use in shopping to select the furniture she wanted.

The sitting room, in its pale shades of blue, was empty as she swept through it. She ignored the quiescent fireplace and the shelves of books. Too often had she seen the comfortable chairs and large desk to notice them when she was lost in her outrage.

Her bedroom overlooked the ocean on the western side of the house. She loved this room because she was never without the changing temper of nature. Wind, rain, and sun struck uncompromisingly on this side of the house. She reveled in the difference of each day.

Throwing her hat on the clean covers of her tester bed, she caught her reflection in the cheval glass and scowled. Stamping past her dressing table and the couch where she often read late into the night, she glared at her own dirty face. That she had met the new minister while she looked as if she had been cleaning chimney pots added to her fury. She rubbed some of the ashes from her cheek, but succeeded only in making a wider streak across her face.

She shouted for her companion Phipps as she stripped off her gown. Only by getting this aggravating, social obligation completed could she be rid of Reverend Beckwith-Carter. She forced his handsome face from her mind and concentrated on his officious attitude.

Already she could tell the man would prove to be intolerable. Grimacing at her image in the dressing-table mirror, she winced while trying to brush the ashes from her tangled hair.

She paused in mid-stroke as the gray flakes dropped around her like dirty snow. Sorrow dimmed the rage within her. Uncle Wilford, who bore the title of Lord Foxbridge, loved this house as she did. So often when she was younger, he would lead her by the hand and point out the beauty of the ancient house. Together they had frequently stood on the parapets. Leaning on the machicolations between each tooth of stone, they would watch the sun disappear into the ocean at their back door.

Where was Uncle Wilford now? She reached for a well-read letter. The postmark had been blurred by its transatlantic journey: United States of America. She hoped he liked it better than he had Panama. He wrote of mosquitoes and humidity that left him drenched. She was glad to know he was away from there. With the tense situation between Spain and the war-hungry United States, Central America was not safe for travelers.

Tonight she could not delay writing to him at the British embassy, which would forward any correspondence to him at his most current address. She could not soften the news. Her uncle had known such sorrow in the past decade. She did not want to augment it, but she had no choice.

Her frustration with the situation fueled her rage with the new parson's impertinent assumption that she gladly would set aside time in her day for him. She smiled wickedly. There were ways of dealing with such problems. She had done it before. Reverend Beckwith-Carter might be surprised with the result of his presumption.

Walking slowly across the beautifully trimmed lawns of the estate, the object of Mariel's rage simply enjoyed the perfection around him. This lush garden did not resemble the crowded yards of London or even the green carpet of his family's country home. Established here at the time of the birth of the Church of England, it had become one with its surroundings, like the Cloister itself.

He admired the lines of the house, trying to ignore the scorch marks on the stones. Stained glass twinkled at him in the sunshine. Three floors high, the building had weathered over time to match the color of the sea on a cloudy day.

Steps led up from the drive to a pair of plain-looking doors. A servant opened one as the new minister approached it. Curiosity emanated from his elderly face as he asked, "Did you find her, Reverend?"

"Yes, thank you." He stepped into the foyer, noting what he had seen before. A thick, oak banister wove its way up the stairs to showcase an intricate window on a landing. From the first floor, he could not determine its exact pattern, but he suspected it was a depiction of the family crest. "Will you direct me to the front parlor? Lady Mariel asked me to meet her there."

The butler could not hide his shock. "Are you sure you understood her correctly?"

Ian laughed shortly. He did not need to tell the impeccably dressed man that he had been forewarned by many about the headstrong Lady Mariel Wythe. Those who had spoken to him had exaggerated neither her stubborn nature nor her incredible beauty. He did not intend to let her waylay him from doing the work he had come here to do.

"The front parlor she said," he answered.

Dodsley, the butler, nodded. He appreciated the parson intentionally misunderstanding *him*. It would not be proper to show that Lady Mariel seldom bound herself to such normal conventions of behavior. "Please follow me, sir."

The room to which he led the auburn-haired man was warm with spring sunshine. After the butler said he would see to the tea tray, Ian sat on a green upholstered sofa. He glanced at the fine collection of antiques. Some of the pieces looked as if they had been purchased at the time the house was built. Heavy with wood and dark with age, they clustered in the corners of the huge room. Near the center, where he sat, the furniture was of a

more current style, with horsehair upholstery and carved
rosewood arms and legs. To one side, a huge piano
waited with its keyboard exposed. He smiled as he noted
it had not been draped to hide its legs, as society
dictated was proper. He should have guessed Lady
Mariel's family would not accept such prudish practices.
From her outspoken reaction at their meeting, he was
sure that she did exactly as she wished.

The musical instrument sat beneath a portrait of a
woman dressed in the Elizabethan style. Her coloring
matched Lady Mariel's enough for him to guess this
must be some distant ancestress of hers. He dismissed
the portrait as he glanced at the ceiling. A plaster ceiling
medallion was surrounded by designs he could see
needed refurbishing. Like the weathered stone on the
outside of the Cloister, the interior showed signs of its
many centuries. He rose politely as Lady Mariel Wythe
entered the room accompanied by another woman and,
surprisingly, an enthusiastic spaniel. He ignored the
black and brown dappled dog as he regarded his hostess.
Although his face remained serene, he was shocked by
the transformation. The dirty-faced scamp had become
the archetype of a titled lady in this sixtieth year of
Queen Victoria's illustrious reign.

Her gown of deep green perfectly accented the
decor of the room. Black lace hung from the high collar
and draped across the front to hide the curves of her
body. Matching lace at the cuffs accented the glistening
sable of her hair, now demurely pulled back in a perfectly coiffed bun. The one thing that had not changed were
her snapping eyes. They looked at him and away,
obviously dismissing him as nothing more than a pest.

"Reverend Beckwith-Carter, please sit down," she
said with what he knew was mock warmth. "Tea should
be here soon. I anticipated that you would like refresh-
ments before your journey back to Foxbridge."

"Assuredly, my lady." He hid his smile and his
glance shifted to the other woman in the room. Her
position as companion to the irascible Lady Mariel
Wythe was proclaimed by her severe dress and the
conservative style of her iron-gray hair.

"This is Amanda Phipps," Mariel said offhandedly. "She wishes to join our conversation, for she has wanted to meet you." She did not add that she had been disgruntled to have Phipps announce she was attending this meeting. Having her companion with her would mean she must watch her tongue. She did not want to distress Miss Phipps again by being impertinent to a man of the cloth.

Ian shook the older woman's hand gravely. "Miss Phipps."

"It's a pleasure to meet you, Reverend," she said in her scratchy voice.

"Reverend Beckwith-Carter?" Mariel asked sharply. "I meant to ask you before. Are you related to the family at Beckwith Grange?"

He returned his attention to Lady Mariel, and willingly. She was lovely, and he admitted to himself that he enjoyed looking at her. He was glad others had prepared him for facing this adversary.

"Distantly. I do have cousins at the Carters's home of Avelet Court to the north of Foxbridge. As they are related to your neighbors, I assume I must be as well."

"Do sit," she repeated. When she saw he would not until the ladies did, she dropped to a settee. Her lips tightened as he sat next to her. To rise and choose another chair would be too impolite.

Mariel shook her head absently as Phipps asked if she wanted to pour. Such rituals did not appeal to her today. All she wanted was to have this meeting over so she could escape to the privacy of her room and the pain burning as hotly as the fire which had destroyed the old Cloister. She glanced down at the dog lying by her side and wondered how people could not understand her anguish when the spaniel did so readily.

She glanced up to see the minister watching her with an amused expression on his face. Tightly, she stated, "This is Muffin."

"Muffin?" Ian could not halt his laugh. The idea that the coldly correct Lady Mariel Wythe had given her dog such a charmingly sweet name was amusing.

"Is there something wrong with that? I don't believe it's a curse unfit for the ears of a godly man." A

glare from Miss Phipps warned her to be silent, but
Mariel felt rebellion bubbling within her. After all, she
had not invited the minister to the Cloister. That she
must suffer his mockery simply because he wore an
ecclesiastical collar seemed the worst kind of foolishness.
She refused to be intimidated by her companion. Passing
a filled cup to her guest, she did not look at him. Crisply
she asked, "What do you want with me, Reverend?"

"Lady Mariel," he said quickly as he heard Miss
Phipps's sharp intake of breath. He saw a scowl aimed
at her charge. It was evident his hostess was more bothered by his presence than he suspected. With a silent
chuckle, he wondered what had been discussed upstairs.
"I have come simply to make your acquaintance. I had
understood you were at home on Thursdays."

"You could have delayed a day or two." She did not
meet his eyes as she stirred her tea endlessly.

He said in a hushed tone, "I was very sorry to hear
about the fire. I had no idea the damage was so exten-
sive until I walked through there myself. Can you salvage
any of it?"

"I don't know." Her voice softened again as she
spoke of the house. "It doesn't seem possible the old
Cloister is gone. It has weathered so much and watched
all the changes of modern England. Now it is gone."

Her blue eyes rose to meet his. As he expressed his
sympathy for her loss, he saw something other than rage
in her volatile eyes. He could tell that for her the old
Cloister was more than a building. A bit of her had died
with its destruction.

This side of Mariel Wythe he had not been told
about by those eager to introduce him to all the gossip
of the shire. He had listened with half an ear to what
was said, for he liked to form his own opinions of
people.

"Will you rebuild?"

"Why? The building was an anachronism." She
shrugged. "It is Uncle Wilford's decision." When he
regarded her with confusion, she explained, "Wilford
Wythe is the name of the current Lord Foxbridge. He is
abroad now."

Miss Phipps spoke when the silence swelled to eat at them. Her questions of how he liked Foxbridge and his new position were ones he had answered often since his arrival.

He gave her the appropriate replies—he had honed them to perfection—while his eyes strayed again and again to the woman next to him.

She did not taste her tea or take a cake from the plate offered by Miss Phipps. Such a rigid stance he had seen taken by those who tried to mask the mourning for a family member. Never for a pile of stone. When he inadvertently cut off Miss Phipps in mid-word by turning to the younger woman, he noticed nothing but the sorrow billowing out like a dark cloud from Lady Mariel.

"I understand you are very involved in community projects, Lady Mariel."

Starting, she looked up at him in surprise. Lost in her grief while she mentally composed the letter to her uncle, she had forgotten Reverend Beckwith-Carter sat next to her. Drawing a shade over the vulnerable openness of her face, she straightened and said, "Yes, I am. It has long been the policy of the Wythes to be concerned with the welfare of the shire. I am simply continuing that tradition."

"I would be intrigued to hear about it."

"Would you?" She bit back the words she wanted to hurl at his perfectly composed, too handsome face. If only his hair did not curl so correctly across his forehead or his collar fold exactly as style commanded. Then she might not have made every effort to unruffle him to repay him for invading her home during her grief. She did not like people who made her feel inadequate.

"Yes, my lady. I have heard—"

"I am sure you have." She rose, forcing him to do the same. She smiled coldly. Sometimes convention could be used to her advantage instead of being simply a prison. "Perhaps we can continue this conversation at a later date."

Ignoring Miss Phipps's hissed displeasure at his hostess, Ian nodded. He lowered his untouched cup of tea to the tray. He picked up his cane and dark hat.

When he offered her his hand, she pretended not to see it and became involved with rearranging the tea table.

"When would be convenient?" he asked.

"Convenient? For what?" Mariel turned to him in surprise. She had hoped he would be offended and leave. It appeared he had thicker skin than the previous parson.

"To speak of your involvement in the village."

"I was not under the impression that my secular activities were of interest to you, Reverend." She moved past him to the door, her dog following like a variegated shadow. Putting her hands on the dark-green velvet portieres, she stated, "If, and I stress if, I find the time to discuss this, I will inform you. Good day, Reverend."

Her footfalls racing up the stairs echoed back into the parlor. Ian shook his head when Miss Phipps began to apologize. "No need."

"She is not usually like this." The woman wrung her hands, wanting to ease the situation. "It is the fire. Losing the Cloister like this has broken her heart."

He nodded. "I understand." He did comprehend what she could not say. Miss Phipps's devotion to her difficult lady showed him that Lady Mariel might not be as immovable as she wished to portray.

Wishing her a good day, he left the house. His carriage waited. The household staff had known the interview would be short in duration. Smiling, he picked up the reins. If Lady Mariel thought she had daunted him, she guessed wrong.

Upstairs, Mariel listened to the renewed reprimand on her unacceptable behavior. She had learned long ago to act as if she was hearing Phipps while she thought of other things. The older woman had been with her too many years for Mariel to say what she truly felt. It made Phipps happy to think her lady heeded her advice. When her companion took a breath, Mariel hastily agreed to be kinder next time she met the new minister.

As soon as she was alone, she changed into an old dress. Taking ink, paper, and a pen, she skulked down the stairs. No one stood in the foyer. She slipped around the base of the steps to flee along the hallway that led to the original part of the house.

She easily threw the new bolt on the door separating the two sections. At first, as she entered the spartan building, she could imagine nothing had changed. Within a half dozen paces, the signs of the fire dissolved her dreams. By the time she had walked a few more feet, the roof was gone and the destruction complete.

She found the bench where she had been sitting when Reverend Beckwith-Carter interrupted her. Putting the ink bottle on the stone next to her, she began the most difficult letter she had ever written.

"Dear Uncle,
"I wish I could find words to soften the blow of what I must tell you. I can think of none.
"Two nights ago there was a fire in the old Cloister. The new Cloister is relatively unharmed. The wind, in addition to the well thought-out design of the house, saved it. As for the monastery section, it. . ."

Her pen halted. She could not write the words. To do so would legitimize them. She did not want to lose the hope that she could waken and find this all to be a nightmare.

Mariel did not like to admit something had happened she was unable to fix. This helpless feeling was so strange she did not know how to handle it. Anger overwhelmed her. Whom or what she was furious with, she did not know. Having no one to blame this on increased her irrational rage.

Her toe toyed with a small pebble fallen from the wall. Even without Phipps's lecture, she had known her behavior toward the reverend was unacceptable. Although she did not care what the man thought of her, she knew her uncle would have been ashamed of her lack of hospitality. She adored her uncle and never wanted to give him cause to think badly of her. He was her only living relative, and despite his journeys to the farthest realms of the earth, a closeness existed between them that no distance could lessen.

A stone tumbled to the floor. She looked up, her sorrowful thoughts interrupted, but saw no one. She sighed.

The fire had made her too jumpy. Tomorrow she had to go into the village to deal with the problem at the Ladies' Aid Society. Then she would fulfill her promise to apologize to Reverend Beckwith-Carter.

Smiling, she collected her writing materials and rose. That would shock the new minister. Her atonement for taking out her frustration on him would be the last thing he expected. Soon he would learn that Mariel Wythe was not like the other ladies of his church.

As she walked through the rubble, Mariel decided that she would relish her relationship with Reverend Beckwith-Carter. He was not easy to cow with a sharp word. She thought they would have many confrontations during his tenure in Foxbridge. She anticipated the next gleefully.

Chapter Two

Ian heard a strange clanking from beyond the parsonage, but could not break away from his work. The prose flowed so perfectly from his pen, he hated to pause to see what was causing the sound. He enjoyed working in the cozy study. From the moment he arrived and discovered that this small house would be his home during his assignment to the church in Foxbridge, this had been his favorite room.

Far less formal than the drawing room across the hall, its walls were covered with an Oriental paper of pale cranberry. More chairs than the room should contain crowded around the paisley settee with its carved arms and cabriole legs. The centerpiece of the room was the massive, rolltop desk situated between the two front windows overlooking the village green. A side window gave him a view of the hills between the settlement and the glory of Foxbridge Cloister near the ocean.

As the noise continued, his mind refused to concentrate until he satisfied his curiosity. He pushed his chair back on the gray rug, which showed the signs of many such motions over the decades.

He arranged the pages on the top of his desk and stood to straighten his collar. As he pushed aside the cream lace curtains at the window, his eyes widened in shock. Moving along the green was a sight more bizarre than any from his wildest dreams.

Grasping his cane, he rushed to the foyer and out onto the porch just as the vehicle slowed to a stop directly in front of him. The driver of the horseless carriage lifted wide goggles and removed a full hat covered with veiling to reveal shining dark hair and a pert nose between sparkling, blue eyes.

"Lady Mariel!"

"Good morning, Reverend. I hope I haven't interrupted you. I drove in for the Ladies' Aid meeting at the schoolhouse, but I am a bit early. If you have time, I thought we could discuss the matter you hinted at during your visit to the Cloister."

Mariel had not discovered the proper phrase to allude to her behavior of the day before, so she acted as if they had parted amicably. Guessing the reverend was a gentleman, she assumed he would not correct her outrageous statement.

He offered her his hand as she stepped lightly from the strange vehicle. "What is it?"

With a laugh, she realized he was so astounded by her automobile that he had heard nothing she'd said. "This is the latest form of transportation. It is an electric automobile."

"Electric?"

"Yes. I have a generator in the stable to recharge it. We have no electricity in the Cloister, so it was easiest to put the generator in an unused building. Every night, I connect the cables to the batteries behind the seat. In about ten hours, they charge enough so I can get a day's driving out of it."

"An automobile," he repeated in awe. He ran his hand along the chrome decorating the outside of the blue machine.

Outwardly, it looked little different from a normal buggy. The four wheels could have been exchanged for the ones on his carriage. The seat was positioned slightly farther back. Instead of reins, a lever sprouted up next to the driver's seat. Pedals on the floor must deal with starting or stopping it, but he did not have enough knowledge about these new automobiles to guess which. On the floor in front of the driver, gauges had been inserted into the dashboard. All of it was as alien to him as if it had been brought from the moon.

Stretching to look closer at the interior of the vehicle, whose top was lowered, he asked, "How far can you travel?"

She shrugged, watching his eager examination of the automobile. "I am not exactly sure. I use it only around Foxbridge. I can drive myself without tying up the time of one of the workers in the stables. The man who sold it to me told me it has a top speed of nearly fourteen miles per hour, and it can go for thirteen hours before it must be recharged. Of course, on these twisting roads, I must travel much slower."

"Amazing." He glanced at her and saw her knowing smile at his boyish awe. "I am sure you get this reaction wherever you go."

"All the time." She looked with affection across the green to the small, white church and the two storied schoolhouse. Grouped around them were small houses much like the parsonage. "Fortunately, the people here in the village are accustomed to 'Lady Mariel's contraption.'"

When he stepped closer, he gazed at her with the same intensity he had used to appraise the automobile. She did not back down before his regard. Her eyes appraised his reaction to his inability to intimidate her this way. Slowly, her gaze traced the uncompromising line of his jaw and the firm planes of his face. He was an undeniably handsome man. His clerical collar and the subdued color of his white shirt and black vest flattered his masculinity.

Softly, he asked, "You came to speak with me, Lady Mariel?"

"Although I hate to admit it, I came to apologize." The words were not as difficult to say as she had feared. "Reverend, I can only hope you will excuse my intolerable actions yesterday."

"You were bereaved by your loss."

"Yes," she whispered, astounded by his ability to discern what she tried to hide. She shook herself mentally. Compelling green eyes could not be allowed to make her forget herself. "Yes, I was," she continued in a

normal voice, "but that was no excuse to act as I did. If
you want to learn about the community groups I am
involved with, I would be glad to answer your questions."

"Won't you come inside, my lady?" He offered his
arm. For a second, she hesitated, then tossed her hat
and driving goggles onto the passenger seat. Her fingers
touched the fine linen of his shirt sleeve to rest on the
strong muscles beneath. Instantly, she had to fight the
desire to pull away. A tingle, like a low electric shock,
raced through her. Only her desire to hide her reaction
kept her hand on his bent arm. As if they had talked of
nothing more personal than the automobile, he asked,
"You like being different, don't you?"

"Yes," she answered hastily. She was pleased he had
not noted how his nearness disconcerted her.

She did not understand why she reacted this way.
Reverend Beckwith-Carter did not like her particularly,
and she expected he would cause her trouble. She
should not be so thrilled by the warmth of his skin,
separated from her by only a single layer of fabric.

Mrs. Reed, the parsonage's housekeeper, came
forward to greet her as they entered the front hall of
the small house. The silver-haired woman had kept the
parsonage for Reverend Tanner before he retired.
Mariel smiled. She had worked on church projects with
this lady, who was as thin as her name suggested. She
respected the older woman's common sense and ability
to deal with pettiness, which exasperated Mariel to
distraction.

"Good morning, Lady Mariel. I just took biscuits
from the oven. You will have some?"

Unbuttoning the heavy mackintosh she wore to
protect her clothes from the dust blown up by the
wheels of the automobile, Mariel nodded with a smile.
She smoothed her simple skirt and the wide sleeves of
her cream, voile shirt. "You know I can't resist your
biscuits."

"Jam?   Strawberry is your favorite, if I recall
correctly."

"If it is no trouble."

"Certainly not. Reverend?"

He had been watching the young woman hanging her coat on a hook as if she was as at home here as he was. Aloud he told Mrs. Reed that whatever she had would be fine. He admitted to himself it should be no surprise Lady Mariel was familiar with the parsonage. She had lived in Foxbridge all her life. He had been here only a few weeks.

When he motioned toward the study, she smiled coolly. His lips tightened. The open friendship she showed Mrs. Reed would not be wasted on him. He had hoped Lady Mariel would not be an adversary, but it appeared she did not share his feelings.

He waited while Mrs. Reed brought in the tray, and he listened to the two women talk about people he barely knew. When the housekeeper excused herself, he rose to close the door. He met Lady Mariel's wide blue eyes. Secretly, he was pleased to see she was astonished at being alone with him unchaperoned. Perhaps she was not as immune to the pressures of society as she pretended.

"Will you pour, Lady Mariel?"

"Of course, Reverend."

"My name is Ian," he said as he took one of the warm biscuits from the plate on the painted tray.

She glanced up in surprise before returning her attention to her task. "I am aware of that. Sugar, Reverend?"

When he did not answer, she found her eyes captured by his again. With the sugar tongs in her hand, she sat motionless as a warmth she could not halt sifted through her, bringing a rose tint to her cheeks. His smile teased a similar reaction from her lips.

Breaking the bewitchment, she said far more serenely than she felt, "Sugar, Ian?"

"Two, Mariel. I trust I may call you that."

"I am sure I have little choice," she retorted with a touch of sarcasm. When he disdained the offer of cream, she handed him his cup. "You are incredibly difficult to deal with."

He smiled as she poured her own tea. "That is odd. I was thinking exactly the same thing about you."

With a laugh, she leaned back against the prickly horsehair upholstery. She raised her cup to her lips, but grimaced as the steam from the hot liquid billowed in her face. "You have the advantage over me. You must have heard of my recalcitrant nature."

"Recalcitrant was not the word your adversaries used. Stubborn is the one I heard most." He picked up a biscuit, lathered it with strawberry jam, and offered it to her. When she accepted it graciously, he continued, "The people around Foxbridge admire you very much, Mariel."

"I know what they think of me, but I only want to help. With Uncle Wilford gone so much, it behooves me to assume those duties normally done by Lord Foxbridge."

"And those are?"

"Helping out in the community, making sure that there is food for the hungry and shelter for the poor." When she saw the twinkle in his eyes, she retorted, "It is important work!"

He smiled. "Undoubtedly. But I find it strange a woman with your remarkable temperament would be satisfied with such tame organizations."

Mariel started to reply, then wondered if his words were meant to offend. "Remarkable temperament" could mean almost anything. She had come to beg his forgiveness, and he threw derogatory, incomprehensible comments in her face. When she rose, he did the same. He asked her what was wrong, but she ignored him as she walked toward the door. His hand on her arm kept her from reaching for the knob.

"Reverend Beckwith-Carter," she stated with icy hauteur, "do not presume that your backward collar allows you to forget the manners of a gentleman."

She gasped as he spun her to look at him. Her black skirt belled out in the movement. Anger transformed his face. She tried to pull her arm out of his grip, but he refused to release it.

"Reverend!"

Auburn brows accented the anger in his eyes. "I will act as a gentleman should when you show me you can be a lady."

"How dare you?" She raised her hand, but halted it before it could strike his face. She could not imagine striking a minister. That was what she told herself, not wanting to admit his green gaze daunted her.

"Why are you trying to make everyone dislike you, Mariel?"

She swallowed harshly. Why could this man with a few words, cut to the quick of her soul? He did not know her, but revealed the secrets she could not admit to herself.

Slowly Ian released her arm. Viewing the bare emotion on her face, he could not ask more of her. More than anyone he had met in his life, Mariel needed to heal the pain within herself. He might not be the one to help her, for she did not fail to show him on every opportunity how little she wanted him to play a part in her life.

When she had arrived this afternoon, he had thought . . . He erased the intriguing image from his mind. As if a sudden lassitude had dropped on him, he sat again. He looked at her confused features.

"Forgive me, Mariel. I had no cause to speak to you like that." His mouth tilted in a wry grin. "Sometimes I have this yearning to solve all the problems of the world. An egotism shared by too many clergymen."

She stood uneasily by the door, torn between the urge to spit out angry words and leave, and the urge to stay and learn more about this surprising man. Her feet seemed nailed to the floor and her voice frozen in her throat. She knew there must be something she could say, but her normally facile mind could think of nothing. As each moment passed, her embarrassment grew. The hot flush along her face warned her she could not hide it.

The door opened abruptly into her back. She was jolted forward several steps. With a hurried apology, Mrs. Reed peeked into the room. When she saw Lady Mariel's reddened cheeks and the reverend's tight lips, she knew she had interrupted something important.

"Reverend, I knocked, but no one—"

He rose with the aid of his cane and waved aside her apology. "What is it, Mrs. Reed?"

"It is Mrs. Albion. She wants to talk to you about the new altar cloth she is making."

"Have her wait in the parlor. I will be there shortly." When the housekeeper nodded and closed the door, he looked at Mariel. "Will you stay while I deal with this?"

Unwilling to lose her chance to flee from this uncomfortable situation, she said quickly, "You are busy. I can return at a later date."

"I won't be long. Five minutes."

"I can come back."

He stepped closer to her. When he took her fingers in his hand, she looked from them to his mysterious eyes. The gentle stroke of his thumb across her palm sent strange sensations through her. He lifted her hand and sandwiched it tenderly between his own.

"Mariel, don't leave when we are unsettled with one another. That happened yesterday. We are going to be working together while I am in Foxbridge. Must we argue all the time?"

"Probably." She dimpled as her sense of humor reasserted itself. "I argue with everyone else I work with."

"So I have heard." He became serious as he asked again, "You will wait?"

"Yes."

He squeezed her fingers gently. His face mirrored his reluctance as he released them. "It will take no longer than five minutes. Make yourself at home."

"Thank you."

Mariel watched as he walked to the door. He moved so smoothly with his cane, she could forget it except for times when it hit the door with a hollow sound or when it brushed her skirt. She whirled about to look out the window past the sofa. Wrapping her arms around herself, she regarded the activities on the green.

Children chased a hoop and played with a ball. Two women with baskets of laundry resting on their hips talked soundlessly. A man staggered from the direction of the village pub, which bore the odd name of "Three Georges." In front of the parsonage, she could see her automobile and a carriage she assumed belonged to Mrs. Albion.

She did not know the woman, although she was well acquainted with her husband, for he served with her on the school board. Mr. Albion fought every idea she expressed. He denounced her outlandish plans, as he was fond of calling them. To her thinking, he disliked everything she said simply because she was a woman. He made no effort to hide his opinion that women should stay in their homes and serve their husbands and raise children.

Thinking of the intractable Mr. Albion always brightened her spirits. She so enjoyed baiting him at the meetings, just the anticipation of the next time brought a wicked smile.

She wandered around the study, noting the changes Ian had made: only small things which evaded the casual eye. Photos of people she did not recognize rested on the fireplace mantel. New pieces of bric-a-brac shared the cluttered spaces on the few tables between the chairs.

By the desk, her dress brushed against pages hanging over the edge. She did not utter her curse, which would have been out of place in a parsonage. Bending, she scooped up the papers, which had fluttered in every direction, and sat in the nearest chair as she tried to put them in order.

Her eyes widened as her attention was caught by a phrase in the bold handwriting. Flipping the page, she saw a date on the top of it. This must be Ian's sermon for the coming Sunday. She glanced at the crossed-out words and the insertions. Never had she thought about the work necessary to lecture a congregation on the need for a sinless life.

Although she knew she should not be reading it, his words captured her imagination. That he would be preaching a lesson from the Book of Ruth about the special love of a parent for a child deepened her interest. Since her early adolescence, she had been delighted by the romantic tale of a poor widow who finds, through her mother-in-law's intervention, the man of her dreams.

Leaning back in the chair, she read through the first page. She smiled at a sally she knew would be enjoyed by the members of the church. Reverend Tanner never would have thought to lighten his dolorous lessons with levity. She put the first page on the table in front of her and searched for the next one. Concentrating on following the arrows moving sentences from one part of the page to the other, she paid no attention to the passing of time.

"Enjoying it?"

She whirled as if she had been caught in a crime. "Ian! I—I—" She tried to choke out a few coherent words. "The pages fell. I picked them up, and—and—"

With a laugh, he sat in the chair next to hers. "So what do you think?"

"What do I think?" she repeated witlessly.

"About my sermon?" He pointed to the pages. "What do you think of it?"

Lowering the page she had been reading, she met his eyes for the first time without rage or trepidation. In a serene voice, she said, "I think it is wonderful."

"Do you?"

"Fishing for compliments, Ian? I wouldn't have told that if I didn't mean it!"

He leaned forward to fold his arms on the back of her chair. "You wouldn't, would you?" Pointing to one of the most rewritten areas, he asked, "What did you think of this part?"

"You want my opinion on your sermon?"

In the exact tone she had used with him, he retorted, "I would not have asked you, if I did not want to know." He smiled when she chuckled. "You are an intelligent woman, Mariel. You must be if you like my sermons."

While they laughed together, she did not think about the harsh words they had traded less than a quarter of an hour before. They discussed the sermon with the ease of longtime friends. If she startled him with her Biblical knowledge, or if she was surprised by his liberal attitudes to many things Reverend Tanner thought should never be changed, neither spoke of it.

Their heads bent closely together over the pages. Taking a pen from the desk, Ian marked her comments next to his words. When they were finished, he folded the crumpled papers and placed the sermon back on the blotter. The letter opener secured it, so it would not fly away again.

When he offered her another cup of tea to replace the one she had not tasted, she accepted happily. From the discussion of his sermon, it was an easy transition to her work in Foxbridge. He seemed very interested in her position on the school board and her ideas to better the school.

"It is not easy," she concluded. "Many people resist anything that is new. Unfortunately, the other members share their opinion."

"Nothing good comes easily. I—" He paused as he heard shouts from across the green. "School is out."

"Already?" She looked at the small watch pinned to the bodice of her blouse. "Look at the time. Ian, I have taken your whole afternoon."

"And I have made you late for your meeting."

She shrugged. "I can get there very quickly in the automobile." As inspiration struck her, she asked, "Would you like to go for a ride in it, or do you think the dignity of your office would be compromised?"

He laughed with young-hearted enthusiasm. "I suppose I should be concerned with my safety in such an infernally modern machine, but . . . why not?"

"I suggest you wear something other than your ministerial blacks. The dust is worse than a carriage."

As he stood, he remembered her reason for coming into the village. "What about your meeting?"

She smiled mischievously. "The Ladies' Aid Society will delight in my absence. I was going to demand a report on the fair last fall. The ones in charge are delaying because they used the funds inappropriately."

"They stole them?" He could not hide his astonishment.

"Borrowed might be a kinder way to phrase it. You should not be so shocked, Ian. They will replace it, but they can't do it all at once." She glanced at his outstretched hand as he offered to help her to her feet, unsure if she wanted to touch him. Knowing she had no choice, she put her fingers on his palm.

He drew her slowly from the sofa. As he had done on the porch, he examined her face minutely. This time he acted as if he wanted to memorize her features. She found nothing to say as she was wrapped in a warm cocoon of unfamiliar feelings. Standing here with Ian made her happy.

Already, she discovered, he had created sensations within her she had not guessed she could feel. No one else could rile her so quickly or soothe her fears with a gentle smile. That she had known him only a day seemed the strangest thing of all. It was as if he had been a friend forever.

"Shall we go, Mariel?" he asked with what sounded like regret.

She wondered if she had done something wrong. She had done nothing. Perhaps she should have said something, but when she gazed into those everchanging eyes, she thought only of how fathomless they were, like the sea they resembled.

"Of course. Let me get my coat in the hall. Do you have something to wear?" She colored as she realized what an inappropriate question that was.

"Do you always blush so much?"

"No!"

He put a single finger to her cheek. "You should. Every emotion is lovely on you, Mariel. Even embarrassment." With a smile, he moved toward the door. "I will get my coat and meet you on the porch."

Overwhelmed by his compliment, and the way her heart leapt at it, she went into the hall. Mrs. Reed popped out of the parlor as Mariel was putting on her driving mackintosh. She wondered if the housekeeper had been eavesdropping on their conversation. Even as she told herself that was an unjustified thought, she soothed her conscience by reminding herself they had spoken of nothing unseemly.

"The biscuits were wonderful. Don't tell Mrs. Puhle I told you that. She wants her kitchen at the Cloister to be the best in the shire."

The housekeeper smiled at the joke they had shared often in the past. When she started to speak, unease bright on her face, she seemed to think better of it. She scurried toward the kitchen at the back of the house as Ian's uneven steps could be heard through the ceiling.

Staring after her, Mariel tried to guess what had caused Mrs. Reed to act so strangely. Certainly there could be nothing wrong with her calling on the new minister or offering him a ride in her automobile. As she did so often, Mariel decided she did not care what another thought. Surprisingly, today, she was enjoying Ian's company and did not want the day to end so soon.

By the time Ian came onto the porch, Mariel was seated in the driver's seat. She smiled as he eased himself onto the narrow seat. Inserting the ignition key, she released the brake. The car started with a sound not unlike a swarm of bees. Her passenger put his hand on the wrought iron decoration near the seat as the automobile lurched into motion.

He watched, fascinated, as she shifted the car easily. The car turned smoothly onto the shore road and wound its way up the hill. Mariel waved gaily to a group of people walking along the path. She drew to the center so the cloud of dust in their wake would not cover the pedestrians.

"So what do you think?" she asked, taking her eyes from the road momentarily.

"It's wonderful!"

She laughed. "I felt the same when I rode in it the first time. As soon as I drove it, I knew I must have one for my own use. I guessed you to be a fellow adventurer."

"Adventurer?"

"That does not offend you, does it?" she teased. "Perhaps it is not a virtue for a minister to be daring. I was raised to scoff at anyone who shrank from trying something new."

He leaned back on the comfortable velvet cushions. Except for having no horses to pull it and the stick in her hand, this vehicle resembled a standard buggy. It had been many years since he went for a ride with such a pretty lady.

Angrily, he forced those images from his head. He did not want to think of the past when he could enjoy Mariel's company. Nothing he did could change what had been. To wallow in rage at what was over would taint the present.

When he noted the dimming of the smile on her face, he realized she thought his anger was directed at her. Again he saw the gentle, sensitive Mariel she tried to hide. He thought of what she had said, so he could give her a joshing reply.

"I have not been adventuresome recently." He offered her his most friendly smile. "I guess I have never considered what a minister should or should not do differently from other folks. Perhaps because temptation has not come my way."

"No?" she asked in disbelief. "You must have lived a most boring life. Temptation comes my way often." Her eyes crinkled in malicious joy as she added, "Usually at the school-board meetings when I feel the urge to tease one of the other members."

Their laughter drifted in the dusty wake of the automobile. The few people they met did not seem awed by the machine. Horses appeared more frightened of it than humans. Ian noted she was careful to pull to the far side of the road when they met another vehicle. She did not want to cause some hysterical beast to bolt, tipping its cart into the dirt.

Ian listened with concealed amusement as she pointed out, with sharp commentary, the various landmarks along their path. No one could accuse Mariel Wythe of trying to spare someone's feelings by hiding her opinions. When her comments varied from those of others he had met, he noted what she said and why. He was coming to see that she formed no opinion haphazardly. If she liked or disliked something, it was because she had thought out every side of the issue.

Mariel stopped the automobile on the section of shore road nearest the cliffs beyond the Cloister. Trees clung tenaciously to the soil on the windswept plateau. Hardy stalks of marsh grass waved like a second sea. The marsh ran from the road nearly to the edge of the land, which dropped into the ocean. Although the walls of the Cloister could be seen in the distance, no other signs of human habitation were visible.

Pulling off her goggles, she placed them on the seat. It took her almost a minute to undo the hat and coat. Shrugging them off, she rose to step onto the running board. When she saw Ian in front of her with his arms out as if to help her from a carriage, she smiled and put her hands on his shoulders.

Lifting her easily, he did not hurry to put her on the ground. When her eyes were level with his, he held them and smiled.

"Is there something wrong with me?" she asked.

He placed her on the grass and brushed dust from her nose as he laughed. "Except for a dirty face, I'd say you are about perfect."

"That's because you don't know me very well," she stated pertly, afraid of the powerful emotions that could build so easily between them. "Have you visited the beach yet?"

"No." He followed as she walked away through the tall weeds. "If you please, Mariel, a bit slower. It is not easy to part this grass with my cane."

"I—I'm sorry." Buried in her own uneasy thoughts, she forgot his need for the cane. It was easy to do, for he stood as straight as a beefeater.

Smiling, he drew even with her. "Do not sound so embarrassed. I don't want my problem to make you unhappy."

"Does it bother you often?" She lowered her eyes, knowing her question was far too personal to ask a man who was barely an acquaintance. Yet, it seemed that she knew him well. In their short conversations, much of what he said struck a chord with her. Perhaps that is why she saw him as a fellow adventurer seeking excitement in the mundane things of life. "Forgive me if that question is—"

"No, it is no problem for you to ask. The leg does not trouble me too often." He sighed. "It concerns others more than it does me. I have become accustomed to it."

She wanted to ask what had happened to him, but she did not want to continue in this personal vein. If she did, he might ask her some things about herself and the other Wythes she never wanted to discuss.

"I am sure you have been warned how dangerous these cliffs are." She gazed out at the surging waves, which created an even pattern as far as the horizon. The crash of the breakers swelled over the rim of the stone wall to spray the scent of the salt water over them. "From the earliest days of my childhood, I remember being told never to come here alone."

He walked to within a few feet of the jagged lip of the precipice. "So wild and untamed. It is odd to think this is here so close to the cities of England."

"This shire clings to the old ways, but I think the residents will change long before the sea does." She laughed. "Or maybe not."

Flashing a smile over his shoulder, he walked along the edge to look at the slender strand below. She pushed through the grass to join him. When he held out his hand and offered her a challenging smile as she hesitated, she slipped hers onto his palm, discovering it fit perfectly.

They wandered along the cliffs until the sun dipped toward the western horizon. Its crimson touch dyed the fluorescent waters. The lonely cry of the sea birds grew more poignant as the night winds tugged at the clothes of the two silhouetted against the multi-hued sky.

"I think we should return to the automobile," Mariel said quietly, loath to end this pleasant walk. "It is too dangerous to stay here after dark."

"The piskies will get us?"

She smiled. "No, not the little people, but I do not trust my footing along the cliffs when I cannot see well. Ian, will you come to the Cloister and have dinner with us?"

"I can't. It's Friday. I have to finish that sermon tonight. Tomorrow I am marrying Louis Bradley and Molly Gray." When she laughed, he asked, "What is so funny?"

Picking her way around a stump, she did not let go of his hand. He drew her back next to him as they continued toward the car. Reflectively, she queried,

"How does it feel to say a few phrases and know you have married someone forever and ever?"

"Wonderful." He mused, "The first time I officiated at a wedding, I was more nervous than the bride and groom. Such an awesome power to join two lives, knowing that the worse might come more often than the better. I no longer dread saying the wrong thing. Everyone usually is joyous at weddings, even when the vows have been anticipated and the girl's father is insistent she marry immediately."

When she laughed, he regarded her shadowed face. Most women he knew would be shocked by such a statement. Not Mariel. She might be conventional about her own moral behavior; she did not judge others harshly. As they reached the automobile, he released her so she could don her odd driving costume.

She sat next to him and reached for the ignition. His hand halted hers. Drawing it back to him, he lifted her trembling fingers to his lips. In the purple glow of the twilight, he could see the warmth in her eyes.

Mariel did not move as she felt Ian's other arm slide along the back of the seat to bring her to face him. Highlighted by the setting sun, the intensity of his emotions was engraved upon his face. He released her hand, and she moved to start the car again.

Again he stopped her. His hand on her cheek brought her face back to his. Refusing to release her tense shoulders, his arm contracted to tilt her toward him. When she saw he intended to kiss her, instinct alone saved her. With her hands against his chest, she broke his gentle hold on her.

Inserting the key into its slot, she refused to be waylaid from starting the motor. She put the automobile into gear and turned it to go back to the village. By her side was a small lantern connected to the batteries. She lit it, not to help her see, because it obscured her vision more than helping it, but to let others know the vehicle was on the road.

She said nothing during the long trip back to Foxbridge. Several times, Ian asked her a question, but she did not answer. When she drew the automobile even with the porch, she stated coolly, "Good night."

"Do not be angry," he said, refusing to leave until they had this misunderstanding solved. "If you do not want to be kissed, that is your prerogative. If I want to kiss you, it is mine."

"Which you have no right to inflict on me!"

He smiled. "Which I did not inflict on you, as you so nicely put it." He leaned toward her and spoke in a low voice no passersby could hear. "Do you think you could have prevented me from kissing you if I had wanted to?" When she gasped, he went on swiftly, "I know what you are thinking. I am a minister. I should not be thinking of such things."

His vehemence disconcerted her as much as his shadow flowing over her in a dark caress. "That's right."

His hands framed her face. "Mariel Wythe, I like you. You have a wonderful sense of humor and a cockeyed way of looking at the world. Something about you revitalizes me. If you do not want to be kissed, I can accept that." He grinned ironically. "I can accept that reluctantly, but I do not want to go back to the spitting catfight of yesterday. Can we be friends?"

"Friends?" Her eyes moved from his to the line of his lips. Her breath felt tight in her chest as she imagined how wonderful they would have felt over hers. Forcing that thought from her mind, she murmured, "I would like that, Ian. Just don't press me. I do not like to be cornered. Then I fight nastily."

"I noticed." He alit from the quietly purring automobile. "Will I see you Sunday?"

"No," she answered.

"When?" He knew he was ignoring the advice she had given him only moments before, but he wanted to be sure this day was not a fluke.

She hedged. "I have to come into Foxbridge on Tuesday for the school board meeting. Until then, I will be busy with some work I must do to prepare for it."

"I will see you soon."

Taking the statement as the command it was, she said, "Perhaps." She pressed on the speed control, wrenching the automobile from the rectory in a spurt of dust.

Ian brushed off his coat as the buzz of the motor disappeared into the distance. She had warned him not to pressure her, and he had risked her wrath. He grinned. He told himself he had not expected she would attempt to use that odd conveyance as a weapon against him.

Walking toward the door, he greeted Mrs. Reed warmly. He suspected Mariel would be as anxious for their next time together as he was. Her behavior had not changed his mind. It would be soon.

Mariel Wythe was not the only one determined to have her way.

Chapter Three

Mariel swore under her breath. When she thought of how Phipps would reprimand her for such language, she repeated herself more vehemently and much louder. Nursing her aching wrist, she kicked the hard, rubber tires of the automobile. It did nothing to get it running, but made her feel better.

Reaching for the key, she decided she had to give the ignition another try. If she could not get it started, she would have to walk all the way back to the Cloister. She grimaced as she looked at her narrow silk gown. As she had so many times, she cursed the current styles, which effectively swaddled women.

This time she released the brake before the key snapped back to burn her fingers. The motor remained as silent as before. If she did not return to the Cloister in time for dinner and a chance to change her clothes, she was going to be late for the meeting of the school board.

She looked at the dark bag on the floor. All her materials were prepared. She had worked late into the night for the past three evenings to be ready to answer all the stupid questions the other board members were sure to pose to her. The task had kept her from thinking about the strong desire on Ian's face when he spoke of kissing her. She could not ignore her own reaction to that tempting invitation.

As she had too often in the days since their walk along the cliffs, she forced the thoughts of him from her head. She did not want to find her life tangled with Ian Beckwith-Carter's quiet existence as minister of this shire. What she longed for she did not know, but she was determined to find it alone.

"Damn automobile!" she snarled as she refocused her frustration on the unmoving vehicle.

"Need help, miss?"

She whirled to see a man standing in the middle of the road. She wondered where he had popped out of so suddenly. He was far too tall for an elf, and his graying, once-dark hair did not seem to fit in with any of the other residents of fairydom. Well worn clothes announced his profession as a landsman. Her eyes rose to meet his midnight black ones. Tall and thin, he seemed as much a part of this silent road as the trees behind the stone wall.

Swallowing her shock, she said in a normal tone, "It's the automobile. It won't start."

"I have heard of these, but I have never seen one before." He placed his hand on the chrome of the fender and stroked it with admiration. His fingers were long and slender, not the short, stubby ones she expected from a farmer. "Shall I look at it for you, miss?"

"If you don't know—"

He smiled, showing even teeth. "I can't hurt it if it's broken. I might be able to fix it. I have worked on other machines."

Reluctantly, she nodded. She stepped back to allow him to check all the wires she had never bothered to study. The car always worked, so she had not prepared for the time when it might break down. She explained the sounds it had made just before it coasted to a stop. With a nod, he leaned over it to check the motor and electrical connections.

She rubbed her sore fingers and watched him. When he stepped to the front and gave the key a sharp turn, she jumped as the motor purred to life. She laughed uneasily as he turned to see her astonishment.

"Thank you, Mr.—?"

"Walter Collins, miss. You are welcome. Just a wire needed wiggling. Have your mechanic check it for you right away. I would not guarantee you could start it again tonight. You'd be smart to head straight for home."

With a nod, she acknowledged his sound advice. She leaned across the front seat for her reticule. When she straightened, she found his eyes following the narrow lines of her gown. She bit back her normal sharp retort to such impudence. The man had helped her. She must be gracious to him. As always, her conscience spoke to her in Phipps's voice.

"May I offer you something for your kindness, Mr. Collins?"

"Nothing, miss." He tipped his broad-brimmed hat. " 'Twas my pleasure to help you."

"But, Mr. Collins, I must insist." Inspiration dawned, lightening her expression. "At least come to Foxbridge Cloister and let us offer you a meal and a night's shelter."

His eyes narrowed slightly. "You are very shrewd to see I am in need of a roof over my head tonight, miss. Or I should say 'my lady'?"

Waving aside his words, she stated, "I am Mariel Wythe. My name does nothing to change my obligation to you, Mr. Collins. Let me offer you a ride in my automobile that you have gotten started so efficiently."

A slow smile spread across his face. He could not hide his boyish delight at having a chance to ride in the horseless vehicle. Although she guessed him to be more than a decade her senior, he leapt like a child into the passenger's seat.

On the journey back to the Cloister, Mariel was kept busy answering his questions about how the automobile worked. She showed him the acceleration lever and how the floor pedals regulated the rear wheels. He was properly impressed when she spoke about the automobile's speed. That she could drive in one hour what it took many a day to walk seemed miraculous.

Many of his questions she could not answer. She discovered her technical knowledge of her vehicle was sadly deficient. At the same time, she listened intently as he spoke of how much this motor was like other machines he had worked on. As they drove through the open gate of the Cloister and turned onto the road leading to the stables, she dared to voice the question nagging at her thoughts. "Mr. Collins, may I ask you something personal?"

"Personal?" He looked at her uneasy face shadowed by the coming twilight.

"Somewhat." She wished her voice would not try to quiver as if she was begging for favors. "Do you have a position somewhere?"

"A job?" With a laugh, he leaned back on the plush seat and put his foot on the running board. "I could say I am between positions right now, my lady, but the truth is that I am broke. I am heading to Liverpool to look for something on the docks."

She hesitated as she concentrated on driving the automobile over the lip of the stable floor. When it was garaged, she turned off the motor. In the uncomfortable silence, she said, "You have impressed me with your knowledge of machinery, Mr. Collins. Would you consider accepting employment here at the Cloister?" She smiled gently. "I am afraid it would not be simply taking care of the automobile."

"Stable work?"

"We need someone."

Taking the electrical cords from her, he stepped out of the car and plugged them into the generator at one side of the room. He came back to the car and leaned on it. With a grin, he shrugged his shoulders. "Why not? It's a job. If I don't like it, I can leave, right?"

"We pay well. I can offer—"

"No need, Lady Mariel. I am sure you pay fairly." His hand caressed the leather decoration on the seats. "I am looking forward to working with this vehicle, and for you."

"Wonderful. It's settled then. I will let Alistair know. He is the head groom," she explained hastily. "You will be reporting to him."

"Sounds fine."

Unsure what else to say, she picked up her bag and stepped out of the vehicle. Telling him she would stop to see the groom on the way to the Cloister, she left him inspecting his new responsibility. She smiled, pleased with her decision to hire him. He clearly loved the car as much as she did. No one else on the grounds wanted anything to do with her toy. Phipps was kindest about it, and she called it a "noisy contraption."

After enduring the head groom's grumbling about hiring a stranger with no references, Mariel returned to the main house. Dodsley greeted her with surprise as he crossed the foyer on his nightly inspection.

"Are you going to be able to get back to Foxbridge tonight? You are quite late for supper, Lady Mariel," he said with his usual curiosity about what she did. She knew he never went to sleep before she arrived home safely on the nights of her late meetings at the school.

"The automobile was not cooperative this afternoon. I decided it would be better not to trust it. I am sure Mr. Gratton and the other members of the school board will not be sorry I am a bit late." She laughed lightly as she placed her hat and veiling on a chair in the hallway. "They probably wish I would not come at all. A quiet meeting would seem like a welcome respite."

"Would you like a tray, Lady Mariel? It might save you some time."

She nodded, remembering she had skipped luncheon. "That would be lovely. Have it sent upstairs. I must rush if I want to get to the village this evening. Would you please tell Mrs. Puhle that I hired a new man to work in the stables? He will be taking his meals in the house."

Although he could not hide his interest, he said only, "Of course, my lady."

Racing up the stairs to her room, Mariel threw open her door, nearly into Phipps's face. The older woman frowned at the habitually disheveled appearance of her lady. When she started to reprimand Mariel, her comments were ignored.

"Not now, Phipps. I have to hurry. The automobile malfunctioned."

"Malfunctioned?" she repeated, aghast. "My lady, are you—?"

Mariel interrupted impatiently, "I am fine. So is the automobile, but it must be recharged tonight, so I will have to take the buggy to Foxbridge. If I don't hurry, I will miss the meeting."

"Lady Mariel, I want to talk to you."

Grabbing a serviceable dress from her wardrobe, she hurried behind her dressing screen. She called from behind it, "Can this discussion wait?"

"I think not."

A sigh of resignation was lost in the folds of the black satin skirt Mariel drew over her head. She straightened her blouse and tied the sashes at the waistband. As she rounded the screen, she dropped the dress she had been wearing onto the bed. She scowled at her reflection in the mirror and wondered how other women had mastered the skill of always being neat.

When she heard Phipps's foot tapping impatiently against the floor, Mariel turned. "All right. What did I do wrong now?"

Blue eyes paler than Mariel's own sparked with the frustration the older woman considered unladylike. Although she had been with Mariel since the girl outgrew the need for a nanny, Mariel had never seen Phipps lose her temper. Not that the gray-haired woman had not been given cause. Mariel had delighted in trying to see how far she could push the limits her companion imposed.

"You know as well as I," stated Phipps quietly as she sat on the couch by the bed.

"If I knew, I would not have asked!" Mariel failed to understand how anyone could not speak her mind. Counting on her fingers, she went through the misdemeanors Phipps considered major crimes. "You have told me of the evils of going out without a hat and gloves. You have warned me about raising my voice to an incompetent underling, suggesting I teach each gently, as I would a child. You have lectured me on the state of my pink gown, which was ruined while I investigated the damage from the fire. That was this week. Do you want to talk about what we discussed last week?"

Phipps pointed to a chair. "Sit down, Lady Mariel."

"I am going to be late!"

"Yes, you are going to be late, for you must listen to reason."

When the young woman ran to answer the knock on the door and thanked the maid who brought the supper tray, Phipps leaned against the back of the sofa and closed her eyes. Although she never had told Lady Mariel, she loved her spirited charge as much as if she had been her own child. The candid, warmhearted woman did things Phipps never would have dared, despite the urgings of her sometimes rebellious heart. She never would change Lady Mariel, but she wanted her to learn to question the impulses that could send her on a headlong course with disaster.

Mariel set the tray on a table. Holding up the plate of sandwiches, she asked, "Would you like one, Phipps?"

"Yes, thank you." She smiled as she selected a roast beef sandwich. It would be difficult not to like her lady, although Mariel let few know the real woman hidden behind the efficient Lady Mariel Wythe. Watching the young woman choose the sandwich she wanted, Phipps said, "I want to talk to you about Reverend Beckwith-Carter."

"Ian?" She gulped to swallow the unchewed bite of bread and meat in her mouth. When Phipps's eyebrows arched at her use of Ian's given name, she lowered her eyes. She had given away too much by her reaction. Unsure how she felt, Mariel did not want to reveal those nascent emotions.

"I understand you took him for a drive in your infernal machine last week."

"He was interested in how it worked, so I asked him if he wanted to ride in it." Taking a large drink of tea, she demanded, "Is there anything wrong with being neighborly? You were angry before because I was impolite to him. Am I going to be disciplined for being gracious?"

Phipps sighed and placed her sandwich on the plate between them. "No, Lady Mariel. You are no longer a child. I cannot confine to your room when you misbehave." She leaned forward and added, "You are a young lady."

"Not so young." She smiled. In a good approxima-
tion of Reverend Tanner's officious style of speech, she
stated, "My dear Lady Mariel, I daresay you do not see
that the days pass you by too quickly. Instead of flitting
about the countryside like a flibbertigibbet, you should
remember the greatest calling a woman can have. A
husband. A family. A hearth, which reflects the serenity
she brings to her home." With an inelegant snort, she
added in her own voice, "The old fool!"

"Lady Mariel! Do not try to change the subject."

"I thought that was the subject."

"Reverend Beckwith-Carter is the subject." When
she saw Mariel's face close up to hide the truth, Phipps's
concern grew. "You should not go riding with a man
without a chaperone. The automobile is no different
from a buggy. A lady has a gentleman call on her at her
home if he wishes to court her."

Rising, Mariel went to the dressing table for a final
glance at her appearance. All appetite had vanished. She
kept her face hidden as she said, "He has no desire to
court me. Very specifically, he told me that we would
be friends."

"And how do you feel about that?"

"Fine!" she snapped, already sick of lying to herself
and her friend. "Don't wait up for me. I may be late."

Mariel threw her cape over her arm and stamped
out of the room. She could not speak of this now. As
she waited in the foyer for the small buggy to be brought around to the front steps, she glared at the design of
tiles on the floor.

Unsatisfied rage billowed through her. First Ian,
then the automobile. Now Phipps, and even the Cloister.
Everything seemed determined to conspire to change or
control her life. She intended to put an end to that
tonight. Her life was hers to live alone.

Whether she wished it or not.

Mr. Gratton pounded his gavel on the table which
normally served as the teacher's desk at the front of the
small classroom. Staring at the pages in front of her,
Mariel hid her involuntary smile. She suspected that the
chairman of the school board enjoyed his power when

he stood before them each month. In the weeks between the meetings, he ran the pub. Under the watchful eye of his nagging wife, he served ale and enjoyed the conviviality of his patrons. That all changed when he entered this building to oversee *his* school board.

"Quiet, everyone! Let's get this meeting underway." He glared at Mariel, although she was silent. When she merely smiled at him, he scowled. Lady Mariel planned something tonight. That would mean hours of debate about her latest radical idea on how the school should be run.

When he came into the classroom for the meeting, he had seen her by the blackboard talking to Mr. Jones, the upper-level teacher. Mr. Jones was receptive to her ideas, while Mr. Knowles, who taught the younger students, felt she was simply a troublemaker. What she and Mr. Jones had been concocting, Mr. Gratton feared he would learn all too soon.

The door at the back of the room opened. All heads swiveled as Reverend Beckwith-Carter entered and took a seat in the last row. His knees reached higher than the child-sized desktop. He said nothing as he placed his hat on the desk in front of him.

"Reverend, is there something we can do for you?" asked Mr. Gratton.

Ian smiled when his eyes met Mariel's. As her lips softened to give him the expression he had seen while they walked along the seaside precipice, he forced his attention back to the bulbous chairman. "I was under the impression that these meetings were open to the public."

"Of course. Of course," said the chairman quickly. A stray thought entered his head, and he added more enthusiastically, "You know you are always welcome, Reverend." He did not glare at the perfectly attired lady sitting on his left. Perhaps with the minister here, Lady Mariel would act as she should, instead of voicing her opinion as though she were a man.

He asked for the minutes of the previous meeting to be read. Mr. Jones volunteered to read the pages sent in by the absent secretary. Mr. Stadley's cow had gone into labor tonight with the usual complications, so no one was surprised to discover him absent.

Throughout the normal, mundane business of the school board, Mariel remained aware of Ian sitting at the back of the room. She kept her head lowered as if the papers in front of her revealed matters of the greatest interest. If she looked up, she was afraid her eyes would stray toward him and display what she must conceal.

She did not understand why he had chosen to attend the meeting. If he wanted to see her, he could have waited until the end of the session. She admitted she did not want him to be here this evening. When she brought up the subject on her mind, Mr. Gratton would not be the only disgruntled boardmember. She was accustomed to this, but she could not guess what Ian would think.

Angrily, she spun her pencil in her fingers. Although Ian invaded her thoughts far too often, she should not allow herself to become overly concerned with his opinion of her. Long ago, she had vowed never to change to suit someone else. It was simply that she wanted him to think well of her. For the first time in her life, another's opinion of her truly mattered.

That Lady Mariel remained silent startled Mr. Gratton. He had expected some outburst from her immediately. His jovial smile brightened his face as he glanced in the pastor's direction. If Reverend Beckwith-Carter had this type of settling influence on Lady Mariel, they must discover a way to coerce him to attend each board meeting.

"No old business? Any new business?" He did not pause to take a breath, before adding, "If there is no—"

With a serenity that deceived no one, Mariel interrupted, "I have a question which would be considered new business, Mr. Gratton."

"Yes, Lady Mariel?" he asked with obvious reluctance.

"I am wondering why there is no money earmarked for the purchase of new textbooks. I know I am not the only one in the community concerned with the appalling condition of the books our children use."

"*Our* children," corrected Mr. Albion, "have used these books for twenty years."

She smiled at him coolly. More than the head of the school board, this rail-thin man, whose head was covered with sparse gray hairs, abhorred her ideas. He termed each one revolutionary or decadent. Although her voice was not raised, everyone was aware of her disgust with him when she replied.

"I may not have had twelve children attend this school as you have, sir, but I do know that many things have changed in two decades. How do you expect the children of this community to deal with the problems of the approaching twentieth century when they know nothing of the new advances in the second half of this one? If they leave Foxbridge to seek their fortunes in the bigger world, they will be ill-equipped to handle it."

"We don't want our children to leave!" he retorted with a sniff.

"But they are. They are going to the cities, to America, to the next town." She warmed to her topic. With her elbows on the table in a most unladylike pose, she pointed the pencil directly at the four men at the table. "We can offer the children of Foxbridge only one thing: a quality education, which will prepare them for the future. Even if they don't leave Foxbridge, they will have to deal with outsiders coming here. Do you want your children to be cheated by hucksters who prey on their ignorance?"

When he saw Mr. Jones nodding in eager agreement, Mr. Knowles leapt to his feet. A pompous man, he always reminded Mariel of a posturing blue jay, decked out with brightly colored feathers, but as empty-headed as the squawks coming from his mouth. The buttons on his forest-green waistcoat strained as he took a deep breath to remonstrate with her. She watched with amused fascination, for she considered him a fool in love with the sound of his own voice.

"Now see here, Lady Mariel. It is all right for you to express your ill-thought-out opinions, but I will not have you disparaging the education the children receive in our school. We do the best with the materials at hand."

"Exactly." She smiled as her agreement knocked the next words from him. "You do the best with what you have, but think of how much more you could do if you had up-to-date materials for these hungry young minds! They want to learn. I know that, for I have spoken with both your students and their parents. They appreciate what you have done with the shoddy materials you have here, Mr. Knowles."

He puffed several times, but could think of nothing to say. Glancing at the other members of the board for aid, he found none. They were as startled by her reaction as the teacher was. He dropped back into his chair and stared at the floor, unsure how she had twisted his words to use them to prove her point.

Mr. Jones seconded her argument as he said enthusiastically, "I agree with Lady Mariel. She has shown me some of the literature she has gathered from various textbook publishers. Science books, history books, the classics. Our children could learn about the people of the far-flung countries of the Empire. Who knows what ideas might come from these young minds if they are properly taught?"

"Ideas?" Mr. Albion refused to be intimidated. "Like hers?" He hooked his thumb toward the smiling woman.

"No," Mariel replied quietly. "New ideas, original ideas, ideas which we in our plodding conventionalism cannot conceive, Mr. Albion."

He sniffed. "Old ideas were good enough for me and mine."

"Old ideas are the building blocks for the future." She glanced around the table. "Or is that what you want to avoid? I can tell you, gentlemen, that the future is coming whether you wish it or not. Hiding like a ferret in a hedgerow will not stop the days from passing. Look at this school. It is an outgrowth of the school my great-great grandmother started with the newfangled ideas she brought with her from America. Would you go back to that time when your children were ignorant of booklearning?"

"Change simply for the sake of change is useless," stated Albion, but more weakly.

When she agreed with him, the resigned faces of the board grew longer. "Of course, Mr. Albion, but not change for the sake of the children of Foxbridge. Who wants to stand and be counted as one willing to deny them the best?"

Mr. Gratton saw no one else was willing to joust verbally with Lady Mariel. Not that he blamed them. The woman was too damn glib! Guiltily he looked at the minister sitting silently at the back of the room. He could not tell what Reverend Beckwith-Carter thought, for his face was emotionless. His hope for an ally dimmed. Reverend Tanner had agreed with the male members of the school board, but had not been able to convince Lady Mariel to seek more ladylike pursuits and leave government to men who knew how to handle it. Rumor had it Reverend Beckwith-Carter had been seen riding with Lady Mariel in that blasted contraption of hers.

As the clock on the wall struck nine, he sighed. He must get back to the Three Georges. "Very well, Lady Mariel. I assume you have this information on the books you wish to purchase, but I must adjourn this meeting because of the late hour. For our next meeting, please have that information, as well as costs, available for us."

She closed the folder in front of her. Although she had not won the battle tonight, she knew when to accept her small victories and retire gracefully from the contest. "I will send a copy of the information I have to each of you a week before the next meeting. That will give you time to peruse it, so you can be adequately prepared to discuss this."

Mr. Gratton said quietly, "Thank you, Lady Mariel." He bristled internally at her easy efficiency. Although she made no suggestions that she could run the board more effectively than he, others had. Loudly and often, he had heard about the fine work Lady Mariel did. It aggravated him more each time. That he liked her despite her outlandish ideas irritated him even more.

Closing the meeting before anyone else could speak, he avoided Mr. Knowles's eyes. He knew the older teacher wanted to talk to him about this newest twist Lady Mariel was bringing to the board. Until he had a chance to organize his thoughts out of the chaos roiling through his head, he did not want to discuss this with anyone.

The pubkeeper hurried to speak to the minister, who was rising slowly from the cramped school chair. This way he could avoid the teacher. "Thank you for coming, Reverend Beckwith-Carter. I trust you enjoyed yourself."

Ian smiled. "Without a doubt. She certainly speaks her mind, doesn't she?"

"Yes!" he snapped. His frustration found an easy outlet with the clergyman. "She comes in here with her strange ideas and thinks she can change what has worked for years. It all comes from allowing women to vote in local elections. As soon as that happened, she convinced some fools to nominate her for the school board. Since her victory at the polls, she has been creating havoc at each meeting."

With studied nonchalance, Ian asked, "I am sure the election results were close."

"The first time," admitted Gratton reluctantly. "She was challenged last winter for a second term and won by a wide margin."

"You might wish to listen to the opinion of the voters, Mr. Gratton. It may be that only the school board is upset by her so-called newfangled ideas." He smiled as the man regarded him with shock. Deciding he had made his point, Ian added, "Good evening, sir. I trust I will see you on Sunday."

Mr. Gratton mumbled something and heard Lady Mariel's lighthearted laugh as she approached. He stepped back to watch while she greeted Reverend Beckwith-Carter. His eyes narrowed when he noted the visible softening of the unyielding edges she presented to the school board. Instantly he knew the new minister would not help them in keeping Lady Mariel from railroading her plans through the school board.

He should have guessed. The pastor was a young man, just the right age to have his head turned by the beautiful Lady Mariel. With a spurt of malicious glee, Mr. Gratton decided it would be gratifying to watch the minister receive his comeuppance. Lady Mariel, in the barkeeper's opinion, was destined to be an old maid. She had turned away too many suitors of wealth and title to be interested in the village parson.

Mariel had no such cold intentions as she smiled at the auburn-haired man who set her heart to beating too rapidly. "Ian, you have met Mr. Jones, haven't you?"

Ian looked at the small man, not much taller than Mariel. Mr. Jones was a pale man with a sallow complexion, nearly colorless blond hair, and drab clothes. Yet when he smiled and extended his hand to the new minister, Ian knew Mr. Jones was a man who loved people and loved his profession. Shaking the proffered hand, Ian said, "It is nice to discover Mariel has one ally on the school board."

"I am not really a member," he explained in a voice that seemed incredibly deep for a man of his stature. "I come more as a cheering section for Lady Mariel. In her short term on the board, she has grasped an understanding of the needs of the children which others have not learned during their many years."

When Mr. Gratton cleared his throat gruffly, Mr. Jones bit his lip to keep from smiling. Mr. Knowles shooed them out of the building, so he could extinguish the lamps. Mariel moved to the steps of the building where she listened as Ian continued his conversation with Mr. Jones.

The other men drifted away into the shadows, leaving the three on the stairs. When Mr. Jones excused himself with the explanation that he had papers to correct for his class, he smiled at the woman waiting with uncharacteristic silence.

"I think we might be able to convince them, Lady Mariel."

She laughed lightly. "Your suggestion of making it sound as if it was my idea shall work wonderfully."

"I was sure Knowles would refuse to cooperate," the teacher explained to Ian. "Then it would be a battle between the two instructors here."

"By making it seem to be Mariel's idea, you could maintain your working relationship with Knowles." Ian smiled. "You two have created your idea and sprung it on the others masterfully. I think you will succeed by wearing them down."

Mariel said, "That is the whole plan. Ian, if—"

"No one will learn of it from me."

With a chuckle, Mr. Jones bid them a good evening and followed the others toward the far edge of the village. When he had approached Mariel with his concerns, she had understood immediately. Not only did Mr. Jones work with Mr. Knowles, but the two bachelors shared a small house not far from the Three Georges. By reaiming the outrage at her, she protected him.

"Where is your automobile?"

The question drew Mariel out of her thoughts. She smiled when she saw that Ian's eyes were on a level with hers, for he stood on a lower step. "It is recharging. I had to drive out to the orphans' home this afternoon. It refused to cooperate on the way home, but I think it is in good hands now. I hired a mechanic to take care of it."

He took her hands in his. "I have been anxious to see you, Mariel. I hope we don't always have to part in anger."

"Ian—"

"No, don't say it. Forget the quarrels we have had. I have to go to the church to retrieve the records book I left there after the wedding Saturday. Do you want to walk with me? Afterward, we can go to the parsonage for another sampling of Mrs. Reed's biscuits."

Searching his face, she saw the longing, which tormented her. Phipps's words rang in her ears, but she could not see any reason to refuse such a kind invitation. No one would think ill of them for walking to the church.

The thickness of the close air of the building swirled over them as he opened the door. She paused as she stepped into the foyer. When he lit a candle from the box on a nearby stand, she smiled uneasily. More than Phipps's warning, this place forced her to recall proprieties. She held her hands clenched in front of her as he picked up the leather-bound book he needed.

"One other thing," he murmured as he walked into the sanctuary.

She followed, for she did not want to be alone with her uneasy thoughts. Her hands ran along the backs of the pews until she reached the foremost one on the right side of the aisle. Unlike the others, this pew had a door secured with a lock. So often she had come with her uncle to sit here and try to remain quiet through the sermon. If Reverend Tanner had written ones like the lesson Ian had let her read, he might have held her attention.

"It is always empty," came a gentle reprimand in a velvet, dark voice.

Mariel turned to see Ian had returned to stand directly behind her. His strong, masculine allure could not be ignored even in the church. She fought her hands which wanted to raise to caress the uncompromising lines of his face. To touch him would be wrong. Her fingers clenched onto the door as she faced him.

"It is reserved for the Wythes," she said quietly.

"I know."

"Ian, don't start lecturing me, too!"

"Too?" He put his hands on her shoulders to halt her as she was ready to walk back up the aisle. "Mariel, what is wrong?"

She shrugged his hands off her. "Nothing. I just don't like having people telling me what I should or should not do. If you want us to keep from quarreling each time we meet, you must remember that."

His laugh resounded off the high ceiling of the church, startling her. "I doubt if you will allow me to forget." He sobered as he said, "I have heard talk that the fire at the Cloister was not accidental."

Her eyes in the candlelight showed her shock at his sudden alteration in the course of the conversation. Inanely, she said, "That is always said after a fire."

"But?"

"I don't know, Ian." Tears of sorrow at the loss of part of her beloved home glittered brightly as she flung out her hands. "Why would anyone want to destroy the Cloister?"

"Do you have any enemies?"

She laughed coldly. "You were at the meeting tonight!"

"Those are adversaries, not enemies. There is a difference." He refused to let her escape from his hands as they grasped her shoulders again. "Mariel, if it is true that the fire was intentionally set, you must contact the constable. There may be a madman in the Cloister. Who knows what such a person would do next?"

Terror wiped all other emotions from her face. Ian stared at her in disbelief. He had seen Mariel sparkling with happiness and fiery-eyed with rage, but not totally incapacitated like this, quivering in fear. When he asked her to tell him what was wrong, she did not move. Not knowing what else to do, he drew her into his arms.

As her face pressed to his chest, she blindly sought for comfort. Her arms went around him as she buried her eyes against his waistcoat. She did not cry as the unforgotten screams soared through her memory. In the past, she cried, but she learned that nothing could soothe the pain and the impotence, which raced over her when this bolted door in her mind chanced to open.

Ian's broad hands clasped her face and raised it to meet his concerned eyes. She saw a small portion of the pain she felt mirrored in them. The shivers ceased racing through her as she let his silent compassion flow over her. He did not need to speak. She was sure he had no idea what to say. Just knowing that he cared was enough, and more than enough.

"Mariel?"

"I am fine," she whispered. As she spoke, she knew the words were the truth. The horror had been submerged again to allow her to pretend it had never existed. "I think I will go home now."

He released her as she stepped away. Juggling the book, the candle, and his cane, he called after her, "Do you want me to drive to the Cloister with you?"

"No, but thank you." She turned to look at him. "You still have not accepted my invitation to dinner. Tomorrow night?"

"Tomorrow night will be fine."

A sad smile could not erase the shadows of the more horrible emotions that had overwhelmed her.

"At least we did not part snarling at one another tonight, Ian. I will see you tomorrow."

Leaning his cane against the pews, he listened to the sound of her footfalls and the closing of the heavy door at the back of the church. What he had said had hurt her, but he could not understand why. When she discussed the damage at the Cloister previously, she had expressed rage against whatever whim of fate had destroyed her beloved home. This reaction was so different. It showed him he had learned too little about her.

That was something he intended to remedy soon. He never wanted to view such naked terror on her face again.

Chapter Four

Mariel smiled as Walter emerged from the shadows of the barn, wiping his blackened hands on an oily cloth. Her nose wrinkled as she smelled the heavy scent of machinery. A gasp of dismay emerged from her lips when she saw pieces of the automobile scattered on the floor.

"What happened to it?"

"Nothing, Lady Mariel." His eyes roved along the machine affectionately. "I am adjusting the chains, which drive it. If they aren't oiled regularly, they could bind and break. That might leave you stranded again."

"I didn't know." Again she was awed by his innate knowledge for dealing with the vehicle. She never had been interested in mechanical things. While other children took apart their toys to see how they worked, she had been busy reading and creating a world within her imagination.

"I hope you didn't want to use it today."

She shook her head. "It deserves a day of rest. I have been scurrying all over the countryside the past week. I will take the buggy."

Instantly his face fell. As if she had reprimanded him, youthful sorrow wiped the years from him. In a small voice, he apologized, "Lady Mariel, if I had known you wanted it today, I wouldn't have—"

"Nonsense," she stated with too much enthusiasm. Walter must learn Foxbridge Cloister was not a place where reprimands were dealt out on the slightest whim. Mariel loved her home and wanted the others who lived here to be as happy. "You know what the automobile needs and when it needs it. I must defer to your judgment. It's no problem to take the buggy." She grinned playfully. "Have fun with all your chains and whatever."

He nodded as she went out the door. Walking to the wide opening, he continued to wipe his hands over and over while he watched her crossing the courtyard. She paused to chat with one of the other workers. The light sound of her always-charming laughter drifted on the spring breeze. Turning back to his chore, he tried not to think of the dark times the sound recalled. He wanted only to think of his task here at Foxbridge Cloister.

Mariel sang to the tempo of the horse's hoofbeats on the hard road. When she missed one note badly, she grimaced and was glad no one else had heard her. Music was her secret joy, but she shared it with no others. Once it had been different, but that was long ago. Occasionally she would play the pianoforte for Uncle Wilford when he was home, but since he left, nearly a year ago, she had had no interest in touching the spinet in the drawing room.

The hills became softer and more frequent as she drove inland. Only near the cliffs were the ridges uncompromising. These mounds wore their spring brown of overturned earth ripe for planting. Stone walls wound uneven paths to the horizon. Everything smelled of the fresh rebirth of spring.

Raising her hand high to match the crescendo of the note she sang, she smiled. This was her favorite time of year. With the promise of summer yet to come bringing its many activities, and the bane of the cold weather banished for many months, she could revel in the wealth of color returning to the fields.

She slowed the carriage as she drew even with a wall higher than the ones dividing the farm plots. She paused at the gate as she waited for it to be opened. A plaque riveted to the stones did not draw her eyes. She had seen the words too often. She knew "The Ladies'

Aid Society of Foxbridge Orphanage" was banished far
from the village so as not to bother the others of the
shire. Few wanted to remember the parentless children
living in the compound.

"Good afternoon," she called gaily to the gatekeep-
er. Like most working at the orphanage, he had been
raised here.

He waved to her before reclosing the gate. Once
some of the children had run away. Since then, the iron
bars had to be secured each time someone entered or
left. That precaution troubled her. She could not imagine being caged for any reason.

Mariel stopped the carriage before a huge house,
which needed painting. On its ornate scrollwork on the
porch, and along the eaves, hung tatters of loose paint.
Empty windows on the upper levels contrasted with the
ones on the ground floor. There the glass was decorated
with many examples of childish artwork. Spring flowers
made of colored paper marched in a row along the
windows overlooking the broad veranda.

Knocking on the door, she waited for the familiar
sound of sharp heels striking the floor. Before the door
opened, small arms wrapped around her waist. She
laughed as she turned in the embrace and patted unruly
blond hair.

"Hello, Rosie," Mariel said happily. "I thought you
would be taking a nap now."

The child grinned, showing the gap-toothed smile of
a five-year-old. "Snuck away, I did. Nurse's busy cleaning
up the mess Donny made. He ate too much. I thought
I'd see if you were calling today."

Mariel knelt to bring her eyes even with the petite
child's. Rosie was a beautiful child, growing lank out of
her toddler form. Like many of the orphans here, she
had lost her parents to sickness and alcoholism. Her
older brother and sister lived with relatives who could
use them to labor on their farms. Rosie was unwanted
by everyone. When she was old enough, she would be
taught a trade and apprenticed to someone willing to
take a chance on an orphan.

"Rosie, go back with the other children!" came a
gentle admonition from behind Mariel.

The little girl dipped in a quick curtsy, blew a dirty faced kiss to Mariel, and scurried away like a pert chipmunk racing through the grass. From across the courtyard, they heard the relieved sound of the housemother's voice as she discovered the return of the "lost" child.

"Lady Mariel, you spoil that youngster."

"It isn't difficult." She brushed the wrinkles from her gown as she stood. When she met the smile on the moon face of the director of the orphanage, she grinned.

Mrs. Parnell, for all her commanding presence, was nearly as short as her young charges, but rounder than three of them together. She had a lap meant for holding children and a soft voice that could comfort them in the middle of a nightmare. She loved her job, and the children adored her.

"I didn't expect to see you today. Do you want to come in for tea?"

Mariel shook her head. "No, for I have other errands to run. I just wanted to let you know that I have approached the school board about ordering new books for the village children. If they do agree to purchase them, I will make sure the old ones are brought out here for your use. I wish it could be more, but the orphanage board refused to consider such an extravagance as buying books for the children."

"We will be very pleased with any books you can bring us from the village. The ones we have are in such sorry condition that anything will be an improvement." She clasped Mariel's hands between her pudgy ones. "Thank you, Lady Mariel, for all you have done for us."

With a sigh, she repeated, "I wish it could be more."

Mrs. Parnell started to speak, then changed her mind. "Good day, Lady Mariel."

"Good day, Mrs. Parnell. I'll let you know as soon as the board has made its decision."

Mariel stepped down the uneven stairs and began to walk along the brick sidewalk, which clinked with her footsteps as if it was made of metal. When she heard her named called, she turned. "Did you forget something, Mrs. Parnell?"

The orphanage director's usual smile had fled from her face. Quietly, she said, "Let us speak in my office."

Although she was instantly curious why the woman's voice sounded strained and why she insisted they meet inside, Mariel went back to the porch. She smiled uneasily at Mrs. Parnell, who held the door for her.

Their shoes sounded hollow along the long hall. The scent of cleaning fluid hung in the air. The hall was dim with the small amounts of light filtering past the closed pocket-doors of the formal front rooms. Ostrich feathers decorated a huge decanter near the base of the stairs, which stretched up into the darkness.

Mrs. Parnell motioned toward a chair in her office, which was crowded with paperwork, bags of donated clothes for the children, and everything that could not find a place elsewhere in the main building. She sat at her desk and moved aside two mountainous piles of folders to enable her to see Lady Mariel. For a long moment, she did not say anything.

Mariel did not hurry her. She could tell the orphanage director was composing her thoughts. That they never had difficulty speaking in the past added to her concern about what bothered Mrs. Parnell.

Slowly the gray haired woman opened a folder before her. Without looking up, she said, "I know you have a special interest in Rosie."

"She's an adorable child."

"But is she special to you?"

"I'm afraid I don't understand what you mean." Mariel removed her gloves and draped them on the arm of the chair. She clasped her hands in her lap to maintain her pose of serenity. It was one of the few tricks she had learned gratefully from Phipps. "You know I care for her dearly. Is there some problem?"

Mrs. Parnell cleared her throat while she folded and refolded the edge of the page in front of her. "May I be blunt, my lady?"

"Please." She laughed. "I admit I'm totally confused."

"Would you be interested in adopting Rosie?"

"Adopting her?" she gasped. Her eyes widened as she tried to think of an answer to such unexpected request.

More than once, Mariel had considered succumbing to the urge to take Rosie home to Foxbridge Cloister. She would enjoy having the little girl brightening the too-quiet hallways of the house. Mrs. Parnell warned her when she first came to the orphanage that she must be able to maintain a distance from the orphans and not become too involved with any of them. That had been impossible with Rosie. The child was so adoring, she made Mariel want to shower her with love.

"I know this is sudden, and I have asked you inappropriately, Lady Mariel. It is simply that I received this yesterday. To tell you the truth, I don't know what to do about it."

Mariel took the crumpled paper from her friend. Smoothing it on her lap, she read the poorly written letter. Fighting her way through the misspelled words and incomplete sentences, she saw it had been composed by Rosie's uncle. He wanted the child to come and live with him now that she was old enough to work.

"She's barely five!" she cried. "He wants her to work? Doing what?"

"Her uncle owns a small manufacturing enterprise."

Her eyes snapped with beryl fire. "That is illegal! Worse than that, it is irresponsible to ask a child of that age to work in a shop."

Mrs. Parnell shrugged. "It's a family business. The authorities hesitate to become involved in such matters." Quietly, she added, "I thought, if you were willing, I would convince her family to sign the child over to you."

"How?"

"Don't worry about that," the orphanage director said with a secretive smile. "I shall be happy to handle that, if you are willing to take the child."

"I don't know what to say." She chuckled nervously at her own words. "That is a novel experience. How soon do you need to know?"

"By tomorrow."

"Tomorrow?" Her voice emerged as a squeak.

Mrs. Parnell apologized. "I'm sorry, Lady Mariel, but the board of directors meets tomorrow night. If I present this letter as I must, they will have no choice but to send Rosie to her uncle. If I can offer them an alternative, perhaps she might be spared a life of hell."

Rising, Mariel clutched the back of her chair. She leaned forward to retrieve her gloves. "I will let you know tomorrow. I promise I will let you know first thing in the morning." She mused, as if to herself, "I doubt if I will sleep much tonight."

Mrs. Parnell came around her desk, stepping with practiced ease over the containers on the floor. She patted the younger woman on the shoulder. "Just listen to your heart, my lady. It can tell you what you need to know."

Silently, she nodded. Some instinct guided her out of the office and house without mishap. She climbed into the carriage and turned it toward the gate. Her brain was enmeshed in confusion.

Should she take this child? Fantasies of having Rosie at Foxbridge Cloister vanished as she contemplated the reality. Twice weekly visits to the orphanage gave her little clue as to what life would be like if she brought the child into her home.

She liked her free life. Busy with various community activities, she could avoid the emptiness of Foxbridge Cloister. Although there was much missing in her life, she did not know if she wanted to trade the knowns for the unknown of having Rosie as a responsibility she could shrug off on no one else. Others would question her ability to parent this child alone, but she cared little for their opinions. All that concerned her was the day-to-day experience of having Rosie living at the Cloister.

Mariel did not realize she had stopped in front of Ian's house until the door opened and he came onto the porch. He smiled as he offered her his hand to help her from the buggy. When she stood next to him, she did not allow him to release her hand. Her fingers tightened on his.

"Ian, I must speak to you."

His smile dimmed. Knowing few would be on the common at this hour of the afternoon, he put up his hand to stroke her dark hair. She closed her eyes in unspoken delight and leaned toward him. Although he wanted to tug her into his arms and kiss her until his hunger for her lips was satiated, he simply asked, "Is something wrong?"

The tip of her tongue dampened her lower lip. When she saw his eyes following its course along the pale surface, she put her other hand on his, resting on his cane. Standing face-to-face, she smiled tremulously. He made her forget everything but the promise in his green eyes of joys unknown. When he repeated his question, she shook off the tantalizing thoughts in her head.

"Can we speak inside? I am not interrupting, am I?"

He stepped back to hold the door for her. "Mariel, you know I'm always happy to see you."

"In a professional capacity?" she teased as he drew the silk cape off her shoulders and placed it on the peg.

With his hands on her arms, he gazed into her smiling face. "In any capacity you wish," he answered without a hint of jesting. When her lips softened in a breathy invitation, he forced his eyes from them.

It would be so sweet to taste her lips, but he did not want to frighten her away. He continued to be amazed that this same woman, who fought her battles with such fervor, reminded him of a butterfly when she stood next to him. She urged him to capture her, but he knew he would destroy her ability to fly if he wiped the magic down from the wings of her soul.

"I think I need this as a friend, Ian. I need someone to listen to me. I need advice," she whispered. She could not withdraw her gaze from his. The barely perceptible stroke of his fingers against her sleeves weakened her knees as she was swept by unfamiliar sensations.

Motioning toward his study, he urged, "Go in. I will see what Mrs. Reed has to offer in the kitchen. She's busy baking for the potluck tonight."

"Is that tonight?" She shook herself, as if awaking from a heavy sleep. Reaching for her cape, she said, "I'm sorry, Ian. I forgot."

"Don't worry," he said hastily, knowing what she was thinking. He drew her hands away from the pegs on the wall. "You aren't keeping me from doing anything for it. Let me offer you something to eat. If you don't mind the informality, I will get the tray. Mrs. Reed is so busy running back and forth to the church, she has time for nothing else. After that wonderful meal you served me at the Cloister last week, I know Mrs. Reed is anxious to see if her food can top Mrs. Puhle's."

Allowing him to lighten her spirits, she laughed. "What a grand contest! The two cooks compete, and we garner the rewards. I'll wait for Mrs. Reed's luscious treat and you in the study."

Mariel found it impossible to sit. Her fingers ran along the gleaming wood at the back of the sofa. She noted a book open on the desk, next to a pile of papers. Ian must have been working on his weekly sermon when she arrived. Although she knew she should contain her curiosity, she peeked at the words.

She heared Ian's irregular steps and smiled as he entered the small room. It did not surprise her when he closed the door. Today she welcomed the privacy for a reason that had nothing to do with the yearning she could not release.

"I'm guilty!" she announced when he cocked an eyebrow in her direction.

"Reading my work again?"

She stepped forward to take the tray he balanced precariously in one hand. Carefully, she placed it on the table in front of the settee. When she was going to sit in the chair opposite, he took her hand and drew her down next to him. His finger ran along the sensitive skin of the inside of her arm until reaching her shoulder. He smiled as he caressed the half circle of her ear.

"It—it is very g-g-good," she stammered.

"This is very, very good," he agreed.

"Ian, I meant your sermon."

"I didn't."

She shook her head to force him to remove his finger moving along her jawline. Continuing as if he had not spoken, she said, "You write with a great deal of insight into the people of this shire."

Handing her a cup of tea, he said, "You did not come here to discuss my ability to preach. Tell me what's bothering you, Mariel."

"Must you always sound like a minister?"

"Must you always argue with me when you are afraid to be honest?" he countered. When she stared at him in astonishment, before lowering her eyes from his clear gaze, he added in a more gentle tone, "Forgive me, Mariel. I can tell something is distressing you. I don't like to see you unhappy, but I can't help you if you refuse to let me."

Staring into the cup, she told him about the letter Mrs. Parnell had received. He watched her mouth twist with loathing as she could not hide her outrage with the child's uncle's proposal. Only when she spoke of how the orphanage director planned to solve the problem did he react.

"Adopt her? You? That is ridiculous."

His immediate rejection of the plan startled her. "Why?" she demanded in a far sharper tone than she wanted to use.

He leaned forward and took the cup from her. After placing it on the table, he grasped her fingers. "Mariel, you are a young woman. This child is not your responsibility. Why do you want to saddle yourself with a child?"

"Saddle myself?" She ripped her hands out of his and stood. Walking across the room, she stared at the intricate pattern on the wallpaper while she tried to subdue her fury. It was impossible. Cold fire burned in her eyes when she whirled to face him. "Are you trying to say that having Rosie as my child will harm my chances for a fabulous marriage? That is what Phipps will say. I know that without speaking to her. If I wanted to hear this, I can listen to her lecture at the Cloister."

"Maybe Miss Phipps is right," he said slowly.

"And I'm wrong?" She flung out her hands in emphasis as she stated, "I am twenty-six years old. I have no plans to get married, but I do have love to share with a child. She needs someone. It seems perfect. Maybe it will ruin my chances for marriage, but is that enough reason to deny Rosie the opportunity for the life I can offer her? While I wait for some nonexistent suitor, I am supposed to let this child be sentenced to slavery in her uncle's shop?" Her words faded into incoherent rage. Blinking back the tears, she managed to ask in a lower voice, "Why are you looking at me like that?"

Ian forced his smile from his lips. This was the Mariel who stirred his blood most strongly. Vehement, caring, ready to fight anyone to do what she thought was right. He rose and walked toward her.

"I am looking at you like that because I think you are incredible, Mariel Wythe." He paused when he stood directly in front of her. His cane pressed against her skirts as he put his hand on her arm to draw her closer. "What do you want from me? A blessing on this project? I think if you feel that strongly about this child, you should bring her to the Cloister for a trial period. See if you truly want the burden of raising a child."

She did not protest when he placed one hand at the side of her head. "I hadn't thought of that. I think Mrs. Parnell would find a trial period acceptable." She smiled. "If this works out, Mr. Albion will no longer be able to tell me that I don't know about the needs of the children in the school."

"Are you prepared for this responsibility?" he asked with sudden seriousness.

"It isn't as if I am alone, Ian. There are many at the Cloister to help me."

"But you will be her mother."

Fear and joy mixed in her voice as she reflected, "Mother? I find it difficult to see me in that role, although I can imagine myself caring for her." She spoke more evenly as she added, "I can! Not just in the good times, but when she is frightened or ill."

He regarded the strong emotions fleeing across her face. Although his common sense told him that she was embarking on a foolish quest, he could not convince his heart to tell her that. Anyone but Mariel Wythe would have cringed from accepting this sudden responsibility. If it was possible for anyone to succeed at this venture, she would do it.

"You can try, Mariel. That is all Mrs. Parnell is asking." His hands caressed her shoulders. "No one should ask more of you. Not even you."

"Thank you, Ian," she whispered as she looked up into his eyes which mirrored the longings within her.

As quietly he vowed, "I will be here to help you in whatever way I can."

"I know you will."

She added nothing more as she allowed him to draw her back to the sofa. Sitting side by side, they spoke of the changes she would have to make at the Cloister to welcome the child. If Mrs. Reed had eavesdropped from the hallway, she would have heard nothing but the enthusiasm of her plans. She would not have known that Ian did not relinquish Mariel's hand during the long conversation.

Two days later, in Mrs. Parnell's office, Mariel paced the narrow floor space between the cartons and piles of paper. She did not understand why she was so nervous. It was not as if she was meeting a stranger. She had loved Rosie since she met her six months ago, during her first visit to the orphanage.

All her doubts and fears of failing surged forth to torment her. What did she know about being a mother? She could not remember her own. She had been raised by a succession of nannies unable to deal with life in the eccentric Wythe household. Her own childhood seemed ages ago. Even Ian's comforting words of support failed her now.

When she heard the door open, she spun to discover Rosie, looking far neater than she had ever seen her. The stubborn blond curls had been coaxed into two braids, which stuck out at strange angles. One was directly over her ear, the other several inches back, giving her a lopsided appearance. A dress slightly too big and decorated by a wide blue sash at its dropped waist hung past her knees. One button was missing and another was unbuttoned on her high topped shoes.

Mariel noticed all of that in the second before she looked at Rosie's face. Her own disquiet was reflected there. Suddenly she knew any fear she felt would be diminished by the fright suffered by this child, who was leaving the only home she had known.

Kneeling, she held out her hands to Rosie. Without her normal vitality, the child walked toward her. She took the little girl's trembling hands in hers and smiled.

"Rosie, has Mrs. Parnell told you that I would like you to come to Foxbridge Cloister for a visit?"

She nodded mutely. Eyes too big for her elfin face were bright with tears.

"Tell me," urged Mariel. "If you don't want to go with me, tell me. I don't want you to be unhappy, Rosie."

The words jolted the child out of her uncharacteristic quiet. "I want to come with you, Lady Mariel." She paused, then blurted, "I just don't want you to make me come back here. Then they will send me away, and I will never see you again."

Sweeping Rosie into her arms, Mariel looked up at Mrs. Parnell. Both women ached with sympathy for the child, but knew they could make no promises before this trial was completed. The board of directors had been emphatic on that point. Lady Mariel and Rosie would have a month to decide if they wished to live as a family. If Lady Mariel did not start adoption proceedings at that point, the child would go to her uncle, who stubbornly continued to demand Rosie come to live with him. How Mrs. Parnell had convinced the board to allow this unprecedented arrangement, Mariel did not ask. She was not sure if she wanted to know.

Mariel tipped back the youngster's tear-dampened face and said, "I want to work hard to be a family with you, Rosie. You must, too. It won't be easy, for the Cloister is different from here. There will be days when I get angry very quickly. I shout a lot, but that does not change my love for you. Shall we try?"

Rosie nodded, watching as Mariel stood. The child slipped her small hand into her friend's and did not release it even when she kissed Mrs. Parnell farewell. A small bag of her few personal possessions waited in the hallway.

Mrs. Parnell said quietly, "If you need any help, Lady Mariel. . ."

"I think we will be fine." She grinned at the child, who smiled tentatively. "At least, I hope so. Rosie needs to be patient with me while I learn to be a mother."

Many of the children were waiting by the automobile when they emerged from the main house of the orphanage. Mariel urged Rosie to go and tell her housemates that she would be returning for visits when Mariel came to do business. The child shook her head, refusing to let go of the woman's hand.

Understanding what the little girl could not verbalize, Mariel lifted her to the seat of the automobile. She placed the too-small satchel in the back, wondering if any of her childish clothes remained in the attics of the Cloister. They might do until she could have proper things made for Rosie.

She climbed into her own seat. Picking up her goggles from the floor, she pulled them over her head and tied her hat's veiling under her chin. With a smile at Rosie, she said, "We will have to get you some driving clothes soon. All set?"

"Yes, Lady Mariel," she answered too politely. That perfectly correct expression disappeared as Rosie flashed a superior smile at her friends while Mariel was turning the automobile to drive through the gate. She crowed with delight, "They all wish they were me!"

"Because you are riding in the automobile?"

"No, because I am going home with you."

She risked a grin in the child's direction. "I thought you might want to sleep in the room next to mine instead of in the nursery. The nursery is on the third floor. No one goes up there anymore." She laughed. "Besides, there is plumbing in a few rooms on the second floor. I don't want you coming down those steep stairs in the night to find the bathroom."

"Bathroom?" The little girl's eyes widened until Mariel feared they would pop out of her head. "You have bathrooms at Foxbridge Cloister?"

"We have many things I think you will enjoy," she promised. "Shall I take you on a tour when we get home?"

Overwhelmed, Rosie simply nodded. She shyly placed her hand in Mariel's. With a smile, Mariel urged the automobile faster along the road. For the first time, she believed this could be successful. It had been years since she had experienced this sense of being part of a family. She savored that feeling as she allowed it to soothe some of the pain she could not let anyone see.

Not even Ian.

Chapter Five

Rosie's eyes grew wide again as Mariel drove the automobile through the front gate of Foxbridge Cloister. On the few occasions when the orphans came into the town of Foxbridge, the little girl had seen the impressive house crouched like a sleeping giant at the edge of the marsh. Only knowing her beloved Lady Mariel lived there kept her from being frightened by the gray monster overlooking the village. Now she would live there. The thought seemed too preposterous to be real.

She did not fire her normal barrage of questions while Lady Mariel pointed out the various buildings connected to life in the Cloister. The little girl had not guessed so much was hidden behind the walls of the Cloister. It was bigger than the grounds of the orphanage. When the car stopped in its private barn, she found herself frozen to the seat. A man stepped out of the shadows, and she squealed with heartfelt terror.

Mariel chuckled. "Rosie, this is Walter Collins who tends to my car. Walter, Rosamunde Varney. She will be staying with us at the Cloister for a few weeks." Taking Rosie by the hand, she withdrew the small bag from behind the seat. "Shall we go up to the Cloister, Rosie?"

Keeping her eyes on the strange man, the child nodded. She did not like this man who gazed at her so strangely. She risked a glance at Lady Mariel and saw she was still smiling. There must be nothing wrong with this man, because Lady Mariel treated him with kindness. She tried to shake off her instinctive distrust of him, but was glad when they stepped out into the spring sunshine and away from his glowing eyes.

"Go ahead," urged Mariel when they paused before a clump of exultantly yellow daffodils. "You may pick one, if you wish. Just don't take too many of them. The gardeners get cranky if we take all the blossoms. They like to enjoy the beauty of their labors as well."

"I think I will leave them," Rosie said regretfully. "They are so pretty here. If I take one, it will die too quickly."

"Shall we come back tomorrow on our way to Foxbridge and see them again?"

"We are going to Foxbridge tomorrow?" the child asked enthusiastically. "In the automobile?"

With a smile, Mariel began to walk toward the house. "Tomorrow is a school day. I think it would be best if you attended at the village school." This was one point Ian had been emphatic on when they discussed Rosie coming to Foxbridge Cloister. He felt the child must be with others her own age instead of imprisoned with only adults at the Cloister.

"School? Do I have to go to school?"

"Of course." She laughed. "Don't worry about it now. Shall we go inside?"

Mariel felt Rosie tighten her grip on her hand as they entered the Cloister. Briefly Mariel wondered what it would be like to be entering this impressive house for the first time. She no longer noticed the plastic scallops edging the ceiling or the silk wallcovering glistening in the gas lights.

Only Phipps and the butler stood in the expansive foyer. Mariel appreciated the thoughtfulness of the staff in not overwhelming the child on her arrival. Calmly, she introduced the two adults to the wide-eyed child.

"Rosie?" asked Phipps. "What is your full name, child?"

"Rosamunde Varney, but everyone has always called me Rosie. . .ma'am." She added the last as an afterthought.

"Then that is what we shall call you here also."
Phipps smiled, and her stern demeanor vanished.

Although she had done all she could to talk Lady
Mariel out of involving herself in this crazy plan, Phipps
welcomed the idea of a child in Foxbridge Cloister
again. In the past year, she had shunted aside her
dreams of staying on at the Cloister as the nanny of the
children Lady Mariel would have. When the young
woman showed no inclinations toward marriage, she had
resigned herself to the solitary life of growing old with
her charge.

She followed as Lady Mariel led the child up the
stairs. Her lips pursed in disapproval as she saw the
woman allow the little girl to touch the stained glass
window on the landing. The expression softened as she
heard Lady Mariel proudly explain that this was the
crest of the Wythe family. She began to smile as Rosie
exclaimed over the two wolves holding up the herald
flag.

Phipps was sure neither Lady Mariel nor Mrs.
Parnell had paused to consider the impact of this
adoption on the community. Lady Mariel was the sole
heir to the wealth of the Wythe family. When her uncle
died, the Cloister would come to her to be passed on to
this orphan.

As the two raced up the few stairs from the landing
to the second floor, the older woman paused by the
window. Undimmed by the centuries of sunlight which
had passed through its light green glass, the family
motto written in Latin wafted on a scarlet banner
beneath the flag. *Always Prepared, Truth's Champion,*
she translated mentally. Phipps often wondered if the
creator of that phrase could have guessed Lady Mariel
Wythe would embody it four hundred years later. When
she heard the giggling from the second floor, she hurried
after the others.

Mariel pointed out the door to her uncle's now
unused rooms and the suite where she slept. Pausing by
her door, she opened it. Out burst a dark brown blur.
She grasped Muffin's collar just as he was about to put
his nose directly into Rosie's face. The little girl was
staring at the springer spaniel as if he was a monster.

"Rosie, this is Muffin," she said as she dragged the dog back from the child. "She's just enthusiastic. She loves children."

Regarding the dog's brown eyes and the full coat covering its chest, she whispered, "To eat?"

Mariel laughed and shook her head. "To play with. Do you want me to put her back in my room?"

"You sleep with her in your room?" she asked incredulously.

"Yes."

"Oh." For some reason that Mariel could not decipher, that fact seemed to change Rosie's mind. She held out a tentative hand and stroked the dog's head along the white stripe between its eyes and along its wide nose. Suddenly she grinned. "She's soft."

"Just like butter melting on a muffin." Mariel chuckled again. "That's how she got her name. Now would you like to see your room?"

"Do I have a Muffin, too?"

Taken aback by the abrupt reversal, Mariel glanced at Phipps. The older woman was trying not to smile at the odd request. Mariel answered honestly, "No, there's only one Muffin, but I'm sure you can convince her to sleep with you sometimes."

Rosie's smile broadened as she patted the dog before skipping after the others. Opening the heavy door next to hers, Mariel ushered the child into the spacious room. It was a simple room, once a servant's quarters, but the single room and attached bath would be perfect for Rosie. A chair and a small table would provide space for school work. Books clustered on the shelves, and a well-used dollhouse waited in one corner beneath a window overlooking the ocean. A jumbled selection of stuffed animals and dolls sat on a chest at one edge of the slightly worn Oriental rug.

"For me?" cried the little girl. She ran to the tester bed and threw herself on its neat covers.

Mariel laughed until she heard Phipps's outwardly outraged sniff. Hating to dampen the child's excitement, Mariel went to the bed. In a stage whisper, she warned, "We don't jump on beds with our shoes on, Rosie." Her voice dropped as she added, "Only with them off, and when Miss Phipps is not around."

Rosie giggled, but slid off the now-rumpled bed. Her eyes were caught by the toys, which she had not seen in the first moments of discovering this luxury of having a massive room for her own use. Awed, she approached a doll dressed in a creamy white nightdress. Her fingers reached out to touch the china curls, but hesitated.

"Go ahead," urged Mariel when the child looked over her shoulder for permission. "She endured my kisses when I was your age. I think she will enjoy being played with again."

Dropping to the floor, the little girl pulled the doll into her lap. Gently she examined every inch of the eyelet gown and the tiny leather shoes. Her face beamed with happiness as she asked, "Can she sleep with me? Can I name her?"

"Of course. I called her Alice, but you may name her whatever you please."

"I like Alice."

"I did too." Mariel sat on the small chair, savoring the joy of having a child in the house again. She pointed to the chest. "She has more clothes in there. Uncle Wilford always had a dress made for her each time he had one made for me."

"So you and Alice could be twins?"

Mariel's smile vanished. Rosie looked from her suddenly shattered features to the shocked expression on Miss Phipps's face. Something she had said was horribly wrong, but she could not guess what it was. A wave of homesickness washed over her. At the orphanage, she knew everyone well. She did not have to worry about every word she spoke.

Struggling to escape the horror such innocent words allowed to run free in her mind, Mariel forced a fake smile on her too-tight lips. "Yes, so we could always look alike." She took a deep breath. "Phipps will unpack for you. I have some work to do. Why don't you play here? I will be back in a few minutes."

Rosie watched, disconcerted, as the woman walked out of the room without further explanation. Needing

to know the truth, she turned to Miss Phipps and asked
bluntly, "What did I say wrong?"

With a sigh, the older woman looked back at the
unhappy little girl. She had thought Lady Mariel had
put that sorrow behind her, but it appeared the lady
simply had fooled everyone into believing she had
accepted her past. The truth was not for this youngster
on her first day at the Cloister.

"You said nothing wrong, child," Phipps assured
Rosie quickly. "It is Lady Mariel. Sometimes she is very
sad. When she is like that, I think you can help best by
giving her a big hug and by not asking any questions."
She absently patted the curls escaping from the uneven
braids. Again she sighed and shook herself to break free
from the tentacles of the past. "Now, shall we see what
you have to wear to supper tonight?"

With the door to her own rooms closed, Mariel
groped for a chair and dropped into it. She hid her face
in her hands, and she began to cry as she had not been
able to do in many years. Such open words laid bare the
wounds which would not heal. She had thought having
Rosie here might help, but already it seemed the child
would only make things worse.

Although she had tried to tell herself there was
nothing she could have done to change what happened
the night Lorraine died, guilt continued to plague her.
She should have guessed what would occur and worked
to alter it. In retrospect, all the signs of the disaster had
been firmly in place weeks before that night.

Her hands pressed against her ears as she heard the
childish screams in her own younger voice. Other sounds
of destruction and death ricocheted through her head.
She could not close them out, for they came from within
the treasury of her memories.

"Oh, Lorraine, why did you have to say that to
him?" she moaned. "Why did you have to teach that
rhyme to me?"

As in the past, there was no answer for any of her
heartfelt questions. Only when the last burning tear
coursed along her cheek did she raise her head. The
shadows crossing the room told her it was nearly time
for the evening meal. A surge of present-day guilt

washed over her. She had brought Rosie to the Cloister, then abandoned her to Phipps's care. Hurrying to get ready for the evening meal, she vowed that would not happen again.

When she knocked on the door of the neighboring room, Phipps answered it. Mariel nodded to her whispered question. She was all right, at least until the next time the horror oozed from the secured vault in her head. She put it from her mind as Rosie ran to her, chattering about the treasures she had found in the toy box. Mariel let the little girl's joy fill the emptiness in her. She drew the child onto her lap as she laughed with her.

"So you like this room?" she asked, although Rosie's glowing face spoke of her happiness.

"I love it, Lady Mariel!"

"Why don't you call me Mariel?"

Rosie gasped. "Mariel? You want me to call you Mariel?"

"Only if you want." Mariel smiled with a shyness she was unaccustomed to feeling. "Maybe later, if everything works well for us, you can call me something else, but for now I thought you might want to call me Mariel."

"Yes." Her head bobbed so hard it appeared as if it might bounce off at any moment. "Yes, M-Mariel!"

Placing Rosie on the floor, Mariel rose and offered her hand. "Shall we go and explore some other parts of the Cloister? I know you will want to know where the kitchen is. When I was your age, I liked to 'help' there. That way I got to sample everything while it was cooking."

Rosie giggled as they walked out of the room hand in hand. She had already decided that she wanted to stay with Lady Mariel. No, she corrected herself mentally, simply Mariel. She vowed to try not to bring the sorrowful expression to her friend again.

Each room they visited Rosie enjoyed more than the previous one. As Mariel expected, she was welcomed royally by Mrs. Puhle. The woman, who always had a sweet for any child who came to the kitchen door, could not hide her delight with having a youngster to spoil again.

Mariel was laughing at Rosie's impressions of the house as they entered the solarium. Of all the rooms on the ground floor, this was Mariel's favorite. Built three steps up from the hallway, the room offered a special haven in the big house. Not that it was cozy. Its ceiling, fifteen feet from the floor, was crisscrossed with heavy beams. A circular iron chandelier accented the ornate metalwork on the arched tops of the tall windows.

Rosie ran to peer out. She squealed with excitement as she pointed to the gardens and the strip of light at the horizon, gray against the dark sky. No child of the shire could be unaware of the sea. Its rhythms controlled the life of the land by bringing storms and balmy breezes.

For a moment, time telescoped for Mariel. She saw another little girl running carefree through this room, intent on discovering what mischief the new day would bring. That youngster, with black pigtails flapping against her back, had not learned yet of the sorrow waiting for her in the near future. Then, she had known only the joy of childhood. Rosie brought that happiness back to her.

Sitting on an oak chair upholstered in the pale green of the Foxbridge crest, Mariel watched as Rosie skipped from window to window. When the child turned to her, she held out her arms. Rosie hesitated for a brief second, then, with a smile, threw herself into Mariel's embrace.

"Can we go for a walk? Can we go and see the gardens?"

"Not tonight, but soon," Mariel promised. "It is nearly time for dinner. We do not want to be out when Reverend Beckwith-Carter arrives."

The child's face froze into distress. "The minister? He is coming here? Why?"

Mariel smiled. "I invited Reverend Beckwith-Carter to join us, Rosie. He is eager to meet you."

"Will I have to listen to him preach about the orphans' obligations?"

"What? Oh, that would have been Reverend Tanner!" Mariel patted the child's hand as she grimaced with her own recollections of Ian's pompous predecessor. "Reverend Beckwith-Carter is nothing like that old bore."

"Don't believe her. I am much worse," came an amused voice from behind them.

As Mariel stood, Rosie could not miss how her guardian's eyes glistened with an emotion she did not recognize. She looked from one adult to the other as Mariel greeted the minister pleasantly. Some unseen thread held them together in a sweet caress, although they did not touch.

"Ian, I did not hear you come in."

"I know I'm early. I wanted a chance to talk with your friend before we sit down at the table." He pulled his eyes from the beautiful woman to look at the scrawny child in the too large dress. Offering his hand, he said, "Hello, Miss Varney."

She dipped in a quick curtsy to avoid shaking his hand. She did not want Mariel to tell Mrs. Parnell that Rosie Varney had no manners. A mumbled, "Hello, Reverend Beckwith-Carter," was barely audible.

"Reverend Beckwith-Carter?" he repeated with a laugh. "Why don't you call me Ian, as Mariel does?"

With a scowl, she realized this man would demand some of the precious time she had with Mariel. Rosie knew too well that this magic might not last forever. She did not want to share the few days she might have at the Cloister. Clasping her hands behind her back, she eyed Reverend Beckwith-Carter suspiciously. She knew what ministers were like. They treated you nicely, then warned you about the need to be grateful to anyone who might give you clothes filled with rips and holes. Every bite she had eaten she must be thankful came from someone more fortunate than she. She did not want to be reminded that Mariel might only be doing her Christian duty. She longed to think her friend welcomed her to Foxbridge Cloister simply because she might care for Rosamunde Varney.

"Mrs. Parnell told me to be polite, Reverend Beckwith-Carter," Rosie said pointedly.

Ian glanced over her head to see Mariel's amused grin. The youngster made her opinions very clear. In this way, she and Mariel should get along well. When she put her hands on the child's shoulders, he listened without comment.

Mariel turned Rosie to face her. "Mrs. Parnell is correct, Rosie. You should always be polite. Now Ian is asking you to be his friend and call him by his given name. I think it would be most ungracious to refuse such a kindness, don't you?"

"Yes," she said grudgingly. She did not want to lose Mariel's love. Vowing not to call the man anything, she nodded her head. She just wanted him gone.

Knowing that to push the issue might cause permanent damage, Ian spoke of the news from the countryside. He had been making calls all day and had much to share. When he motioned for the others to sit, he saw Rosie stay close to Mariel. He understood the child's need to cement her relationship with the woman she adored. He would not intrude tonight, although he longed to sit next to Mariel and hold her slender fingers in his.

This was one thing he had not mentioned to her when they discussed bringing the youngster to Foxbridge Cloister. Not only would Rosie complicate Mariel's many activities, but she would make it difficult for her guardian to have any time alone with him.

Both sets of blue eyes brightened with enthusiasm when he mentioned the rumor of a band of Gypsies bringing their circus close to the shire. Whether their meandering journey would enter Foxbridge, no one knew. The thought of such entertainment suggested new and strange delights.

"Let us know as soon as you learn if they are coming here," urged Mariel. "We would love to go, wouldn't we, Rosie?"

"Oh, yes!" Her smile dimmed as she looked at the man in the seat across from them. She wondered if he would be included in the invitation as well.

Mariel saw her jealousy and wondered what she could do to convince Rosie there was no reason to feel this way. Sitting here would not help. Rising, she said, "I was giving Rosie a tour of the Cloister, Ian. Would you like to join us? I was about to show her the portrait gallery. You might be interested in that."

When he politely offered her his arm, a small whirlwind stepped between them and grasped Mariel's hand. He tried to keep the frown from his lips, but failed. She drew Rosie to the other side and placed her fingers on Ian's arm as if there had been no interruption.

"How wonderful!" she said with too much warmth as she sought to cover the unease in the room. "To have both of my friends here with me. Shall we go?"

By the time they reached the door leading to the long, narrow gallery, Rosie had recovered her good spirits. She chattered nonstop about everything she saw. Mariel answered her questions as quickly as they were posed and with a patience that startled Ian. The sharpness she presented to others was muted when she spoke to the child.

Rosie ran ahead to turn on the gaslights. Ian took the opportunity to ask, "How is it going?"

"Better than I expected," she said with a sigh. "I imagine it will be easier when we become accustomed to each other. She likes her room and has charmed the staff. I am sorry she is being so cold to you. That is not like Rosie."

He smiled. "She is averse to sharing you. I understand how she feels." He drew his arm away so he could take her hand. Easily he turned her to face him. "My dear Mariel, I understand all too well."

"I thought you would. You have learned—"

With his finger on her lips, he silenced her. "This has nothing to do with my work, my dear. These words are directly from the heart. I find myself wanting to spend more time with you, not less, and not time I must share with that cute youngster."

"Ian, I did not know," she whispered. She swallowed harshly as she realized how stupid she sounded. Her trite words covered the truth. She had known his desire to have her to himself. He took advantage of every opportunity that presented itself for them to steal a few minutes alone. As she did. Daring to open her heart slightly to him, she asked, "Why haven't you said something?"

"I am." He picked up her fingers and pressed them to his lips. His keen eyes did not miss the softening of her face as she breathed a sigh of delight at the touch of his mouth against her skin. Without releasing her hand, he added, "I would like another chance to be alone with you soon."

Flustered by the strong emotion in his words, she mumbled, "I am so busy with Rosie now. I don't know when—"

"You will find time soon." He grinned, the desire in his eyes replaced by good humor. "Somehow you will find time. Mariel Wythe can do anything she is determined to do."

With a laugh at the lopsided compliment, she said, "Next Saturday—not this one, but a week from this coming Saturday—shall we go on a picnic?"

"The three of us?"

"The two of us." Her voice muted as she gazed up at him. "I cannot promise, for so much depends on Rosie. If she adjusts well to school and to the Cloister, I—"

An impatient young voice interrupted her. "Hurry, Mariel. I want to see the paintings."

With a smile, Ian offered her his arm again. "Shall we?"

Rosie ran forward to take Mariel's hand as the adults entered the narrow gallery of the Cloister. Although the gaslights burned in their regularly spaced sconces, the room was dim with shadows. There were no windows to admit the starlight. The smell of a room too long unused assaulted their senses as their footsteps echoed along the long room.

Mariel watched as Ian paused before each of the portraits. The Wythe family had been living at Foxbridge Cloister since the early sixteenth century, so there were many pictures to enjoy. Proudly, she told him about the painter who did each portrait. She never grew blasé about the glories of her home.

"Your family certainly is an awe-inspiring group," he said admiringly as Rosie raced ahead to look at the other pictures. "Your ancestors glare out of their portraits as if they intend to take on the world even now."

She smiled. "The Wythes have been known to be assertive, even before this generation. Uncle Wilford told me many tales of the pranks he and my father perpetrated during their boyhood. They were twins. Twins have been in nearly every generation since the time the Lords Foxbridge took up residence at Foxbridge Cloister."

"But not your generation?"

When she did not answer as she bent to speak to Rosie, Ian was sure she had not heard him. He repeated the question. This time, when she began to speak of something else, he suspected he had touched on another subject Mariel would not discuss. He wondered why she should be secretive about something so harmless, but did not continue to ask. If he truly wished to know, he could check the church records. All births in the parish were recorded there.

Mariel did not look at him as she pointed out various ancestors and told a tale about each. There seemed to be gaps in the family history, but she either did not know of those times or did not reveal the stories.

He listened to tales of violations of every tenet he taught in the church. Not always against the Wythes, for the family fought for what they believed was right. That Mariel had made her battleground the relatively sedate school board did not lessen her determination to continue in that tradition.

As he viewed each painting, he thought of the many lives spent within this house. All of these who had come before depended on this young woman to be what they had been. Dozens of Wythes had lived and died here. Only Mariel and her uncle remained. Ian knew she did not intend for the sunset to fall on the glory of this house.

"Here is the same woman as down in the front parlor," he said with surprise. No other figure had been repeated. A single portrait had been painted of each Lord and Lady Foxbridge. Knowing Mariel, he doubted if any of them would have had the patience to pose longer than that.

Mariel shook her head and smiled. "Everyone thinks that, but the two women lived nearly two hundred years apart. That is my great-great-grandmother, Rebecca Wythe. She came from America."

"The one who started the village school?"

"Yes, that one. The woman in the painting downstairs lived during the time of Queen Elizabeth."

"Amazing!" He leaned closer until his nose nearly touched the one in the painting. The poor light in the gallery protected the artwork, but made it difficult to view the faces easily. "Perhaps this is where you inherited your blue eyes. Most have the darkest brown eyes I have ever seen."

"Like my uncle's. They are nearly black. Are you finished?"

Although he would have enjoyed spending more time studying the different styles of painting, he nodded. He could tell Rosie was determined to be on her way. The child paced from the doorway to Mariel and back in a clear signal to go on to the next adventure. He guessed the viewing of paintings was too sedentary for a five-year-old.

"Which ones are your parents?" he asked as Rosie ran to turn down the lights.

"Can't I show you some other day?"

He turned to see her watching the little girl. Slowly he nodded. "Of course. Are you sure you can handle this, Mariel? I am here to help you in any way I can."

"Ian, don't become the minister with me today," she teased. "I need to know how to entertain a child, not to hear a sermon."

"I can't help it!" He chuckled. "It becomes habitual."

She placed her fingers on his dark coat. "Just be my friend. I need a friend far more than I need anything else."

Her honest supplication surprised him. His hand stroked her upper arm, visible through the fine material of her wide sleeves. "You know I am your friend, Mariel. I did dread coming to this small parish, although it offered the challenges I wanted. Meeting you has told me my time here will be infinitely more enjoyable and infinitely more challenging than I planned."

"I don't know if that is a compliment." Her eyes twinkled as she watched his moving along her figure with candid admiration.

Slowly his fingers tightened to bring her closer. His voice was subdued as he put them under her chin. While he spoke, his mouth descended toward hers. "Rest assured, my dear, it is a compliment."

Mariel's eyes widened. With a gasp, she stepped backward to leave him awkwardly hovering over a nonexistent woman. She whirled, so her back was to him. In a breathless voice, which displayed the reaction he could not see, she called, "Rosie, I think we should return to the solarium. Phipps will be wondering where we are."

The child ran to take her outstretched hand. At the same time, Rosie shot him a triumphant smile. She had the attentions of Mariel, which both of them wanted. Chattering, she tried to monopolize the woman, but Mariel turned to ask, "Are you coming, Ian?"

Before he could answer, she had opened the door at the end of the gallery. He shared a joking grimace with her long line of ancestors before following. Now he had two females to win over if he wanted to gain the chance to taste Mariel's inviting lips. A challenge was what he had called her. It was one he would not hesitate to accept.

Chapter Six

Mr. Knowles smiled with superiority as he motioned for Mariel to sit in the chair she normally used during the board meetings. "It was good of you to come so quickly in response to my note, Lady Mariel. Your devotion to that orphan reflects upon your gracious and open heart."

"That orphan," she stated curtly, "I consider my daughter. I trust you will remember that, Mr. Knowles."

He sniffed. Even after nearly a month of having to deal with the child, he could see that she was not ready to admit this episode had been a grievous mistake. No one would ever accept that urchin as Lady Mariel's daughter. She was a fool even to attempt this grand exercise in futility.

His eyes noted the packet of information she had brought with her, and he scowled. This would be the propaganda on the textbooks she expected him to read and agree with. He refrained from glaring at the ceiling. Jones was correcting work upstairs. That the young idiot thought Lady Mariel's idea was as fabulous as if it had been his own continued to irritate Knowles. Heated words had been exchanged in the small house down the street on this very subject.

"Be that as it may, my lady, the child is out of place in this school."

"Out of place?" Mariel asked. She glanced around at the bare walls. Mr. Knowles did nothing more than the basic necessities with the children. Until they graduated upstairs to Mr. Jones, they learned nothing of music or art.

At the Cloister, she tried to fill that void for Rosie by teaching her to play simple tunes on the piano and giving her bits of material and baubles to make imaginative creations of color. Phipps was helping her learn to do the needlework, which had always bored Mariel, and was discovering an eager student. Rosie enjoyed anything she could do to make a pretty picture.

"Your *daughter,*" he said with snide emphasis, "is creating havoc in my classroom."

"Is she?" Mariel drew the pins from her hat and placed it on the table. She folded her arms in front of her and returned the man's glare. "That is a surprise, Mr. Knowles. Rosie acts fine at the Cloister."

"Perhaps you have different standards of behavior there."

She laughed shortly. "I might, but I can assure you that Miss Phipps demands a very high standard of behavior from all of us under that roof."

"Is that why you behave as you do when you are not at the Cloister?"

Her blue eyes locked with his. Although she knew the man despised her, he had not made it so blatant in the past. She refused to retort with the comments rolling through her brain. "Mr. Knowles," she said coldly, "I understood that you wanted me to come here to discuss Rosamunde Varney, not to throw childish insults at me."

Knowing he had overstepped the bounds of polite society, he mumbled a hurried apology. Over and over, he had told himself before this meeting that he would not allow her to anger him so much that he forgot himself. Now barely five minutes into it, she had succeeded in doing just that.

He rose and put the width of his desk between them. In a strained voice, he stated, "The child is a problem, Lady Mariel. She and the Lyndell boy have been disrupting the class every day."

"How?"

With eager delight, he listed the multiple crimes the two youngsters had committed. Mariel's eyes grew dark with anger as she listened to the pettiness of the teacher. A piece of broken chalk and a tipped water bucket were not more than accidents. If a book fell on the floor from another child's desk, it must be Rosie's fault.

"Is that all? Why not blame Rosie for the Original Sin? It is the only evil done in this world you have omitted. Are you sure you haven't missed something?" she demanded when he was finished. "May I say something, sir? You are far more guilty than the child. Not only have you wasted my time by asking me to come to this worthless conference, you have shown yourself as a bigot who should not be teaching our children."

She placed her hat on her head and jabbed the pins into it with the furor she wished she could reserve for tormenting him as he had Rosie. Until now, she had not understood why the child hated coming to school every day. She had spoken to Mrs. Parnell about this. The orphanage director had been just as baffled about Rosie's reluctance, for the child had loved attending the school there.

Standing, she said, "I bid you good day, sir, unless you have something of value to say to me."

"She deserves to be expelled!" he snapped.

"Because you cannot handle her high spirits? I thought one of your duties is to maintain decorum in the classroom. If you cannot handle a five-year-old—"

He slammed his ruler on the desk. Mariel started at the sharp crack. Her lips tightened to a straight line as she recalled the red welts on Rosie's hands. This must be Mr. Knowles's favorite method of punishing his students.

"That child does not belong here with decent children."

Trying to restrain her temper, she answered, "I said I would be glad to listen if you had anything to say of value. As you wish only to discuss your prejudiced ideas, I can see no reason to continue this further, Mr. Knowles."

"I will speak to the orphanage board about this!" he shouted at her back.

Mariel paused. Turning, she walked to the front of the room. He was so startled when she pulled the ruler from his hand, that he released it. She cracked it over her knee and dropped the two pieces onto the desk.

"Do not threaten me, Mr. Knowles," she said with icy calm. "I realize you think of me as only a bothersome woman, but do not forget that the Wythe name has considerable influence. Touch my child with that stick or any other again, and you will find yourself looking for another position without a recommendation."

"Lady Mariel, if you think you—"

She smiled at his reddened face. "No, Mr. Knowles, I don't think that I can have you removed. I *know* I can. Good day, sir."

Feeling his glare in the center of her back, she regally crossed the room. She could not let him guess at the distress within her. That Mr. Knowles would use Rosie to rid himself of his frustration with Lady Mariel Wythe was something she had not considered. She did not want to pull the little girl out of the school, although it would not have been difficult to find a tutor for her. She wanted her to be with other children, instead of alone in the world of adults at the Cloister.

Suddenly, she felt overwhelmed. Bringing Rosie to the Cloister had not been as simple as she expected. Although the staff adored the little girl, and she returned that affection freely, she refused to lower her guard to Ian. It made his now more infrequent visits to the large house uncomfortable. Nothing Mariel did could convince the child to change her mind. Stubbornly she continued to call him "Reverend Beckwith-Carter."

Ian had said nothing to Mariel about Rosie's coldness, but she knew it bothered him. As she wanted to have him come to the Cloister more often, she found herself desperate for a solution. The added problem of Mr. Knowles did not make this difficult time easier. Within a week, Mrs. Parnell would want her answer, if she wanted to keep Rosie permanently. Only Mariel's longing to do nothing to ruin the newborn relationship with Ian made her hesitate.

She strode across the green. As she knocked on the parsonage door, she glanced over her shoulder to see Mr. Knowles watching her with a frown on his face. That the man would judge her for the simple act of calling on a friend increased her rage until it blinded her to everything else. Without bothering to wait for an answer, she swung open the door.

Ian stepped back as Mariel burst into the foyer. When she spat a terse greeting to him without pausing in her march to the study, he sighed. He put his hat on the peg and unbuttoned his coat while he followed. Mariel broadcast her furor broadly.

When she turned to face him, tears of frustrated rage brightened her eyes. Without giving him a chance to speak, she exploded.

"How dare that pin-sized brain tell me that I am taking Rosie into my house only because I want to prove my charitable concerns! He says Rosie is incorrigible. He says she has no place with decent children. He blames her for every misdeed perpetrated in that school. He wants her expelled. Can you believe that? He says—" She paused to take a breath and looked at him curiously. In a sorrowful voice, she asked, "Are you going out, Ian?"

He laughed. Stripping off his coat, he dropped it over the back of the settee. He held out his hand. "I was, but I think I am needed here. Sit down, Mariel."

Dropping to the sofa, she leaned against him and whispered, "Hold me."

"Certainly."

He masked his surprise at her amazing request. Until now, Mariel had been very careful to keep the barrier between them. As he drew her into his arms, he felt the quivering remnant of her rage draining away into grief. Gently, he stroked the delicate line of her shoulder.

Fiercely, he fought his smile. He would not want her to suspect how he was taking advantage of her sadness to enjoy feeling her so close. With his cheek against the top of her head, he savored the touch of her slender fingers.

Comfort eased Mariel's anger. With her face on his chest, she could hear the steady pumping of his heart. The sound welcomed her to nestle closer. She sighed softly as she moved closer to the sturdy strength of his body.

When Ian's fingers brought her chin up so he could look into her eyes, she smiled. "Thank you."

"For what?"

"Helping me."

A single finger moved along the silken texture of her face. "It was my pleasure, my dear Mariel."

She drew back when she heard his husky tone and saw the glitter in his eyes. With a soft chuckle, he moved away from her. She pressed against the back of the settee as the disappearance of her fury left her empty. His left arm rested on the top of the settee while his right hand continued to caress her face.

Dampening her suddenly dry lips, she said, "Ian, you should not do this here."

"Not here? This is my home, my dear."

"This is the parsonage!" she gasped.

"So?"

Mariel pushed him farther away and rose. Pointedly she sat in the chair opposite the sofa. When she saw his amusement, she spat, "I have no intention of being seduced in a parsonage!"

"No?" He leaned forward and retrieved his cane from the floor. He twirled it between his fingers as he asked, "Where exactly do you intend to be seduced?" When her cheeks tinted pink, he chuckled. "Forgive me, Mariel. That was an inappropriate thing to say. It is difficult to think of you so often and see you so seldom. Each time I do, Rosie is with you. It is not easy to enjoy your company when she makes it so clear how much she loathes mine."

"I have tried to talk to her about this," she replied. "I never realized how stubborn Rosie could be."

He stood and took her hand. Without speaking, he brought her back to the settee. She watched as he sat next to her. His hands sandwiched hers between them. When he smiled, she tried to hide her unease.

"Mariel, what do you want me to say? That you have tried your best, so it is all right to give up? You don't want to hear that." His brows formed a straight line across his forehead. "Or if you do, you aren't the woman I thought you were."

"Ian! It is not easy! I have been trying so hard, but it doesn't seem to help. She refuses to be pleasant to you."

"Don't press her. I remember another lady from that house who made her dislike of me clear. Rosie reminds me of a smaller, less resilient copy of you, Mariel. Let her find her own way. She will come around eventually."

She waved aside his reasonable words. "Until then? I-I-I—" She paused as she fought her shyness to say what she wanted to tell him. When she saw his gentle smile, she forced the words past her trembling lips. "I want to see you more often, Ian, but each time the three of us are together, there is trouble."

"Then the two of us. You promised to join me for a picnic last week."

"It rained."

"This Saturday we shall go. Just you and I, Mariel." He released her hands to frame her face with his warm palms. His intense green stare cut into her to reveal the yearnings of her her soul. "Just the two of us. Yes?"

"Yes," she answered as if caught within a spell. Her fingers came up to cover his. "On Saturday."

The muted gong of the mantelclock broke her mesmerism. She stood so hastily her petticoats flared behind her. When she heard him step toward her, she moved to the door. Her hand settled on the knob, although she was loath to end this meeting.

"I will see you Saturday, Mariel."

She looked up at him and wondered if touching his face would thrill her as much as when he stroked hers. When she realized her fingers were rising to do exactly that, she dropped them hastily to her side.

"It will be fun."

He laughed. "I hope you sound more enthusiastic about it then than you do now. If—" He paused as a knock resounded through the house. "Mrs. Albion. That woman is obsessed with her altar cloth."

His frustration with the wife of her nemesis on the school board brightened Mariel's spirits. It would be fun on Saturday. And she would take Ian's valid advice. Perhaps by allowing Rosie to make her own decisions, the child would learn to like Ian as much as her guardian did.

With a cheery farewell to him and a quick greeting to the dour-faced woman at the door, she ran across the green. If Phipps had witnessed such childish behavior, Mariel knew she would be reprimanded harshly. It was simply impossible to be sedate when her heart sang. Saturday was only two days away. Then she would have a chance to be with Ian as she had only dreamed.

Saturday dawned with the clear perfection of spring. The morning sun peeked over the top of the Cloister to find its way into Mariel's room. Slithering past the drapes and the curtains of her bed, its warmth tickled her nose.

After eating breakfast with Rosie and Phipps, Mariel returned to her room. She sang as she took a quick bath. The luxury of the claw-footed tub was something she took for granted, although she had been thrilled when it was installed five years before. Wrapping a towel around her, she danced across the room to the melody she hummed. It was impossible to deny her happiness. It had been building within her since Ian suggested this outing.

From her closet, she selected a pale blue gown, one which would withstand the punishment of the salt and sand. The frock of dotted swiss muslin was decorated with an organdy square bib on the bodice. It had been embroidered with an intricate pattern of green and blue to match the silk sash accenting the narrow line of her waist. The three-quarter-length sleeves ended in a half cuff edged with lace. A straw hat embellished with a rose sat on the back of her head. It would relieve her of taking a parasol to the beach.

Mrs. Puhle had the picnic basket ready when Mariel came into the kitchen. When she handed the young woman the basket covered with a linen towel, the plump cook stated, "Roast beef sandwiches, potato salad, pickles. . ."

"Wonderful," Mariel interrupted before the cook announced everything in the basket. She peeked in to see that all she had ordered had been packed.

"Have a pleasant day, Lady Mariel."

She met Mrs. Puhle's knowing grin steadily. A bit of mischief entered her voice as she said, "I intend to. Oh, don't forget Rosie is having a guest for lunch."

"I remember, Lady Mariel." Her delighted laughter followed Mariel out of the kitchen.

Crossing the garden bright with blossoms, she reached the garage. She smiled when she saw the automobile was ready. A glance at the gauge on the floor told her it had been properly charged. The cables were coiled neatly to the side.

She looked quickly around the barn, but Walter was nowhere to be seen. Vowing to commend him for his efficient work the next time she spoke to him, she loaded the basket into the back of the automobile. She checked that she had everything she wanted.

With a half-spoken curse, she realized she had forgotten the blanket to protect her dress from the relentless, rough particles of sand. She left the basket on the fender of the car and raced back to the Cloister.

Dodsley opened the door and was halfway down the steps as she sped across the emerald grass. Laughing, he held up the heavy wool blanket. "Miss Phipps thought you would want this."

"Thank you." She bundled it under her arm as she spun to return the way she had come. Over her shoulder, she added, "Tell Phipps I appreciate it."

The butler chuckled again. Lady Mariel never failed to act as if she was late, even if she had plenty of time to get where she was going. Her impatience drove her hard, but she seemed to thrive on the fast pace of her life.

Mariel tucked the blanket between the seat and the batteries at the back of the automobile. She picked up the cloth, which had blown off the top of the picnic basket. Stuffing it down into the sides of the container, she placed the basket on the floor by the passenger seat. In the small vehicle, they would be crowded, but it was not a long ride from the village to the easiest path down to the beach.

Ian was waiting for her on the porch of the parsonage when she brought the automobile to a smooth stop in front of the steps. She smiled as she saw how handsome he appeared even through the dust on her glasses. Raising them, she allowed her eyes to rove along the surprisingly light tan of his frock coat. A plaid vest covered his white shirt with its high stock closed by a perfectly arranged tie. Dark brown trousers matched the band of his Panama hat. Seeing him in something other than his sedate ministerial blacks was a charming change.

As he settled himself on the plush seat, she readjusted her driving goggles. With a wave to Mrs. Reed, she turned toward the shore road.

The small vehicle protested as she drove it up the hill beyond the rectory. Concentrating, she kept their speed constant and did not let it stall. When they reached the top, she smiled at the accomplishment.

"You truly love this automobile, don't you?" asked Ian as he leaned back against the comfortable, royal blue upholstery. His arm rested behind her, but he did not touch her.

"It is wonderful."

"Because it is new and different?"

She laughed. "Partly. You know my affinity for anything I feel will be important in the next century. I do like it simply because it can be so efficient. Now that Walter is taking care of it, I have not had any breakdowns."

"It seems odd to be riding in it again." He grinned. "I have been waiting to have a chance to be with you without Rosie, but I must admit I miss her sharp comments today."

She smiled. "She must have a chance to be a child, instead of being with adults all the time. Tip Lyndell came up from the village to play with her today. I am sure they will give Phipps and the others a busy day."

She listened as he spoke of the news from the village. Although she could feel his eyes on her, she did not dare to take hers from the road. The ruts left by the spring rains did not gibe with the axle width of her vehicle. They bounced along toward the shore.

When she parked the automobile in the short grass near the edge of the cliff, she wondered if her eyes would settle back in one place. It seemed as if everything still jounced unevenly across the horizon. She admired how the blue of the sea stretched to its meeting with the sky. The brisk wind ripped her hair from beneath her hat to float in front of her face. She wanted to pull off her hat and race along the strand.

Ian smiled as she looked in his direction. "It is beautiful, isn't it?" he asked.

"Beautiful and powerful and forever. I cannot imagine living away from the sea." She placed her thick coat on the seat and brushed the wrinkles from her dress. "How boring it must be never to have the song of the waves rumbling in your ears!"

She reached for the blanket, and her fingers met Ian's. Instantly, as it had the first time she touched him, the spurt of electricity raced along her, creating a glow on her face she could not dampen.

"I will take the blanket, Mariel," he said softly. "The basket is lighter."

"Yes," she agreed. With her face afire, she could think of nothing else to say.

When he held out his hand to her, she slowly raised hers to place it on his palm. His fingers closed over it as he drew her closer. She gazed up into his face. Beneath his auburn brows, his green eyes caressed her sweetly. She felt her lips part in a breathy sigh. Suddenly she shook herself.

"Shall we go, Ian?"

"Of course." He put the blanket over his hand holding the cane. "I am anxious to sample this beauty on the sand below."

Mariel hid her concerns as Ian led the way down the steep path to the beach. By the time they were halfway to the strand, she realized she need not worry. He was as surefooted with his cane as she was with her two good legs. Soon they stood side by side on the pebbles at the base of the cliff. She sat on one of the larger rocks.

Without modesty, she drew up her skirts to reveal her calf-high shoes. She unbuttoned them, removed them, and drew off her black stockings. Stuffing them into the shoes, she glanced up at Ian.

"With all the sand, I don't. . ." Her voice faded as she saw his expression. Heat swept over her that had nothing to do with the warmth of the summer sun.

His hands settled on her arms and he drew her to her feet. Without her shoes, she discovered her eyes were even with the fullness of his lips. As they tilted up in a smile, she lifted her gaze to meet his. His fingers created a tingle against the skin of her neck as he moved her head into the perfect position for his mouth descending toward hers.

Unable to move, mute, and captured by the sweet sensation of his arms around her, she welcomed his kiss. Her hands slid along his arms to clasp behind his neck. The crash of the waves and the screech of the seabirds vanished into the vortex of the passion drawing her to him.

A muttered oath severed the magic. She clutched onto Ian as she felt them sway together. With a grin, he stabilized himself on his cane. "Damn leg!"

"Reverend!" she stated with feigned shock. "Such language!"

"Compared to what I was thinking, it was mild indeed. I have been waiting so long for that kiss. I think such an expletive is appropriate." His eyes sparkled as he traced her slim lines with his eager gaze. "It was not difficult to be godly, until I met you, Mariel. Are you my temptation?"

She laughed. "Such a thing to say, Ian!"

Taking her hand, he watched as she picked up the basket and her shoes. As they walked closer to the water, he said softly, "I meant it as a compliment. You are the most beautiful woman I have ever seen, but it is more than that. I have never met anyone as full of life

as you. Since the—since I hurt my leg, I have found it
more comfortable to watch life as a bystander. You
could never be that way."

"No," she said with characteristic honesty. "I can't
imagine letting the world pass me by. Ian, what happened to your leg?" Hastily she added, "If you don't
want to tell me, you don't have to, of course."

He took the blanket from her and shook it out to
settle slowly to the sand. As she sat on one corner, he
said, reflectively, "The question sometimes bothers me,
but not when you ask it. You don't want to know simply
because you are curious."

"Yes, I do!" she retorted with her pixie smile
brightening her face.

"It is not simply that. You care about me, don't
you?"

Her lips parted in a breathless invitation as she
looked up into his face. "You shouldn't have to ask that,
Ian. You know you are very special to me."

"As you are to me." He sat by her, watching the
wind course through her hair, loosening the pins holding
it in a sedate bun. "I hurt myself in a stupid hunting
accident at a house party after I was graduated from the
seminary. I was riding with some friends and others.
Overwhelmed by the zeal of the chase, I tried to jump
my horse over a thicket I knew he could not take. He
went down. I went down under him. My leg was
crushed." He said the words with the dull resignation he
had learned since the accident. "By the time my friends
found me, they did not know if I would live. At that moment, they did not think of anything as inconsequential
as whether I would ever walk again."

"But you did," she whispered as she gazed at his
handsome face. She wanted to take the sorrow from his
face so it would be alive with happiness once more. Her
hands slid along the sleeves of his frock coat.

She sighed softly as he pushed aside her thick hair
to place teasing kisses against the side of her neck. Her
fingers tightened on his shoulders. When his mouth
moved to cover hers, her eyes closed in eager surrender
to the passion swirling through her. As he leaned her
back onto the blanket, she drew him with her. She had

found what her heart craved, and she did not want to lose it.

As the pace of his kisses grew frantically, she felt the answering surge of longing within her. She gasped with the power of the desire overtaking them as his tongue slipped between her open lips to conquer the interior of her mouth. It jabbed and retreated, caressed and cajoled until she found herself moving with its rhythm, yearning to feel it touch all of her as succulently.

His lips roved along her face again to seek the hidden joys of her skin. Although she heard her own voice whispering his name in a breathless tone, she was only aware of the ecstasy urging them to satisfy it.

He drew away from her slightly, and she opened her eyes slowly. "Must you stop?" she whispered.

A wry grin crossed his lips. "You always read me so well, my love. I *must* stop, for to continue would be more than I think you want now."

"But, Ian, I want you to kiss me."

"And I want to kiss you." He did so very lightly. When he heard her moan of longing, he moved away from her. That she responded so ardently to his caresses should not have surprised him. He could not imagine Mariel being halfhearted about anything.

He reached for the basket. Uncorking the bottle of wine, he poured two glasses. He tried to ignore how her fingers shook as she reached for the one he held out to her. He admired the fall of dark hair swirling around her shoulders, shadowing the form he wanted to learn intimately. As he lifted his goblet to drink, her hand touched his wrist, halting him.

"One moment," she whispered. "I want to make a toast."

"A toast?"

She lifted the glass and said softly, "To our hearts' dreams. May they come true soon."

While she drank delicately, he watched her. He had come to this distant shire to escape those he knew in London. Their pity and unintentionally cruel remarks cut into even the thickest skin. Coming to Foxbridge had been a mindless race from what had been. He had not expected to find this special treasure here.

"Drink up, Reverend," she urged with a laugh, which severed his serious thoughts. "Or do you think of your sermon tomorrow? Will you be preaching on the virtues of abstinence?"

He drained the glass easily. "Why not the sin of wastefulness? Your uncle keeps a fine cellar, Mariel."

"I hope you will meet him." She drew her knees up to her chest. Her full skirt covered her demurely. "Uncle Wilford is like no one else I know. He does exactly as he pleases. He comes home when he wants and goes wherever he chooses. Each place he goes to, he brings me home a present. I have a closetful of the most exotic outfits you could imagine."

Taking her glass, he moved closer to her. His avaricious gaze swept over her as he murmured, "You might be surprised what I could imagine." He traced an invisible path of rapture along her cheek. "If I could select one exotic costume for you, I would like to see you dressed in the crimson glory of a sheikh's favorite." His hand moved to stroke the silken wisps of hair floating aimlessly on the breeze. "To see the entire length of you hidden only in filmy silk."

"Ian!" She was startled to feel the heat of a blush rising along her cheeks.

He laughed at her rosy face. "You didn't think clergymen had fantasies?"

"Not of that sort!" She chuckled. "By the way, it is not crimson. It is royal blue. Almost the same shade as the automobile's upholstery."

"What is royal blue?"

"My harem outfit, which Uncle brought home from the Ottoman Empire. He told me he bought it from the man who makes them for the sultan's harem." She folded her arms on her knees and watched the clouds racing the sea wind. "It is blue velvet with gold tassels. The girdle is embroidered with strange symbols and set with carnelians. He even purchased the matching pointed-toe slippers."

When Ian did not join with her laughter, she met his steady gaze. She gasped as she saw the naked hunger on his face. His mouth captured hers once more, licking the drops of wine from her lips. Instantly she felt the longing envelop her in its heated mists.

His kisses along the angles of her face were tantalizing. Their gentle teasing made her long for the return of the fire of his touch. He smoothed her hair from her forehead so he could kiss the soft skin. He felt her stiffen against him at the same time he saw the puckered line of a scar. Now he understood why she wore her hair in unstylish thickness across her forehead. It hid the one thing that detracted from her perfect features.

Pushing away his fingers, she rearranged her hair to conceal the mark. His strong hands kept her next to him. A cry of horror erupted from her lips as he moved the hair aside again so he could see the three-inch-long scar.

"Don't, Ian," she begged in a tone foreign to the Mariel he knew. He could not have imagined her pleading with him about anything.

"How did it happen?" He sensed her pain. Although from the look of it, he guessed this had happened years ago, he could tell the anguish of whatever had caused the injury still burned within her.

"I was hurt in an accident."

"An accident? What type?" he pressed.

She turned tear-bright eyes to him. "Ian, the day is so lovely. Do we need to discuss this now?"

"I think you do, honey."

With her eyes closed, she fought the horror, which rose in her whenever she thought of that nightmare time. "I was hurt the night my twin sister died."

"Twin sister?" He released her, his shock too intense to allow him to be still.

"My sister Lorraine. There was an accident. She was killed. I was hurt." She refused to look at him. Softly, she said, "I don't want to talk about it."

"How old were you?"

"Ten." Her hands reached for his. "No more now, Ian. Please."

He drew her head against his chest and stroked her back. "As you wish, honey. Just remember I don't want to do anything but learn everything there is to know about the fascinating Mariel Wythe."

"Let's eat. Then we can take a walk along the water." She smiled weakly, trying to regain the joy she had known moments ago. "The water is so cold this time of year. You will not want to put your toes in it for at least another month."

Although he wanted to discover why a frightened Mariel hid behind the brash front she exposed to the world, he did not want to ruin their brief hours together. He listened to her light chatter and responded. At the same time his mind was busy with unanswered questions. He was sure if he asked them in the village, he would hear the story of the night Lorraine Wythe was killed and Mariel hurt. Those queries he would not make. He wanted her to open her wounded heart to him. Only when she trusted him with that pain could she allow herself to bare her heart to other emotions.

The picnic luncheon met the high standards Mrs. Puhle insisted were kept in her kitchen. It did not take them long to enjoy the sandwiches and salads while they sipped on the sweet wine.

Mariel waved aside the offer of dessert. "You can eat both, Ian."

"I just may," he said with a laugh. "Chocolate layer cake may be my downfall, especially Mrs. Puhle's." He shook his fork at her, and dark crumbs fell to the blanket. "Don't tell Mrs. Reed I said that."

"I will not do that. There is no wrath like a cook scorned." She giggled as she packed the napkins and dishes back into the basket.

He yawned as he finished the last bit of the frosting. "All right. Let's go for that walk. I think I have had too much sun. It's made me sleepy."

"Not too much of Mrs. Puhle's delicious food?" She stretched as she stood and looked out over the water. Not seeing Ian's eyes on her appealing silhouette, she said, "I think I shall sleep well tonight."

His arm snaked around her slender waist to draw her close to him. Careful this time to lean on his cane, he drew her lips beneath his once more. He felt the soft lines of her body and yearned for far more than this chaste kiss. Her innocent words painted an image in his mind of her sharing his wide bed in the front bedroom of the parsonage.

Suddenly he laughed. Mariel had made it quite clear how she would feel about any seduction in that building.

"What is so funny?" she demanded.

"You, my dear."

"Me?" Her nose wrinkled as she looked up into his face. The sun was glaring into her eyes. "I don't think I like the sound of that."

"How about the sound of this?" He whispered in her ear, "You are the most enticing, most—"

Mariel whirled away and chuckled as his words were lost in another gigantic yawn. Weakly, he grinned at himself. He certainly would never charm her this way.

"I think we should go before you fall asleep, Ian," she teased.

Knowing anything he said would bring more merriment, he simply offered her his hand. She smiled as she slipped her fingers between his. They wandered along the beach while she pointed out various sights among the craggy rocks.

Pools of water were warm in the sun, but the splash of the ocean reminded them of how close they still were to winter. Sand squished between their toes as they left deep footprints behind them. They walked about a mile before turning back toward their blanket.

She paused by a wide crack in the cliff wall he had noticed at the beginning of their stroll. "Wait here."

Before he had a chance to reply, she raced away across the sand. He watched as she searched for something in the basket. A smile reflected the joy within him. He could never guess what Mariel would do. To discover the lush sensuality hidden beneath the prim clothes she wore had been a true delight.

Mariel glanced over her shoulder as she felt Ian's gaze on her. Bending to her task, she fought the soul weakening strength of her longing to feel his lips on hers again. She could not lie to herself and pretend that was all she wanted. With the fierce power of the kisses he placed on her skin, she wondered how much more potent would be the love they could find together.

Despite the strictures of society, her uncle had felt she should know about the physical side of the love shared by men and women. He had answered her questions with an honesty unacceptable in Victorian England. Mariel knew well the danger of the strong yearnings overtaking her.

With a grin, she told herself she was being foolish. Although Ian enjoyed kissing her, he was the village pastor. He might think of kissing her in his study, but he would hardly be imagining the delights in her mind. She remembered the many sermons Reverend Tanner had repeated Sunday after Sunday about the evils of lust.

She shook her head. That wicked desire could not be what she felt for Ian. As she looked at him surreptitiously again, she knew there could be nothing evil about this sweetness binding their hearts together.

Finding what she wanted in the basket, she rose. When she returned to where Ian stood, she held out a candle. She also carried a box of matches. Pointing to the crevice which was two feet wide and nearly five feet tall, she asked, "Shall we go into the cave?"

"I would guess you have come this way often if you are so well prepared," he teased.

"You have been curious about the Wythe family. I thought I would show you something here."

His forehead furrowed. "About your ancestors? Is this where you have buried them?"

She smiled mysteriously. "Not exactly." Striking a match, she held it out of the wind as she lit the candle. "Are you coming?"

"With the suggestion of past mayhem to be unearthed, do you think you can keep me out?"

"Be careful," she warned. "The floor is uneven. This is a tidal cave and fills up at high tide. The waves have carved out the floor in very strange patterns in several places."

Offering her his arm, he motioned with his cane for her to enter. The sound of the waves was magnified as they stood within the cool dankness. Troughs of briny water filled the lowest spots on the floor, but they had hours to explore before the tide resurged through this opening to fill it dangerously.

Mariel stumbled suddenly. Ian caught her before she could fall. When he teased her that she should listen to her own advice, she smiled. He turned to examine the striations of rock in the walls, and she rubbed her eyes. She felt strange. Her head was as light as a child's helium balloon floating away into the sky.

Not wanting to worry Ian, she said nothing. She was glad when her eyes refocused and she felt normal again. *Too much sun,* she surmised. It had been a long time since she had come to the beach to spend a day in quiet happiness.

"This is fabulous," said Ian, his voice echoing grotesquely between the walls. He held up the candle. The light gave up the attempt to reach the ceiling. "Does the cave lead anywhere?"

"This is just the entrance. What I want to show you is farther on."

He offered her the candle. She took his hand again as they walked along the slowly rising, cracked floor. Beneath them they could feel the steady pulse of the waves reverberating through the rock, but the rest of the world ceased to exist in the silence of the cave.

When she warned him to go more slowly, he glanced at her smiling face, distorted by the flickering light. They stopped before a gap in the floor of more than seven feet wide.

"This is where my great-great grandfather saved his wife from a man who wanted to kill them both," announced Mariel with pride. "Way back in the eighteenth century. The man abducted my greatgreat grandmother and imprisoned her on the far side of this crack. Grandfather saved her. Her kidnapper ended up dead at the bottom of that." She pointed to the shadowed slit. "I'm sure his bones are still there if they haven't rotted in the dankness."

Ian took the candle and held it over the chasm. "Down there?"

She nodded as she took a studied step back from the edge. Her eyes had begun to bother her again with their strange blurring. Normally heights did not bother her, but today she felt the need to be cautious. Trying to mask her disorientation, she spoke lightly.

"We Wythes have a long history of taking care of our enemies effectively." She sat down with her back against the wall. The nausea in her stomach eased when she leaned her head on the stones behind her. Drawing her bare feet up, she watched as he peered into the bottomless hole. "Your family, too, if I remember the tale correctly. There was a Beckwith involved."

"Really?" He walked over to where she sat and lowered himself to the stone floor of the tunnel. Resting his cane over his knees, he drew her closer. "Hero or villain?"

She laughed lightly. The sound sparkled along the tunnel. "What a question! I thought the background of pastors would prove to be without a blemish." She leaned against his arm, which encircled her shoulders. After a moment of deep thought, she said softly, "I think it was a she, and I think she was a good person." She paused, battling the lightness of her head to find the strength to speak. He did not hurry her. When she was able to talk again, her words came slower and slower. "To tell you the truth, I don't remember the story too well. Grandmother told it to me. It was about her grandparents. Too long ago to think about."

Her eyes blinked several times as she looked up into his face. She rubbed them, but nothing cleared the fog in front of her. When Ian put his hand on her cheek, she tilted her head against his chest. She relaxed and let the world spin wildly around her. Resting here with Ian was heavenly. She did not want to move.

He regarded the top of her head placed so trustingly against him. With a yawn even wider than the ones earlier, he bent forward to kiss her hair, which smelled of the sun and salt. As he tried to raise his head, he felt as if weights had been placed on the back of his neck. Closing his eyes, he accepted the inevitable. He was asleep before another thought could form in his head.

Chapter Seven

Mariel felt the cold before anything else. As she fought to open her eyes, she shivered. More than the cold, she felt dampness. Water sprayed her face, and she forced her heavy eyelids open. Darkness, unbroken by any light, surrounded her. Memories of another black night, filled with horror, burst into her mind. Never-forgotten panic swelled through her.

"Help!" she screamed. "Uncle Wilford, help me! Help—"

"Hush, honey," came a moan not far from her ear. Strong hands caught her flailing arms as she fought off a nonexistent tormenter.

The soft words broke the grip of terror. She whispered in a voice still thick with fear, "Ian? Is that you? What—where are we?"

Gentle fingers touched her face and turned it to where he must be in the ebony darkness. "The tunnel. Don't you remember? You brought me to show me the chasm."

"I remember," she answered as memory burst into her head. "What happened?"

His voice grew as chilled as the water as he stated, "That I have no answer to. The last thing I remember is being so tired I could not move."

"I was dizzy."

"There must have been something in what we ate. Someone wanted us to fall asleep out here."

"But why? To ruin our reputations?" She laughed bitterly. "That could not hurt me. Everyone knows the crazy Wythes do as they wish. And you have not been here long enough to gather any enemies."

He chuckled with more sincerity than he felt. "The wine may simply have been tainted. It weakened us until we slept it off."

"But who would have done it? Mrs. Puhle packed the basket. It was never out of our sight."

"It doesn't matter now." He stood. "It's cold in here. Shall we go?"

"Where?" She did not move. When another pulse of the water splashed against her skirt, she added, "This is a tidal tunnel. Remember? The entrance must be filled with water if it is reaching us here. We won't be going anywhere until the tide goes down." She reached up to touch his trousers. "Please sit down, Ian. That chasm is so close. We could fall in so easily in this dark."

With a sigh, he did as she suggested. "We must have been asleep for quite a while. The candle has burned out, so this is the night tide."

"Damn!" Giggling, she said, "Excuse me, Ian."

"I've heard worse. What is wrong?"

"My favorite slippers and my new hat were on the blanket on the beach. By this time, some fish is enjoying them." As he wrapped his arm around her, she laughed lightly. "Go ahead and tell me I shouldn't complain when we are alive."

His fingers stroked her face. "Why do you expect me to be a saint? I am a man like any other, simply trying to do my best to help this world. In that, I am no different from you with your community work. Do not try to imbue me with such wondrous qualities all the time. I have my faults."

"I know."

"You can be very vexing!" he snapped, but he was smiling.

"That I know, too."

Her laughter faded as she leaned against him again. Whatever had been wrong with their food or drink remained to ache in her stomach. She did not want to be sick in front of Ian, so she fought the distress.

The hours passed slowly as they waited for the water to ebb along the tunnel. In the dampness, they pressed close together to keep warm. They spoke infrequently, but the silence was not uncomfortable. They had passed the point where they must not allow the conversation to falter. It was enough simply to sit quietly and listen to the whisper of the water slipping across the stones.

Whenever the water failed to reach them, they moved closer to the entrance of the tunnel. Ian used his cane to test the depths ahead of them, but no amount of impatience hurried the ebbing of the waves.

The first hint of the end of their vigil was the sparse glitter of moonlight peeking through the top of the crevice. Mariel cheered when she pointed it out to him. Although the light vanished almost immediately, to reappear with the motion of the sea, it meant that soon the water would lower enough for them to escape.

Ian drew her to him and tasted the smile on her lips. He teased, "Are you so happy to be done with our picnic, my dear?"

"It will be memorable."

"Because of this escapade?"

Her fingers rose to the wilted collar of his shirt. She could feel the layer of salt on the material as her hands clasped behind his neck. Softly she said, "You know I cannot forget this, but it is what we shared on the beach I will remember first when I think of this day."

"That part we will have to repeat soon." He lifted her matted hair aside so he could outline the half-shell shape of her ear with his tongue.

Mariel leaned against the wall as her knees threatened to fail her. When he stepped closer, she put her fingers on the back of his head to steer his mouth through the darkness to hers. At her eager gasp of joy, he pressed her tighter between him and the unbending wall. In the soaked dress, every inch of her slender form could be felt through the layers of clinging material.

They parted with a laugh as they were splashed by a wave higher than the others. With his hand on her cheek, he brought her face toward him. In the dim light filtering into the cave, he whispered, "We shall do this again soon."

"Yes, we—" A shiver raced along her, and she smiled. "But not in this cold water."

He joined in with her amusement, although he would have preferred to continue kissing her. That she had not complained once about the bone-chilling cold did not surprise him. He guessed the layers of skirts and petticoats she wore would be heavy and uncomfortable hanging from her waist. His own clothes had lost any semblance of their original shape.

Releasing her, he stepped forward cautiously to test the depth of the water. Within a few paces, he paused and called, "I think we can get out now, Mariel. Here!" He extended his hand to her. "Let's try."

"Good!" She started to raise her skirts in an automatic motion to keep them from the water. Laughing at herself, she dropped them back into the waves. She could see Ian stood up to his knees in the cold blackness. It might be deeper before they reached the exit.

Her grip tightened on his hand as the motion of the water buffeted them. The undertow threatened to pull her feet out from beneath her. More than once, she clutched desperately to Ian as they reeled toward the moonlight. The pressure increased near the crevice.

Ian paused as he measured the tempo of the water. Warning Mariel to move when he gave the signal, he watched for when they would have the least resistance as they attempted to follow the water through the hole.

"Now!"

Mariel did not release his hand as they surged forward on the flow of the ebbing wave. That they were too slow she learned as an incoming one slapped her in the face and against the stones. She swallowed her moan of pain with a bitter dose of salt water. Ignoring her shoulder which had struck the wall, she continued toward the beach.

When they emerged from the waist-high water swirling through the entrance of the tunnel, she was spun into Ian's arms. His victorious exultation was silenced as he kissed her joyously. He started to speak, but they heard shouts far down the beach.

Lanterns glowed on the strand like giant fireflies.
When Ian bellowed in the tone he reserved for Sundays,
the movement of the lights froze. Exclamations rolled
along the water to reach them. Almost instantly they
were surrounded by the townspeople who had been
searching for them.

At first no one asked what had happened. Warm
blankets were placed over their wet clothes. Mariel was
swept away from Ian as helpful hands drew her toward
the path up the cliff. She peered over her shoulder, but
could not see which one he was among the press of the
crowd on the strand.

Then everyone around her began pelting her with
questions. Kept busy responding, she was able to forget
her aching shoulder and her feet sliced by the rocks in
the cave. Gentle hands lifted her into a carriage she
recognized as one from Foxbridge Cloister. She only had
to time to identify the driver as Walter Collins before
the door closed and the carriage lurched into motion.

She peered out of the window as they turned in the
direction of the Cloister. Another buggy waited for Ian
among the scattered vehicles on the marsh grass.
Nowhere did she see her automobile. She wanted to ask
about it, but realized someone would have mentioned it
if there had been trouble. She suspected it had been
driven back to the Cloister.

Leaning back against the lush cushions of the
carriage, she sighed. Phipps was sure to be outraged,
even though their adventure had been accidental. She
wondered what Rosie would be thinking. As vehement
as the child had been about her not going with Ian,
trouble was guaranteed. If only Rosie would relent. . .

Mariel sighed again. After today, nothing could be
the same for her and Ian. The first kiss by the path had
forced her to face what she had been fleeing for a
month. She could easily love this man she had despised
on first meeting. His gentleness, which covered the
steely strength he fought to subdue, fascinated her. On
the beach, she could dream of happiness. Back among
the rest of the world, she wondered if it could be as she
wished.

The harsh light of flares penetrated the windows of the carriage as it stopped by the front stairs. Dodsley swung open the carriage door before it had halted completely.

"Lady Mariel!" he cried. Over his shoulder, he shouted, "She is here! Unhurt."

"Almost," she answered with a grimace, as he helped her to the ground. She could not stifle a moan when he took her left arm to help her up the stairs. "My shoulder," she whispered. "I bumped it."

Moving his hand to her other arm, he assisted her up the steps. He shouted orders for Walter to bring Dr. Sawyer from the village. When she mumbled that the doctor was not necessary, he hushed her with uncharacteristic sternness.

He did not allow her to pause in the foyer, but led her directly up the staircase, which must have lengthened while she was away from the Cloister. She feared they would never reach the top. When the butler spoke to someone, she forced her eyes to leave the floor to meet Phipps.

The reprimand she expected was left unspoken. The older woman quietly urged Dodsley to take Lady Mariel into her rooms without waking Rosie. He assisted her to a chair and watched as she lowered herself into it gingerly.

"I have sent for the doctor, Amanda."

"Thank you," Phipps said without taking her eyes from the disheveled woman. "And the reverend?"

Dodsley started. "I didn't think to ask. I can go—"

"He is fine." The two glanced at Lady Mariel who was cradling her left arm in her right hand. "We were caught in a tidal cave by the high waves. We simply had to wait for the water to come down."

The gray-haired woman's lips tightened in anger, but she spoke to the butler. "I am sure they will bring him here. The guest room is available for Reverend Beckwith-Carter's use."

"Yes, Amanda. I will see to it."

"Try to keep everyone hushed, so the child can sleep." Her glare riveted on Mariel as she continued, "She had a great deal of difficulty going to sleep tonight, worried as she was. I hope she can rest enough so she does not take ill."

Dodsley left to do as requested while Phipps went to run water in the tub. Mariel forced herself to her feet to follow. She saw her companion bent over the Dutch tiles, which decorated the claw-footed tub. Dropping the damp blanket on the Grecian vase styled water closet, she began undoing the hooks on the back of her dress. Involuntarily, she gasped as she stretched her aching shoulder.

"Here," stated Phipps in her most no-nonsense voice, "let me help you with that." As Mariel turned compliantly, she continued, "You know better than allowing the tides to catch you off-guard, Lady Mariel. There will be much talk about this."

"Not if the truth is told." She winced as she lowered the ruined sleeve along her arm. Meeting Phipps's eyes squarely, she stated, "Ian and I were doing nothing illicit, if that is what you are suggesting."

Phipps's mouth became a straight line of disapproval. "I did not suggest that, Lady Mariel. Others will. How could you be so foolish?"

"Something in our food put us to sleep."

"To sleep?" The older woman could not hide her horror. The thought of her charge curling up next to a man she was not married to insulted her most Victorian sensibilities. "Lady Mariel, you will not be able to show your face beyond these walls again."

Mariel scowled as she untied her petticoats. "My face and I will continue as we have in the past. I am alive. Ian is alive. That is all that should be important. If I had not shown him the cave where my great-grandparents triumphed over their enemy, we might have drowned on the beach. That strip is covered totally by high tide water at this time of the moon."

Phipps mumbled something and flounced out of the room, her insulted dignity evident. Untying the stiff ribbons of her underclothes, Mariel wanted to shout after her. She knew it would be useless. Phipps considered reputation to be of the ultimate importance. On this one thing, they had argued often in the past.

Sinking into the lusciously warm waters of the tub, Mariel closed her eyes to savor the heat. She wanted it to ooze all the way to the center of her bones. Only the sting in the cuts on the soles of her feet broke into the perfection. She ran her hands along the ceramic and delighted in the luxury of this bath tonight.

A knock on the bathroom door roused her from her half-slumber. When Phipps informed her the doctor had arrived, Mariel called that she would be out in a moment. Rinsing the soap from her hair, she hurried from the tub. She pulled a dressing gown over her. The loose garment would allow the doctor to examine her shoulder.

Hobbled by her sore feet, she went to greet the doctor. Dr. Sawyer did not smile as she walked unevenly toward him. His broad jowls, accented by his wide sideburns, quivered with barely suppressed emotion. Dark eyes appraised her clinically, and his frown deepened. As he motioned for her to sit on the settee, his sparse silver hair glistened in the lamplight.

"Lady Mariel, the reverend is unfamiliar with the dangers of the Cloister beach. His ignorance I can forgive, but how could you have been so foolish?"

"Please, doctor," she said tiredly. "Miss Phipps has already regaled me with my idiocy. I will tell you what I told her. There was some impurity in our picnic food, which made both Ian and me ill."

His rage vanished as if with the flip of a switch. "Ill? How?"

"Tired, dizzy, sick to the stomach. Just a general malaise. We lost our battle with it in the tidal cave. When we felt better, the water was too high to escape. We had to wait for it to lower." She carefully said nothing about the unspeakable sin of falling asleep so innocently in Ian's arms. Dr. Sawyer would be as unaccepting of that as her companion had been.

"Hmm. . ." He added nothing to that, but ordered her to show him the soles of her feet. Opening his bag, he pulled out a salve and lathered them generously, then he bandaged them until she was sure she would not be able to feel the floor through the many layers.

Phipps added from the shadows, "Her shoulder also, Dr. Sawyer. I understand she struck it when they were coming out of the crevice."

Examining her through the thin material of her dressing gown, he frowned. He apologized before asking her to loosen the robe so he could see the shoulder. She tried to submerge the blush rising along her skin as his fingers moved competently along the curve of her shoulder and across the front of her chest. As soon as he was finished, she pulled it closed again.

"I think you have only bruised it, my lady. I can feel no broken bones. If it continues to bother, I can send you to the city for a Roentgen ray picture of the bones. I believe there is a technician in Liverpool."

Emerging from the shadows, Phipps stated, "No, doctor. I will not allow such. I have heard of those so-called X-ray photographs. People have been burned badly by exposure to them."

Dr. Sawyer nodded. "I agree. I think soaking the shoulder in epsom salts and warm water will suffice. The Roentgen rays have not yet proven that their value is greater than the risk." He looked directly at Mariel as he ordered, "Rest, Lady Mariel. No more larks on the beach or about the shire until that shoulder is better. Do you understand?"

"Of course, doctor." She smiled at him, knowing she had no intention of being quiet simply for a bruise on her shoulder.

In spite of his wish to intimidate her into listening to his suggestions, he could not help returning her smile. He admired Lady Mariel. More than anyone else, he understood the tragedies she had suffered. He had arrived in Foxbridge shortly before the typhoid epidemic that had killed her parents. He had been called to the house the night her twin died and often in the horrible years before then. What he knew of the Wythes, he spoke of to no one else. That Lady Mariel had survived with this resiliency impressed him.

"Very well, my lady. I am going to check on our adventuresome parson now. I suggest you go to sleep. Do not hurry to rise in the morning."

"Soon," she promised. "First, I want to relax with a cup of hot chocolate to take the last of the cold from me. The water is frigid this time of year."

When the doctor chuckled and went to the room down the hall, Phipps offered to go for the cup for her lady. Mariel thanked her, but asked her to bring it to the solarium. At that moment, she did not feel like sleeping. She was not tired, for she had slumbered for hours during the afternoon.

She was not surprised to see many of the household staff waiting in the room when she entered. With pleasure, she soothed their concerns. That her disappearance had caused this much worry surprised her. She had known the Wythes were well loved by their servants, but had never expected this outpouring of emotion.

Within minutes, she was sitting on the sofa and laughing with them over her misadventures. Her voice faded as she heard the distinctive sound of Ian's cane on the stone floor of the hallway. She stood as he limped into the solarium. Aware of the others around them, she did not rush to throw herself in his arms as she wished. Instead she asked, "What do you think of this reception?"

In the same light tone, he said, "More than I expected." Phipps arrived with a tray. She handed him a cup of steaming chocolate and urged him to drink it. He took a sip, but did not remove his eyes from Mariel. Dressed in a mauve silk dressing gown with her hair in dark waves along her back, he wondered if anyone could be more desirable than this blithe spirit.

"Reverend," repeated Phipps insistently before he realized she had spoken to him once.

"Yes, Miss Phipps?"

"Please sit down. You must be exhausted. If you will give me a list of what you need, I can have clothes brought for you from the parsonage."

Tightening the belt of the too wide smoking jacket he wore over trousers which did not reach his ankles, he shook his head. Lord Foxbridge's wardrobe had yielded little to fit him. This was the best available. He placed the barely touched cup on a table. "There is no need to put yourselves out like this, Miss Phipps. If I can impose on one of our rescuers to give me a ride into the village, I will—"

"Nonsense!" she retorted. "Neither you nor Lady Mariel are stirring from the Cloister until you are rested. I cannot understand why you chose today to go to the beach. It is barely spring. If you do not take care, you may catch your death of cold."

Mariel put her hand on Ian's arm as she moved to stand next to him. "Orders," she said with a light laugh. "I have learned it is better not to argue with Phipps when she uses this tone."

Much later—long after all of the searchers had left to seek their own homes and hours since they had washed the salty crust from their skin, the adrenalin of their adventure having seeped away to leave them so exhausted they could not think of moving—Ian found himself alone with Mariel. Phipps had reluctantly gone to bed when she could stay awake no longer, but had left no doubts that the two would be well chaperoned by the staff of the house.

He smiled at that thought and regarded Mariel with her feet hidden beneath the silk folds of her robe. She reclined on a settee. He rested his feet on a hassock as he stared at the dance of the flames on the hearth.

"I should go home."

"In the morning," she murmured. "It must be nearly dawn already. You are welcome to stay here to sleep, Ian."

He smiled. "Yes, I would say you have the room. Now I can understand why you welcomed the idea of bringing Rosie to live with you. Did you ever get lonely here all by yourself?"

"Yes."

At her strangely terse answer, he lifted his head from where it leaned on his fist. All fatigue vanished when he saw her sorrowful expression. Softly, he said, "You still miss your twin sister?"

"It sounds odd, but I do. When she died, it was as if a part of me did, too. Not that I always liked her. Sometimes I hated her. We were sisters, after all, and she was as strongwilled as I am. Maybe it comes from being together before memory begins." Suddenly, she sat up and said in a tight voice, "I don't want to talk about this, Ian."

"I'm sorry."

"Don't pity me!" she cried. "Disagree with me, call me a fool, hate me, but never pity me!"

He rose and sat next to her on the settee. Slipping his arm around her shoulders, he drew her trembling body back against his chest. "Mariel Wythe, I can't imagine pitying you. Nor can I think of a time when I could hate you. What I want is to learn more of you, sweetheart, and to taste the honeyed warmth of your lips."

"Ian!"

He paused as he was bending to kiss her when he realized a younger voice had called him. His mouth became as round as his eyes when he met Rosie's smile. He moved to greet the child who had called him by his first name, but she glanced past him.

"Mariel!" With a sob, she rushed forward to throw her arms around the dark-haired woman's neck.

"It's all right, baby," soothed Mariel as she stroked the trembling child. Even as she repeated the phrase over and over, she shrugged her shoulders in response to Ian's unspoken question. Why Rosie suddenly called him something other than "Reverend Beckwith-Carter," she could not guess. Her eyes widened as Rosie whirled out of her arms and looked at Ian in indecision.

With a laugh, he motioned for her to come to him. As her exuberant form bounced toward him, he laughed. "What are you doing up so late?"

"So late?" demanded Rosie. "It's morning."

The adults looked toward the western facing windows, but no lessening of the dark had forewarned the sun rising on the other side of the house. When the child asked if he was staying for breakfast, Ian smiled.

"Of course. How could I resist such a wonderful invitation to have a meal with two of the loveliest ladies in Foxbridge?" He sat her on his good knee and asked quietly, "Are you sure you want me to stay?"

She nodded. "I'm sorry, Ian. I prayed you would go away and leave us alone. Last night, I was afraid you had gone and taken Mariel with you. Miss Phipps told me my wishes would not come true, because only loving prayers are answered. She told me I was foolish to think Mariel would love me less just because you are her friend. She told me you could be my friend, too."

"I would like that." He smiled and tweaked her nose. "I would like to have a special friend named Rosie."

Mariel said quietly, "Rosie, go to the kitchen and tell Mrs. Puhle we would like breakfast as soon as possible. Ian needs to get his sleep if he is going to preach later this morning."

With a yelp of enthusiasm, Rosie raced away to seek out the cook, who spoiled her more than anyone else in the house. In her wake, Mariel put her hand on Ian's arm. He drew her into his embrace.

"I never suspected. . ." She shook her head in disbelief. Just when she had thought Rosie would never accept Ian, she welcomed him to the Cloister.

"What is the old saying? 'An ill wind blows no good'?" He smiled. "Surely there must be one about the sea washing unexpected treasures onto the shore after a storm."

"I'm sure there is something like that." She smiled as he reclined her head back against the hardness of his arm.

He pressed his mouth over hers. His hand sliding along the silk of her robe discovered her softness, which was hidden beneath her daytime clothes. As he sought deep within her mouth for her delight, she tightened her grip around his shoulders. The treasure Mariel had found on the beach today she did not intend to lose again. In the twilight of the dawn, she could not guess how she would have to fight to keep what she had discovered.

Chapter Eight

Ian rubbed his nose as he heard Mrs. Reed greet someone in the foyer. The tickle did not ease. Fighting it, he smiled as he saw the man at the study door. "Come in, Mr. Turner," he urged. He turned his head when he could control the oncoming sneeze no longer. "Excuse me. I think I caught a cold after taking a chill on the beach below Foxbridge Cloister. Come in. What can I do for you today?"

The senior member of the church board did not respond to the warm welcome. His granite-like square face refused to crumble as he gruffly stated, "May I sit, Reverend Beckwith-Carter?"

"Of course. Shall I send for tea?"

"No, I shan't be long. What I have to say should be said quickly."

The smile fled from Ian's face as he gauged his guest's nervous demeanor. Mr. Turner was concerned about something. What could be worrying him, Ian did not attempt to guess. It was clear he would learn the truth soon enough. He placed his pen on the desk and put the stopper in the bottle of ink. He wondered if he would have a chance to catch up on his correspondence. A letter from his mother demanded his attention. He had not written to her in more than a fortnight. Each time he began this task, someone interrupted him.

Rising, he went to the settee. He sat and motioned for the other man to do the same. Mr. Turner hesitated for so long, Ian began to wonder if he would move at all. Finally, he perched himself on the very edge of a chair.

"Now, Mr. Turner, as you cannot stay long and want to get this over with quickly, I suggest you begin. What is the crisis bothering the church board?"

"It's Lady Mariel," the older man answered reluctantly.

"Mariel?" His eyes widened with surprise. This was the last thing he had suspected would be troubling them. "The church board has a problem with her?"

Mr. Turner frowned. "Not with her, Reverend. With you and her." When Ian did not reply, the man continued uneasily, "The church elders would not like to report to your superiors misconduct between you and Lady Mariel."

"Misconduct?" Unless they could convict him for the crimes he had committed in his heart, there was nothing he had done wrong. Many had joked with him over the past week about his initiation into being a true resident of Foxbridge. He learned it was part of nearly every childhood to be caught by high water in the tidewater caves. It could not be that which had upset the church board. Coldly, he stated, "I suggest you clarify your words, Mr. Turner."

The man cowered before the emerald anger burning in the minister's eyes. He had not wanted to confront Reverend Beckwith-Carter alone, but had allowed the others to convince him to do this. He did not know what to say. Inspiration struck. "Reverend Beckwith-Carter, I think you should attend the next meeting of the board."

"When?" His terse reply showed he was not willing to accept this treatment docilely.

"Tonight at the church."

"I will be there, Mr. Turner. I suggest you be able to validate these claims of impropriety." He stood to tower over the seated man. "*I* would hate to report to my superiors of such allegations being created by the senior members of my parish. It would cast a most dreary pall over the Foxbridge church."

Mr. Turner had been rolling the brim of his hat in his hands. Angrily, he pressed it onto his head. "Rest assured, Reverend, that we feel these claims are not without basis. Tonight."

"Good day."

"Good day." He stamped out of the room, startling Mrs. Reed, who was coming from the kitchen with the unwanted tea tray.

She leapt back, the tea splashing from the teapot onto the plates and onto her crisp apron. When he did not pause to apologize, she scowled in disgust. Putting the tray on the table next to the settee, she used a napkin to dab uselessly at the dark spots on her white apron. She started to speak, then saw the rage on the minister's face.

"Reverend?"

Ian almost spat an answer at her. Controlling his wrath, which should not have been directed at Mrs. Reed, he tried to smile and failed. "Excuse me, but I do not want tea."

"What did that old fool want?"

A grin tilted one corner of his lips. "Old fool is right. What he wants is to cause trouble."

She nodded sagely. "I knew it was just a matter of time. If you were calling on any other woman but Lady Mariel, there would be no trouble. It is simply that the church board does not wish to see its minister involved with one of the Wythes."

"Why?" It shocked him that Mrs. Reed spoke immediately of the source of the problem. He had been surprised by the subject Mr. Turner wished to discuss. Seldom had he misjudged anything as much as he had the community's stance in regard to Mariel. He said exactly that to the housekeeper before adding, "The family, if Mariel is representative, is civic minded. They have been involved with the church here since its beginnings and have contributed more than money to its survival."

"It's just that—" Her head swiveled. "My cookies!" She raced toward the door as if she had been blown by a sharp northeastern wind. "Later, Reverend. They are burning."

"By all means, go!" He laughed until she closed the door behind her. Then his smile faded.

He should have guessed there would be trouble. Enough hints had been dropped when he talked to the more bigoted members of the church board. Like the ones sitting on the school board, they felt Lady Mariel Wythe had stepped out of a woman's role by becoming involved in politics. Seeing their minister talking to her, they carried the courtship to what they saw as its inevitable end. A parson married to the outspoken, seldom conventional Lady Mariel Wythe was not acceptable to them. They intended to prevent it.

The clanging of the school bell broke into his thoughts. Walking to the window, he drew aside the curtains to see the children exploding onto the green. By the steps waited the electric automobile. Several of the children paused to talk enthusiastically to the young woman sitting in the driver's seat, but only one climbed aboard. He watched as the passengers waved to the others before the vehicle began its swift journey back to Foxbridge Cloister.

If he bowed to pressure, these quick glimpses would be the only interaction the church board would allow him to have with Mariel. He dropped the curtain back into place and went to his desk. Sweeping aside the papers, he withdrew a clean sheet from the cubbyhole. He dipped his pen in the ink and began writing furiously. Only when he had said all he must did he lower the pen to the desktop. He folded the note and placed it in an envelope. Inserting it in his pocket, he went out of the study.

He needed fresh air to relieve the stench of bigotry, which pervaded the manse. Telling Mrs. Reed he would be very late for supper, he went to the stable. He hitched the horse to the buggy. As soon as he was aboard, he gave a command seconded by a slap of the reins. He hoped the cleansing winds of the ocean would wash away the sickness within him.

Twilight had descended onto the village by the time Ian returned to park the buggy in front of the church. His time by the shore had strengthened his resolve to do what he had known from the beginning must be done.

He would not hesitate, although it might destroy his career in the church. If he accepted their dictates, he would destroy his soul.

He did not feel the welcome he normally experienced when he entered the church. The sanctuary slept in the spring darkness. From beneath the meeting room door, at the right of the entry, light beckoned. Nothing could be gained by delay. Feeling the acceptance of an innocent man about to be executed, he opened the door.

The jumbled blare of conversation ceased instantaneously. "Good evening," he said with false warmth. "As you requested, ladies and gentlemen, I am here to attend this meeting."

Mr. Turner glanced at the other members of the board, but none of them met his eyes except for Mrs. Parnell. The orphanage director lost her smile as she saw the odd expression on his face. With a glance she noted the fury he could not hide. Her fingers gripped tightly on her pen as she wondered what had preceded this meeting.

"Come in, Reverend," urged Mr. Turner with sudden hospitality. "Please have a seat."

He shook his head. "As you told me earlier, I am not staying long. What must be said should be said quickly."

"Now, Reverend," began Mrs. Rivers, "there is no need to take such a defensive attitude." Her multiple chins quivered in a copy of upper class outrage. Although the silver-haired woman tried to pretend she was nearly at the same social level as the Wythes, no one acknowledged her claim. This had augmented her hatred for the whole family at Foxbridge Cloister.

"No?" he asked sharply. Stepping to the table, he hung his cane over his left wrist. He leaned on the table top and glared at each member until he came to Mrs. Parnell. Her questioning expression dimmed his rage for a moment. He had forgotten Mariel's friend sat on this board.

"Of course not," the officious Mrs. Rivers stated. "We simply want to be assured that you do not do something foolish, like becoming involved with a woman who is inappropriate for a clergyman's wife."

His auburn eyebrows made a pair of identical arches over the green fury beneath them. "I did not realize that I must have the approval of this board before I choose a bride. Your continued interest in my well-being astonishes me. I did not realize that a picnic on the strand constituted a betrothal. I am sure Lady Mariel would be as shocked as I am to learn that."

"Now, Reverend—" began Mr. Turner. He was interrupted when Ian turned to him.

"What do you want?" he demanded with an anger that would lie quiescent no longer. "To have Lady Mariel excommunicated? Would that satisfy you?"

"That is a fine idea," growled Mrs. Rivers. "She is just another of those crazy Wythes. She should be sent—"

"Enough!" Mrs. Parnell stood. "I have heard enough of this witch-hunt. I agreed to ask Reverend Beckwith-Carter to come here tonight to speak of community concerns. Never did I suspect you planned to put our good parson and Lady Mariel on trial."

Mrs. Rivers leapt to her feet. In a vituperative tone, she stated, "We have the moral standards of our children to consider. What do we tell them when they have seen Reverend Beckwith-Carter riding with *her* in that horseless carriage? It's immoral, I tell you! They should be censured. Or worse! They—"

The sound of the door opening halted the tirade. Shocked silence held the room captive as Lady Mariel Wythe entered. Her lips tightened slightly when she saw the strain on Ian's face, but her voice was steady as she spoke.

"Mrs. Reed told me you were here, Ian." She refused to play the hypocrite and call him Reverend Beckwith-Carter before the church board. Mrs. Reed had told her far more than where Ian would be this evening. Trying to control the rage boiling within her, she kept her tone conversational. "As I needed to get this message to you immediately, I trust you will forgive this brash interruption."

"Of course, Mariel." Ian dared anyone to dispute his right to call this woman by her given name. He sensed that she was determined to stand with him on this issue.

"It may not sound important, but I did not want it to become garbled in repetition." She smiled with faked sweetness at the people seated at the table. "You know how easy it is for things to become misunderstood when they are repeated again and again . . . and again." She gave Mrs. Rivers her most charming smile before she turned back to Ian.

He struggled to keep from grinning. He knew that Mariel despised the gossipy Mrs. Rivers, but she would not lower herself to calling names. "I appreciate your concern. What was it you wanted to tell me?"

She wrung her gloves as she gave Mr. Turner a glowing expression of pure innocence. "I am sorry. I know you must have many things of great importance to discuss. What I wanted to tell you was that I cannot drive you to Reverend Tanner's tomorrow, because Rosie has a program for the closing day of school. If you wish, we will take you on Friday afternoon . . . not the morning, because I have to be at the orphanage then."

She gave Mrs. Parnell an honest, half-smile, the best she could dredge up in the heat of her outrage. If her friend had known of this beforehand, she would have warned Mariel.

"Thank you, Mariel." His piercing eyes cut into each nonplussed face. "Friday afternoon will be fine."

"You will join us for dinner as well?"

He smiled as he regarded the furnace of fury dressed in a dark skirt and ecru blouse. The sedate coverings could not conceal from anyone that Mariel was set to explode. "Of course. I promised Rosie I would build her a boat to sail on the garden pond."

"Fine." She turned to go, pausing at the door when he called her name. "Yes?"

Ian looked at the members of the church board. "I think I have completed my business here this evening. Or do you have something else for me, Mr. Turner?"

The man glanced guiltily away from his stern regard. "No, no, Reverend, nothing else. Thank you for coming this evening." He swallowed convulsively, then said in a small voice, "Thank you for coming, Reverend."

"It has been my pleasure. I am glad we will have a clearer definition of our duties and responsibilities in the future." He added as he offered Mariel his arm, "I trust we will not have to deal with this matter again."

Mrs. Parnell piped in with a smothered chuckle, "I am sure you are correct. Good evening, Reverend, Lady Mariel."

No one else spoke as Ian led Mariel from the room. The buzz of conversation cut through the door when he closed it behind him. He said nothing while they walked out into the warm evening. When he heard the sound of her soft laugh, he drew Mariel closer to him.

"The hypocrites!" she snapped.

"Hypocrites?"

"Oh, Ian, you should listen to the gossip more closely. Some of it is true. Like Mr. Turner keeping a mistress on the other side of the shire. Or Mrs. Rivers and her consistent habit of having a bottle of brandy in every drawer of her house." She smiled maliciously. "Yet they dared to slap you on the wrist."

"For riding with you and enjoying your delightful company."

She paused as they were walking across the green toward the manse. "Ian, I am sorry. I did not want to make things difficult for you. Now that Rosie has accepted you so wholeheartedly, I thought things would be better."

"My dear, the comments of a hypocritical church board will not change me." He tilted the flat brim of her pert straw hat. "Determination and stubbornness are bred in my family as they are in yours."

She gasped as he leaned forward and kissed her lightly. Such an inappropriate action in plain view of the church board was an insulting challenge to them. When she started to step away, his arm swept around her waist and kept her next to him.

"Ian!" she hissed. "You are asking for trouble!"

"Funny. I thought I was asking for a kiss." He muted her laughter by seeking her mouth in the darkness.

She forgot all her objections as she drowned in the power of the longing he created deep in her center. Every inch of her skin begged to be close to him. She was vitally aware of the hard breadth of his chest pressing against her. His blatant masculinity sparked a complementing softness in her. She wanted to be nestled in the strength of his arms.

Her eyes sought the shadows of his as he moved away from her slightly. He kept his arm around her shoulders and steered her toward the parsonage. It seemed exactly right that her head should rest on him while they walked.

An anxious Mrs. Reed met them at the door. Her smile seemed broader than usual when she saw them walking so close. Although she had not thought the board would daunt either of these two, she worried the controversy would sour their love.

"Tea and biscuits in the study," she announced, as if it was a royal command.

"I cannot stay long." Mariel's voice was low with regret.

"Long enough for tea surely," returned the house-keeper before she bustled to the kitchen.

Ian chuckled. "You cannot disobey such an edict." He walked into the crowded room with her. Taking off his coat, he tossed it on the back of the settee. He started to speak, then scowled. "Forgive me a moment, Mariel. I forgot the horse and buggy by the church. Let me take care of them, then I will be right back. Why don't you read my sermon for this week? I'd like to hear you comments."

"Is that why you want me to stay? To critique your latest masterpiece?"

Tugging her into his arms, he bent to whisper in her ear. "Shall we use that as an excuse to satisfy everyone's curiosity? I want you for this." His mouth captured hers with a passion she had never known. The kiss was as swift as it was fiery. Watching Mariel put her fingers to her lips in wonder, he chuckled. "I will be back in a moment."

She nodded, astonished by the reaction that had detonated within her at his actions. More, her heart screamed. She wanted to feel the glory of this desire again.

Her fingers trembled as she reached for the pages on the desk. Sitting on the nearest chair, she began to read. As with the others she had read, Ian had found a way to reach directly to the heart of the lesson he wanted to teach. He did not preach down to his parishioners as Reverend Tanner had. His phrases lilted across the page, leading his congregation with him as he explored the problems they faced.

She smiled as she restacked the handwritten pages and placed them back on the desk. Although he could not have known when he started composing this, many would suspect he spoke directly of the church board when he preached about the moneychangers using the temple for their own purposes. It was sure to cause some comment.

Mariel crossed the room to pick the frock coat up from the settee. It would wrinkle unless she hung it in the closet. She was brushing off the fine layer of dust when something crackled under her hand. From the pocket she pulled an envelope. She placed it on the desk.

"Why don't you read it?"

She turned to see Ian standing in the doorway. He held the tea tray. With a smile, she said, "I think you have caught me too many times reading your private works." She hung the coat on its peg and closed the door.

Crossing the room, Ian picked up the envelope and handed it to her. "Read it."

She glanced at him to see a queer smile on his lips. Lifting the flap of the envelope, she unfolded the slip of paper. Her eyes widened as she read the first few sentences. "Ian, this is your resignation!"

"Yes."

Again her eyes were caught by the strong intensity in his. She bent to finish reading the letter, but could not complete it, as her eyes blurred with tears. When he put his hands on her shoulders, she looked up into his face.

"You would have done this for me?" she whispered. "But, Ian, you love this church. You love the work you are doing here."

He drew her into his arms. "I love all that, but I love you, too, Mariel."

With a gasp, she tried to avoid his mouth descending toward hers. He captured her lips, telling her with his kiss what he had with his words. She wanted to escape, but the tantalizing caress of his mouth held her prisoner more than his embrace. Only when he felt her breath mixing rapidly with his did he relinquish her.

"I love you, Mariel. Whether you love me or not is not important now." He smiled as he brushed a stray strand of hair from her pale face. "I know better than to hurry you, pretty one. I just wanted to let you know what is in my heart."

"I know," she said nearly silently. "I know, Ian." She whirled and dropped to the settee. "I know because I love you, too." There was no relief in speaking finally the words that had been burning on her lips.

He sat next to her and took her fingers in his. His other hand brought her downcast face up to look at him. "If you love me, Mariel, then why are you so sad? I feel as if I should paint the sky with my happiness."

"Happiness? What is that?" She sighed when she saw the joy fade from his eyes. She did not want him to share her misery. "I am sorry, Ian. You saw what it was like tonight. The people of Foxbridge care deeply for you. They do not want to see you become mixed up with me."

"Why? I don't understand." He stroked her downy cheek. "They love you also, or at least I thought they did."

She shook her head. "Why doesn't matter. What I worry about is what would happen if you told the rest of the shire what you have just told me that I worry about. I think I should go home."

"Mariel?" he asked as she rose.

"I will see you Friday afternoon."

Softly, he said, "I will be at the closing activities on the last day of school. I am sure to see you and Rosie there." He rose to where she clumsily was trying to tie the ribbons of her cape. Taking them from her, he quickly made a bow. Framing her face with his broad hands, he added, "Mariel, I cannot pretend to understand why you feel this way. Love should make you delirious with joy."

"It should, shouldn't it?" She tried to smile, but failed. "Good night, Ian."

"Good night, my love." When he saw the flicker of happiness in her eyes, he bent and kissed her lightly. He watched as she ran from the room. The sound of the door closing behind her urged him to go to the window.

Even as he was sweeping aside the curtains, the hum of the electric automobile could be heard through the glass. Twin lights marked the passage of the vehicle as she turned it toward the shore road.

He dropped to his favorite chair as he tried to puzzle why Mariel loved him, but fought that feeling, which could bring them only joy. It was only another puzzle he could not solve centering around the huge house on the cliffs.

Mrs. Parnell held out the piece of paper. Mariel took it and smiled. "This is it?"

"This is it. File that with the court to begin proceedings to adopt Rosie. I trust the Wythes have a barrister."

She nodded. "Yes, we have always done business with Mallory and Sons of London."

"Send this to them. They will know what to do with it." She hesitated a moment, then said, "Lady Mariel, have you written to Lord Foxbridge about your plans to adopt Rosie?"

"Yes." She tucked the page carefully into her bag.

"And?"

"I haven't heard from him." She smiled with the joy she could not hide as she reassured the orphanage director, "Don't worry. Uncle Wilford will not be upset by this. He has been concerned about me living alone. It is a topic he mentions with frightful frequency in his letters."

Mrs. Parnell said softly, "Perhaps he meant a husband, not a child. You have understood why there has been so much ado about this adoption? Not every orphan is advanced so quickly in wealth and position as to become the child of the heir to the Wythe fortune."

"I have not been obtuse to the envy." She sighed. "If just one of those who hate Rosie for this would think about the other side of the coin, they would know that she is accepting more than just the promise of money along with the Wythe name." Standing, she offered Mrs. Parnell her hand. "Thank you for all you have done for us."

"It has been my pleasure."

Opening the door, Mariel called softly. Rosie burst into the room. As usual, her stockings were awry and her shoes misbuttoned, but her snaggletoothed grin brightened the office. Until Mariel was sure of the outcome of the directors' meeting, she had not wanted Rosie to hear the news.

Mariel admitted to herself now how deeply worried she had been. Mr. Knowles was not the only one who had been determined to keep this from proceeding. Many had shown the jealous outrage Mrs. Parnell discussed. She had feared that one of them might come to the board with a falsified deposition to keep her from being granted custody of the child. If she had announced she would keep Rosie simply as her ward, there would have been less trouble. She wanted to give the little girl more than that. She wanted to give her what Mariel had lost so many years ago. A family to love and comfort her.

Rosie did not wait to hear the news. She could see the good tidings on Mrs. Parnell's smiling face. With a cry of joy, she wrapped her arms around Mariel's waist and hugged her.

Tears distorted the orphanage director's vision as she watched Lady Mariel bend to place a loving kiss on the unruly curls. It told her how right she had been to urge the board to allow this adoption. When the two walked from the room hand in hand, she smiled at her piles of paperwork. If all problems could be solved as satisfactorily as this one, her job would be a delight.

As they walked down the steps of the old house, Mariel said, "I promised Ian I would take him to visit Reverend Tanner today. Would you like to drive with us?"

"In the automobile?"

"Assuredly." She smiled. Rosie had not lost her thrill of the automobile. "It will be crowded with three of us."

"I don't mind. Ian will let me sit on his lap if I promise not to tickle him."

"Then let's go. We don't want to be late."

Mariel kept her thoughts to herself. In the days since the picnic, Rosie had thrown aside all her jealousy and had welcomed Ian into her life with a vengeance. She enjoyed teasing him. Slowly Mariel was beginning to believe her dreams could be coming true. She began to sing as she turned the automobile toward the gate. Being with the two she loved made even a dull errand something to anticipate.

Chapter Nine

Mariel tossed the ball high into the air and listened as Rosie squealed, running to catch it before Muffin could snatch it away. She laughed when the little girl slipped on a patch of the vividly green grass. Rolling with the dog, Rosie crowed with happiness as Muffin lapped her face enthusiastically. She bounced to her feet with the ball in her hands. Ignoring the stain on her white stockings, she flung the black orb wildly toward Mariel.

Trying to guess where it might land, Mariel raced across the lawn. She held her sports skirt high so she would not fall as the child had. She heard Muffin bark, but could not turn to see who was arriving. Her full concentration was on the ball. When she leapt forward to snag the ball, she heard cheers. Spinning, she smiled.

"Ian! I didn't hear your buggy." She hurried to where he stood by the carriage.

Her eyes took in his appearance as she neared. Forsaking his clerical collar today, he wore a normal stock. His dark walking suit flattered his slim form. With his black top hat and ivory decorated cane, he looked every inch the role of the country gentleman on an outing.

He took her hands and bent forward to kiss her quickly. Before Rosie and the residents of the Cloister, she would allow nothing else. With a smile, he ordered, "You should listen to Muffin. She greeted me."

131

Putting her hand on the dog's silken head, she teased its full ears. "Muffin is not the most reliable watchdog. She barks at the geese on the pond as well as at guests."

"I'll try not to take that personally." When she grinned at him, he ordered, "Change into something for a ride, my love. Both you and Rosie."

"Where are we going?" demanded the child as she threw her arms around his leg.

"It's a secret, Petunia," he teased. "Hurry. The quicker you are ready, the quicker we will be there."

As the child sped toward the Cloister, Mariel asked, "What should we wear?"

He laughed. "No clues, even if you are trying to be a bit more subtle than Rosie. Wear what you would to go on a picnic." He gave her a gentle shove away from him. "Go, or I will take only Rosie with me. Then you will die of curiosity before we return."

"At least walk me to the house." She held out her hand.

"Gladly." Leaving the carriage in the middle of the road, he entwined his fingers with hers. "How is your shoulder?" he asked in a more serious tone.

"Fine. It has not been aching for several days now." She dimpled as she said mischievously, "With the presentation on the textbooks for the school board and the parents coming up next week, I need to be ready to weather any storm."

He looked up at the unblinking eyes of the Cloister. The sun shone like molten gold on the glass. With a smile, he waved to Rosie, who peeked from the upper foyer to urge Mariel to hurry. Softly, he asked, "Do you expect trouble?"

"From the parents, no. From the school board, of course. It is nothing I cannot handle. We *will* have new books when the school opens next term."

"I don't think anyone doubts that." He smiled at her grimace of disagreement. "All right, perhaps Mr. Knowles."

"And Mr. Gratton, Mr. Albion, and Mr. Stadley."

"That's the total of the school board. You still expect to pass this measure?"

Devilishly, she nodded. "Of course." She thanked Dodsley when he held the door open for them. Leaving the two men talking, she rushed up the stairs.

From her closet, she selected a pink tulle blouse accented with black veiling and trimmed along the front with penny-sized sequins. The black taffeta skirt had seven rows of pink braid near the hem. With her patent-leather-toed button-up shoes and her favorite straw hat with its black bow, she felt ready for any activity Ian had planned.

Rosie was waiting impatiently with Phipps in the hall. The gray-haired woman was adjusting the ribbon at the hip of the dropped-waist dress. Thick cotton shirring created a vee along the front of the green frock. Rosie pulled at her drooping stockings while Mariel glanced quickly to be sure all the buttons were secured on her shoes. Forsaking a hat, which never would stay in place on the little girl's head, bows clung precariously to her braids.

"Can we go?" she cried when Mariel turned to speak to Phipps.

"In a moment. Go down, if you wish, and tell Ian I will be with you as soon as I am done here."

Forgetting all the lessons Phipps had tried to instill in her about manners and being seen and not heard, Rosie scurried down the stairs, whirling around the landing, which was decorated in the green light from the stained glass window.

Mariel smiled at the disapproval mixed with love on Phipps's face. No one could fail to be won by Rosie's enthusiasm for life. It pleased her that the other important people in the Cloister cared for the child as she did. She said only, "We may not be home in time for dinner. Ian has a surprise for us."

"Do not stay out too late, Lady Mariel. The night air can be dangerous."

"Yes, Phipps," she replied as she had so often. With a wave, she followed Rosie, at a slightly more moderate pace. She would have preferred to run to Ian's arms, but knew Phipps would be watching.

After giving Rosie a chance to extract a promise from Dodsley to take her fishing, the threesome went to where the buggy waited. When the little girl climbed nimbly aboard and sat directly in the center of the padded seat, Ian started to speak.

Mariel put her hand on his arm and shook her head. The new love Rosie had for him was still so precious, she did not want to do anything to threaten it. Not even when her heart yearned to have no one between her and Ian.

Reluctantly, he nodded and smiled. "If you will take a ride with me alone later, Mariel."

"That would be lovely," she answered politely while she sang with silent joy.

Warmth suffused along her as he put his hand beneath her elbow to assist her into the vehicle. As low to the ground as her automobile, the buggy was easy to enter. When she sat on the leather bench, she put her gloved hand in Rosie's. The child chatted nonstop as Ian walked around to the other side and stepped aboard.

The black horse lifted its feet jauntily as they drove along the road to the front gate and the shore road. When they passed the electric automobile stopped by the side of the path, they waved to Walter. He smiled in response.

"Problems?" asked Ian.

"No, not anymore." She turned to watch the automobile come to life as the mechanic drove it toward the garage. "Walter checks it every day I don't drive, so there will be no breakdowns when I do take it out. Since he came to the Cloister, it has run perfectly. I wonder now what I did without him."

They quickly forgot the automobile as Rosie began to pester Ian about the secret he was keeping from them. He teased her, but refused to divulge a single clue. Mariel listened to them and leaned back against the seat to enjoy the lovely day.

As always, the breeze came from the ocean, refreshing the air with its salty tang. The warm sunshine urged her to give in to the lackadaisical daydream of closing her eyes and allowing the day to pass to the easy rhythm of the hoofbeats on the dirt. Birds called sharply above the whirring of the insects among the growing plants. From far away along the hillsides, puffs of white bleated their mournful cries. The tinkling of sheepbells drifted with the even-whiter cotton of the clouds.

Ian slowed the carriage as the road became crowded with other vehicles, all traveling in the same direction. Mariel smiled as she realized where he meant to take them. When the little girl saw the brightly colored caravan of wagons scattered across a freshly harvested hay field, she gave a squeal of delight.

"The circus!" Rosie cried.

"Shall we stop here, Daisy?" Ian teased, winking broadly at Mariel. "I had planned to take you and Mariel for another charming visit to Reverend Tanner, like the one we had yesterday."

"My name is not Daisy! It's Rosie!" She gripped the dash of the buggy as she stated, "And I don't want to visit that old fool."

"Rosie," admonished Mariel, "you should not call Reverend Tanner an old fool."

"*You* do!"

With a laugh, Ian brought the carriage to a stop in the shade of the trees growing along the hedgerow. "She has you there, Mariel. I have heard you call him that on more than one occasion. Right, Iris?"

"Rosie!" she retorted, but she giggled. This had become a private game between the two of them.

He tweaked her nose and said, "I will try to remember that. Do you want to go now?"

Rosie could not contain her excitement when Ian lifted her from the buggy. She bounced from one foot to the other as she waited for him to assist Mariel. Her head turned to follow each delight waiting to be discovered.

Ian grinned as he put his hands on Mariel's waist. It was nearly as narrow as the child's. He did not want to release her when her feet touched the ground, but Rosie's excited demands gave him no time to enjoy the woman. With a flourish, he offered Mariel his arm.

After opening her wispy pink parasol, which matched the lace of her blouse, she placed her fingers on Ian's wool coat sleeve. Secretly, she thought the three of them looked like the perfect family on an outing in the country. Such thoughts she would not voice, for she

did not know how Ian would feel about such presumption.

"Where first?" he was asking the little girl.

Rosie glanced about at the wagons painted with
stripes and flowers. Each one had a garish awning
attached to it where the owners could present their
wares. In the center of the camp was a huge tent where
the circus would be held. The performance did not start
for a few minutes, so they would have time to explore
the alien delights of the wagons.

Without hesitation, she urged, "The ponies. Please,
Ian. Can I have my picture taken on a pony?"

He laughed. For Rosie everything was new. Her
sparkling enthusiasm spilled over onto the adults to
allow them to enjoy anew the delights of childhood. "Of
course. Come on. Do you think Mariel should have her
photograph taken as well?"

"Yes!"

"Some other day," said Mariel with a smile. "When
they have full-sized horses. I am afraid I am too tall for
the ponies. Run ahead and choose which pony you want,
dear."

She kept her eyes on the child as they walked
through the crowd. The circus was little more than a
half dozen gaudily painted wagons, but many of the
residents of Foxbridge were taking advantage of the rare
entertainment on this warm afternoon.

Rosie went up to the man with the camera, which
was perched like a three-legged sea bird on its tripod.
When he smiled at her, she was not daunted by the
patch over one eye and the long ragged scar on his
cheek. She pointed to the cream colored Shetland pony.
Its saddle was inlaid with fake gems and stitched in an
outrageous pattern. Long blankets nearly touched the
ground on each side of its short legs.

"Is that the one you want, young lady?"

"Yes!" she breathed with candid excitement.

"Do you have any money? The photos are—" He
straightened as he saw the woman with her eyes on the
child by his side. His single eye narrowed as the little
girl raced to her. No one had to tell him who this was.
He made it his practice to know such details as the

names and descriptions of the gentry before he opened his circus to the public.

He smiled as he put his fingers to his forehead. "Good afternoon. Have you come to have your photograph taken?"

Mariel grinned at Rosie's rapid list of reasons why she must have her picture taken on the light brown pony. "My daughter would like to be photographed on that one there." Her happiness glowed on her face as she spoke of the little girl as her child.

"Daughter?" the photographer asked involuntarily. He had heard nothing of Lady Mariel Wythe having a child. As far as he knew, she was a spinster. Recovering quickly, he added, "Would you like to be in the picture also?"

"No, this picture is for Rosie."

He nodded and led the little girl by the hand to where the pony waited with infinite patience. Lifting her onto it, he adjusted her frock and hair. He warned her not to move, then returned to his camera. Peering from beneath the dark cloth, he adjusted the lens to the correct focus.

Ian watched the process with interest. He put his hand on Mariel's arm and drew her back closer to him. She smiled at him swiftly before looking at Rosie again. As soon as the picture was taken, she lifted the child from the horse. She took the slip of paper from the photographer and nodded when he told her to come back after the show to purchase the picture.

She thanked him and placed the identifying slip in her bag. As they walked away to visit the next wagon, she did not notice that his eyes followed her until they were lost among the throng of revelers.

Rosie ran from one wagon to the next, pointing excitedly to everything offered for sale. She convinced Ian to buy her a candied apple, which immediately turned her face to sticky scarlet. Music called to them, and they paused to watch a dancing bear.

They cheered loudly with the rest of the crowd as the trainer put the animal through his routine. Mariel's cheer subsided as she felt an unease she could not name. Nothing was wrong, but something had changed. She had the sensation of being observed clandestinely.

Slowly, she turned. She was right. Someone was watching her. Although she wanted to ignore the man, she could not. Even without the paisley scarf over his head and the golden hoops in his ears, she would have known he was a member of this traveling band. Bulging muscles were revealed below the sleeves of his tattered shirt.

His slightly tilted eyes hid in his wide face, but she could feel his gaze on her. When she saw him take a step toward them, she looked back at the antics of the trained bear.

"Mariel?"

She should have guessed Ian would sense her disquiet through her fingertips on his sleeve. "There is a man staring at me. No, don't look."

"Don't worry," he said with a smile. "The constable is here with his brood. None of these Gypsies wish to cause any trouble for us. They would rather take our gold for their entertainments." His arm slipped around her shoulders as he added, "I am sure he simply enjoys looking at such a lovely lady."

"I wish he would look at someone else."

"There is no one prettier." When she did not respond to his compliment, he called to Rosie. "Let's go into the tent and get our seats on the benches for the show. It will be starting soon."

Mariel waited impatiently as Ian purchased their tickets. Herding Rosie before her, she walked with him into the tent. The summer sun had heated the interior, and the air was thick with the scent of mildewed canvas and animal droppings mixed with the sawdust of the ring. When they found seats in the front row, they considered themselves lucky.

While Ian talked with their neighbors, Mariel stared at the center of the ring. She did not understand why the stranger had stripped her of her joy in the day. Ian was right. The man had done nothing but look at her, and that could not be construed as any sort of a crime. Forcing herself to forget him, she tried to respond to the anticipation around her.

The show began with a blare of off-key music. Horses raced into the ring under the watchful eye of their trainer. The master of the circus shouted out the name of the performer and the tricks the woman in the sparse costume would attempt, and Mariel felt Ian's fingers slip over hers. His nearness comforted her and allowed her to become enraptured by the acts of skill and finesse.

Clowns displayed their antics between each act. When one grasped Rosie's hands and invited her to join their comical dance, she hesitated only as long as it took Mariel to urge her to accept. Mariel laughed until she felt weak, with tears in her eyes as Rosie wholeheartedly played with the men disguised behind their stage make-up. When she returned, breathless from laughter, she continued to giggle at the games they played.

More performances followed, some beautiful and graceful, others terrifying with the fearsome daring of the circus members. Mariel's hands grew sore from applauding and from Rosie clenching them as she watched the show in open-mouthed awe.

Too soon, it was over. The ring lost its magic as it again became only a wooden circle filled with well trampled sawdust. They waited for the others to leave, unwilling to let the enchantment end. As they stood, a man approached. He bowed and handed Rosie a flower.

The little girl took it and looked from the pale pink blossom to him in bafflement. He grinned a lopsided smile as he winked at her companions. "For your assistance today, young lady. Don't you recognize me?"

Only when he did a backward flip with an ease that seemed impossible did she clap her hands and crow with delight. Without his stage makeup, she could not see him as the clown who had invited her to participate. His everyday looks would not be noticed in any crowd. His mousy brown hair and clear brown eyes did not hint at the joy within him.

"Thank you for making the day special for her," said Mariel sincerely. "She has never been to the circus before."

He smiled. When he spoke, she noticed the heavy accent of his speech. Most of the people connected with this circus must be from one of the far eastern parts of Europe. "I thought so. I cannot remember the first time I saw a circus, for I was born to this one. Yet, when I see the delight in the eyes of these children, I, too, can enjoy the performance as if for the first time." He patted Rosie's head. "Thank you, little one, for making this day special for me, also." With a hearty farewell, he raced across the ring to disappear through the performer's entrance.

"Look, Mariel," urged Rosie. "Isn't it beautiful?"

"It's lovely. We shall put it in a vase, and you may keep it in your room."

"Forever?"

"Forever, if you wish." Mariel looked up at Ian and wondered if anything could be more wonderful than this moment when love surrounded them.

He took her hand as she took Rosie's. "I think we should go see the rest of the wagons. What do you think, Lilac?"

"Rosie!" She skipped as they left the tent.

The hours passed too quickly as they visited with friends they met among the wagons and watched the entertainment. Music created a constant undertone for all conversation. The smoke of outdoor fires was filled with the tantalizing scents of exotic foods. The circus members had thought of many ways of making a profit from the local people.

When they passed the fortune-teller's wagon, Rosie asked if they could go in. Ian told them to go ahead. He would go to get a cool drink. He laughed as he explained, "It would not do for my parishioners to see their minister seeking advice of the future from such a source."

Taking Rosie by the hand, Mariel went to the open door. Inside this wagon, set slightly away from the others, a solitary woman sat. She smiled and waved for them to come in and close the door.

A quiet settled on the cool interior as the bustle of the fair was closed out of the room. The walls had been painted midnight blue. Wispy cloth draped the corners of the ceiling to soften the angles of the room. A single chair faced the woman.

Her face was painted as garishly as the wagons. Black kohl lined her eyes, drawing them out like an Egyptian's. Brilliant red slashed across her lips and made her face seem even more pale. A black veil edged with gold coins covered her dark hair. Her gown was shot with threads of the same color. Wide sleeves dropped back to reveal her slender arms.

"Sit. Let me open the door of the future for you. I can pull back the curtains of time and let you peek at what will be." She smiled as Rosie stepped forward shyly. "Come, child. Offer me your palm, and I will tell you what will be."

Rosie climbed onto the chair and leaned across the wide table. She giggled as the fortune-teller traced the lines of her palm with her long fingernail. "That tickles!" she said.

The woman smiled indulgently. She enjoyed telling fortunes for children, who did not react with disbelief to her knowledge. After prophesying a long life and a fine family, she watched as the child scampered down from the velvet covered chair.

"And now you, Lady Mariel?"

Mariel started, but did not demand to know how this woman could know her. Any woman who dared to speak so assuredly of the future must be a good judge of human nature and very observant. Almost anyone could have overheard her conversations with the others reveling in the circus. When she came here with Rosie, the fortune-teller would have been told immediately.

"No, thank you. I have no interest in having my palm read." She dropped a coin on the table and turned to take Rosie's hand.

"My lady, let me read the tarot cards for you."

"Tarot cards?"

The fortune-teller bobbed her head so hard that the coins sewn to her veil flapped against her forehead. She drew a pack of the oversized cards from beneath the table. "Come. Sit. For few do I do this. Most are satisfied with learning the truth written in their skin. Let me read them for you."

Mariel hesitated. Her uncle had told her about having his fortune told with tarot cards while on the continent. Although he admitted little of it had come true, he had spoken of the incident fondly. Fascinating was his exact word.

"All right," she said with sudden enthusiasm. "Rosie, Ian is waiting outside. Tell him I will be with you in a minute."

"May I have an ice?"

"A small one! You have had too many sweets already."

The little girl raced out of the narrow wagon and down the ladder steps. Her chatter faded as the door closed. Clutching the handle of her parasol, Mariel leaned forward to hear the words intoned by the seer.

"I will shuffle the cards. Think of your life. When you think the cards are right for you, tell me."

Unable to wait for long, Mariel said almost immediately, "Now."

In an obscure pattern, the woman laid the cards on the table. She started by placing a single card on the table. Putting one over it, she stated, "This card covers you." She continued, "This one crosses you. This one is over you. This beneath. This behind you. This ahead of you."

Mariel's eyes followed her lovely hands as she dealt the cards. When the fortune-teller put the rest of the pack on the table, she looked at the woman expectantly. Uncle Wilford was right. It was fun to imagine a door could be opened to reveal the future. She scanned the cards, wondering if any would speak of what waited for her and Ian.

The silence grew long in the wagon. Suddenly the woman scooped up the cards and began to shuffle them again. In a tight voice, she mumbled, "I made an error."

"An error?"

"Let us try again, my lady. Tell me when the cards are right for you."

Although Mariel felt a twinge of uneasiness, she simply watched the slender hands competently reorganize the large cards. With less enthusiasm, she stated, "I think, now."

The fortune-teller smiled. "Forgive me, my lady. Sometimes the cards make no sense. I thought you would be wanting to get an accurate reading. Shall we?" She repeated the patter in the identical, singsong voice she had used the first time.

Different cards sat in the center of the table, but none of the odd pictures made any sense to Mariel. The obscure symbols belonged to another time and place. When they were arranged, she waited for the woman to speak.

With a cry, the veiled woman swept the cards from the table. Mariel ducked instinctively as several flew toward her. "What is wrong?"

"Go, my lady! I will not read for you today!" Her voice rose in undisguised terror. When Mariel stared at her in astonishment, she repeated more shrilly, "Go! Go away!"

Before Mariel could rise, the thick curtain behind the fortune-teller was shoved aside. A huge man stepped around it. She gasped as she recognized him as the one staring at her while she watched the performing bear. Fear froze her voice in her throat. Stumbling to her feet, she groped for the door.

A huge hand on her arm halted her. In a voice as broad as his size, the man spoke to the fortune-teller in a language Mariel did not comprehend. When the seer answered, waving her hands in open distress, he looked at the woman standing next to him.

"Lady Mariel Wythe?" he asked.

"Yes, that's my name."

"Nadia will not read the cards for you today."

She tried to pull her arm out of his painful grip, but he refused to release her. "I understand," she said when she saw he wanted a response.

"Do you?"

The threat inherent in his words sent icy fear burning through her middle. She had no idea what he meant or why the fortune-teller refused to read the cards after being so anxious to tell her future. None of this made sense. All she wanted was to be done with these crazy Gypsies and return to the Cloister.

"You are a pretty woman," he continued when she did not answer. "Do you have intelligence to match your beauty?"

"Raoul!"

He glared at the woman removing her veil. Spitting a command at her, he smiled as she lowered her eyes in a submissive attitude. Mariel looked from one face to the other and could not guess what was being said between them.

A knock on the wagon door broke the frozen tableau. Muted by the thick wood, she could hear Ian's voice, calling to ask if she was still within. She looked at the twisted mouth of the man holding her. He bent toward her, and she cowered away.

"If you want to know the truth in the cards, come back here tonight. Raoul will explain them to you."

"I don't want to know. Good day, sir."

He laughed at her icy manners. "Go, then, my lady. When the darkness falls on you, you will be sorry you did not listen to me."

"Raoul!" cried the fortune-teller again. "Do not speak of that. The cards must be unreadable today." She glanced with a desperate apology to Mariel. "Sometimes they do not speak clearly to me."

The man snapped, "What she means is that she is too squeamish to reveal the truth of the tragedy awaiting you, my lady."

Suddenly, Mariel laughed. She eased herself away from the man and reached for the door latch. All of this heated talk about what was no more than a joke—she did not want to waste her time with it. The man's last threat was only half spoken as she shut the door behind her. When she saw Ian waiting at the base of the steps, she held out her hand to him.

"So, Mariel, what great mysteries have been solved for you?" His smile faded when she did not tease him in the same light tone.

"She decided not to read the cards for me." She added, "Can we go home, Ian? I think we have had enough of this carnival today."

His eyes swept her face and saw the unhappiness there. Something had happened in the small wagon to upset her. Tales of the future would not have bothered her. She was too prosaic for such flights of bizarre fantasy.

Rosie barely protested leaving. With her half-melted ice in one hand and her precious flower in the other, she was ready to go home. Before the sounds of the circus disappeared in the distance and the lights were swallowed by the twilight, she fell asleep against Mariel. The flavored water melted stickily on her skirt, but her fingers remained tightly around the blossom.

Mariel stared into the thickening darkness. She wished they had not gone into the fortune-teller's wagon. It tainted the memories she would have of this day. Just the suggestion of evil made her uneasy.

"Why didn't she read your fortune?" asked Ian as if she had been speaking her thoughts aloud. "Rosie said she was insistent about using the tarot cards."

"It was strange," she admitted, glad to speak her concerns aloud. "At first, the woman could not wait to do the cards. Then she refused, telling me she could not read them today." She hesitated about adding more. Telling Ian about Raoul's half-spoken threats would do nothing but cause trouble.

He put his arm around her shoulders and leaned her head on his shoulder. "What a shame she would not read them for you. Who knows what fabulous things you might have in your future?"

"Ian, I thought you did not believe in such nonsense!"

"I don't." He chuckled lightly so not to disturb the sleeping child. "I don't, but it is fun to imagine such was possible. It would have given you such a pleasant remembrance for the day."

Suddenly she sat up. "Oh, no! I forgot to get Rosie's picture."

He smiled. "No problem. We can get it after we take Rosie back to the Cloister. Miss Phipps can put her to bed. It will not take long."

His words proved true. Miss Phipps bustled out of the house to collect the exhausted child. When she heard about their errand, she said, "I will tell Mrs. Puhle to hold supper for you. Come, child."

"Miss Phipps, see my flower?" Mariel heard a sleepy little girl say as Ian urged the horse back toward the gate.

The road was nearly deserted. They passed a few vehicles on the way home from the circus, but for most of the trip only the night insects and an occasional owl accompanied them. Even when they reached the fair-grounds, the few lights gave the area an uninhabited appearance.

Before Ian alit from the carriage, the door of the closest wagon opened. A silhouette emerged to disappear momentarily in the night. Only when he was a few steps from them did they identify him as the man who had been taking the pictures. Grateful that he did not have to search for the man, Ian greeted him and told him their reason for returning.

The photographer nodded. "Of course, I remember the little girl. I was going to stop by Foxbridge Cloister in the morning to see if my lady had forgotten to pick up her picture. It is in my wagon. Reverend, if you wish to come with me. . ."

"Mariel, I will be right back."

She smiled as she tightened her silk cape around her shoulders. "Do hurry. Phipps will be troublesome if I arrive home too late."

With a grin at her mock compliance with her companion's edicts, he followed the one-eyed man toward his wagon. The moonlight had stripped the caravan of its flashy colors. All of the reds and golds blended into grays.

She leaned back against the raised top of the buggy. The excuse of coming here to the circus grounds again had allowed her the chance to be alone with Ian without tongues wagging too harshly. She smiled as she wondered what quiet, winding road he would choose to take them back to the Cloister. Certainly they would not go the most direct, shore route.

"My lady, I see you have decided to accept my invitation."

In shock, she opened her eyes to see the impudent smile of the man the fortune-teller had called Raoul. She stared at him, unsure what to say. He leaned across the buggy so that his broad face was too close to hers. She tried to retreat, but he simply laughed. The motion set his golden earrings to bouncing.

"Come," he ordered.

Finding her voice, Mariel stated haughtily, "I can assure you, sir, that I have no intention of going anywhere with you. As soon as Reverend Beckwith-Carter returns with my daughter's photograph, we are leaving."

"He will not return quickly."

"Nonsense! He just has to go to the wagon over there." She pointed to the well-lit glow of the photographer's wagon. "He will be back any second now. I suggest, sir, you leave before you find yourself in trouble."

"You are the one in trouble, Lady Mariel." His broad hands spanned her waist easily as he lifted her from the buggy. As she opened her mouth to protest, he threatened, "Speak, and you will be sorry. Come, for Nadia will read for you now."

Deciding that it would be easier to go through this charade, Mariel sullenly walked with him to the wagon set apart from the others. He opened the door at the top of the steps and bowed her into the tiny room.

The woman who had worn the veil in the afternoon was now dressed in a loose caftan. Without the cosmetics she wore for her work, she appeared far prettier and gentler. Her long fingers, now devoid of the garish rings, clutched the pack of tarot cards tightly.

"Lady Mariel," she whispered as she pointed to the chair opposite her.

"Nadia, you do not have to do this."

She glanced past Mariel. Her dark eyes glowed with fear. Lowering them to the tabletop, she murmured, "I must." Louder she said, "Think of the cards, Lady Mariel. Think of your life. Concentrate on your dreams. Tell me when the cards are right for you."

Mariel could not doubt that the other woman was terrified. Whether of the man standing nearby or of the fate she must read in the cards, she did not know. This had gone on long enough.

"No!" she said, slapping her hand on the table. "I will not think of that. I do not want you to read the future for me. It is only a game."

Raoul pressed her into the chair. "Do as Nadia says, my lady."

"You cannot force me!" She bounced out of the chair and was at the door before he could move. Flinging it open, she halted, swallowing a scream as she stared at the smiling face of the photographer. "Move aside, please. I am leaving."

He spoke to the others in the wagon in the strange tongue she had heard Raoul use during her first visit to the wagon. His faked smile dimmed as he listened to them. Then he shrugged. What he replied brought peals of cold laughter from Raoul.

The photographer stepped aside and held out his hand to help Mariel from the vehicle. "Go then, my lady. Remember that you could have been forewarned of the evil surrounding you. Now you will have no choice but to fall victim to the darkness Nadia has seen."

"I don't believe you!" she stated, but with less vehemence than she wanted to project. She looked back at the other woman's sorrowful face. "Nadia, I do not want to belittle you, but I cannot believe in this."

Nadia rushed past the huge man to kneel in the doorway. Her glistening black eyes were level with Mariel's. "Be careful, my lady," she whispered. "Whether you believe in the gift of my ability to read the tarot or not, I urge you to be careful. The evil one is within your house now. He wants to steal the light of life from you. More than that, I cannot tell you, for I could not bear to read more of the darkness. Please, my lady, take care."

"I—I will," she heard herself promise. Nadia must feel very strongly about this. This woman would not put on such a performance if she did not give some credence to her own talents. What she meant, Mariel could not guess.

Raoul growled and dragged Nadia to her feet. Even as he was closing the door, he clearly was berating her in the language they spoke. When Mariel started to step toward the wagon to defend the woman who wanted only to help her, the man who had taken Rosie's picture took her arm.

"Do not interfere, my lady. Raoul does not like Nadia to give away the fruits of her sight. He sees her gift as a way to make money." His teeth glittered in the moonlight. "Do not worry. He will not strike her hard. He knows she must be able to work tomorrow if he is to eat."

When he tugged on her arm, she compliantly went back to where Ian was waiting. Telling her farewell, he walked away to blend into the shadows.

"So you decided to have your fortune told after all?" teased Ian as he assisted her into the buggy.

She did not answer as he lifted the reins and turned the carriage onto the road. Instead, she slid across the seat to feel the comforting strength of his body close to her. Slipping her hands around his arm, she clutched onto him as if she feared she would be swept away without him to anchor her amid this madness.

Nothing was said while he drove onto a road leading more indirectly to the Cloister. When he had put more than a mile between them and the fairgrounds, he halted the horse in a pool of moonlight. He turned to look into her shadowed eyes.

"Tell me, Mariel."

This time she revealed everything that had been said during both of her visits to the fortune-teller's wagon. When she was finished, he drew her to him and kissed her on the forehead. She whispered his name as she felt his mouth hovering close to hers. At its touch, she forgot all her trepidation and remembered only the glory of the feelings Ian brought forth from her.

As he leaned her back on the buggy seat, she closed her eyes to better savor the caress of his lips searing their path along her neck. His fingers traced rapture among the sequins on her blouse. As they stroked the responsive curve of her breast, she moaned with a longing she could not deny.

Her hands found their way beneath his coat to the fine lawn of his shirt. The wide strap of his suspenders teased her fingers to push it aside. They clenched on the elastic as his mouth replaced his fingers exploring her through her clothes' thin fabric. Her body pressed against the lean line of his, demanding satiation.

Looking down into her face lit by the soft glow from the night sky, he wondered how much longer they could wait to satisfy this craving. Whenever he was away from her, he thought of the enticing shape of her body and the teasing sound of her laugh. At night, he spent hours thrashing in his lonesome bed, infected with desire for her.

"Mariel?"

She opened her eyes lazily. Happiness brightened her face as her fingers followed the planes of his whisker harsh cheeks. "What is it? Why are you talking instead of kissing me?"

"Let me kiss you every night, my love, before I close my eyes."

Bafflement furrowed her brow. "What do you mean?"

With an irreverent grin, he picked up her left hand and kissed the fourth finger. "Do I need to be less subtle, my love? Marry me, Mariel. I have thought long on it today. I know I want you with me forever. You know we belong together. Marry me."

Instead of answering him with the joyous abandon she exhibited when he kissed her, she drew out of his arms. Sitting up, she moved away from him to straighten her blouse. Her hand shook as she lifted her cape over her shoulders again.

"This is so sudden," she answered with a triteness she hoped would cover her true emotions.

"Then think on it," he urged. "Think on it, and give me your answer soon."

She wanted to reply that she could give him her answer now. She could not marry Ian Beckwith-Carter. That she loved him with all her heart changed nothing. She had not needed the woman with her tarot cards to speak of the curse hanging over Foxbridge Cloister. Every day of her life, it had been her constant companion. Never before had it hurt her as much as it did tonight by ripping her dreams from her once again.

Letting him put his arm around her as he picked up the reins, she tried not to show him the fear within her. She spoke of Rosie and of the circus while they drove to the Cloister, anything but the marriage proposal and the reason she could never reveal why she would never marry him. They drove into the night, which was less dark than the void of horror within her.

A horror she could share with no one. Not even the man she loved with every ounce of her being.

Chapter Ten

Mariel opened the heavy, time-stained door of the pub. She blinked as she tried to adjust her eyes to the dimness of the interior. When the door slammed loudly behind her, all light from the outside world vanished.

Within seconds, she could see again. Picking her way through the maze of tables and benches, she sought the bar. The woman working there did not hide her surprise when she saw who had entered the Three Georges.

"Lady Mariel! I—I did not expect to see you here."

She smiled politely. No proper lady would enter this place, especially unescorted, but she had business with the owner. "Good morning, Mrs. Gratton. Is your husband here?"

"Yes. Yes, my lady. He is in the back. One moment please." The woman scurried away after a respectful half-curtsy in Mariel's direction. From the room behind the smoke-darkened bar, her voice sounded shrilly as she called to her husband.

Mariel turned away to hide her amusement. She glanced about the room. She had never seen it before, although she had heard much about the revelry shared here by the men of the shire. A dart board hung on a wall pitted with misfired darts. The huge fieldstone fireplace smelled dank as it sat waiting for the winter.

"Lady Mariel?"

She greeted the tavernkeeper. Dressed in his chambray shirt, with black suspenders struggling to hold his trousers around his girth, he appeared far more at ease than at the school board meetings. The men constantly tugged at the unaccustomed stiffness of high stocks and ties while Mariel worked with them to make the school a success. "I told you I would bring this information to you, Mr. Gratton. It took me so long to copy it all. I did get Mr. Knowles and Mr. Jones their copies before the term was completed. I thought they would need the most time to peruse it." She smiled charmingly at him. "When I spoke to you at the meeting about arranging to bring this to you, I had no idea how much time Rosie would take out of my day."

"Thank you," he replied as she handed him the thick packet. It would take him hours to struggle through just the first few pages of this material. He wondered if he should simply tell her to do as she wished and save himself the trouble.

"I will see you tomorrow night, then. Good day." She raised her voice slightly. "Good day, Mrs. Gratton."

Walking along the green, she waved to women hanging their freshly washed linens in the summer sunshine. She hesitated as she stepped onto the porch of the parsonage. She wanted to see Ian, but she could not bring herself to tell him what she must. Her distress had kept her awake all night. No answer had appeared with the dawn. Without telling him the essential bit of truth she could not reveal, he would never understand why she could not follow her heart into his arms.

Her knock on the door went unanswered. She frowned in bafflement as she peered into the front window. As she expected, Ian was working furiously at his desk. Lost in his task, he probably had not heard her.

Knowing it was bold of her, she opened the door and admitted herself. No sounds of industrious preparation came from the kitchen. She stopped by the open door of Ian's study and rapped lightly on the molding.

Ian smiled. "Come in. What are you doing in Foxbridge so early on a Monday morning?"

"I had papers to deliver to Mr. Gratton." She drew the pins from her hat and placed it on the forest-green chair. "Where is Mrs. Reed?"

"Her sister is ill, so I sent her to stay with her. I think I can manage alone for a few days."

"Nothing serious?"

He shook his head as he bent again over his work. "No, but her sister is not young. I knew Mrs. Reed was worried, so rather than have her moping around here, I sent her to York until her sister feels better."

"Such a sacrifice," she teased as she wrapped her arms around his shoulders and placed her head against his. "What are you working on?"

"Sunday's sermon." He peered up at her. "Sometime you should come and hear me." He swiveled to face her. "I think I will be most inspired this week."

Dropping to sit on his lap, she smiled. "You always inspire me, Ian." When he wrapped his arms around her, she asked, "Why should I come Sunday when I have already been regaled by a private service here?"

"You do listen well." He stroked her arm as he said in a more serious voice, "Honey, I think you should attend the services."

"Are you worried about my eternal soul?"

"It is not something to joke about, Mariel." His hands tightened around her as she scowled. "I know you used to attend every Sunday with your uncle. After he left last time, you have not set foot in the church for Sunday services. Can't you tell me why? If it was just because you did not like Reverend Tanner, that should not keep you from attending now. After all, you do like me."

In a small voice, she said, "I do not want to attend by myself."

"Bring Phipps. Bring Rosie." He turned her face so he could scrutinize her distressed features. "Why won't you be honest with me?"

She stood and moved away from him. Picking up a small statue on the fireplace mantel, she examined it as if it was of the greatest interest. She put the china shepherdess back and she said, "I must get home. Phipps will be beside herself if I am late again."

"Will you stop by tomorrow?"

"I don't know. Tomorrow is the first Tuesday of the month. I have the school-board meeting with my report due on the new textbooks."

Ian did not intend to let her leave when she was this upset. She had come into the house a bright spirit and was leaving a hollow phantom. Rising, he took her hand and did not release it until she looked at him.

"Have you thought about what I asked you last night?"

"Yes." Her whisper could barely be heard.

"And?"

She put her fingers on his arm. "Ian, can we forget you asked me to marry you? Can't we go back to the way things were? It was so wonderful to be with you and feel your arms around me. I have never known anything so fabulous."

"All the more reason to stay together forever." His green gaze cut through the flimsy defenses she offered to keep him from seeing the truth. With his wide hand warm against her icy cheek, he said, "I don't know what frightens you so, my love, but I want to help you. I love you."

"I love you, Ian."

"Then be mine."

As if it was the most sacred vow, she whispered, "I am yours."

"You will marry me, then?" He could not keep the joy from his voice.

"No!"

"No?" His question hung in the empty room. Before he could speak, she had fled. The sound of the front door crashing against the wall echoed through the house.

His eyes went to her hat sitting on the chair. Slowly, he walked to the door and reached to close it. He saw the automobile racing up the hill toward the Cloister as if demons were chasing it.

Demons. Mariel could not hide her fright from him. What dark curse lay over that house and its inhabitants that would not allow her to do as she wished?

Suddenly, he smiled. Perhaps he was seeing horror where there was none. Despite her eager yearning for all that was modern in thought and manner, she could not hide her charming modesty when he touched her. Pretty Mariel might be afraid of marriage simply because she clung to popular ideas that a woman should be frightened of what awaited her in the marriage bed.

He closed the door and regarded the staircase with satisfaction. If that was Mariel's problem, he could think of a way to solve it without much ado. With a laugh, he went back to his work. The words flowed with inspiration from his brain to the paper. It did not surprise him. He wanted to get this done today, so he could attend the school-board meeting tomorrow night. He was sure it would be delightful.

Mariel's eyes swept the filled classroom. She had not expected so many of the parents to accept her invitation to attend the meeting. If there had been a larger room in Foxbridge, they would have reconvened elsewhere. Each desk was occupied, and other people stood against the walls.

"If you have any questions on this proposal, I would be quite happy to answer them now." Her gaze settled on Ian's smile where he stood near the door. Hastily, she looked away. She had been trying to avoid meeting his eyes all night.

A man stood up in the first row of desks. He ran a hand nervously through the sparse hair on his head, making it spike into strange angles. "Lady Mariel, I don't know about the rest of these folks, but I just want to say I think this sounds like a fine idea. My kids have complained about being jeered at by their city cousins. I say we should get these books for our kids."

Cheers met his words. She risked a glance at the board members to see their faces set in carefully immobile lines. They would not want their constituents to guess how much they hated the thought of spending some of the school board's reserve for books. That plenty of money would remain after the purchase did not change their opinions.

Other, equally supportive comments were offered by the parents. More than one woman took the courage to stand and speak for herself and her family. Before Lady Mariel had been nominated for this position, no woman in Foxbridge would have considered coming to a meeting like this. The idea of a woman stating her opinion at a political gathering would have been scoffed at as farfetched.

Mr. Gratton signaled for quiet when he discovered no one was going to make a statement against the plan. Recognizing defeat when it slapped him in the face, he cut short the discussion. "I want to thank Lady Mariel for all the work she has done. This will be voted on next week at a special meeting. I thank you for coming tonight. This meeting is adjourned, although I understand Mr. Knowles and Mr. Jones request you remain for further information on next term. Good night."

All the board members rose to file stolidly from the room. Only Mariel was stopped by the townspeople. More than one repeated the enthusiasm expressed earlier. She thanked each one for their support.

Ian stepped forward to join her as she reached the door. Quietly he said, "Good evening."

She smiled as they left the schoolhouse. Her joy at seeing him forced aside her unease at the conflict within her. "Ian, I did not expect to see you tonight. How did you like my report?"

"I am sure it will have them talking for weeks."

"I don't say such things simply to shake them up, you know. This world is changing with incredible speed." She pointed to her automobile parked in front of the building. "Just a few years ago, even I would have called anyone who said I would be driving such a vehicle a fool. So many things are changing. Our village children must be prepared to meet those new challenges—the girls as well as the boys."

He tucked her hand into the crook of his arm. "A cup of tea before you go home?" When she hesitated, he added, "At least come and retrieve your hat."

Not wanting to speak of her actions yesterday, she agreed hastily to his invitation. "Let me bring the

automobile around to the rectory. Then I won't disturb
the parents' meeting when I leave."

"May I drive it?"

"You?" She laughed. "I thought you despised this
modern vehicle."

"I do, but I want to drive it." He tapped the rim of
the broad hat she wore when she drove.

She gave him quick instructions on how to run the
vehicle while they walked over to it. Leaning over the
side, she watched intently as he inserted the key. Its
muted rumble was loud in the night undisturbed by
other mechanical sounds. With a skip in her step, she
ran around to the passenger's side. She grasped Ian's
hand and leapt into the seat.

"It seems strange from this perspective," she said
with a laugh. "All right. Just be careful."

Ian found it simple to steer the machine around the
green. He had ridden with her enough times to know
exactly what the few controls did. When he drew even
with the rectory, he passed the house.

"Ian! The brake! There on the floor!"

"Don't panic, honey. I don't intend to hurt your
precious automobile."

She clutched the wrought-iron decoration on the
side of the seat as he jounced the automobile onto the
driveway leading to the stables at the back of the
parsonage. The wheels grabbed the small stones and
spurted out them behind them. They rolled to a stop by
the back door leading to the kitchen.

With a flourish, he doffed his cap to her. "Door-
to-door service, my lady."

"I am impressed." She jumped out and smoothed
her skirt as she waited for him to descend more slowly.
When he offered her his arm again, she took it with a
smile. "I shall have to let you drive more often. You
are clearly overwhelmed by it."

He opened the door and turned on the gaslight in
the white kitchen. The light cut like a hot knife through
the darkness. When she started to walk toward the coal
stove to put the cast iron kettle to heat, his hand tightened on her arm and spun her back to face him. Her

joking retort died unspoken as she met the desire glowing in his eyes.

In a voice thick with longing, he whispered, "It is not your automobile which overwhelms me, my love. It is you. I love you, Mariel Wythe. Stay here with me tonight."

"Stay here?" she gasped. "All night?"

"Why not?" His hands encircled her face. "You know I love you."

She nodded. "Of course. Ian, I love you, too. But—" He silenced her protest by pressing his mouth over hers. For a second she acquiesced to the lure of his lips. Then sanity reasserted itself. She pushed herself out of his arms.

"Ian, what is wrong with you?"

"Nothing but that I cannot get the thought of loving you from my mind."

Refusing to be enticed by his fingers, moving in slow, sensuous circles along her arm, she stated coldly, "You are a minister, Ian. What you are asking me to do is "

"Sinful?" he supplied. "Come with me, my love. I have something I want to show you."

He stepped away from her and opened a door by the broom closet. He took a candle from a shelf and lit it from the gaslight. He turned the light down and took her hand in his. With his eyes holding her gaze, he led her up the kitchen stairs to the second floor of the house. Through the narrow hall, she followed until he opened a door near the front of the house. He ushered her in without comment.

Her eyes widened as she saw this must be Ian's bedroom. A wide tester bed sat in the middle of the opposite wall. Its crocheted canopy drooped into tassels. The design was repeated on the covers. A desk smaller than the one in the study bore its burden of papers and books. It stood on a worn rug. Other pieces of furniture lurked beyond the light of the single candle.

"Ian, I shouldn't be here." She turned to go, but his arms halted her again. Looking up into his handsome face, she murmured, "If anyone was to discover this, it would ruin you. How can you forget what the church board—?"

"No one will learn you slept in my arms tonight." When he heard her soft sigh of desire, he leaned forward to whisper in her ear, "Think of how you feel when I kiss you and touch you. Think how much more wonderful it will be when you and I have nothing between our hearts but the loving caress of our skin. Mariel, I love you. Be mine."

Sorrowfully, she shook her head and pulled away from him. When several feet of empty space lay between them, she regarded him with tears in her eyes. "Don't you understand, Ian? That is why I can't do as I want with all my heart." She spread out her hands. "This is your life. You love your work. I cannot let you risk all that for me."

"You may be right," he admitted slowly. When he saw the flicker of pain in her eyes, he added, "If you feel that way, you should probably go."

"Yes," she answered in a dull tone.

She did not look at him as she secured her hat ribbons under her chin. As she crossed the room, he said nothing. She hoped this would not destroy the love between them. If only he would not urge her with his deep green eyes to forget what she should do. They continued to tease her to do as she wanted.

As she stepped past him to leave the room, the door closed in her face. She whirled to face Ian. His hands grasped her upper arms and tugged her to him. Any chance she had to remonstrate disappeared as his mouth captured hers. As one arm held her tight against him, his free hand untied her hat and tossed it to the floor. Easily, he sent the pins in her thick hair flying across the room as he loosened it to cascade over his hands.

When he stepped backward from the door, he drew her with him. Although her mind shouted warnings, she refused to listen, and she followed. He smiled as he raised his head from hers. Bewitched by the magic of his desire, she could not look away as he undid the buttons of her driving coat. The mackintosh fell heavily to the floor.

His fingers reached for the buttons of her blouse. Despite herself, her blush betrayed her. Even in her own room, she undressed behind her screen. Although she acted very outspoken on other subjects, on this most intimate one, she was charmingly shy. Her hands folded in front of her. Only his fingers beneath her chin would bring her eyes up to meet his.

Bending, he placed his lips against the heat of her cheeks. He sighed with regret. He must not push her, for he did not want to lose this opportunity, which might never come again. In his fantasies, he had disrobed her with unhurried pleasure, delighting in each newly discovered treasure. He would submerge that longing tonight. Somehow, he hoped, there would be other times.

Quietly, he said, "The dressing screen is over there." He reached in his closet and withdrew his satin collared robe. Its ruby colored, quilted material would cover her sufficiently to ease her discomfort.

"I don't know if—"

"My love, do you think I would do anything to hurt you?"

Her voice strengthened. She regarded him without her azure eyes sliding away from his. "Of course not. Just be patient with me."

"There is no need to hurry, honey." He teased her earlobe with the tip of his tongue. "We have all night."

The tingling from his caress swept all the way to her toes. With a gasp, she drew away from him. She ran to the dressing screen and put it between him and her yearning heart.

Her fingers trembled as she drew her shirt from her skirt. Flustered, she paused. She did nothing more, until she realized she could not stand behind the screen all night in indecision. Bending to undo her shoes, she stepped out of them and drew off her stockings. Easily her skirt untied to fall to the floor over them. The petticoats followed like huge snowflakes. It was more difficult to undo the buttons of her shirt.

Beyond the screen, she could hear Ian's movements through the room. She did not satisfy the curiosity to discover what he was doing. A small voice in the back of her head taunted her by accusing her of being afraid to look. For the first time in longer than she could remember, she did not listen to her more daring self. She clung to the anonymity of the screen, frightened by the strong desires whirling through her.

She had the strange feeling this was not really Mariel Wythe here. Never had she considered staying with Ian in his house alone. Yet no more than he, could she turn her back on this chance to share what her heart ached to know. Forever could not belong to them, but this one stolen night could be theirs.

The light dimmed just as she drew the robe around her. It clung to the silk of her underclothes and outlined her body easily. Closing her eyes, she took a deep breath to strengthen herself. She stepped from around the side of the screen.

"Come here," came a soft command from out of the twilight.

Slowly, she walked to the bed and stood on the opposite side from where Ian reclined under the covers. As he reached across to take her hand, the blanket slipped to reveal far more of his muscular body than she had ever seen. Her eyes followed his silhouette from broad shoulders to the leaner line of his waist. The blanket covered him lower than that, but her imagination, honed by nights of fervid dreams completed the fantasy of the man she loved.

"Sit with me, my love. If you wish only to sit and talk now, we will." From the warmth of his voice, she knew he longed to do far more.

"I want you to kiss me." As she said the words, she knew he was right. Tonight belonged to them. Whatever might happen in the future, this one night was set apart to be spent in magic. She sat next to him and held out her arms, nearly lost in the wide sleeves of the robe. "I want you to love me."

His eyes burned with green desire as he leaned over her. Timidly her fingers reached out to touch the dark matting across his chest. The flame leapt from him to ignite her longing as she touched him. His lips on hers fanned the spark to a conflagration. Easily he pushed the ties of the robe apart. When his fingers touched the silk beneath, he smiled. This modesty was a part of her hidden behind her brash exterior. He knew how difficult it was for her to combat it. At the thought of what she did for their love, his yearning exploded within him to submerge every other thought.

She barely noticed as he drew the robe from her. Her fingers were enrapt in learning the thrill of his bare skin. The hard texture of his body was so different from her own. When his fingers settled on the curve of her breast, her eyes opened wide. The involuntary gasp of his name brought a smile to his lips. She did not see it, swept away as she was in the lyrical melody he played upon her skin.

With his love lacing his words, he murmured, "I want to see every inch of your beauty. Now, my love."

Rising to her knees, she reached for the hooks which held her chemise in place. His hands slowly drew hers away as he brought her to rest over him. One hand at the back of her head kept her mouth against his while he loosened the fine silk shadowing her body.

Her gasp of unbridled rapture spiraled through his mouth as he pulled aside the opened camisole to introduce the sweetness of her skin to him. The soft sound became a cry as he raised her so his mouth could taste what he had touched so infrequently.

A spring tide rose deep within her as his tongue teased the tip of her breast before seeking its way along the downy surface. The moist rhythm of his kisses urged her body to a tempo she did not recognize. With the blankets between them, she could sense only slightly his reaction to her craving.

Before she quite realized what was happening, his fingers were drawing the last of her underclothes from her. When they settled onto the jumble of clothes on the floor, he flipped aside the covers and reclined her on the cool muslin sheets.

She took a deep breath of astonishment as she saw him naked before her for the first time. The embarrassment she had expected to feel when she shared herself with the man she loved never materialized. All she could think of was how much she wanted to touch him in the same enticing way he was stroking her.

When her fingers raised tentatively, he smiled. That expression gave her the courage to do as she ached to. Each caress along him brought her more delight from his fingers.

His mouth wove a fiery web along her skin as his fingers sought the most secret delights she had to offer him. Every spot he touched came alive as never before. Her breath sounded loudly in her ears as she moved to the pattern his fingers were teaching her.

When he brought her beneath him, her eyes opened again to touch the love-softened lines of his face. One arm wrapped around his shoulders as her hand stroked his cheek. Her whisper of love escalated into a gasp as he sought the total of their love in the depths of her body.

Murmuring his name, she clutched his shoulders. The joy became exquisitely agonizing. She became a pulse, beating in time to the powerful sensations crashing through her. . . wilder, faster, uncontrollable, until she splintered apart into starglow, billowing up to mingle with the heavens in the love of the man who shared her heart.

Leisurely kisses against her neck roused Mariel from the luscious lethargy weighting her limbs. She whispered Ian's name as she lifted her arms to bring him back against her.

"My sweet love, how have you hidden this passion from the rest of the world?"

She opened her eyes to see his face directly above hers. Her finger followed the outline of his lips, which brought such delights to her. "I have been waiting for you, Ian. While others laughed behind their hands at the spinster of Foxbridge Cloister, my heart knew I should wait for you to set it free to soar."

"I love you, lovely lady."

"And I love you, Ian." She grinned impishly. "I love the way you make me feel when I lie here with you."

He laughed as he brought her head to rest on his chest. His fingers slowly moved along the silken texture of her skin so he could feel the power of their ecstasy drain from her. Biting back the words he longed to say, he did not ask her if she had changed her mind about marrying him. Later was time for such plans. Now all he wanted to do was savor the sweetness of Mariel in his arms.

"Shy?" he teased when she reached for the rumpled covers.

"No, chilly." She gasped as he rolled her onto her back and leaned over her. The leer on his face distorted it from her image of the kindly Reverend Beckwith-Carter.

"Let me warm you."

Her fingers touched his shoulders. She discovered she was trembling with the anticipation of the joys she would know as he held her. She pushed thoughts of the danger of this love from her mind.

Tonight she would do nothing to harm what she should never have done. She would not think of the consequences of this love affair. For this brief moment, the ecstasy was worth the chance of losing everything she held dear.

"Love me, Ian."

"For as long as you want, my love."

She swallowed her moan of desperation as she gave herself over to his loving once more. Only in the very thing that could destroy her could she find happiness.

Chapter Eleven

An unfamiliar sound broke through Ian's dreams. He opened his eyes to a brilliant splash of sunshine. When he heard his bedroom door close, he sat upright. His astonishment at his room being invaded became a lazy, loving grin.

"Good morning," sang Mariel. She placed the tray she carried on the night table and sat on the edge of the bed.

When he wrapped his arms around her slender form dressed only in beribboned camisole and cotton petti-coats, he brought her to rest against him. With as much yearning as the first time he held her the night before, his mouth explored the pearlescent warmth of her lips.

Softly, he whispered against her ear, "Good morning to you, my love." His fingers traced the gentle roundness of her skin above the lace of her chemise. "Breakfast in bed? I did not know you could cook. I figured you left that to Mrs. Puhle."

"I do have talents other than upsetting the stuffy school-board members," she retorted saucily.

He pushed her back into the pillows and put one hand on either side of her head. Seeing the love in her sapphire eyes, he smiled. "I agree. You have many talents. Are you sure your esteemed uncle brought you only the costume of the sultan's favorite and not her secrets of keeping her husband satisfied in her bed?"

166

"Ian!" As always when he pleased her with his admiration, she flushed and failed to find words to reply to such open emotion. She sat and reached for a steaming cup. "Do you want to try my coffee?"

"It cannot taste as good as you." He pressed his lips to her bare shoulder. When she gasped a sharp warning, he took the cup from her quivering fingers. "Very good," he said after he took a sip. "Do I smell eggs?"

"Scrambled." She giggled with childish amusement. "They started out as fried, but I am afraid I make much better scrambled eggs than any other kind."

He raised the cloth covering the tray. The aroma of the food tantalized him. When she leapt from the bed to serve him, he reached for his trousers. He felt her eyes on him and glanced at her. Guiltily, she pretended to be busy spooning eggs onto a plate.

Reaching out for her hand, he pressed it to his weakened leg. With gentle compassion, he said, "You seem afraid to touch me here. You cannot hurt me. The leg is healed as much as it ever will be."

"It feels no different from the other," she said with wonder as she ran her fingers along the finely muscled leg. The now familiar surge of longing burst within her as she touched him.

"It differs only on the inside, my love. It is not the limb of a monster."

"Ian, I did not mean for you to think—"

He interrupted her with a lingering kiss. "I know, Mariel. You would never be cruel to me unintentionally." He grinned wickedly. "You would be sure to say it outright."

With a laugh, she asked, "Do you want to eat your breakfast now or wait until it is cold?"

"I would like to make love with you."

"Breakfast first. I worked too hard while you were sleeping to let it go to waste."

His hand stroked her bare arm. "Breakfast first, then I want to enjoy you again."

Putting her palms to her forehead, she bowed, "Your wish is my heart's desire, my sheikh."

In spite of her vow to let no one daunt her for spending the night away from the Cloister, Mariel found herself sneaking into the house at mid-morning like a thief. She tiptoed through the foyer and up the stairs lit by the stained glass window. Along the hallway she skulked, hoping to see no one.

Hastily she changed out of her clothes, which showed the abuse of a night of lying on Ian's bedroom floor. She shoved them to the back of the closet. Somehow she would find a way to explain their condition. Not now. She was tired and wanted only to take a nap. Ian had left her little time for sleeping during the night.

"So you decided to come home?"

Mariel twirled to see Phipps. The older woman had her arms folded across her chest in the uncompromising position she had often chosen when a younger Lady Mariel refused to desist in her latest antics.

"Phipps, can we talk about this later?" She rubbed her dry eyes.

"My lady, you must remember your place in this community." She crossed the room to stand directly between Mariel and her bed. Unless Mariel wanted to cut through her companion, she must stay and listen.

With a sigh of resignation and a longing look at the soft welcome of her bed, she said, "All right. I am listening. Lecture me."

Phipps shook her head. "There is nothing left for me to say. I have tried to teach you to be the proper young lady you should be. It appears I have failed."

"Because I was late coming home one night?"

"Lady Mariel, you know as well as I do that you have only now come home. I will not ask you where you have been or whom you have been with. All I want to say is that you have an honored place in this community. You must ask yourself if what you are doing is worth the risk of losing that."

Angrily, she stated, "Right now, I can tell you I do not give a damn what the rest of Foxbridge thinks about me!"

"Lady Mariel!"

"What upsets you more?" she demanded sharply. "That I cursed or that I was late arriving home?"

Pain crossed Phipps's face as she looked at the young woman's stubborn stance. "What upsets me is the example you are setting for that child next door! How do you expect to raise her as a moral, chaste woman if you spend the night elsewhere?"

"Leave me alone!" cried Mariel. All the joy she had shared with Ian vanished when Phipps forced her to realize that what she had done in the midst of desire had blinded her to everything else. She did not want to think of that now or to admit to herself that she would be returning to the parsonage later to go eagerly to Ian's bed again.

Phipps started to speak, then clamped her lips closed. Over and over during the night as she waited for Lady Mariel to come home, she had told herself that if she was delayed, she must be with Reverend Beckwith-Carter. She expected her lady should have no concern about her chastity with the parson, but Phipps discovered she had been wrong. Lady Mariel could not hide the glow of her newfound joy behind her icy exterior.

With a sigh, she wondered what would come of this love. It would be less easily accepted than a young woman from the village carousing with her lover among the shadows of the hedgerows. Already the church board had made its feelings clear on a relationship between Lady Mariel and the minister. This could cause only more trouble.

Mariel watched, perplexed, as Phipps excused herself and left the room. She had expected far more argument. Then she recalled her companion's words. A scolding and being sent to her room without dessert would not suffice as a lesson for this misdeed. Hurt burned with hot tears in her eyes. She did not want to be punished for doing the only thing she could to satisfy her heart before the love she had waited for all her life disappeared.

Throwing herself onto her bed, she buried her face in the cool fluffiness of her pillows. No one could possibly understand the hell she lived in except for Uncle Wilford. Perhaps she should run away, as he had. But to do that would mean never seeing Ian or Rosie again. She could not throw away her love to escape her unhappiness.

Dreams soothed her as she relived the rapture of those precious hours in Ian's arms. It was her only comfort as she escaped the truth for another few hours.

The sun burned in the western sky when Mariel left the Cloister. She did not drive the automobile. Leaving it behind the parsonage again tonight would be an invitation for troublesome gossip. Anyone who saw the buggy would assume it was Ian's, left in the yard for an early errand.

She drove around to the back and left it in the driveway. Unhooking the horse, she led him into the barn. After making sure he would be secure for the night, she went toward the house.

Mariel opened the kitchen door of the rectory. The aroma of roast beef tantalized her senses. She smiled as she walked to the stove. That Ian could cook such a luscious meal surprised her more than he had been with her breakfast that morning. Peeking into the oven, she closed her eyes as she enjoyed the wondrous scent.

The door crashed shut as she released it. A kiss sent a wave of delight along her. She whirled to be enfolded in Ian's arms. His lips silenced her greeting. The sweet flush of desire burst through her again. His hands reacquainted themselves with her. When his mouth explored her skin, she became breathless with longing.

"I love you, Ian," she whispered as her fingers stroked his face. Her eyes remained on his lips, which could delight her so easily.

"Mariel, this day has been a century long. I feared the end would never come." He tilted her face back so he could see her expression. "I feared you would not return."

"How could I stay away?" Her eyes lowered as she added with less happiness, "Phipps lectured me this morning and dropped hints all day about my less than exemplary behavior, but I want to be with you."

He searched her features and saw the stubbornness that was her tool to deal with any blockade in her life.

"Then stay with me forever."

"Forever?"

His hands caressed her shoulders leisurely. When he drew her head against the strength of his chest, she did not protest. He spun the future before her. "Think of being able to share forever what we discovered last night. Think of the other ways we give each other happiness. Mariel, no woman has ever irritated me as much as you do. No other woman ever made my heart sing just to look into her eyes."

In a whisper, she replied, "I think about it, Ian. I think about it all the time. I just do not want to talk about it tonight. Not when I want to be in your arms tasting the ambrosia of our love." She flung her arms around him. "Love me, Ian. Now!"

"Now? Dinner is nearly ready." He chuckled. "I understand your impatience, my love, but—"

Her fingers drew his face toward hers. "Now, please. I need you, Ian. I need the warmth of our love to wash away the fear within me."

"Fear?" He stepped back to see her ashen face. "Mariel, what is it? What is wrong?"

Tears clung to her eyelashes as she whispered, "Don't ask me to tell you what I cannot. Ask no promises of me except that I will love you forever."

He refused to be satisfied with such an obscure explanation. Taking her shoulders, he stepped away to view her face. "What is frightening you so? It must be more than what that Gypsy told you."

"I haven't thought of that since," she lied. *Not much,* she amended to herself. That Nadia's words matched her own fears of the future had startled her, but she had been warned. She could not do anything to change what would happen, just as she had been unable to do anything about the past. Softly, she added, "Don't make me beg you, Ian. Please allow me this much."

"I will give you everything I can." He reached past her to open the oven door. The heat spiraled out into the kitchen as they walked up the back stairs. At that moment, their feet moved in the perfect rhythm their bodies soon would know. They did not worry if their meal would be ruined. All they wanted was to cure the

anguish in their hearts by delighting their senses with
rapturous kisses and caresses.

The days passed in a flurry of joy and agony for
Mariel. Whenever she was not with Ian, she tried to do
all the other things she normally did to fill her days.
Sleep became something she could experience only in
her memory. She refused to spend the whole night with
Ian again after that first night, but she did not sleep in
her own bed.

Through the night, she paced endlessly. A warm
bath or a cup of heated milk did nothing to help her
sleep. She wanted to be in Ian's arms, to slumber
dreamlessly, as she had that one night. To do that might
decimate everything she wanted for herself and for the
ones she loved.

She realized how distant she had been to everyone
in the Cloister when she went looking for Rosie on
Saturday. It disturbed her to be unable to remember if
she had had time alone with her daughter since the day
of the school-board meeting.

Searching through the house yielded her no clues to
the location of the child. Finally, she asked one of the
maids. The woman looked at her as if she was insane.
"Why, Lady Mariel, today is the day Dodsley promised
to take Miss Rosie to the pond to go fishing. Don't you
remember?"

"Yes, thank you." She said nothing more as she
walked toward the solarium. Peering out the windows,
she could see the line of trees edging the small pool at
one end of the gardens.

She remembered that Dodsley meant to take Rosie
fishing. She also recalled the day before she was to have
gone with the child to visit Mrs. Parnell. Rosie's best
friend at the orphanage turned six yesterday. There was
to be a party which they should have attended. Instead
she had forgotten in her desperate dreams of loving Ian.

When she heard crisp footfalls, she said, "Good
afternoon, Phipps."

"Good afternoon, Lady Mariel." The iciness of her
perfectly correct voice did not thaw when Mariel turned
to face her.

Without preamble, she said, "I forgot to take Rosie to the party yesterday."

"She asked for you, but I could not find you."

"I—" There was no sense in lying. Phipps would know the truth anyhow. Mariel had never succeeded in telling her companion a falsehood. "I was with Ian. I should have remembered, but I didn't."

"No," she said, sitting on the settee, "you did not remember. Walter drove Rosie to the orphanage. I understand they had a grand time." Her censure resounded through her voice as she added, "I hope you did also."

Suddenly, Mariel felt the overwhelming need for someone to understand why she was acting this way. She went to the sofa and sat on the green cushion. Leaning forward, she took Phipps's gnarled hand in hers.

"I love him," she said simply.

"Does he love you?"

"Yes."

"And this is how he shows it? What kind of minister is he to bed you without marriage?"

Anger tainted Mariel's voice as she defended Ian. "He is a wonderful minister. He has been responsive to the needs of his parish. And he has asked me to marry him."

"He has?" Phipps' scowl disappeared instantly. "Then when will the wedding be held? Oh, my lady, why haven't you shared these wondrous tidings with us?"

"There will be no wedding."

Phipps gasped. Her voice squeaked as she repeated, "No wedding?" She cleared her throat and asked in her normal voice, "But why? You clearly love him. He loves you. Why won't you marry him?"

Tears filled her eyes as she whispered, "I thought you would comprehend why I can't bring Ian into this family."

"That was years ago, Lady Mariel. Why should any of that resurface now?"

"Why not? Or in our children? Should I be ecstatic because the curse passed me by if my children must suffer the consequences of their parentage?"

Tersely, the gray-haired woman stated, "It may be too late to be thinking of that now."

The residual color in Mariel's face vanished as she asked herself how she could have been so stupid. She knew it was simply because denying herself Ian's love required more willpower than she possessed. Children did not come only from marriage beds.

Pain ripped through her. If it was not too late now, she had to put a stop to this madness. She shuddered as she thought of that word. Perhaps she was not exempt from the curse, after all. She could not have been sane to allow him to lure her to his bed when she was aware of the horror that could follow.

Pushing herself to her feet, Mariel said, "I must go out, Phipps. I will be back before dinner."

"Lady Mariel, do—"

"I am fine," she interrupted. "I will see you at dinner."

Phipps wanted to follow her lady and urge her to be careful. She did not want her to have a mishap while so upset. Instead of chasing after Lady Mariel, she simply sat on the settee again. It would be a waste of time and breath to offer such warnings. She sighed and prayed her distraught lady would return to the Cloister safely.

Ian glanced up at the study doorway, astonished to see Mariel there. He had not expected her for several hours. When he saw the distress on her face, he rose and held out his arms. With a cry, she ran to him. He held her without asking why she wept.

"Hush, my love," he murmured against her ear.

"Ian, I love you," she gulped between harsh sobs. "I love you." He urged her to sit on the sofa. Smoothing her dampened hair from her face, he watched as she tried to recompose her shattered self.

"I came to tell you that I cannot stay with you tonight."

A swell of disappointment washed over him, and he tried to keep her from seeing it. He knew he had failed when he saw the pain in her eyes. Softly, he asked, "Why?"

"It's Rosie." During the short drive to Foxbridge, she had decided to use this excuse to serve in place of the truth. If only she could tell him . . . She could not! Trying to keep her voice calm, she said, "I have barely spent a minute with her in the past days. I love her, too. She needs me."

He leaned against the back of the sofa and nestled her against him. As his fingers stroked the line of her arm, he whispered, "I have been selfish. I would like to have all your love for me."

"I have enough for both of you."

He chuckled. "That Rosie has learned. I do not want to be as jealous of you as she was when she first came to the Cloister." He glanced at the mantelclock. "I have an appointment in two hours. Do you want to help me pass the time until then?" Heated kisses against her face accented his words.

With a gasp, she ripped herself out of his arms. "I I can't! I have to be back to the Cloister."

"Why?" He rose to put his hand on her arm. He did not allow her to escape him.

Mariel stared up into his face and felt the yearning that never lessened. She wanted to know his loving again; to feel his lips touching her skin, searing it with the heat of their love; to caress him and hear his eager response to her fingertips moving along him in a spiral path.

Her feet moved to bring her close to him before she could form a thought. By the time she realized how foolish she was being, it was too late. His mouth had wooed hers into believing that this one time would be the last time she would risk their love by giving in to its rapture.

When he moved to latch the door and draw the drapes, she knew what she had from the beginning. She did not want to escape from the sweet web of love Ian had woven about her. Knowing that it would not last forever, she could not waste any of the time they had been given now. If later she rued the decision of this day, she would remember the enchantment of watching him slip off his dark coat while he walked toward her. The memory of his green eyes bright with passion would accompany the thought of his body pressing her into the soft cushions of the sofa.

All fear left her mind as she gave herself up to the love that knew no limits. Only later, when the soft glow of happiness had faded, did the tears fall to stain the fabric of the settee. When Ian could not comfort her, he ached for the pain within her. He did not ask her again why she acted this way, for she had devised too many stories to cover the truth. Until she opened her heart completely to him, he would not be able to help her heal the wounds festering deep in her heart.

When she left the parsonage half an hour before his meeting, he wondered if he had helped her or harmed her by professing his love for her. It was something he might never know.

Rosie was thrilled the next morning to have her beloved Mariel offer to take her for a ride. The young woman asked, "Why don't you come, too, Phipps?"

"A ride? Where to, Lady Mariel?" She reached for the sugar bowl to sweeten her morning coffee.

Offhandedly, Mariel said, "I thought we would go to church."

The older woman choked on her sip. She lowered her cup to the Wedgwood saucer and asked, "Do you think under the circumstances, my lady, that is a good idea?"

"I think it is a wonderful idea under the circumstances." She turned to Rosie, who was planning excitedly what she would wear. "What you have on is fine, my dear. Now, you must remember that Ian is working today, so you cannot tease him as you normally do."

"That won't be as much fun!"

Mariel patted her hand as she picked up her own coffee cup. "After the service, I am sure you will have plenty of time to play with him. Just be quiet and make him and me proud of you."

Phipps hid her concerns as the three of them finished breakfast and went to the garage to get the automobile. She said nothing while Lady Mariel chatted easily with Walter Collins. The man unplugged the vehicle from the generator and folded the cables neatly on the floor. He looked up to see Miss Phipps watching him. A strange expression crossed his face, but he was smiling when he turned to bid Lady Mariel a pleasant trip into the village.

The automobile drove smoothly along the steep road into the village. Mariel negotiated the dangerous corner at the bottom with ease. When they stopped in front of the white, clapboard church, the bell overhead was clanging in joyous abandon.

"That's Tip Lyndell," confided Rosie as Mariel lifted her from the vehicle. "He told me he gets to ring the bells every Sunday."

"What a lucky lad!" she agreed. Taking the child's hand in her gloved one, she led the way up the steps.

A welcoming sense of peace reached out for Mariel as the sexton unlocked the pew reserved for Lord Foxbridge and his family. She thanked Mr. Stadley, pretending they would not be foes in the argument over the textbooks on Tuesday evening.

"My pleasure, Lady Mariel."

Her smile broadened as she noted the humor in his eyes. Despite the harsh words she often shared with the residents of this small town, she saw they understood that she cared deeply for the future of their children. The ties binding the Wythes to Foxbridge were older than she could imagine. She felt like a member of an extended family.

Phipps brushed invisible dust from the unrelieved black of her skirt. She handed Rosie a hymnal and sat in correct silence. Opening her own to the first song posted on the board at the right side of the altar, Mariel wondered if Phipps had ever fidgeted when she was a girl or if she had always exhibited such perfect behavior.

Hiding her smile, she told herself this was not the time to be plotting devilment to tease her companion. She handed Rosie a piece of candy and told her to chew it quietly. If she would behave during the service, Mariel promised her another. A door on the opposite side of the church opened. At the same time, the choir accompanied the organ in a rousing song to brighten the summer morning.

Mariel hoped no one could see the admiration she was unable to hide, as her eyes took in the transformation of Ian into the imposing Reverend Beckwith-Carter. A white surplice decorated with thick lace covered the dark suit he wore on calls to his parishioners. With his auburn hair and emerald eyes the only colors in his outfit, he seemed so different from the laughing, loving man who had caressed her and introduced her to paradise. Despite that, the familiar yearning to feel his arms around her suffused her with warmth.

As he greeted his congregation, Ian smiled. The church was full today. Continuing attendance meant he was serving the needs of these people. He hoped he could find someone willing to chair the committee for the annual summer fair. One of the ladies was sure to volunteer if he charmed her. When he first came to this small church, he would not have considered such tactics, but he learned quickly that politics played a part in his position. He forced those thoughts from his mind as he bent his head to lead the prayer.

He stumbled on a word and paused as he saw the bowed heads in the first pew to his left. This was the first time anyone had sat there since he assumed his duties in Foxbridge. Hastily, he continued with the supplication, before anyone could think he had done more than hesitate to catch his breath. His eyes remained on the Wythe pew. When Mariel peeked at him from under the wide brim of her picture hat, a slow smile spread across his face. Her eyes twinkled at him mischievously.

Easily recognizing the challenge she posed to him, Ian found himself caught up in an attempt to impress her. He ignored the pages in front of him on the altar as he spoke from his heart of the need for love in his congregation's lives. Too often, he found his eyes straying to Mariel. Each time, he could see the love emblazoned on her face, which urged him to forsake his task and take her in his arms.

A flush brightened his cheeks as he finished his sermon in grand style. The organ resounded against the rafters as he gave a signal to the choir director. That he had touched more than Mariel with his words he discovered as the churchgoers enthusiastically joined in with the final hymn. He walked to the back of the church as he did each Sunday and spoke the benediction.

With the ease of habit, Phipps straightened Lady Mariel's hat as they rose. The younger woman's silky hair refused to allow the wide hat to stay in place. It continually slipped toward her right ear. She listened as Lady Mariel chatted with the people sitting behind them, and she wondered if the young woman had any idea how special her life was. That she was trying to ruin it with this latest escapade, which took her to the bed of the man who led this church, seemed insanity to her.

The gray-haired woman blanched. Such words could never be voiced in Foxbridge Cloister. The taint of the past haunted Lady Mariel. The dark-haired woman needed no reminder of that horrible night when her life was altered forever.

Mariel could not have guessed Phipps's dark thoughts. Today her heart swelled with the joy of seeing Ian. Although she could not show the love she shared with him, being near him made her happy. She wondered if he would be able to find time tonight to hold her again. Although the horror continued to hover over her, she could not wait to drown it in the depths of their love.

"My, you are happy this morning," crooned one of the spinster ladies who had sat behind them.

"I am," she responded with a smile. "It's been a very good summer so far. Such good weather for the crops, and I have such high expectations for the future of the school. All in all, it is a day for jubilation."

The second lady could not restrain her nosiness. "We were quite surprised to see you here, my lady. It's been so long since you and the lord joined us for services. It's been since. . ."

Mariel interrupted her hastily. "The reverend shared your concerns about my laxness, so I thought I would come to see what all the adulation of his sermons was about. He did so well." She smiled as she found she had changed the subject with ease. The two ladies, dressed in the most somber style of their day, began to discuss every detail of Reverend Beckwith-Carter's sermon. Leaving them to their debate over some minuscule matter of scripture, Mariel walked with Phipps to the door of the church.

She waited while Ian spoke to the people in line ahead of her. As if they were the merest of acquaintances, Mariel offered him her hand. "I enjoyed the service, Reverend." Her smile caressed him as she added more softly, "Truly inspiring."

"I am glad, *my* lady." The slight emphasis was heard only by her heart. "It is such a pleasure to see you here."

"I am happy I came. Until now, I had not realized how much I missed these services." When she realized others waited to speak to him, she added, "Would you take luncheon with us?"

"It would be an honor."

She smiled with the love burgeoning in her heart. "We will wait for you by the automobile."

"No. Why don't you and Phipps go to the rectory? Mrs. Reed made lemonade this morning. She will be delighted to give you a glass."

"Mrs. Reed is home?" Her voice faltered before she added, "I trust her sister is better."

He nodded as he released her hands, which he had been holding publicly too long. She lowered her eyes and stepped away. Although he had hoped to find another way to tell her, there was no way to soften the truth that the sweet interlude was over. Even as he talked to other members of the congregation, he watched her walk slowly across the green, wavering in the heat. He understood the sorrow in her heart.

Rosie greeted Mrs. Reed with her usual enthusiasm. While the adults talked, she found her way to the kitchen table for a glass of lemonade accompanied by one of Mrs. Reed's incomparable biscuits.

"I am glad you have been able to return," said Phipps. She did not look at her lady, who would not be sharing her relief at the housekeeper's returnend. "How is your sister?"

The thin woman held out two more glasses of lemonade. Frost clung to their sides. "She is doing quite well. A heart palpitation, but she understands what she must do to stay well." She smiled. "I am happy to be back in my own home. I can tell the reverend missed me."

"How?" asked Mariel before she could halt the question.

"He was very grateful for my cooking this morning." She lost her smile as she said thoughtfully, "He asked for scrambled eggs, although he always has them poached." With a shrug, she laughed, "Perhaps he tired of the way the church ladies served him his meals."

Mariel smiled weakly and left the kitchen on a half-spoken excuse. Wandering to the front of the house, she opened the pocket doors of the drawing room opposite Ian's study. She sat in the cool silence. That this joy would come to an end she had known from the beginning. It was just that she did not want it to be today. One more time she wanted to lie in Ian's arms and lose herself in their love.

"I thought you might be here."

She looked up to see the man she loved standing in the doorway. Without attempting a fake smile, she said, "I did not think you would mind."

"Of course not." He entered, but did not close the doors behind him. "Honey, we must talk."

"I know."

"Not here."

She nodded her immediate understanding. Mrs. Reed was a wonderful housekeeper, but she could not be cured of her habit of listening at keyholes. "After lunch, we shall go for a walk. There are places in the gardens where we won't be overheard."

Taking her hands, he drew her to her feet and into his arms. "I love you, Mariel Wythe. More every day."

"I love you." Her smile was genuine as she added, "And I think you are the most wonderful preacher I have ever heard. You could woo the devil into renouncing his ways."

He grinned at her exaggeration. "Not quite, but thank you for the compliment. You learn early to be charming when you have to talk your way out of punishments in the headmaster's office." Kissing her too quickly, he led her to the hallway.

Rosie bounced from one foot to the other when Ian offered to give her a ride to the Cloister in his buggy. The four of them would not fit in the automobile. Mrs. Reed waved to them as they all drove away, the electric vehicle in the lead so as not to frighten Ian's horse.

Throughout the succulent meal, which was tasteless in Mariel's mouth, he continued to tease Rosie in the way she knew she loved. Somehow, Mariel found herself responding to the conversation and laughing with the child. She wanted only to have the meal completed, so she could be alone with Ian.

She was surprised when Phipps said, "Why don't you take Reverend Beckwith-Carter out and show him the roses, my lady?"

"Me, too?" piped in Rosie.

"No," said Phipps. "You must practice the piano this afternoon."

"It's Sunday!"

"I am quite aware of the day, young lady, but you skipped both Friday and Saturday. Lady Mariel will expect you to do well at your lesson tomorrow afternoon." Taking the child by the hand, Phipps led her from the room.

Ian pushed back his chair. "Shall we?"

"I don't think we have any choice. When Phipps gives commands in that tone of voice, I have learned to listen."

"But not to obey?"

She grinned. "Not always."

They went through the French doors in the dining room onto the stone terrace at the edge of the lawn. The gardens shimmered in the midday sun. Walking through the quiet, they could hear the soft song of the waves in the distance. The ever-present breeze puffed and faltered under the heat of the day.

Ian drew her into a rose-covered arbor. Within it, the power of the sun was diminished. When she sat on the narrow bench, he wrapped his arms around her and kissed her with the passion he could deny no longer.

"I wanted to send you a message when Mrs. Reed arrived last night, but I could not think of a way to phrase it." He brushed her hair back from her cheeks.

"My love, there must be other places."

"Name one!" she demanded bitterly. "Name one where we can have even a few minutes of privacy."

He shook his head. "I don't know, but we cannot let this destroy what we have found. This could be solved very easily in the three weeks it would take to post the banns."

"No!" she stated firmly.

"Why do you resist every time I suggest marriage?" He forced her face to turn so he could see the emotions she could not control. "You love me. This is the easiest way to solve our dilemma. It was what I intended from the beginning."

"From the beginning?"

Taking her by the shoulders, he snapped, "Do you think I would have made love to you otherwise? I thought then that you refused to marry me because you feared what we would share in our marriage bed. If I could prove to you how wonderful our love would be, I thought you would accept my proposal. But that is not what you fear, is it?"

"Ian, I don't want to talk about this now."

"Then when?" he demanded in growing anger. "I love you. You love me. What we feel is potent and should last all our lives. I have married couples who do not share a love as honest as ours. Why do you prefer to sneak about when all you have to do is tell me yes?"

She would not look at him. "I said I don't want to talk about marriage."

A gasp of pain escaped her lips as he shook her, but he did not apologize. "Why don't you simply say the truth? You don't want to marry me. You enjoy the times you share my bed, but the lovely Lady Mariel Wythe cannot lower herself to marry a cripple."

"Ian, don't say things like that!" She wanted to soothe his pain, but his anger refused to let her bridge the chasm it created between them.

"Why not?"

"Because it's not true!"

"Then why won't you marry me?"

She opened her mouth, then closed it tightly. If she told him the truth, she feared he would reject her outright. She loved Ian. For that reason, she could not ask him to share the nightmare waiting to take her without warning. When she did not answer, she saw his face hardened into a prison for his fury.

Ian rose. She leapt to her feet, but he brushed aside her hand as she tried to halt him from leaving. "Please, Ian," she cried. "Listen to me!"

"Listen to what? You have made your feelings clear." He placed his hat firmly on his head. "Good day, Lady Mariel. Thank you very much for the fine luncheon."

Gathering her skirts in her hand, she ran to catch up with him. She stood in front of him, but jumped aside as she realized he would not stop. "Ian!" she shouted. "Don't be like this! I love you."

Over his shoulder, he stated, "I am sure you think you do. Good day."

Mariel sank to a stone bench. She watched as he descended the hill toward the road. Within minutes, she saw his buggy leave a cloud of dust in its wake as it sped through the gate. A void aching deep within her told her that her heart went with him as he stormed away from Foxbridge Cloister.

She hid her face in her hands and she sobbed. Even as she told herself it would have come to this sooner or later, she did not want to think of losing this love, which had been the keystone of her life for the past weeks. She did not want the love to end.

Forcing herself to cross the lawn, she went up to her room. Behind the locked doors, she wept at the inevitable which had come too quickly. She refused to answer the door when she heard a soft rapping on it. Just now, anyone's sympathy would decimate the bit of Mariel left in the aftermath of her rejection.

That day and the next dragged by as Mariel tried to think of some way of convincing Ian of her love without telling him the truth. Slowly, she discovered that was impossible. She spent part of each day walking to and from the front windows to peer out into the sunshine.

Not once did his carriage pull up in front of the house.

Only the work she needed to do to prepare for the special board meeting kept her busy. She poured all her energy into it, but found it was not enough. During the day, she spent her empty hours with Rosie in a desperate attempt to find the love she feared she had lost. During the long hours of the night, as the starlight created a crisscross pattern through the diamond-shaped mullions of her windows, she once again paced the floor, trying to tire herself enough to sleep.

That she knew Ian did the same in the smaller bedroom in the manse did not ease her sorrow. His stubbornness and her fear drove them apart when they needed each other most. Too many times during the day, she thought of something she wanted to share with him—a joke, a comment. Each time that happened, her pain increased.

Phipps left her lady to her own devices. Although Mariel never had been easy to work for, she became impossible as her pain erupted in sharp words. Phipps guessed that the reverend had hurt Lady Mariel in some manner.

The older woman kept Rosie busy, so she would not disturb Lady Mariel. The child did not notice any problem. She simply was happy to have her beloved Mariel at the Cloister all the time.

The night of the board meeting, Mariel delayed as long as possible leaving the Cloister. She wanted to have to hurry. That way she could be sure not to have the time to speak to Ian if she saw him on the village green.

Walter was waiting for her when she arrived at the barn. She could not find a smile to answer his grin. Instead, she said, "I thought you would be at the Three Georges by this time."

"I knew you wanted the automobile, my lady. I polished it for you today, so you can be proud to drive it into Foxbridge." He stretched his tired muscles. "I doubt if I will go into town tonight. It has been a long day. I think I will simply pack away my tools and call it a day."

"Good night, then," she said as she climbed into the driver's seat. She envied him his apparent ability to sleep

with such ease. It seemed as if it had been an eternity
since she found her slumber so easily.

The key started the motor purring. She backed it
carefully from the barn and turned onto the path leading
to the gate. Mr. Gratton would be fuming by this time,
wondering why she was late. He knew she would not
miss this meeting.

As she drove, Mariel rehearsed the speech she
would use to convince the school board they had no
choice but to vote for the textbooks. She knew they
would be as unaccepting of her ideas as usual. Sometimes she wondered why she bothered to run every year
for the position. She smiled into the rose-colored sky.
The answer was simple. If she was not there, they would
do as they wished and ruin the school in Foxbridge. She
intended for the town to move into the twentieth century
with the rest of the world, but it was not easy for people
who clung to the ancient ideas of another era.

She turned the corner and checked her watch.
Delaying over supper had made her later than she
wanted to be. She increased her speed. With a smile, she
thanked Walter silently. Under his care, the automobile
worked perfectly. Since he had come to the Cloister, she
never had to worry whether it would get her about on
her errands.

When the lights of Foxbridge appeared in the valley
below, she tightened her grip on the lever. She knew
this road well and respected the steep hill leading into
the village. Many years ago, she had seen an overturned
carriage at the bottom. The image of the crushed vehicle
returned to her mind nearly every time she came this
way.

Keeping her foot near the brake, she watched as the
trees fled past. She frowned as she pressed the pedal to
slow the vehicle. In the dusk, she felt she was traveling
too fast.

Panic replaced her misgivings as she stamped the
brake again with her foot. Nothing happened. If anything
she was moving more quickly. Concentrating on what
she could do, she realized she must steer the car around
the wide corner at the bottom of the hill. She nearly
bounced off the seat as one wheel hit a stone. With her

grip painfully tight on the lever and her feet striking the pedals controlling the rear wheels, she struggled to bring the vehicle back into her control.

Nothing happened.

In terror, she swung the lever back and forth. No response came from the wheels, which were spinning too fast. She screamed as she looked up to see the stone wall directly in front of her. Releasing the useless lever, she instinctively raised her arms to protect her face.

"Ian!" she shrieked, fearing she would never see him again.

A burst of pain rushed through her as an explosion of sound crashed around her. As the automobile impacted with the ancient wall, her scream faded into silence. Metal screeched at a higher pitch than a human throat could create. It fell in on itself as sparks brightened the twilight. One spark fell on the battery terminals, instantly igniting. A second detonation echoed through the night.

Chapter Twelve

Ian struggled to concentrate on his sermon for Sunday. Last night, he had found an old one he could reuse. He did not want to do that, but he might have no choice. Since his argument with Mariel, he had not been able to think of anything but the mystery surrounding her refusal to marry him. She loved him. That never had been the issue, only the reason for her stubborn rejection of his proposal.

He dropped his pen to the table. Tired palms eased the weariness of his eyes. This battle to try to pretend he could exist without her was foolish. He could not sleep at night in the bed, which seemed too lonely without her softness next to him. All day his mind dwelled on her, blocking every other thought.

For the past two evenings he had sat here, succeeding in doing nothing. He drew curlicues in the margin of the empty page. Ashamed to admit before Mrs. Reed his inability to think of anything but Mariel Wythe, he continued to pretend he was working. His ears longed to hear the sound of her light footsteps on the wood floors. He wanted to feel her fingers massaging the tightness out of his neck before they roamed along him to inflame his desire to its fervid pitch.

Suddenly, he jumped from the chair. He glanced around, baffled. Picking up his cane from the floor, he went to the window. The housekeeper looked up in concern from where she sat on the other side of the lamp.

"Reverend, is there a problem?"

"Did you hear that?" he asked. When Mrs. Reed did not answer, he ignored her confused expression. "She called to me, but she isn't here."

"She? Who did you—?" She interrupted herself as a flash of lightning cut through the darkness. A crash of thunder followed too closely. "A storm? I saw no clouds tonight."

Ian crossed the room and grasped his cloth coat from the peg by the door. "That is no storm."

She followed him to the door to watch as he raced away into the darkness faster than she thought him capable. Across the green, the lights from the small schoolhouse next to the church poured out onto the jeweled grass. Other figures rushed from the building. They called to Reverend Beckwith-Carter, but he did not answer as he continued toward the shore road.

Mrs. Reed put her hands over her mouth as she knew suddenly what the pastor feared. Lady Mariel would have been coming from the Cloister for the school-board meeting. Tonight she intended to demand acceptance from the other members on the textbook issue. None of the silhouettes emerging from the school was skirted. If she drove that infernal machine of hers. . .

Pain burned in Ian's side as his cane struck the ground again and again in rhythm with his pumping legs. He paid no attention to it, or to the anguish in his weakened leg. As he rounded the corner at the bottom of the hill, he stopped. The horror of the scene stripped him of every voluntary motion.

Flames lapped the dark sky. Only because he knew the automobile must be at the center of the inferno could he guess its original shape. Heat scorched his face, although he stood a good distance from the fire. Small fires began and died in the dew wet grass.

Moans could be heard behind him. Others were discovering what he had seen. Shouts called for volunteers for a bucket brigade to keep the fire from spread-

ing. He forced himself to move. There must be something he could do. A hand grabbed his coat sleeve.

"Reverend, you can't! Don't kill yourself! She's
dead."

The words broke his shock. He shook off the hand
and rushed forward, but more cautiously. The warnings
of the people behind him did not impact on his brain.
Only one thought remained. Somewhere in that twisted,
burning mass of metal and wires, Mariel had been
riding. She could not be dead. The voice that had called
to him had been desperate, not resigned to her fate.

Someone appeared next to him with a lantern. He
did not look to see who it was as he ripped its handle
from its owner's grasp. Ignoring the fire, which held
everyone else's attention, he swung the light to see the
deep ruts where the tires had left the road to cut across
the grass and smash the automobile against the wall.

With a gasp, he ran to a spot twenty feet from the
fire. He dropped to his knees and picked up the slender
wrist of the form crumpled on the grass. It took his
tremulous fingers several seconds to find her pulse. He
whispered a fervent prayer as he felt it thready beneath
his touch. Although she clearly was hurt, Mariel lived.

"Someone! Help! Over here!"

When a man raced up, he was surprised to see it
was Walter Collins from the Cloister. He had not
thought to see him here. Then he remembered the
handyman often came into Foxbridge to enjoy the
camaraderie of the Three Georges.

"Reverend? I'm sorry. I—"

"Be silent!" he ordered. "Tell some of those people
over there I need help. Then hurry back to the Cloister
and let Miss Phipps know Lady Mariel has had an
accident, but is alive."

"Alive?" Involuntarily the gray haired man looked
at the burning automobile. Only when the pastor turned
back to regard something on the ground did Walter
notice the shadow in front of Reverend Beckwith-Carter.
"She survived that? How?"

"She must have been thrown free before the impact." Ian looked up, his face twisted by his fear.
"Hurry, man!"

Collins turned on his heel to race along the road toward the Cloister. He did not need to get aid from the others. The pastor's raised voice had caught the attention of the firefighters. Shouted orders sent a boy running to find the doctor. No one dared move Lady Mariel until Dr. Sawyer checked her.

Unashamed of the tears coursing along his face, Ian whispered, "Stay with me, Mariel. Don't die now. Don't die when you think I am angry with you." He found no comfort in knowing her heart had called out to his in the seconds before the crash. During the horrid hours of the last two days, he never once doubted she loved him.

A hand patted his shoulder awkwardly, but he did not look up as he pressed her limp fingers to his cheek. In the glare of the fire and the pale light of the lamp, he saw blood etched across her face. Dirt outlined the pattern of the scratches distorting her features. Her heavy coat was ripped. Someone bent to smooth her skirts around her ankles, careful not to touch her.

"Reverend, the doctor is here." When he did not appear to have heard, Mr. Gratton cleared his throat as he did when he wished to gain the attention of his quibbling boardmembers. He repeated the words.

Dazed, Ian glanced at the crowd around them. His eyes settled on the doctor. He rose slowly. Someone pressed his cane into his hand. His thanks was automatic as he watched Dr. Sawyer.

"Will she live?" he demanded, afraid to know the answer.

"Let me examine her first, Reverend." The doctor's voice softened as he said, "Your house is closest. Can we take her there?"

Numbly, he nodded. He would play the doctor's game. The McNaughtons' house was nearer, but there was no use acting as if Mariel was only another of his flock. Before all these people, he had bared his love for her tonight. He did not worry if it would surprise them or not. All he thought of was fighting for Mariel's life. Without her in his, he knew he would never regain the joy she had taught him.

"Get a bed ready for her. We will bring her."

Ian followed the orders, with several trailing him to be sure he did not hurt himself as he staggered toward his house. Mrs. Reed ran forward, the question she did not dare to speak displayed on her face.

"Mariel is alive." As he spoke those words to console her, he felt a strength he thought gone settle on him. He took Mrs. Reed's arm and turned her toward the house. "Come. We will put her in my room. It is the best in the parsonage." He did not add he wanted Mariel to be in familiar surroundings until she could be moved to the Cloister. That truth could not be revealed now.

"Reverend, what happened? Why did the automobile crash like that?"

"Later," he ordered coldly. "Now all we must think of is making sure Mariel stays alive."

Pain cut across her head. With a moan, Mariel raised her hands to her face. Gentle fingers blocked her motion. She moved her head to look at the one who held her, but only darkness surrounded her.

"Don't move, honey. Let the doctor finish checking you. You seem to have escaped the accident with only a few scratches and bruises." Relieved laughter filled her ears. "You were very lucky."

"Ian!" Hot tears stung her aching eyes. Her hand slid along the bed covers and recognized the pattern of his coverlet. Being in his bed where she had learned of the power of his love for her urged her to speak the truth. "I thought I was going to die without seeing you again. I did not want to die when you thought I was angry with you."

"Hush," he ordered. He leaned forward and kissed her tenderly on the forehead. "Let Dr. Sawyer tend to you."

"Doctor?" In confusion, she noted the fingers moving along her left arm. "Ian, will you turn up the light so the man can see what he is doing? How do you expect him to examine me in the dark?"

Ian forced his gasp down his throat before it could escape to betray him. Behind him, he heard Mrs. Reed whisper a supplication. He looked from Mariel's face, turned toward him, to the doctor on the other side of the bed. Except for a few scrapes, she appeared normal.

Dr. Sawyer took her face gently in his fingers and tilted it toward him. When she groaned, he commiserated softly, "I am sure your head aches, my lady, but I will be done in a moment." His jovial words did not match his intense expression as he grasped the candle on the nightstand. Holding it close to her face, he watched her reaction intently.

"What is so hot?" gasped Mariel. "Ian, is the car still burning? It exploded." Suddenly her voice rose in panic, "What is wrong? Why can't I see?"

The doctor did not answer her question. Instead, he spoke to the other man, who could not hide his concern. For weeks, it had been a secret to no one in the small village that the reverend enjoyed the company of Lady Mariel Wythe. He wondered if what he must say would change that.

"Reverend, if I could speak to you in the hall-way. . ."

Mariel shoved herself up from the pillows, disregarding the whirling of her head. "No!" she cried. "If it is that horrible, I want to hear it. Now!" Swallowing her hysteria, she forced herself to say more calmly, "I am b-blind, doctor." In spite of herself, she stumbled on the word. She took a deep breath and asked, "Will my sight return?"

He shook his head, then recalled she could not see him. Her clear blue eyes in her bandaged face regarded him as steadily as if nothing had changed. "I don't know, Lady Mariel. What I do know is that you must rest." His hands pressed against the tattered material of her dress. "Lie down and don't move. Mrs. Reed shall wait in here to tend to you until Miss Phipps arrives with your things from the Cloister. I don't want you to do anything but lie there until I check you tomorrow morning."

"But, doctor—"

"No buts. If you cooperate, you might regain your vision. Whether it will all come back, I cannot tell you. Be as stubborn as the rest of your family, and you will throw away any chance you may have."

The stern timbre of his voice terrified her. She was familiar with Dr. Sawyer's honesty. He had tended her during her childhood illnesses. All the confidence she had learned to place in his judgment was put to the test as she hesitated. She did not need to see him to know his basset hound face was longer than usual.

She closed her eyes as she leaned back on the pillows. The covers were drawn over her, and she turned her head. "Ian?"

"Over here, honey." His sorrowful voice came from the opposite direction. It showed blatantly how helpless she was without her eyes. He felt his own burn with the frustrated tears he could not shed. "Mrs. Reed will sit with you now. Rest. I must let your other rescuers know you are awake. I will be back in a short while."

She nodded, but wondered if resting would be all she could do in the future. This blindness might be permanent. Even Dr. Sawyer admitted that. Everything she loved to do required her eyes. She could not read the reports from the school board. She would be unable to be independent, to run about the countryside as she wished. Never would she see the glories of the sunset dipping into the western sea beyond the Cloister.

Until Mrs. Reed murmured, "Don't weep, lamb," she did not realize she was crying. She pressed her hands over her face, but drew them away when she felt the bandages on her cheeks. She had not equated the tightness of her skin with anything but the scratches she knew must be there. Now she discovered her eyes were not the only part of her affected by the accident.

When she found it impossible to stop sobbing, an arm slipped under her to raise her to drink from a cup. The bitterness of the potion could not be hidden beneath the honeyed tea. It worked quickly to soothe her fears into a dreamless sleep.

Mariel opened her eyes to the unchanging darkness. A spark of light at the far left of her field of vision brought a gasp from her lips. When she turned her head to follow it and savor the welcome glow, it disappeared.

"How do you feel, honey?" came a voice as a hand caressed her hair.

A smile creased her lips and painfully pulled the tight skin beneath the bandages. "Ian! When is it?"

"About three o'clock in the morning."

"What morning?"

"Sunday."

Instantly, she gasped, "Sunday? What are you doing up so late with me? You have to preach in less than six hours. You—" She laughed weakly as she heard his welcome rumble of amusement. When his hand settled over hers, she asked, "Who else is here?"

"Just you and me. Phipps has gone back to the Cloister to spend some time with Rosie. Mrs. Reed is asleep in her own room. They are exhausted. You are the only one who has had much sleep in the past few days."

"I'm so scared."

Soothingly, he said, "I know. If it helps at all, I know. I have been sitting here and looking at you and remembering the hours I lay in a bed waiting for them to tell me they would have to amputate my leg."

"I would rather that than being blind," she stated bitterly.

"Enough!"

The sharpness of his voice broke into her sorrow to release all her fears. "Is it?" she cried. "I'm not brave like you, Ian. Look at me."

"I am, my love, and it is wondrous to see you alive."

"Alive? Maybe, but how can it be like it was before? I don't want to be dependent on someone all my life. What else is there for me? To sit in the Cloister and listen to the walls molder around me? I can't read. I can't go anywhere." She gave a sob of her desperate fear. "You might as well shut me away as they did my cousin Georgie."

"Georgie?"

"Hasn't anyone ever told you about Gregory Wythe? I thought you knew." Astonishment softened the edge of her anger. "I'm surprised, but I guess such old news doesn't interest anyone any longer."

Ian leaned forward to stroke her forehead above the small bandage there. It seemed ironic that her crystal blue eyes were the most unchanged part of her face. The doctor had assured them the cuts would leave no scars once they healed, but most of her face had vanished under the salve lathered coverings. When she turned toward him, he could see her eyes searching to find him. He took her hand and raised it to his cheek.

"Tell me," he ordered quietly. "Why did they shut Gregory Wythe away?"

"My cousin was insane. Uncle Wilford tried to keep him home by hiring guards and a nurse. Georgie was smart. Most of the time he acted normal. Then he would explode." Her voice quivered as she continued, "He exploded the night he killed Lorraine. He almost killed me except that his guards found us in the attic room where he had dragged me. I did not think he would do that to me. He hated Lorraine because she taunted him, but he knew I loved him. Every time he came near she teased him with the 'Georgie Porgie' rhyme. When he broke away from the guards and would have hurt me, I used it as she had. He cried. They took him away, and I never saw him again."

Ian watched her face while she told the tale. Suddenly, he understood what she had never wanted him to know. Though modern medicine tried to teach that insanity was a disease, not a curse, Mariel feared to involve him with a family who bore this horrid taint. He longed to draw her into his arms and show her he did not care what had happened to the Wythes of the past. He wanted only to love this one and share his life with her.

Very explicit orders from Dr. Sawyer kept him from doing as he wished. The doctor continued to insist that she not be moved. Forcing his longing back in his heart, he asked gently, "Where is he now?"

"He's dead," she said with a lack of acceptance of the past. Her voice rose steadily as she added, "He died in the asylum in a horrible fire one of the inmates set. His funeral was the last time the old chapel in the Cloister was used. Now he rests next to the other crazy Wythes in the cemetery behind the Cloister. I never had a chance to tell Georgie how sorry I was that I taunted him that night. I know he could not help being the way he was."

"I'm sure he has forgiven you, Mariel."

The venom returned to her tone. "Don't play the pastor with me, Ian. If you do that, the next thing you will be saying is that my automobile accident is the result of God's wrath for luring you into my arms."

"Mariel!" he snapped. "That is enough. Being angry will not help anything now. The doctor has made it clear that you must rest. He is contacting a colleague in London to find you a specialist."

She pulled her hand out of his. "London? How am I to get to London? Look at me! Even if I was allowed out of bed, I couldn't find my way across this room."

"I was going to say I would take you, but if you are going to act so petulant, I doubt if I will offer."

When she heard him rise, she feared he would leave the room. She could not tolerate the thought of being alone. After all they had shared, she thought he would have guessed her sharpness covered her frustration at being unable to fix this situation, as she had so many other things in the past. She was used to being the sensible one in the family. Never had she been unable to do what she wanted once she set her mind on it.

"Ian!" she cried. "Don't go away."

"I won't." His voice was surprisingly close. When the bed moved, she turned to feel his arms around her. Fearfully, she broke away. Her head ached violently at the sharp movement.

"Honey?"

For the first time since she had met him, she lied intentionally, "I am sorry. I just don't feel well."

"I understand."

His kindness hurt as much as the pain within her. She could not tell him the truth. She did not want him to touch her. If he did, she might not be able to deny herself his loving. He did not need to be burdened with her. Between his ministerial duties and his work in the community, he could not spare the time she would require. Now, she was grateful she had another reason to tell him she could not marry him. She did not want to think of how it would be if he refused to break their betrothal simply because he pitied her.

Hot tears burned her useless eyes. She did not want anyone to feel sorry for her. She wanted nothing but to find a hole and bury herself in it. There was no hope for her. Dr. Sawyer had all but admitted that.

"Do you want to rest, honey?" Ian's voice intruded on her thoughts.

"Yes," she whispered.

"Do you want me to hold you?"

A pang cut into her more sharply than any injury from the accident. Although her heart demanded that she agree so she could feel safe in his love, she murmured, "No, Ian. Just let me rest here, please."

"Of course." The pain he felt could not be hidden. The bed moved as he sat again on the chair next to the bed.

She turned her back on him. The tears dampened the many bandages on her face. At first a trickle, the weeping became a cascade of anguish as she realized how much she had lost in the accident.

Ian did not move from the chair through the long hours of the night. Even when Mariel fell asleep, her breath still ragged from her sobs, he sat silently in the darkness. He wanted to pray, but the words froze within him as he watched the broken woman. Never had he expected to see Mariel Wythe give up any fight.

And this one has just begun, he thought. Dr. Sawyer had told him nothing different from what Mariel had demanded to know. The slim chances of her recovering her sight faded with each passing day.

She would have to accept that and rearrange her life to meet the challenges ahead of her. He could help her, if only she would let him. No one else understood as he did the pain dwelling in her, cutting into the sensitive edges of her dreams.

As the first pink glow of dawn began to sneak into the room, he rose and walked quietly from the bedroom. He tried to keep his steps soundless as he walked down the stairs, but was not surprised to see Mrs. Reed waiting for him in the front hall.

"Reverend?"

"I am going to the church for a few minutes. I am sure Mr. Stadley has it prepared for this morning's services, but I want to be sure."

Mrs. Reed wrung her hands in her apron. "You are preaching this morning?" When he looked at her in surprise, she added, "I thought you would have asked for a substitute. No one expects you to be there this morning."

For the first time in days, he offered her the wry grin that signaled his thoughts of Lady Mariel. Pointing toward the ceiling, he said, "There is one who would be astounded if I did not do as I should." His smile faded. "Or she would if she was herself."

"Do you think—?"

He interrupted hastily. "I don't know what to think. I will be back soon, Mrs. Reed. If Mariel wakes, please send across the green for me."

"Yes, sir." She added nothing else. The man could not hide his pain. To augment it now by asking unanswerable questions would be too cruel.

Tears spilled from her eyes to course along her hollow cheeks as she went to the door to watch his slow steps across the empty village green. Before this tragedy, there had been talk of a match between Reverend Beckwith-Carter and Lady Mariel. She wondered how this accident would change that. Wiping her nose inelegantly on her sleeve, she went back to the kitchen.

The soft hush of the church comforted Ian as he opened the door. The sun-heated wood stank within the closed building. With the warmth rushing past him, he strode toward the empty sanctuary. Dropping into the closest pew, he placed his folded hands on the back of the one in front of him. His knuckles bleached with the fierce emotions boiling within him.

He had come here to reach out to all he believed in most fervently to work a miracle for Mariel. Now he found he did not feel the least like petitioning for her recovery. He wanted to rage at the indiscriminate hand of fate, which had chosen her as its latest victim.

His eyes swept the church. Inordinate pride had filled him each time he entered this room. This was his domain, where he could heal the concerns of those hurting in the rapidly changing world. Here he had found something that had been missing from the hubbub of his life in London. His rage erased all that.

"It's not fair!" he groaned. He leaned his forehead against his clenched fists. Knowing that he should be singing with joy that she had not been killed, he thought only of the wraithlike Mariel who refused to fight. Such dependence was so out of character for her, it scared him. If she stopped fighting, he feared she would lose that part of Mariel Wythe that delighted him most.

Footsteps sounded behind him. Irritated that someone would dare to interrupt his mourning, he swung to confront the interloper. His harsh words died unspoken as he saw the tear-streaked face of Miss Phipps. Silently, he stood and watched as she walked toward him with her stiff, uncompromising grace.

She whispered, "I came to relieve Mrs. Reed this morning, but first . . ." She looked at the bare altar and away. "I thought you might be here."

"I am looking for an answer," he said, finally voicing the truth.

"But there is none." She sat on the opposite side of the aisle. Removing her broad-brimmed hat, she placed it next to her. "I have sought within myself for an explanation of why Lady Mariel must be the one to suffer. Of all the Wythes I have known, she is the most giving and caring. Her uncle thinks foremost of himself, although he dotes on Lady Mariel. Lady Lorraine was nothing like her sister. Sometimes I thought Lady Mariel received all the compassion the two were meant to share."

"She told me how her sister taunted Georgie." He was anxious to learn more about this person, whom Mariel had conspired to keep a secret.

Miss Phipps sighed. "Ah, Georgie. Such a haunted soul he had. A brilliant child he was, but it turned within him to destroy that mind. He could not help himself. This family has had so much sorrow. I thought it was over when Georgie died. I was wrong."

Ian was not sure how to console the usually controlled Miss Phipps as she bent her head to weep. Tenderly he put his hand on her shoulder. Sitting next to her, he patted her back awkwardly until she wiped her eyes on a lace handkerchief and waved him away.

"What worries me most," she continued as if she had not started crying, "is her refusal to see Rosie. She adores the child. Rosie is pining for her."

"She is ashamed."

"Ashamed?" The idea was so at odds with what she had thought, Miss Phipps gasped, "What does she have to be ashamed of?"

Ian smiled sadly. If only Mariel would let him help her. He had struggled alone through all the darkness she experienced now. She could be spared some of the sorrow if she would accept what had happened and learn that she could be as she had been despite the changes in her life.

"Mariel is ashamed of being less than perfect." He surprised himself as much as Miss Phipps when he chuckled. "She could allow herself such faults as obsession, inflexibility, and bullheaded determination, but she cannot tolerate being less than perfect physically."

"She must see the child. Rosie is having nightmares. She doesn't believe me when I tell her Lady Mariel is alive. She does not understand why she cannot see her if she is simply resting at your house."

"Have you told Mariel this?"

She shook her head. "She will not let me speak of Rosie. I think she fears the child will despise her." Her pale eyes sought an answer in his. "Should I tell her the truth?"

"No. She will only refuse again to see Rosie. Here is what I think we should do." He bent his head to conspire with her to help the woman they both loved. Something had to be done to help Mariel. If this failed, he feared they would lose her forever to the grip of the despair controlling her.

After services that afternoon, Ian sat on the edge of the bed and watched as Mariel unevenly moved about the room. Although the doctor had not given her permission to leave her bed, he had come upstairs to find her dressed in her robe and attempting to decipher the labyrinth of this unknown room. He said nothing of

his pride at her attempt to escape from the prison of the
bed. Such words of encouragement might cause more
damage.

His eyes followed her intensely. She did not release
one piece of furniture while she sought another. Her
steps were as tentative as if she walked along the edge
of a cliff.

"Mariel, how much longer are you going to delay
seeing Rosie?"

"I don't know!" she cried. "Why are you tormenting
me like this, Ian? Don't I have enough to feel miserable
about without you harping on this?"

Anger burst from him. He had been patient and
generally ignored her sharp comments, but he could not
do that any longer. Grasping her by the shoulders, he
swung her to face him. Her terrified expression showed
him how fearful she had become of any spontaneous
movement.

"Why do you act as if you are the only one to have
suffered? I never thought I would see Mariel Wythe
give up so easily."

"Well, you are seeing it now!" She laughed bitterly.
"'Seeing it'? I never realized how much a part of our
language such words are."

"Sit!" he snarled. Shoving her into the overstuffed
chair, he hobbled to the door. He swung it open and
went out into the hall. He called over the banister to
Miss Phipps.

Mariel clenched her hands on the arms of the chair.
"No," she moaned when she heard what he ordered.
The eager footsteps on the stairs brought fear to her
face. She could not do this. Not now.

Short arms were flung around her neck as curls
scented with her favorite perfumed soap pressed to her
face. Soft tears dripped on her as Rosie climbed into her
lap without releasing her grip around her neck. Awkwardly, as if they were made of the same straight wood as
Ian's cane, her arms moved to enfold the child.

She was startled at how familiar the child felt in her
lap. So many times she had held Rosie in the dark to
comfort her in the midst of some nightmare. Then there
had been no light to let her see the little girl's tear

dampened face. She did not need to see now to know the fear Rosie had been feeling.

In a whisper, she murmured against the twisted curls, "Don't cry, baby. Don't cry. It will be all right."

"I-I-I thought y-y-you w-were d-dea-ea-dead," she hiccuped through her sobs. "Miss Ph-Phipps, sh-she wouldn't l-let me come to-to see you."

"Hush, baby." She stroked the slender line of Rosie's back. "Don't blame Phipps. I did not want you to see me when I looked like this."

Rosie drew back to look at the bandaged face of the woman she loved. She remembered what Phipps had told her. She must not make Mariel sad. "You look beautiful, Mariel."

"Do I?" She laughed with honest delight for the first time since leaving the Cloister. "I thought I must look quite grotesque."

"Your face looks like the turban of the snake charmer at the circus," pronounced the child.

A rumble of male laughter near the door brought Mariel's head up. She had been so engrossed in greeting her beloved child, she had not realized Ian had returned to the room. She wanted to offer him her hand, but did not dare to touch him.

Rosie's voice drew her attention from the man. "What is it like to be blind, Mariel?"

She heard gasps from near the door and knew Ian was not the only one watching this reunion. She could imagine the paleness of Phipps's face as her young charge asked the one question she had likely been instructed not to ask. Ian's expression would be as strained.

Softly, she said, "Close your eyes, Rosie. Put your hands over your eyes so no light can come through. Then imagine you are in the deepest cave on the darkest night. It is something like that."

"I am sorry you are blind, Mariel."

Phipps said in a broken voice, "Rosie, I think you have spent enough time—"

"No, no, it is all right," said Mariel hurriedly. She put her hand on Rosie's face. It startled her how her fingers moving along the child's damp skin reinforced the image in her mind. Rosie's cheeks, as plump as a well-fed squirrel, her pert nose and fine eyebrows. Each touch brought an answering memory. Quietly, she continued, "I am sorry too, Rosie. I am glad you are here to love me despite this."

"Always!" she declared stoutly as she burrowed closer to Mariel's heart.

When she felt a loving hand on her shoulder, Mariel raised her fingers. She did not have to say what she wanted. Ian pressed them to his face. As she had with Rosie, she ran them along the textures of his features, features that were far more rigidly carved than the child's. She touched his forehead, scored with lines far deeper than the day he left in anger from the Cloister. Moving along his patrician nose, she smiled as she felt his upturned mouth.

"Thank you," she whispered.

He pressed her palm against his lips and kissed it lightly. They had far to go to convince Mariel to reach out avidly for life again, but a beginning had been made this afternoon. For the first time, he believed they might succeed.

Chapter Thirteen

Ian did not speak when he took his seat at the back of the schoolroom. No one looked at him or at the empty chair at the table where Mariel should have been sitting with her papers spread before her, prepared to do battle with the stalwart resistance to change.

Mr. Gratton picked up his gavel, then lowered it to the table. There was no need to call for silence. The inside of the school was as silent as a tomb. At the thought, a pang coursed through him. Lady Mariel had been moved to Foxbridge Cloister only this morning. Although that bespoke of her expected recovery, no one wanted to jinx her good fortune with premature celebrations.

When Mr. Stadley started to call the roll, he halted abruptly. In a voice thick with distress, he said, "All present but Lady Mariel."

Rushing through the reading of the minutes of the previous meeting, the chairman asked if there was any old business. For a long moment, no one spoke. This should have been the time for Lady Mariel to ask for a vote on the textbooks she wanted.

A chair scratched the floor at the back of the room. Each one relieved at not having to be the first to speak, the men looked to see Reverend Beckwith-Carter rising. He walked toward them and leaned on the end of the table. When he spoke with anger, they were astonished.

"She is not dead! This is not, thank God, her wake. Will you stop this mournful keening?" he demanded. "She is going to recover. Abusing yourselves because you have thought less than kindly of her in the past will change nothing. If it helps, I can tell you with total honesty that she has belittled each of you in my hearing for your refusal to see things her way. Do not beatify her because of this accident."

Mr. Jones spoke in his bass rumble, "Is it true, Reverend, that the doctor does not expect her to regain her sight?"

"Dr. Sawyer is unsure. As soon as she is well enough, he wants her to see a specialist in London." Ian glanced around the table to view each long face. When his fist struck the top, the men sitting there started. "D-ammit!" he snapped. "You are so shortsighted you will let this accident ruin everything she has attempted. Vote on the appropriation for the books, but don't change your minds because of the accident. You know as well as I what Mariel would be saying if she was standing here."

"That we are pigheaded reprobates."

Ian grinned at Mr. Gratton's muted humor. "Exactly."

When they urged him to sit at the table with them, he shook his head silently. "I will leave you to your deliberations. I came only to observe so I could take her the news of the vote." He crossed the room to resume his seat in the back.

Although he let them think he did not want to intrude, he could not imagine sitting in the only empty chair at the table. It was Mariel's, and it sat as a silent reminder of what should never have happened. Many were asking questions about why the automobile had failed. Some said it was simply that such modern toys were too dangerous and should be banned by Parliament. Others wanted to know how the steering and the brakes could malfunction at the same time. They would never know, for little of the vehicle had survived the ferocious heat of the fire.

The twisted metal remained by the curve at the bottom of the shore-road hill. No one knew what to do with it. Nothing like this had ever happened in Fox-bridge or the surrounding shire. It was a monument nobody wanted to see, for it reminded them how easily it could have been a memorial to a young woman whose life was part of theirs.

Ian did not look at the men speaking quietly at the table. The sorrow that burned directly behind his eyes all the time now might embarrass him in front of them. With Mariel gone from the rectory, it might be days between each time he could see her.

He leaned his head on his fist and listened to the muted debate at the table. The words he spoke so vehemently to others he could not heed himself. He could not pretend Mariel would be the same. Although he knew the accident would change many things, he did not want that to happen.

Those thoughts remained in his head as he drove to Foxbridge Cloister. The starlight guided him and helped to keep his eyes from going to the wreckage by the stone fence. He refused to look at it again. He kept his eyes on a spot directly in front of his horse's nose until the buggy had passed through the gate.

Dodsley greeted him at the door and took his hat. "Good evening, Reverend. Miss Phipps said you may go directly up to Lady Mariel's room."

"How is she doing?"

The butler lost his professional demeanor. "It's like Lady Mariel left here last week and someone else came back today. I don't know how to explain it, sir, but. . ."

"I understand," he said quietly. "She needs to mourn for what could be. Only then can she rebound."

"Will she?"

An expression of fierce determination hardened his face. "If I have anything to do with it, she will."

The sound of his cane preceded him up the stairs. He tried to keep it as quiet as possible, for he knew Rosie would be in bed, but stairs had been his bane since his accident. What he could do easily on a flat or sloped surface seemed much more difficult on these steep steps.

Miss Phipps met him at the door and told him she would be back in a few minutes with a tea tray. She scurried away before he could say anything other than a hurried "Good evening."

He looked about with interest as he entered Mariel's private rooms in the Cloister. It did not surprise him to note the two portraits hanging over the fireplace. The style of clothing and the shape of the faces told him these must be the portraits of Mariel's parents that were missing from the gallery. She must have kept them here to ease the loneliness she had known before he and Rosie came into her life.

That sense of being adrift alone sent a pang through him. Even in his darkest days, when he had been abandoned by the one he thought he could always depend on, he had had his mother and grandfather to comfort him and urge him to do what he thought was impossible. Then his grandfather had died. A feeling of being bereft swept over him again.

His thoughts were interrupted as he heard a soft voice from the next room. "Ian?"

"Yes, Mariel." He went into the luxurious room to see her propped among the pillows on the wide bed. The hopefulness in her voice brought a painful memory from him. He remembered lying in his bed, praying that someone, anyone, would come to break the monotony of the days.

He moved to the bed and sat in the chair by its side. When her hand, nearly hidden beneath the wide lace of her chamber robe, sought his, he put his fingers where she could find them easily.

"It must feel good to be back home."

"I miss you, Ian."

Squeezing her hand gently, he said, "I told you, I will come every morning to read the newspaper to you if you wish."

She leaned her head back against the headboard. Tears balanced on her dark lashes as she fought the rage within her. Every kindness done for her was only out of pity. She did not want Ian to come to Foxbridge Cloister to read to her. She wanted him to hold her, to feel his mouth sliding along her skin, but that was impossible.

"That would be very nice," she replied quietly.

"I just attended the school-board meeting."

"Did you?"

He longed to take her and shake that dull sound from her voice. Even as he thought that, he saw the spasm fleeing across her blank features. Mariel continued to try to hide the truth from him, but when she had offered him her heart, she had opened her soul to him. He could sense the horror she struggled with each waking hour.

"Honey, they voted to appropriate the money for the books you wanted. Mr. Jones is ecstatic."

"I'm glad."

Ian put his hand on the side of her face and turned it to meet his eyes. "Glad? Is that all you have to say after the hard battle you have waged to get this?"

"Why should I be happy about books I will never see?" Sobs ripped from her as she buried her bandaged face in her hands.

He fought his longing to comfort her. Instead, he snapped, "You have every reason to be happy. You have done what I would have said was impossible. That tightfisted board has parted with some of its money for a most worthy project. Not only that, but they agreed to give the old texts to the orphanage as you requested." When she did not reply, he grasped her shoulders and shouted, "Dammit, Mariel! Don't give up on yourself when everyone else wishes you only success!"

"Let me go!" she screamed.

"No."

"I said let me go!" She enunciated each word as she struggled to escape him. When he took her hand and dragged her out of her bed, she shrieked again. Fearfully she clung to him as he led her rapidly across the room. "No! Ian, don't! Let me go back to bed."

He released her. "All right. Go back to bed."

"Where is it?"

Sitting down in one of the chairs, he smiled coldly. "That, my dear Mariel, is something you must find for yourself."

"Ian!" she moaned. "Help me."

"I am." He folded his arms across his chest to keep from taking her outstretched hands. Although he wanted

to assist her back to the bed, only this way could he truly
help her.

Mariel spat a curse at him and heard his outrageous
chuckle. He wanted her to become so angry that she
would bounce off the furniture in the room until she
bumped into the bed. That, he thought, would help her.
Determined not to play his games, she dropped to the
floor to sit cross legged. She glared in the direction she
thought he was.

Hands under her arms lifted her roughly to her feet.
When she was about to fold up, he said sharply, "Do it,
Mariel! Or are you scared?"

"Yes!" she cried. "If it satisfies your sadism, I am
scared."

"Of what?"

She started to reply, then realized she had no
answer. For the past week, she had huddled in bed,
afraid to move, afraid to think. Slowly she turned and
put her hands on Ian's chest. Her fingers moved along
the front of his shirt, past the clerical collar and to his
face.

He was not smiling. That comforted her. In the
midst of her mind numbing terror, she had forgotten
the most important thing. Ian loved her. He would do
nothing to harm her, but would force her to help herself.

"I am afraid of failing," she whispered as his arm
slid around her waist to hold her close.

"You never have been in the past. Each time
someone told you that you could not do something, you
struggled even harder. Now it is Mariel Wythe saying
you cannot be reasonably independent anymore. Are you
going to listen to her, or are you going to do what you
know you must?"

"I don't know."

He held her tightly as he felt her tears wet against
his shirt. Perhaps this was enough for today. He had
pushed her to recognize her fears. It might be too much
to expect her to conquer them in the same day. Recall-
ing his long months of convalescence, he relented.

Mariel said nothing as he turned her to walk the few
steps to the bed. It startled her how close she had been
standing to it. If she had extended her arms, she might

have been able to touch it. When she stubbed her toe against the steps of the bed, she climbed up onto its high surface. Pulling the covers over her, she sighed in relief.

As much as she hated being confined to this bed, it was safe. She knew the dimensions of it and did not have to fear being confronted with something she could not handle. Stroking the chenille bedspread, she waited for Ian to speak.

"Tomorrow," he said.

"Tomorrow what?"

"Tomorrow you will do it by yourself." He took her hand and pressed it to his weakened leg. "I had to learn to walk again. So will you."

The sound of a throat clearing by the doorway made him look up in what he was sure appeared to be guilt. Mariel's hand against his thigh clenched as she heard Phipps's steps entering the room. Moving away from the bed, Ian waved aside the offer of tea.

"No, thank you, Miss Phipps. I must return to the parsonage. I will be back tomorrow, Mariel. You will try again."

"I don't know if I can!" she cried.

He smiled grimly. "Of course you don't know. You haven't tried yet. Good night, ladies." With the determination he had shown Mariel, he walked out of the suite. He could not allow his heart to soften to Mariel's plight.

Mariel leaned back against the pillows. Of all the people in her life, she would have thought that Ian would understand how helpless her situation was now. He had had to struggle to regain his ability to walk. That had been minor in comparison to what faced her.

She took the cup Phipps placed in her hands, but left it on its saucer. She said nothing. All she wanted was to wake from this horror and be well again. To try to live with this handicap would be to admit she expected to be like this forever.

That she could not do!

The days passed slowly. Ian kept his promise to come each day to read to her. Mariel enjoyed his

company until he pressed her to try to regain her
independence. Every visit ended in recriminating tears
and frustrated words. Their shouts resounded through
the Cloister until Phipps hinted to Ian it might be better
if he relented. He refused, sure that only this way could
he help Mariel.

Then one day he did not come. Although they had
exchanged heated words the previous day, Mariel had
been sure Ian would not forsake her. As the morning
ended and the afternoon sun burned into the room, she
wondered if he grew tired of the battle, which she
showed by loud words and uncooperation that she
wanted no part of.

If he did not come to visit her, the last bright light
from beyond the Cloister would die. With the slow
ticking of the clock reminding her of the time, she
wondered if he would return. In the weeks since the
accident, she had not once told him aloud what she felt
in her heart. Her love for him had grown while he tried
to be patient with her.

Suddenly, she felt a yearning for the escape that had
always comforted her in the past. The piano in the
drawing room could fill her with music and wash away
some of the pain. Before she realized what she was
doing, she tucked her loosened shirt into her skirt and
slid to the edge of the bed.

She could reconstruct the room easily in her mind.
The location of the chairs, the tables, where the door
opened to the sitting room, and the hallway beyond. Her
feet moved confidently down the steps of her bed and
sank into the thick carpet.

Afraid to move quickly, she scuffed her feet along
the floor. She smiled as she found the chair exactly
where she remembered it. That discovery encouraged
her enough to keep her going on this strange journey.
Her fingers groped for the doorway.

The carved wood of the molding was smooth and
cool. She walked through the door. When the floor went
from stone to carpet, she knew she stood in the center
of the antechamber. Walking with more assurance, she
swore vehemently as she impacted harshly against a
stand. She rubbed her shin, but did not turn around.

She had come this far. If she returned to her bed, she did not know if she would dare this again.

Opening the door to the hallway, she heard the muffled sound of voices from the first floor. The scent of dinner cooking drifted lazily along the corridor. She smiled as she recognized the scent of roast beef. Mrs. Puhle had been preparing all her favorite meals in the hopes of easing the sorrow of being confined to her room.

"No more," Mariel whispered to herself.

She touched the banister on the staircase. The warmth of its patina, worn by many hands over the centuries, welcomed her. She ran her fingers along its silken texture, and a flare of frustration flew through her. The feeling was too familiar. Although she could discern more through her fingertips with each passing day, it only reminded her that she would be dependent on this for the rest of her life.

Fiercely, she shook off such depressing thoughts. She might not be able to do what she could before the accident, but she was determined to discover what she could do. With care, she dropped her foot to the first riser. Her fingers tightened on the banister as she put her weight on that foot and stepped to the next stair. Fear boiled in her stomach while she sightlessly descended the stairs she once had taken at a run.

At the bottom, she silently congratulated herself. She waited to hear if anyone else had noticed her performance, but it seemed that the foyer was empty. That surprised her. At this time of day, it usually was busy. She smiled. This was perfect. She did not need an audience.

Again she closed her eyes to recreate the scene burned into her memory. The door to the drawing room waited—only a few paces to her right. Trying to walk normally, she stepped toward the room. Her smile faded when she could not find the door, then she chuckled. Of course. She could not touch the wall. She stood in the wide doorway.

Her questing fingers found the doors. She drew them together. The doors closed easily, but she did not latch them. Years ago, she and Georgie had tried to see how the lock worked. Ever since that failed experiment, the doors had not been secured because it was questionable whether they could be unlocked again.

From beyond the open windows, the fresh scent of newly cut grass surged through the room. Sunshine smelled warm on the stones closest to the ceiling-high windows. The room had been cleaned during the last few days. Mariel could discern the oil the maids used to dust the furniture. She wondered if these aromas had been in existence all along or if she was discovering something new.

A soft yip intruded into the silence. Involuntarily she turned toward the sound, which came from the doors opening onto the terrace. "Muffin?" she whispered.

The dog bumped against her leg, and she groped to find its head. With a laugh, she found its tail first. Holding out her hand, she ordered, "Here, Muffin." Instantly she felt its head butt her palm.

She dropped to her knees and wrapped her arms around Muffin's soft furry body. Pressing her face into the fur, she breathed in the rich aromas of the grass where the dog had been playing. Muffin's puff of breath struck her face seconds before the velvet-coated tongue touched her cheek. Slowly she stood, not wanting to let the tears in her useless eyes overflow in the midst of her excursion.

"Later, Muffin," she whispered.

As the sound of the dog's paws on the floor disappeared into the distance, she sighed. She could not understand how everything had remained the same—everything but her eyes. The temptation for self-pity flooded her, but she tried to ignore it.

Crossing the room, she touched the smooth keys of the piano. Her longing to be lost in the complicated harmonies grew. She drew out the stool and gingerly sat on it. Although it made no difference in the darkness surrounding her, she closed her eyes. Instantly her memory supplied the scene her eyes were unable to show her.

Her fingers settled on the keys. The melody flowed from her head through her fingers to the piano. A cascade of music filled the room. Soaring chords crashed

into the ceiling to resound back through her. Her hands
chased the piece as she became immersed in the beauty
of the sound.

When the final notes faded into silence, she placed
her head on her folded arms on the music platform over
the keys. She felt sapped and somehow rejuvenated. It
was her favorite piece. For more than a year, she had
worked to perfect it. Today she had played it through
with no mistakes.

"I should have guessed you would choose Bach."

"Ian!" She rose to turn to the door. Her smile
brightened as she raised her hands to him. The sound
of his uneven steps warmed her heart. "Where have you
been?"

He leaned forward and kissed her cheek. Quickly,
he examined her. As the doctor had said, there had been
no permanent damage from the superficial wounds she
had suffered. Mariel remained as lovely as ever. He
admired the lacy blouse tucked into her black sateen
skirt. Despite his intentions, his hands slipped around
her slender waist and drew her to him.

Instantly, her smile faded. She turned her face from
his. Putting her fingers on his arms, she pushed him
away. He took a step toward her, but she whirled to
flee. Her escape was halted abruptly when she bumped
into a marble-topped lyre table. It rocked violently as
she fought to keep the statue on top of it from crashing
to the floor.

Other hands helped hers right the sculpture. She felt
Ian's eyes on her and knew exactly how his face turned
down with displeasure. When she stood next to him, it
did not seem she could not see him. So often in the past
months they had spoken lovingly and in anger. Those
strong emotions were imprinted in her heart to be
recalled with ease.

"Thank you," she said quietly. She did not want to
argue with him. Since the accident, all they had done
was disagree. It would be pleasant to speak kindly again
to each other.

"You are welcome." His reply sounded as stilted as
her words. "Sit down, Mariel. I want to talk to you."

Her hand reached for the settee. Her lips tightened as she sat. He had not answered her question of where he had been. Without asking, she knew what he would not say. He had been here. He had waited for her to become so frustrated with her self-imposed prison that she would force her way out of it. She suspected he was smiling with satisfaction.

Ian watched her innately graceful movements. In just this short excursion, she had regained her smooth steps and the butterfly-light motions of her wrists. He sat opposite her in the overstuffed chair. Leaning toward her, he asked, "How are you doing, Mariel?"

"If you mean, have I recovered from the accident, I can say I have no more pain. If you mean, am I pleased with falling prey to your tricks, the answer is no."

"You did not have to leave your room," he stated reasonably.

"No?" Her hands swept wide to encompass the house. "I have not been beyond those walls in two weeks. Now that I will no longer scare children with my mummylike bandages, I can wander where I will, right?"

He grinned. "Exactly."

"Wrong!" she snapped. "Coming from my room to here, I managed, but it showed me how helpless I truly am." Her voice softened as she added, "I never knew there were so many endless hours in a day."

"You must get out of the Cloister."

"How?"

He scowled as he heard the pain in the single word. As he feared, Mariel was still ready to give in to her infirmity. "You can ride in the carriage. Most ladies of your class have a coachman. It is nothing to be ashamed of."

"I have no place to go to."

"I find that hard to believe. You never stayed at home before."

Her hands folded in her lap. When he took one and placed something in it, her fingers moved along the slender, smooth surface. In shock, she gasped, "This is your cane, Ian."

"One of them. I want you to have it. With it, you can find your way around easier."

In horror, she released it. The clatter of its ivory clasp against the floor did not enter her mind as she envisioned herself using it. She did not want to have to use something like that. Only old men and beggars depended on canes.

She did not realize she had verbalized her thoughts until she was jerked to her feet. Ian's rage washed over her as his fingers bit into her skin beneath the fine lace of her shirtwaist.

"You are going to learn now how much you need this."

"Ian—"

He handed her the cane again. "Prove me wrong, Mariel. Prove to me that you aren't the woman I thought you were. Show me you have no courage."

Mariel tightened her fingers around the staff. She would try, but not for the reason he thought. Only by doing this could she keep him from shouting at her. With her head aching from her exertion today, she wanted to go to her room and rest. If this is what it took to do that, she would cooperate.

Listening to his instructions, she tried to visualize what he was saying. She bit her lip when he told her this was how he had seen the blind walking in London. Although she wanted to screech out her revulsion at the word "blind," she concentrated on what she must do. It sounded simple, but quickly she learned how wrong she had been.

"Stop thinking with your eyes," he urged. "Think with your fingers. They can show you what is before you." As the cane crashed into the door, sending anguish along her arm, he repeated, "Think, Mariel. You must use your other senses."

"How can I think when you are babbling?"

He fought to keep his voice steady as laughter filled him. This was the Mariel he loved, feisty, refusing to accept defeat. If he could find a way to keep this one here and force the sorrowful waif to leave forever, he would have won the battle.

Mariel tried to concentrate as he suggested, but her mind and feet refused to work in unison. She tripped again and again. When the cane tapped against the stairs, she paused. Taking a deep breath, she put her hand on the banister and stepped up. Instantly, she swayed.

Strong arms caught her before she could fall. She pressed her face against Ian's neck as she shook with fear. His hands moved along her back, holding her closer than was necessary. Breathing in his scent, which brought memories of the love they had shared so briefly at the parsonage, she could not convince her body to move away from him. Only when his hands loosened did she realize how intent he was on having her continue with this lesson.

"Try again," he ordered.

"Ian, I'm tired." She dropped to sit on the stairs. The variegated shades of the stained glass window played over her, tinting the cream of her blouse.

"Once more, honey."

She shoved the cane at him. "No, I said. I am tired." Her lips tightened into a scowl. "Why can't you understand I will not be able to do everything I did before?"

"Because it isn't true!"

"Do you ride to the hunt?" she taunted. Her pain forced her to strike out at him. "No! You drive your carriage, but I have never seen you on horseback."

Cursing, he dropped the cane. It clattered down the stairs to roll to a stop in the center of the foyer. Staring at Mariel's determined face, he did not notice the door opening. Walter Collins bent to pick up the cane, but said nothing as he silently watched the conflict on the stairs.

Ian grasped Mariel's shoulders and lifted her to her feet. She groped for the railing. "Help me!" she gasped.

In a low voice, he retorted, "Help yourself!"

"Ian!" Desperation crept into the single word.

He stubbornly said nothing. If she did not realize how much she needed to be independent, she would be confined to Foxbridge Cloister the rest of her life. He watched as her fingers clutched the banister to steady her.

Only when she was sure she would not fall did she snarl, "Get out of my home, Ian Beckwith-Carter! I hate you! I hate you, and I want you to leave."

"If you feel that way, Mariel, then maybe you are right. Maybe you should stay in this house and never come out again. Maybe you should pretend that you are of no use to anyone. I thought you had learned a lesson today, but I clearly was wrong. If you continue to act this way, you soon will be exactly as helpless as you wish."

Her fears exploded. "Stop it, Ian! You don't know what I feel!"

"I don't? You feel like a burden on everyone you know. You wonder if you ever will be of any use to this world. You pray that this is all a nightmare, and that you will wake soon to laugh in the morning light." When he saw the astonishment on her face, he laughed bitterly. "You are not the first one to lose your dreams. How I longed to become a missionary and take the truth to those in need of my teachings. To assist those who needed me. Instead, when my friends left England I spent the time in my room, waiting for my leg to heal and praying I could die. I didn't, and neither will you." He shook her sharply. "First you have to stop feeling sorry for poor little Mariel."

"Stop it!" she cried again. "Save your sermons for Sunday, Reverend!"

Silence dropped between them as he slowly stepped away from her. "Good day, Mariel. I have been calling on you regularly. If you wish to see me again, I trust you will remember how to find your way to my house."

"Ian!" she called as she heard his footsteps descending the stairs. She followed, nearly falling. The concentration required to remember to place her feet cautiously left no room for other thoughts. Now, all of her mind was centered on Ian. She did not want him to leave.

Her fingers settled on a coat sleeve. "Lady Mariel?" came Walter's voice.

With a half-articulated sob, she pushed herself away from him and grasped the doorknob to swing open the huge door. Her fingers lifted her skirts as her feet remembered the way along the steps leading to the driveway. Dust blew in her face to choke her. The clatter of the carriage driving away silenced her calls to Ian.

She felt hands on her shoulders. When she heard Walter urge her to return to the house, she fought the tears rolling along her face through the dust. Placing his arm awkwardly around her shoulders, he led her up the steps. A strange feeling of having been comforted like this before rushed through her.

Into her mind came the day a lifetime ago when she had been mourning the loss of a rabbit she had found injured in the hedgerow. She had tried to save it, but she had found it too late. It simply slipped away from her, sleeping to escape its pain. That day Georgie had been the one to ease her grief. He told her how it was better for the rabbit to die than to suffer endlessly. From anyone else, she would not have accepted such fatalistic phrases. Georgie had never lied to her, even when the voices within him taunted him to some misdeed.

Walter gave her that same unquestioning comfort. He made no judgments, only that it was better that she rested after her difficult day. When Phipps came rushing toward her, he stepped back to allow the woman to help Lady Mariel to her room.

He held the cane in his hand as he watched the women go up the stairs. For a second, he thought of breaking it, or throwing it in the trash. Then he placed it in the umbrella stand by the door. It leaned drunkenly as he walked out of the house. He decided to walk into the village. Without the automobile, there was little for him to do at the Cloister. No one had spoken yet of him having to leave. He hoped they would not. There was more he wanted to do here.

Phipps hushed Mariel as they walked slowly along the hallway. "Don't worry, my lady. Rosie is with Mrs. Puhle. We thought it best she not get in your way this afternoon."

"*We?* You were part of Ian's plan, too?"

"It was necessary to get you out of your room. I thought his plan was an excellent one."

"I'm sure you did." She tugged away from her friend. Dropping to her bed, she pulled a pillow over her head. From that stuffy haven, she growled, "You two must have had a grand time while I reeled to the drawing room."

"We were very proud of you, my lady, if that is what you want to hear."

"So proud that Ian continues to insist I do more?"

Phipps demanded, "What else could you expect from him? He wants to see you embrace life again."

"He could have the decency to—to . . ." Her voice faded away as she raised her head. When the bed moved, she rolled onto her back to talk to the other woman.

"Is pity what you want? You won't get that from Reverend Beckwith-Carter."

Bitterly, she stated, "I don't want to hear about how he has overcome his own difficulties. I don't want sainthood."

"You are impossible!" In a tone Mariel had never heard her use, Phipps stated, "I did not want to do this now, but I must. I am giving you my notice, Lady Mariel."

"Notice?" Mariel sat up and nearly fell off the edge of the bed. She moved to the center and groped for her companion's hand. "But, Phipps, why?"

Sorrow tinted the older woman's voice. "I did not think you would know. You have been accustomed to doing things exactly as you wish. When you could not have your way, you had a tantrum. A very ladylike one, I will admit. Now, when something has happened you cannot change, you are acting the same way. Polite folk call it headstrong. I will tell you I do not want to work for a spoiled brat any longer."

"That's not fair!"

"Most things aren't."

Mariel rose and felt her way across the room to the window overlooking the gardens to the west. She opened it and leaned on the thick sill. The fresh brine of the sea washed over her. All her happiest memories contained that succulent scent. She closed her eyes to dam the tears behind her lids.

Ian. She did not want to lose him. No one understood why she acted as she did. If she allowed their love
to grow, she was afraid he would ask her again to make
their relationship permanent, whether he truly wanted
to or not. She wanted to break the ties between them he
felt obligated to maintain.

Gentle hands stroked her loosened hair. She whirled
to find solace against Phipps's full shelf of bosom. As
she sobbed against the wool of her companion's jacket,
the older woman calmly massaged the tense muscles of
her back. She did not urge her to stop crying. She let
Mariel release some of the pain, which grew with each
day.

Softly, Phipps said, "Think of the good things you
have, Lady Mariel. Think of the love you have for the
parson. It may not last forever, but don't force it away
from you. What will you have if you deny your feelings?"
She tilted the younger woman's face back so she could
look at the tear-brightened cheeks. "I will tell you. An
empty life of waiting for something you could have had
if only you had opened your heart to the truth."

"But how can I know if he feels more than pity?"
she whispered, allowing her most fearful thought to
emerge.

"You can't unless you stop trying to remold everyone into your image of the world. Let what will happen
happen. If it is wonderful, why would you want to
interfere? If it is not, then nothing you could do will
make any difference." She brushed her lace-edged
handkerchief across her lady's cheek. "Do not throw
away what you have. I envy you, my lady."

In shock, Mariel gasped, "You envy me?" She could
not imagine anyone wanting to be as she was now.

"Think of what you have and what you can have." A
soft smile creased Phipps' wrinkled face. "Think what I
am. A spinster with no one to share her life but other
upper servants and two very headstrong lasses. Is that
what you want for yourself?"

For the first time in the many years they had been
together, Mariel envisioned Amanda Phipps as she truly
was. Since she had come to Foxbridge Cloister, Mariel
had delighted in making her life miserable, especially as

an adolescent, when she sought to bury her pain along with her dead sister. That had not changed significantly as Mariel matured. Many nights when she came home late from some meeting, Phipps would be sitting in her favorite chair beneath the dimmed gaslight doing some bit of needlework or writing a letter to her aged mother in Middlesex.

Like the furniture in her room, and like Foxbridge Cloister itself, Mariel had taken Phipps for granted. She wondered suddenly when her companion had last taken the week of vacation due to her each year, or even a single day, to do something she wished.

"Can I convince you to stay?" Mariel asked in a much more tranquil voice. "All these years you have been waiting to teach me what I need to know of life. I think I may be getting ready to learn."

"Of course I will stay." Phipps hugged her quickly before releasing her. Such shows of emotion were not easy for the gray haired woman. "Foxbridge Cloister is my home, and you, Lady Mariel, are my career. It appears I may be successful yet."

"Thank you."

"Nonsense." In her normal voice, she ordered, "Get in bed, and I will bring you a tray. Rosie may eat with you here, if you wish."

"Of course. That would be wonderful." A smile warmed Mariel's face.

Listening to the receding sound of Phipps's forceful steps, Mariel obeyed her commands. A sense of peace settled over her. Ian had presented her with a challenge. She would accept. Soon she would be calling on him at the parsonage in the village.

The next morning, Mariel awoke more determined than ever to become independent. She waited with barely concealed impatience while Rosie and Phipps came to entertain her. Dr. Sawyer also visited to check on her, as he did frequently. Pleased with her progress, he did not stay long.

Phipps remained all morning while Rosie ran in and out with her normal exuberant spirits. Mariel did not want to be read to, or to speak of the latest news in the shire and the world. And until she was more sure of herself, she decided no one must know what she planned. When her visitors left to have luncheon in the breakfast room, she knew she had her chance.

It was simpler today to find her way along the stairs. She brought the cane with her that Rosie had found and returned to her. Her hatred of the ivory-capped stick had not lessened, but she would use it if it would help.

Sliding her hand along the wall of the back hall, she found the huge door. Her fingers made short work of the lock. She squeezed through and closed the door behind her. If someone found it unlatched, she hoped they would not follow her.

The reek of the long-extinguished fire remained in the hallway of the old Cloister. It brought images of a more recent fire, but with a shiver, she forced them from her mind. She did not like to remember that the explosion of the automobile might be the last thing she would ever see.

Mariel gritted her teeth as she tightened her grip on the cane. If she could manage to find her way through the maze of the ruined Cloister, she would be able to manage anywhere. She took a step forward. Instantly, she stubbed her toe on a fallen timber. With a moan of pain, she put out her hand to find the wall.

This was not the way. There must be some secret to walking without careening into everything. She had done it all her life without paying attention to what she was doing. Surely she could do it now.

Sliding the cane in front of her, she swept it along the floor to determine where the fallen timber ended. She smiled as her fingers finally understood the clues from the slender shaft. The large wooden beam crossed only half of the open corridor. If she stepped to the left, she could bypass it.

Exultation burst from her lips as she moved forward cautiously. It vanished as she tripped over something she had not noted on the floor. She fought back tears as she felt the dampness of blood on her knees. The cinders and fallen stones were as sharp as jagged slivers of glass.

She forced herself to her feet. Angry determination had replaced her longing to traverse this maze. She wanted to prove to everyone that she could do what she once had found simple. No more pitying ladies were going to call at the parsonage and the Cloister and call her a poor lamb. She was no one's "lamb." She was Lady Mariel Wythe. It was time everyone relearned that.

Again she let the cane move from side to side, this time near her feet. As cluttered as this ruined building was, she must take it inch by inch. Closing her eyes, she allowed her feet to follow the path suggested by the cane. She concentrated on her task as she tried to recall the habits honed by twenty-six years.

She would do this. She would. The litany became the rhythm of her feet. She did not know how long it would take, but once she could traverse this jumbled mess without falling, she would know she could show Ian he was right. It would not hurt her to admit she was wrong when she ended up the winner.

Chapter Fourteen

Mariel waved aside Walter's half-spoken suggestion that he walk her to the door. This was something she had to do herself. For far longer than she had anticipated, she had practiced just for this moment. Yesterday she had traversed the old Cloister without a mishap. Visiting Ian at the parsonage was her reward. She tried to still the rapid beating of her heart. It had been more than a fortnight since he had left. She hoped it was only stubbornness that had kept him away. The thought of working this hard and discovering he truly did not want to see her again brought a pang of fear.

Placing the cane in front of her, she found the steps to the rectory's front door. Her fingers grasped the railing with the ease of her memory's eye. She was discovering that if she let her body relax, she could do far more than when she struggled to be perfect.

Confidently, she lifted the doorknocker and rapped it lightly against the brass circle on the door. Although she fought to keep herself outwardly serene, her gloved hands tightened on the head of the cane. Everything depended on her reception.

The scent of freshly baking bread billowed over her. A soft gasp of surprise came from the other side of the door. With a smile, Mariel said, "Good day, Mrs. Reed. Is Ian home?"

"Y-y-yes, Lady Mariel. Come in." Hastily she asked, "Do you need help?"

"I am fine." Her feet found their way up the last stair and onto the smooth wooden floor, which she knew gleamed with Mrs. Reed's loving care. Reaching up, she pulled the pins from her hat. "If you would call Ian—"

"Mariel!"

She whirled to face him. The aroma of his cologne and the strong soap he used delighted her. A feeling of love coursed through her as she raised her arms to him. Her hat fell to the floor when he drew her into his arms. With her arms around his neck, she pressed her face to his broad chest and savored his closeness.

In a shaky voice, she said, "I decided to be the proper lady and allow my carriage to bring me on my calls today, Ian. Remember? You told me I was to call on you before you would come back to the Cloister."

"I remember," he replied, choked by what she had fought to accomplish. The days of waiting to see if she would do as she must had been hell for him. Too often, he found himself at the window, watching for the Fox-bridge Cloister carriage. As the weeks passed, he wondered if she understood he wanted only to help her. The words he could not speak he tried to communicate with the loving caress of his hands along her slender back.

"I thought if you weren't too busy, I would practice my conversational techniques on you before I visit Mr. Gratton. I must become current on what was discussed at the school board meeting if I am to attend next week." She laughed with a return of her malicious humor. "That is, if they haven't closed the school and burned all the books while I have been absent from the meeting."

"You can't attend next week."

Her brow furrowed as she stepped back from him. "And why not? Weren't you the one urging me to stop hiding behind the walls of the Cloister? I am continuing with my life, and you say I shouldn't?"

Ian chuckled as he tweaked her nose. When she glared at him, her lips a straight line, he laughed again. "Honey, I didn't say you shouldn't attend the meeting. I said you will not be able to go. I will let Dr. Sawyer explain."

"Dr. Sawyer? He is here?"

He caught her head between his loving hands as she turned first one way and then the other. "In my study. Mrs. Reed, another cup please."

"Yes, Reverend." The satin of her gown whispered as she moved swiftly toward the kitchen.

He placed Mariel's hand on his arm, but she drew it away. "Like this will be easier," she stated firmly. She put her fingers in his hand in the method she guessed would make walking the easiest.

Ian could not contain his smile as he led her to his study. He was unsure how she would manage in the crowded room. She maneuvered with easy self-confidence. What he had started to teach her, she had been practicing. He glanced at the doctor and grinned as he saw the surprise in Dr. Sawyer's eyes.

"You don't have to look so satisfied," said Mariel, flashing a grin at the man behind her.

"How—?"

She laughed lightly. "Ian, I do not need my eyes to know exactly how you react." Her brow wrinkled with concentration before she turned and held out her hand.

"Good day, Dr. Sawyer."

"Don't tell me. The smell of my pipe."

"And the alcohol you use to clean your surgical instruments. I am continually amazed at how much more I can perceive with my other senses." She sat on the edge of the settee. "I remember lying in an empty field with Lorraine and Georgie when we were children. We would close our eyes and discover what we could guess of the world around us. That is how we learned the sweet smell of the honeysuckle drifting on the breeze and how the sun made the air shimmer on our skin."

Ian said nothing as he sat next to her. Mariel seldom mentioned her sister or her cousin and never so easily. Her hand slid over his, and she smiled as she added, "You need not think I am as mad as Georgie was. There are things I *like* to remember about those years."

While Mrs. Reed bustled into the crowded room and poured a cup of tea for Lady Mariel, they spoke of gossip from about the countryside. While on his calls,

Dr. Sawyer always learned all the latest news in the cottages sprinkled across the rolling hills.

His voice changed nearly imperceptibly as he said, "Mariel, I came to tell Reverend Beckwith-Carter that I finally received an answer from my colleague in London."

"And?" She took a sip of tea to hide her nervous anticipation.

"He will be able to see you next week. Tuesday is the day he said would be most convenient."

Carefully, she replaced the bone china cup on its saucer. She put them on the marble-topped table next to her. With her hands shaking so badly, she did not trust them not to drop Ian's best dishes. A strong arm slipped along her back and Ian's hand rested on her shoulder. She knew he would feel her quaking. It was no use to pretend. Each of them knew how important this trip was. Dr. Sawyer admitted there was nothing more he could do for her.

Trying to keep her voice buoyant, she smiled. "Now I understand why you said I would be unable to attend the school-board meeting next week, Ian." In a more serious tone, she asked, "Do you think the trip will be worthwhile, doctor?"

"I don't know." The honesty he had shown her throughout her recuperation remained in his voice. "I wish I could promise you Dr. Gillette will work a miracle for you, Mariel, but that is impossible. You wouldn't believe me, even if I did."

"I'd like to believe you."

He chuckled. Taking a deep draught on his pipe, he glanced from one young face to the other. Secretly, he wondered who would find it harder to deal with the news if it was not favorable. The reverend could not hide his hopes of finding a cure for Lady Mariel's affliction. At the same time, it appeared the young woman was beginning to accept her handicap.

It pleased him to hear her speaking of returning to her duties in the community. When she had retired to the ancient house behind its high walls, a spark of light had vanished in the shire. Many disagreed with Lady Mariel, many she denounced loudly as incompetents and incapable of a modern thought, but those were the words of respected rivals who harbored a secret admiration of each other. What the residents of the shire had learned in the past month was that they needed their lady to spur them on with her odd ideas. If they did not accept them, at least, her strange notions inspired them to conceive less eccentric plans of their own.

That Lady Mariel appeared here today prepared to tackle the world with the fervor she had lost during her recovery told the doctor she also had been taught a lesson. Her life was in serving others, not herself. If she had been born in a different class, she might have chosen to be a teacher or a nurse. Instead, as the heir to Foxbridge Cloister, she used her influence to bring change to this backward area.

Seeing the others were waiting for him to speak, he pushed aside his thoughts and told them all he could of his friend Lester Gillette. He explained the type of examination the other doctor would perform, adding more than once that this might have changed, for new knowledge continually was augmenting the field of medicine.

"You are going?" he asked quietly.

"Of course!" cried Mariel. "This chance I cannot let pass by. Besides, I would love to go to London. It has been years since I went there with Uncle Wilford." She asked more quietly, "Ian?"

Mimicking her enthusiasm, he said, "Of course, I am coming! I cannot pass up this chance to go home and visit my family." He squeezed her shoulders as he regarded her shining face. "I would not miss this for anything at all, Mariel."

"Neither would I!"

The reek of sunshine on cinders smacked Mariel in the face as she stepped from the carriage. A playful breeze tugged on the brim of her hat, floating the veiling across her face. She checked it quickly to be sure the pins would hold it in place.

When Ian took her hand, she let him lead the way toward the platform. "Eight steps," he murmured with the ease of the habit they had developed during the whirlwind preparations of the last week.

She counted the stair risers in her head as they slowly walked up to the macadam area where they would wait for the train. A rush of voices burst over them as they stepped out of the tunnel onto the platform. Like a prehistoric monster lurking on the iron rails, the train breathed its gusty heat over them.

Phipps said with a girlish wonder she could not curb, "The engine is trimmed with scarlet, Lady Mariel! As scarlet as the ribbon you wear with your navy gown. Imagine that!"

Ian squeezed Mariel's fingers, and she knew he shared her amusement with Phipps's enthusiasm. The older woman had been unable to hide her delight with the forthcoming trip. Rosie urged Miss Phipps to explore the ticket office with her. Happily, she agreed.

In the flurry of activity in trying to prepare for the hastily planned journey, none of them had had a chance to catch their breaths. With the help of the caring residents of the Cloister and the shire, everything had fallen into place quickly. The deacons of the church volunteered to supervise services for as long as the reverend needed to be in London with Lady Mariel. Even the school board cooperated, promising without hours of debate to order the books Mr. Jones had told her were the best for the students.

In the midst of the preparations, Mariel had realized with shock that she had no idea where they would stay in the city. When she asked Ian if he could suggest an appropriate hotel in his native city, he laughed.

"What's so funny? With the queen's diamond jubilee going all year, London is busy. I don't want to get there and find we have no place but the street to sleep."

Putting his arms around her, he drew her down onto his lap. Mrs. Reed was busy in the kitchen, preparing to close the house. The housekeeper would go to visit her family while her employer was away. She granted Mariel and the reverend privacy, although her presence nearby could never be ignored.

"I have taken care of all that already," Ian said with a smile. "A nice place. Five bedrooms, each with its own private bath; a drawing room; a parlor; and a dining room, as well as a full staff."

"We don't need anything that fancy," she gasped, calculating the cost of such luxury. "It will be frightfully expensive."

"It's free."

"Free?" Her fingers on his cheeks noted the laugh lines deepening along his face. "What is all this?"

"When my grandfather died, he left me his London house. We can stay there."

Despite herself, she gasped. She had never considered Ian in anything other than in his role as the country minister. Though she knew his mother lived in London, she could recall little else he had told her of his past. If she had thought about it, she would have realized that the sons of merchants and other middle class families did not ride to the hunt, as he had. That he was related to the residents of both Beckwith Grange and Avelet Court, two of the finer homes in the area, should have told her that Ian came from a monied background.

To cover her reaction, she asked quietly, "At your house? Alone?"

"You will have Phipps and Rosie with you." He did not speak his thoughts. Too many times she had pushed him away when had tried to do more than kiss her chastely.

Ian tried not think of that as he made sure their luggage was taken from the carriage to the wheeled baggage cart at the station. If Mariel would let him breach the wall she had erected again, he could explain that he knew her fears and wanted to help her overcome them. He never was given the chance. She had become a dear friend again, but nothing more. Sometimes he wondered if he had only dreamed the luscious hours of loving her. Then he would feel her fingers on him and know the ache within him came from real memories.

Mariel turned as she heard her name called. "Dr. Sawyer," she said with a forced smile. She did not want him to think she was displeased to see him. All her nervousness centered on the journey ahead.

"I wondered if you would hear me in this crowd."

She tilted her cheek for his fatherly kiss. Laughing, she answered, "I find I hear more than I wish to now, doctor. Maybe I heard it all along, but it seems to invade my privacy much more."

"Mariel, as I told you before, there are no guarantees my friend can help you," he said with his characteristic bluntness.

"Yes, I know that." Her tone grew as serious as his. "I know that, but I continue to hope."

"Of course you do. So do I. That is why I am sending you to see Lester Gillette. He is the very best man in his field. If anyone can help you, it will be him."

She bit her lip to silence the thought that rang in her head. Conversely, if Dr. Gillette could not help her, no one could. She stiffened as she felt a hand against the middle of her back, but relaxed when she heard the doctor greet Ian.

"Have a pleasant trip," the doctor said tritely. She wondered if they had exchanged a look that said more than their words. It did not matter to her. She knew how small the chances of regaining her sight were.

A whistle shrill in the clear air interrupted the conversation, relieving all of them from having to think of something else to say. With the obligatory good wishes and handshakes, the party of four boarded the train. Miss Phipps pointed out everything to Rosie with continuing enthusiasm. She did not pay attention to her lady's morose expression. Once this trip was underway, she expected Lady Mariel would regain her normal buoyancy.

Ian spoke to the conductor, who gave them directions to their rooms. Taking her arm, he led Mariel along the narrow corridor. If he spoke to her, she did not hear him. The sound of her own fear rang in her ears, repeating the words over and over that this trip was useless. She did not know if she could survive the destruction of her hopes. Before, she had told herself she had adjusted to this handicap. She knew how untrue those words had been.

At their door, Ian left her in Phipps's care while he went to speak to the conductor. The older woman followed her into their private quarters. Sunshine was warm on Mariel's face as she sat on the velvet corduroy seat. She listened to Rosie's squeals of excitement as she discovered the other wide bench.

Phipps bustled opposite her in the small compartment, telling the porter where to put their small bags and assuring herself that the other luggage had been secured in another car. Mariel hid her smile as she heard the man's politely resigned replies.

"Good news, ladies," came a familiar male voice. "The gentleman in the hall assured me that the train should be on time bringing us into Paddington Station."

"Wonderful, Reverend," gushed Phipps. "I am glad you are here. Will you sit with Lady Mariel while Rosie and I check on the arrangements for our meals?"

Before he could answer, the woman and child had fluttered out of the tiny room to satisfy their curiosity about the train. He closed the door and walked to where Mariel sat by the window. Dropping to the seat across from her, he watched as she unpinned her hat and placed it on the cushion next to her.

A clank and a sharp squeal announced that the train was leaving the station. She clutched the arms of the chair, but the train moved fairly smoothly from the platform. Slowly, it gained speed, pressing her back against the cushions.

"How fast does it go?" she asked.

He shrugged. "I don't know. You could ask one of the conductors or porters. It moves faster than your automobile did."

"It is so wonderful to be able to travel in such comfort." She did not wince at each mention of the automobile or the accident as she once had. Time was erasing that pain as well as the physical discomfort.

His hands brushed the dirt from the seat where Rosie had soiled it with her shoes. He looked from it to Mariel's face turned in profile to him. Once those soft lips had parted willingly beneath his and warmed his breath with her own. His eyes followed the modest lines of her traveling suit. The worsted jacket of kelly green and the plaid skirt to match gave her a jaunty appearance for the beginning of their trip. He did not have to

search far in his mind to think of her dressed in fine,
nearly transparent silk, laughing with him as they
partook once more of their love.

Aware of the raised window shades, he did no more
than touch her fingers. When she placed her other hand
over his, she smiled. "I'm glad you are coming with me,
Ian."

"Did you think I would let you do this alone?"

"Sometimes I don't know what to think anymore. I
know things weren't simple before, but now. . ."

He moved to sit next to her on the bench. Slipping
his arm around her shoulders, he smiled as her head
rested against him. If he had to court Mariel from the
beginning again, it would not be such a terrible fate. He
enjoyed holding her and knew the reward his persistence
would win him.

"Would you like to meet my family while we are in
London?" he asked as he watched the panorama speed-
ing past the window. "I received a letter from Mother
yesterday. She is having a small party at her house
tomorrow night."

She shook her head. "I haven't been invited, Ian. I
could not possibly attend a private gathering."

"Mother's idea of a small party is no more than a
hundred people. It will hardly be private."

"I haven't been invited," she repeated regretfully.

"I am inviting you. If I attend, I do not wish to do
so alone. Would you do me the honor of allowing me
to escort you, Lady Mariel?"

A faraway expression softened her face. To be with
other people, to hear music, to dress in the ballgown
she had packed in case they attended the theater. . . .
Such dreams she had thought were as battered as the
automobile, never to be resurrected. Ian refused to let
her think anything was impossible.

"Will you dance with me?"

"Dance?" Instantly he realized what she meant. If
she was to be brave enough to enter an unknown house
filled with strangers, he must show he was as courageous
and waltz her across the dance floor. With a laugh, he

said, "It has been a while, but I think I can manage, if you don't mind having your feet stepped on."

"It won't be the first time."

"I am sure of that. You must have been invited to many balls by your young suitors."

She smiled in remembrance. "Uncle Wilford was determined I would be escorted to every dance in the shire, even if he had to do the honors himself. You know, it is funny, but the fondest memories I have are of the dances Uncle shared with me."

"That is because you could not love any of the others who wanted to hold your hand like this or kiss your cheek." He bent to place his lips against her face.

Her face turned to him. A shy smile tilted her lips. "You are right. I could not love any of them. Not as I love you, Ian."

"You still love me?"

Shock wiped the soft expression from her face. "Did you think I stopped loving you? I don't think I can. You are inside me, here." She pointed to her heart. "I love you, Ian Beckwith-Carter. I love your ornery nature and confounded temper. I even love you when you prove me wrong."

"No, my love, I only proved you were right." His fingers framed her face. "You are the same Mariel who won my heart. Nothing could change that. I love you, Mariel." He leaned forward to whisper in her ear. "When we get to London, stay with me."

Her brow furrowed as she said, "But, Ian, I am staying with you. Oh!" She drew away as she realized what he meant. She shook her head vehemently. "I can't, Ian."

"Why not? Don't mention Rosie, for she would not notice if you sleep alone or with me."

The return of their two traveling companions saved her from having to devise a lie to answer him. She could not tell him the truth. One by one, she had overcome her fears until only the one that kept her from marrying him in the first place remained. If she allowed him to convince her to return to the indescribable delights of his bed, she would not be strong enough to continue to refuse his proposal as she must.

Rosie chattered about all the luxurious rooms she had seen in the cars. They were able to quiet her enough to take a nap by promising to wake her in time for dinner. Phipps urged them to go to the lounge car while she sat with the child. Not wanting to be alone with Ian, Mariel decided the public car would be the perfect spot to spend the first hours of their trip.

The motion of the car rocking on the tracks made Mariel's head spin, until she learned to compensate for the rhythm as she walked. When Ian opened the door at the end of their car, sound exploded at her. The muted click-click of the wheels on the tracks became painful in her ears. She thought she could hear Ian speaking to her, but could not decipher the words over the noise. Only when they entered the next car forward did she understand him.

She smiled as he took her hand once more. Quietly, he described the scene before them. The plush beauty of the room, decorated in the highest rococo style, ran the full length of the car. On both sides, by the windows, overstuffed chairs in rich, red velvet offered views of the passing countryside or could be turned to facilitate conversation. Matching drapes softened the lines of the windows. She felt his arm move to point out the arched ceiling, gilded in a floral design. Cut-glass globes lit the narrow room. At the far end, a carved bar served drinks to gentlemen while a porter offered the ladies something of a lighter nature.

Mariel allowed Ian to select a seat for her. From the quiet in the car, she suspected they were the only passengers in it. That supposition strengthened when, as soon as Ian excused himself to get a glass of brandy, a porter appeared at her elbow.

"May I offer madam something to drink?" he asked in a deep voice, which rivaled the rumble of the engine far ahead of them.

"Yes, thank you. A cup of tea would be lovely."

The waiter held out his tray. He frowned when the lady did not select one. Glancing at the cups, he saw that they were clean and that the beverage steamed enticingly. He started to speak when her escort returned.

Ian silently picked up one of the cups and told

Mariel to hold out her hands. Only when he was sure
she had her fingers around it securely did he release the
saucer. When she thanked him, he regarded the steward
as if daring him to speak the thoughts written across his
face. The waiter glanced with candid curiosity from
Mariel to the man wearing a minister's collar before
scurrying away.

Sitting, Ian listened while Mariel spoke quietly.
What she said made no impression on him. He fought
his anger. In Foxbridge, Lady Mariel Wythe would always enjoy the prestige she had won through her hard
work, as well as the loyalty everyone offered the Wythes,
although they were no longer feudal overlords. Elsewhere it would be different. She would receive pity and
ridicule, the very things he had fled from London to
avoid in the company of former friends.

If this doctor could not help Mariel, her world might
narrow to those few miles around her ancestral home.
Everything she might have done beyond those bound-
aries would be denied because strangers would see her
blindness first. He understood through harsh lessons
what she had not yet learned. He wished he could spare
her this torment.

Other travelers came and left the lounge, but did
not bother the two seated close together. Ian watched
the scenery pass in a steady parade and described anything of interest. When he took her hand, she felt the
strong emotions he was keeping pent up within him. She
did not ask him to tell her what bothered him. Instead,
she tried to comfort him by talking about her last trip to
London four years earlier.

Slowly, Ian's anger diminished to frustration. He
could not ruin her trip by being so glum when she was
making such a valiant effort to be cheerful. When a
verbose man and his equally talkative wife sat next to
them, he allowed himself to be wooed into the conversation. Pride blossomed in him to lessen his anger. Neither
of the two newcomers had noticed Mariel's blindness, so
charmed were they by her sparkling wit.

The pompous man lost no time bragging about his
position in Salisbury's Unionist government. He in-
timated that every decision out of the Exchequer bore

his signature as well as the minister's. At the same time, his wife was regaling Mariel with all the important people they knew in London.

"Surely we must know your family, Lady Mariel," she cooed in a tone unsuited for her age. "Wythe, did you say?"

Without showing her amusement, Mariel said, "Perhaps you have met my uncle. He is Lord Foxbridge."

"Lord Foxbridge?" gasped the man. "You are of that family?"

"Yes," she answered, without changing her friendly tone. "Do I take it that you have met Uncle Wilford?"

He stuttered, "N-n-no, I must admit I have not had the pleasure. He is abroad, I believe."

"Lord Foxbridge enjoys traveling." Her fingers on the arm of the chair clenched tightly on the thick upholstery.

Noticing the distress she would not allow to enter her voice, Ian placed his hand over hers. He watched the other couple's eyes rivet on his motion, and he could read their thoughts blaring from their priggish faces. When they hastily excused themselves, he was glad to see them leave.

Mariel sighed as she relaxed against the plush seat. As if to herself, she murmured, "I had forgotten."

"Forgotten?"

She smiled tenderly at him. Just by being with a member of her somewhat notorious family, he could find his name sullied as well. "Rumors grow with the re-telling. Those who heard of the tragedy at the Cloister fear the crazy Wythes."

"They are fools," he retorted to comfort her.

When she laughed, he waited to see what was so amusing. "Don't be angry, Ian," she said. "I have become accustomed to it. Uncle Wilford's life is different enough to make such narrow-minded people think he is as mad as Georgie was. Perhaps he is, but his insanity is more socially acceptable than my poor cousin."

"You loved him dearly, didn't you?"

"I adored Georgie. He was the one adult who always had time to listen to me. Because he never outgrew his own childhood, he understood the traumas of that time as no other adult could." She paused before adding, "I loved him, but he died thinking I despised him."

He took her hand in his, but said nothing. There were no words to ease the pain in her heart. Although only the scar on her forehead remained visible from that horrid time, other scars hid to torment her. When he suggested they return to collect Miss Phipps and Rosie, to find the dining car, she nodded tiredly.

Through the meal, with its less than succulent fare, Mariel remained quiet. She knew they would be coming into the station shortly after dark. Each time the train stopped to discharge or take on passengers, she was reminded how they neared their destination. In two days, she would be going to see Dr. Gillette. Suddenly she wished she had never come on this trip. It might be better to stay at the Cloister and dream the dreams that could be destroyed by this man.

Emerging from the hubbub of the busy station, Ian wasted no time finding a cab. It was barely large enough for the four tired travelers and their luggage. Mariel held Rosie in her lap as they crowded into the small space. Her feet rested lightly on a hatbox, and she could feel Ian's arm around her shoulders. The tightly packed hansom would have been amusing if they had not been so exhausted.

After a ride through the twisting streets of the city, it stopped smoothly in front of a row of houses. Ian helped the two women from the carriage as the driver removed their larger pieces of luggage from the boot. With his fingers on the brim of his hat, he thanked his passengers for their fine tip.

Mariel listened intently as Phipps described the house before them. In the lamplight, she could pick out the Gothic Revival details of the arched windows contrasting with the classic style columns around the door. The brick house closely resembled its neighbors. Hedges edged the short walk and narrow front yard where a stone bench offered a streetside view. Chimney pots of all sizes and shapes clung to the shingled roofs above. A single tree stood guard between the sidewalk and the road.

Ian took her hand and placed it on his arm, he drew her toward the house. "Three steps."

"Thank you."

Noting the stiffness of her voice, he asked, "Honey, is something wrong?"

A smile flitted across her face and disappeared. "Just nervous. So much depends on these next few days."

"Try not to think of that now. Just enjoy your visit here. After all the wonderful visits I have had to your ancestral home, let me play the genial host in mine."

The opening of the door drew his attention away from her wan face. He greeted the butler by name and introduced the two women and little girl with him to Barbon. The round man, perfectly correct in his spotless suit, welcomed his employer's guests without allowing his reaction to show. On short notice, he had been warned to prepare the house for Mister Ian, as he still thought of the man he had watched grow from a child. Although Mister Ian had no use for the house, he arranged for the staff to continue to work there. The house was kept ready for an infrequent visit like this one or for use by the guests of one of his mother's parties.

Mariel thanked a maid as her hat and cloak were taken. She felt the thickness of carpet beneath her feet and smelled the undisguisable scent of gas burning overhead. Listening quietly to Phipps's whispered description, she hid her astonishment.

Her companion described quickly the pair of rooms she could see opening off the central hall. They were furnished as richly as any room at Foxbridge Cloister. Images of the overcrowded chambers of the parsonage, filled with castoff, threadbare furniture, contrasted with this wealth. She wondered what other surprises of Ian's past would be revealed during this trip.

When he suggested they might wish to explore the house in the morning after a good night's sleep, she acceded. She was tired, not physically, but emotionally.

Like a procession of ducklings, they followed the butler up the stairs.

Phipps urged her lady to rest. She would put the child to bed. With a weary smile, Mariel agreed. In her dreams, she might be able to escape the dread churning her stomach to spasms. She kissed Rosie good night and promised to join her in the morning to peek into all the corners of the house.

A maid opened the next door along the corridor. "My lady?" Awe filled her voice as she spoke. She had never met a blind person before and had not guessed one could appear so normal. Answering Mariel's questions, she stumbled on her words in her attempt to act correctly. A mumbled "Good night" accompanied her out the door.

Mariel placed her hat and bag on a chair. The maid had been disconcerted by her questions about the location of the furniture and doorways, but she needed the information. Cautiously she crossed the room to where the bed should be. She found it when her legs brushed the footboard. Running her hands along it, she found the twisted carving of the canopy uprights. This room was lovely. She would enjoy staying here for their visit to London. The thought of renting a room in an unknown hotel had worried her.

"Will this do?"

She spun to face the door. An involuntary smile brightened her eyes. "This is wonderful, Ian. Why are you hiding this part of your life?"

"I never meant to conceal it from you. It has been easier to gain the trust of the people in Foxbridge if they think I share more of their background than of yours. I have not lied."

"I cannot imagine you lying. You are too honest sometimes." She laughed as she walked toward him.

Ian lowered his eyes, unable to meet her smile. If only she could guess how he lied over and over. Every word he said to her was encased in a falsehood. His faked optimism about this visit to Dr. Gillette, as well as his acceptance of her resistance to his love. He wanted to be done with these lies. He longed to pull her into his arms and love her. He yearned to rest his head against her skin as he released the anger and sorrow within him.

"Rosie is anxious to investigate the back garden," she continued as she took his hands in hers. "I am glad we brought her with us. It is so much fun to share her excitement."

He laughed, but the sound was false even to his ears. "I don't know who was more thrilled with the train. Rosie or Miss Phipps."

"Ian?"

Patting her hand, he did not have to ask what was bothering her. It was him. "It has been a long trip, my dear."

Mariel put up her fingers to search his face for the truth. She felt the tightness of his lips vanish beneath her soft touch. When he caught her hand and pressed it against his lips, she felt the too familiar surge of longing. His other arm circled her waist. The hard line of his cane pressed her closer. Her mouth welcomed his.

Hungrily, he kissed her again and again. His lips moved along her face while she laughed with the happiness coursing through her. That sound vanished as he captured her mouth once more. His tongue probed within it to tease awake the passions she had tried to dampen. Her fingers slipped beneath his coat to hold him tight to her. The solid strength of his chest against her softer curves weakened her bones and her resolve not to be his again.

When he raised his mouth from the bewitchment he had been creating along her neck, he whispered in her ear. The warmth of his breath sent a flame along her.

"Sleep well, my love."

She put out her hands to keep him from stepping away. "Ian, must you go?"

"I must, unless you want me here with you all night." A single finger etched delight along her as it moved from her collar down along the front of her jacket. "You hesitate in answering me."

"I love you," she said helplessly.

"And I love you. That is why I am telling you good night now." He kissed her lightly. "I want you to want me without that hesitation."

She clasped her shaking fingers in front of her as he went from the room. The sound of his cane striking the wood floors did not go far before she heard a door open and close. Slowly, she shut her own door.

Undressing for bed, she fought her yearning to run to him and ask to be held in his arms as she once had been. Only because she feared that becoming his lover would precipitate another proposal did she delay. She loved him too much to risk that again.

In the loneliness of her bed, she could not weep out her sorrow. It was too potent for such relief. She felt the darkness weigh on her until she ceded herself to it. In the depths of her sleep, she could not escape her longing to believe in the impossible hope of regaining everything she had had for three short, perfect days.

Chapter Fifteen

Phipps pressed the ostrich-feather fan into Mariel's hand. Stepping back, she regarded the nervous woman objectively. "There, my lady. You look perfect."

"Phipps, I can't do this." Mariel dropped the fan onto a chair.

"And why not?" She busied herself picking up the discarded clothes. "You do not need your eyes to attend this ball. Your ears can hear the music. Your feet can move to the steps of the dance. Go and enjoy yourself."

"I am afraid of shaming Ian." Her fear was so potent, she could hide it no longer.

Phipps put her hands on the shivering arms of the young woman and turned her to face her. "Lady Mariel, you could ride as naked as Lady Godiva through the streets of Coventry and not shame him. Don't you understand? He loves you."

"Did he tell you that?"

"Tell me?" She laughed with easy amusement. "Dear child, did you think either of you could hide the truth from the ones who love you? Nothing stays hidden long in Foxbridge. Still, no one ever spoke of seeing your automobile and buggy parked behind the parsonage for the nights Mrs. Reed was away with her ailing sister."

Her cheeks flushed. "You simply—"

"You are a grown woman, Lady Mariel." She pressed the the feathers back into her lady's hand.

"What you choose to do is a matter between you and your conscience. At first, I feared you would be haunted by the gossips. When I heard nothing other than an acceptance of the fact that you and Reverend Beckwith-Carter loved one another, I knew the people of Fox-bridge cared enough about both of you to leave you alone."

Mariel's fingers tightened around the fan. Never, in the warmth of newly discovered love, had she guessed what others were thinking. Only the bigots like Mrs. Rivers and Mr. Turner had made their opinions known. Those opinions she had discounted as worthless at the time. She had wondered about the lack of interest among their friends, but gave it little thought. Loving Ian in those stolen moments was all she wanted in her heart and in her mind.

That happiness had disappeared. Ian tried to pretend everything would be fine if the doctor gave her bad news, but she could not share his optimism. Although she had regained much of her former independence, nothing would be exactly as it had been.

Telling Phipps to have a pleasant evening, she went out of her room along the narrow corridor. Her full skirt belling out from the narrow waist of the gown brushed the small tables set beneath the gaslights. She placed her hand on the banister and walked slowly down the stairs along its curve. The musky scent of Ian's cologne reached out to embrace her.

She smiled as she held out her hand to him. If she gave no sign of her distress, she might be able to convince herself of her ability to deal with this evening. His eyes moved along her in a heated appraisal she did not have to see.

Ian smiled. Every man at the ball tonight would envy him this vision on his arm. One look at the dress she wore told him her uncle must have brought this gift from 7 Rue de la Paix in Paris. Lord Foxbridge must have known someone to give him cachet to Paris's most selective designer. Only the House of Worth could have created such a luxurious gown.

The ashes-of-roses crepe de chine was embroidered with sequins along the shirred nun's-veiling panel in the front of the open skirt. As she moved, the gaslights glittered off the iridescent flowers cascading in a soft shower of petals from her shoulders to the hem. It whispered softly as she walked.

When Mariel felt his warm lips through the fine mesh of her gloves, she closed her eyes in unspoken delight. She followed her fingers as he drew her into his arms. His mouth caressed hers lightly as they both fought the desire she refused to acknowledge. With his hands at her waist, her arms rose along the silk of his tuxedo coat to his broad shoulders.

Softly, she said, "This is very different from what you wear in Foxbridge."

He laughed as her fingers roamed along his high stock collar and found the onyx studs closing his shirt above his white satin waistcoat. "I am very different in Foxbridge. There I am Reverend Beckwith-Carter. Tonight I am only Ian escorting the most beautiful woman in the world to my mother's soiree."

"Ian—"

"Don't say it, my love. I know how anxious you feel. Simply smile, and every man there will be eager to do your bidding."

"Stay close to me."

He laughed. "I don't think you could convince me to do otherwise. It is already fashionably late. Shall we leave?"

During the long carriage ride to the house in the fashionable suburb of Kensington, Mariel was silent. Any attempt he made to speak to her was met with monosyllables or a brief nod. Feeling her distress, he put his arm around her shoulders and drew her trembling form closer to him.

Too soon for her, the carriage stopped. She clutched-ed tighter to Ian's arm as they slowly climbed the stairs to the door of his family's house. She smelled the many gaslights burning to light their way. The confused mumble of mingled voices swept out to encompass them.

"This is the last step."

"Thank you."

"Honey, relax," he urged as he greeted the liveried doorman. "This is my mother's house. Some of my family will be here tonight. They will not be able to resist you, if you give them a chance to know you."

She dampened her dry lips as she walked by his side. The smooth floor under her feet was cool through her thin slippers. Marble. She smiled involuntarily as she discovered, as if for the first time, how much she could discern without her eyes. The melodic strains of a waltz came from the left. She gripped convulsively onto Ian's arm as he turned her in that direction.

He moved away from her slightly as he said, "Mother, I would like you to meet Lady Mariel Wythe. Mariel, my mother Cynthia Beckwith-Carter."

"So formal?" came a cheerful laugh. "How lovely to meet you, my dear. I am so glad you were able to join us this evening. I trust you had a pleasant journey to London."

The scent of expensive perfume surrounded Mariel. That and the swish of a heavy silk gown brought a picture instantly into her mind. Ian's bright eyes in a feminine face, somewhat older, but no less charming. The image made her feel instantly at ease.

"It was a lovely trip," she answered with a smile. "My daughter has not stopped talking of all our adventures since we arrived at Paddington. I thank you for inviting me on such short notice to your party."

"Nonsense, my dear. This is Ian's home, although he insists on staying in his own house on his few visits to London. My son's friends have always been welcome here. You must come back to have luncheon with me when we can have a chance to chat without all these others about." She chuckled again as she added, "And without Ian about to warn his mother to watch herself and not say the wrong thing. Does he do that to you also?"

"All the time." Mariel giggled as Ian took her hand. "See, he has that exasperated expression on his face because I have said the wrong thing already."

Mrs. Beckwith-Carter started and glanced at her son in shock, seeing that the young woman was correct. Disconcerted, she did not want to blurt out the thought in her head. She had been sure her son had written he was escorting Lady Mariel to London for her to see an ophthalmologist.

"She knows me too well," Ian said quickly to ease his mother's astonishment.

"Why don't you take Lady Mariel into the ballroom and get her something cool to drink? Here comes your father's cousin Godwin. He is a terrible boor, so hurry. You know you want to evade him."

Ian bent forward and kissed her cheek. "Mother, you will never change." With a gentle tug on Mariel's fingers, he added, "A glass of champagne?"

"That sounds lovely. Thank you again, Mrs. Beck-with-Carter."

"Tell him to bring you back soon, my dear. Soon, Ian!"

Her joyous laugh followed them as they descended the pair of steps into a lower level of the entry foyer. The ballroom spread out before them. Ian regarded it with pride. This was a lovely house. Except for the two years when he hated everything, he had loved his visits here from their country home.

Vivid shades of golden velvet and silk glistened in the light from the trio of Waterford crystal chandeliers. The flames of gas soared toward the ceiling and its mural of a Grecian feast, complete with goat-footed pans and floating deities. To one side, nearly hidden by the crowd of guests, the orchestra played on a raised platform decorated with bunting. Opposite, awaited the tables where the buffet would be served at midnight.

He adjusted the bow tie at the collar of his tuxedo. As he was about to lead Mariel toward the punch bowl, he heard his name called. "Ian!" came the enthusiastic female voice, which he recognized all too easily.

Mariel was nearly rocked off her feet as someone pushed her rudely aside and away from Ian. She put out her hand to steady herself and touched slippery satin. "Oh, excuse me!" she gasped, feeling the heat of a blush climbing her cheeks.

"No problem, my dear young lady," came a laughing voice. Her fingers were raised to lips topped by a full mustache. The bristles stroked her hand through her glove as he kissed it. "Colonel Arnold Hoppe, Retired, at your service. You are—?"

"Mariel Wythe," she said quietly. She felt adrift without knowing exactly where Ian was. She smelled his cologne nearby, but did not know if it was only a residual scent. In the blur of voices around her, she could not discern his easily. If she called to him, she could make a fool of herself. Taking a deep breath, she remembered her resolution to act normally tonight. In a steadier voice, she added, "It is a pleasure to make your acquaintance, Colonel."

She could hear his smile in his words. His voice was exactly as she imagined a retired colonel's to be. Rich with aristocracy, snobbish with the presumption that the British were the finest, most civilized people on the globe. "Wythe did you say? You must be Wilford's niece. Where is that chap now? Last time I spoke to him was when I was garrisoned in Cape Town."

"Uncle Wilford is on his way home," she said, pleased to meet someone who did not react with loathing to the Wythe name. "He was in America last. Some place called Chicago. He is taking a steamship from New York to Liverpool. We expect him home within the month. He wrote that he can't wait to tell me about the United States. As always, he was fascinated by the idiosyncracies he found."

"That's Wilford. He would be fascinated if he met his end being eaten by cannibals. I always recreate him in my mind as I saw him in the interior, with his notebook in hand, his pith helmet awry, chasing some poor native to gain information for that book he has yet to write." He chuckled. "Is that why he is coming home? To write that long awaited tome of 'fascinating' information?"

Hedging, she answered, "I believe that is one of the reasons." The man had not mentioned anything about her accident, so she did not want to say the real reason her uncle was ceasing his lifelong travels around the world.

Just the previous week they had received a wire from her uncle. He had received, from the British consulate, the letter Miss Phipps had dashed off to him as soon as they had been sure Mariel would live. Only the difficulty of making reservations, and long layovers, kept him from getting home as quickly as he wanted, to be with his beloved niece.

Colonel Hoppe held out his arm and asked, "May I, my lady?"

"Excuse me?" She could not understand what he meant. Desperately she turned to seek Ian. He must have moved away, for she could discern no sign to let her know of his presence.

"Allow me to escort you into the ballroom."

"I promised to dance first with Reverend Beck-with-Carter."

He picked up her hand and placed it securely on his arm. The wool of his coat was prickly beneath her fingers. "He is busy talking to Portia Muir. I am sure they have much to discuss since the last time they saw each other, seeing as how they once were rumored to be ready to announce their betrothal. By the time they finish chatting, I will have returned you here. A single dance with an old friend of the family, Lady Mariel?"

Before she could answer, he had swept her into the crowded room. She squeezed into herself, afraid of bumping into something or someone. Her full skirts brushed others, but the colonel steered her through the press of people with the élan of one leading an expedition through the jungle. She recognized the dance floor by the pliant texture of wood beneath her feet. The music swelled over her.

The colonel turned her into his arms and began to waltz her unevenly, but enthusiastically, across the floor. All the time he gossiped about people she had never met and places she had never been. She discovered that a simple sound to let him know she was listening proved sufficient for her share of the conversation.

Her thoughts were caught up in the words he had said as he drew her through the crowd. Portia Muir. She could not recall Ian ever mentioning that name. He knew so many of the secrets of her past, but had failed to tell her he had been prepared to marry this London lady with the exotic name. An aching sense of betrayal brought a flush to her face. Not only had he not bothered to tell her about this important bit of his past, but he had left her alone, helpless, in this strange house as soon as this Portia came to reclaim his attention.

She bit her lip as she whirled to the gay beat of the music. Too long ago, she had known the sweetness of Ian's skin against hers as he taught her of paradise. He was urging her to share that bliss with him again, but that might change if he renewed his relationship with Portia Muir. Had he loved this other woman in the same way and whispered identical promises in the warmth of sated love?

Portia. The name brought to mind raven locks and snapping black eyes. For the first time, Mariel feared she had misread Ian. Perhaps he pitied her and brought her to London only to help as a good clergyman should. If he could convince her to warm him in the night, he would not pass by the opportunity while he dreamed of this Portia.

Suddenly her dismal thoughts were interrupted. The colonel released her. "Excuse me a moment, my lady. I see someone I must speak with immediately. I will be right back."

"Colonel Hoppe, please, I can't—" She interrupted herself as she heard his footsteps vanish among the dancers. In horror, she stood in the middle of the dance floor. Where she was in relation to the rest of the room, she could not guess.

One thing she knew. She could not wait here as the others moved past her. Trying to retrace their steps, she guessed the entrance foyer was somewhere to her left. The music now came from her right. Summoning all her confidence, she took a step in that direction. When she did not impact against one of the dancers, she recalled the number of times she had been dancing and her partner had swirled her around someone crossing the floor out of pattern with the dance.

"Excuse me," she murmured when she bumped into someone at the edge of the dance floor. With sudden inspiration, she asked, "Can you direct me to the cloak room?" In most houses of this class, that small room would be off the foyer.

A woman with hard, tight corsets sniffed. "Straight ahead and to your left. You would be wise, young lady, to drink less, so early in the evening. Then perhaps you would not be colliding with people."

"Yes, ma'am," she replied meekly. The heaviness of the woman's perfume and her stilted words identified her as a dowager, assured of her own opinions.

Mariel tried to maintain a straight course, but it was impossible. She held her fan in front of her to warn her of obstructions. The folly of her vanity in refusing to bring her cane taunted her when she needed it so desperately. To miss people and furniture, she had to stray from her path, but tried to return to it, keeping the music always at her back. When she met something she could not get around, she realized she had lost her way.

Her hands ran along the obstruction, wrinkling the silk hanging there. In one direction, she discovered a wooden pilaster carved in vertical grooves. The same waited in the opposite direction. She scowled. This was clearly a wall. She had no choice but to turn about and try to find Ian.

"Miss?"

She whirled to face the speaker. "Yes?"

"Is there a problem?"

She wanted to demand he identify himself, for his words gave her no clue to who stood in front of her. "I am looking for Reverend Beckwith-Carter."

"He is over there by the pillars."

Before she could ask him for better instructions, the person was gone. Pillars? What pillars? Where? Over there could mean any direction. Bravely, she struck out in the one she thought might be correct. Within a few steps, she found herself facing a wall again. Her hand went out to touch glass. It was a window.

She tried to recall where Ian had said the ball would be held. If it was in a conservatory, this would be no help. Many windows would ring the room. If a regular ballroom, she could use this as a reference point. She paused to listen to the music, concentrating on sifting it from the other noises. It was to her right. She must go left.

If she was not so distressed about being lost in this unknown house, she would be outraged at Ian. He promised not to leave her alone for a minute. As soon as they entered the house, he allowed his attention to be monopolized by an ex-lover with the unlikely name of Portia. She comforted herself with vowing to let him know of her displeasure when she found him.

Enrapt in her thoughts of reprimanding him, her concentration wavered. When she bumped into someone, she heard cries of dismay and felt a spray of liquid on her arm. Anger burst from a male voice as he demanded, "Why don't you watch where you are going?"

"I am sorry," she murmured as she touched the damp spots on her gloves. She hoped the wine he was drinking was not red wine. It would stain them so horribly.

He did not seem ready to accept her apology. She backed away as she sensed his face too close to hers. The thick odor of liquor on his breath gagged her.

"Look at my waistcoat!"

"I'm sorry," she repeated as someone she did not know said, "Leave her alone, Muir. It was simply an accident."

"Open your eyes, lady, and watch where you are going. Are you blind?"

Her choked answer was halted by familiar hands on her shoulders. "Ian," she whispered gratefully. She forgot her rage with him in her relief.

Over her head, Ian locked eyes with Rupert Muir. He should have guessed the tall man would be here when he encountered the possessive claws of Portia. Brother and sister never failed to attend these events together. Both enjoyed viewing the trouble the other could be guaranteed to create.

"Is there a problem?" he asked in a calm tone which belied his true feelings.

"Well, hello, *Parson* Beckwith-Carter." The snide emphasis on the title brought snickers from the crowd of dandies around Muir. He smiled as he viewed the auburn haired man. Running a hand through perfectly coiffed hair, his dark eyes drilled into Ian's. It angered him that he could not penetrate that hard wall Beckwith-

Carter could raise so easily. "I had not thought to see you in London this season. I expected you would be out in the hinterlands saving the souls of orphans and widows."

"I have business in London, so I thought to stop in and see my family. I might ask you the same. I thought your family banished you to the country after your last escapade."

He shrugged. "Father relented when he could not tolerate my company at the Hills any longer." His gaze went to the silent woman standing between them and noted Beckwith-Carter's hands stroking her shoulders. For the first time, he noticed how beautiful she was and realized he did not know her. He thought he had met every lovely woman in London—he had seduced as many of them as he could convince to welcome him to their beds.

Mariel sensed the anger in the air and took a half step back toward Ian. She wanted to feel his arms around her. That he did not like this man she could tell by the way he spat his words at him.

"Come, Mariel," came the gentle order in Ian's voice. He took her quivering hand and placed it on his sleeve. As they turned to go, she felt another hand on her arm. She jerked her arm away, sure it was the horrible Mr. Muir who dared to be so forward.

"Mariel? Lady Mariel Wythe?" Laughter sounded in the obnoxious man's voice. His next words were spoken so loudly, she was sure many would hear him. "No wonder you bumped into me like a bat caught out in the dawn. You are blind after that automobile accident. Is that why you hooked up with the good reverend? Is he going to work a miracle for you?"

Ian said too quietly, "That is enough, Muir. At least have the decency to lower your voice if you cannot have the sense to act like a gentleman of your class."

"What a pair!" Muir continued. "The crippled parson and the blind heir to a family of madmen."

When Mariel was released to fall backward several steps, hands supported her to keep her from slipping to the floor. It warned her how many were enjoying the

unexpected spectacle. She gasped as she heard the dull
thud of a fist impacting on bare flesh.

"Ian!" she screamed. "Don't!"

Other shouts drowned hers. The strong fingers
holding her pulled her back as another series of blows
sounded. From across the room, the orchestra ceased
playing in a shrill cacophony.

"Stop it," Mariel begged. "Stop it, please."

The man released her, ordering her not to move.
She heard him yell as he jumped into the melee. More
confusing orders crisscrossed the room. A woman's
scream echoed off the ceiling. A begemmed hand took
Mariel's and pulled her away from the fight.

"Mariel, come with me."

"Mrs. Beckwith-Carter?"

Even as she was drawing her past the spectators, she
said in her no-nonsense voice, "Cynthia, my dear.
'Beckwith-Carter' is too much of a mouthful to say each
time you speak to me."

"Ian—"

She put her hands on Mariel's shoulders, bared by
her ballgown. "Sit here, my dear. Oh, you, there. Champagne for Lady Mariel."

The fragile stem of a glass was placed in her hands.
When she heard Ian's mother order her to drink, she
took a sip. She started to speak again, but Cynthia
hushed her by saying she wanted to watch the fight.

"Is it continuing?"

"Sit." This command was in a sharper voice.

Mariel lowered herself to the very edge of the
settee. She flinched as she heard the semi-intelligible
comments from those around her. Who was winning,
who was losing, who was fighting, she could not determine. When the orchestra started to play again, she
yearned to ask those around her what had happened.

When a handkerchief was pressed into her fingers,
she realized she was crying. Raising it to her face, she
gasped as she felt the embroidered initial at one corner.
"Ian!" Her hand reached out to touch his face.

"Careful," he warned with a laugh. He took her
fingers and moved them to his right cheek. "That one
is fine. The other is a bit tender."

"You're hurt?"

Ian gazed at her shattered expression and wondered how he could ever have thought her love for him had died. Displayed there for all the world to see were her fears for him and the love she was afraid to offer him again. He took her hand and pressed it to his lips. Smiling sent a pang across his head, but he ignored it as he saw her mouth part in a soft invitation he yearned to accept. In this crowded ballroom with everyone watching, he must accede to propriety.

"I am fine, Mariel. Muir's fist grazed me once or twice, but the rotter forgot the number of times I beat him at Eton." He chuckled. "It's good to learn my sedentary life has not ruined my reflexes."

Standing, he accepted the good-natured jesting of his friends and family. He was reaching for Mariel's hand when a white-laced tempest whirled between them. As she had before, she shoved Mariel aside. The sharp sound of her hand on his aching face silenced those around the settee.

Ian's eyes narrowed as he regarded Portia Muir with ill-concealed rancor. Her blond beauty was unaltered, but he had changed. He had not thought of her wistfully in more than a year, not since the last time he saw her at a party in the home of a mutual acquaintance. Before his accident, she had used all her wiles to try to convince him she would be the perfect wife. Not once had she visited him while he was recuperating. The first time he met her when he was on his feet again, she pointedly ignored him.

"You are a hypocrite, Ian Beckwith-Carter!"

He laughed coldly. "And you are proving you have the same lack of manners as your brother, Miss Muir."

"*Miss* Muir?" she exploded. She glanced at Mariel who was moving to stand next to Ian. "Now that you've found yourself a titled lady who will have you, you think you are too good for the rest of us." She sneered at Mariel, "Pity. That is what he feels for you. The saintly Reverend Beckwith-Carter! He sees you as another chance to secure a star in his heavenly crown."

Mariel slipped her hand into Ian's and said, "Miss Muir, I can assure you that Reverend Beckwith-Carter does not pity me. You are mistaken, for you see, I can tell by the way he is speaking to you that you are the one he pities. It is a shame, for even on our short acquaintance, I would say you are not worthy of that compassion."

Portia sputtered, but found herself looking at the back of the woman dressed in the fabulous dress she had identified immediately as a Worth original. Her eyes narrowed as she saw her rival raise a handkerchief to the small cut on Ian's face. She did not miss either his smile or the way his arm slipped around Lady Mariel's waist to bring her closer to him. Their motions spoke of an intimacy she had never shared with the handsome Ian Beckwith-Carter.

Even as she watched the Wythe woman's ministrations, she could hear her brother's gloating voice in her head. When she told Rupert she did not want to marry a cripple, he suggested she spurn Ian after his riding accident. Now she wondered if her brother simply had seen a chance to keep his enemy from becoming part of their family.

Realizing everyone had forgotten her as they crowded around Ian and his too-pretty companion, Portia flounced away to find her brother. Ian had beaten Rupert senseless with only a few blows. Rupert would not stay to face the jeers of his so-called friends.

At the top of the stairs, she drained her glass of champagne and dropped the goblet into a heavy planter. She did not notice as the fine crystal shattered. All of her attention was centered on the woman still standing so close to Ian. Until she saw Ian tonight, she had not remembered how handsome he was. His time in the country had done him good, returning the healthy flush to his skin and the self-assurance to his voice.

She wanted him back, but he had found this Lady Mariel to replace her. That would change soon, she vowed. How, she did not know, but she intended to find some way to get rid of this Mariel and take her place.

Ian felt Portia's intense glare on them. From the tight expression on Mariel's face, he knew she sensed the rage as well. Tucking her hand in the crook of his arm, he asked quietly, "Do you want to attempt that dance now?"

"If you feel well enough."

"At least the blow to my head will give me an excuse for my clumsiness." When she laughed, he placed his cane against a chair and added, "If you will excuse us, Mother."

"Of course." She fluttered her fan to hide her pride in her only child. When Ian had left for his calling to the western coast, she had feared he would shut himself away in his work and not remember the man he had been before the accident nearly destroyed his life. With the help of the woman he so clearly adored, he had recovered that joy.

As Mariel stepped into Ian's arms, she whispered, "Is everyone watching?"

"No. One of the servants is answering the door." He laughed as he drew her closer. "Everyone is curious to see how we do."

"Shall we surprise them?"

Mariel did not admit aloud that she was the one surprised as Ian waltzed her with little difficulty along the floor. Soon she forgot the ones who must still be watching with avid curiosity. Losing herself in the rhythm of the music, she followed his steps easily. To the refrain of the waltz, he twirled her about so her full skirts swept the floor in a wide circle.

He smiled as he saw her eyes were closed. Her face glowed with happiness. His arm tightened around her to draw her closer than etiquette allowed. He did not care what anyone else thought. To enjoy this moment of holding her lithe form against him erased the memories Portia's presence had brought forth. He forgot the other woman. While he led Mariel through the pattern of the dance, his fingers stroked her back. When her head rested against his shoulder, he whispered, "Tired?"

"No." She did not add anything more as she heard the music fade into the night. With a sigh, she stepped away from him.

"Another dance, or shall we let the others have the floor again?"

A warm flush tinted her cheeks prettily. "There are no others dancing?"

He laughed. As the orchestra leader raised his baton, he drew her to him again. "Don't worry about them, my love. Tonight is for us."

Placing her head against the strength of his shoulder, she let the music sweep her away into the love she could not forsake any longer. Softly, she whispered, "Do you have any other old lovers I need to concern myself with?"

"Old?" He chuckled. "I doubt if Portia would enjoy being called that. No, my love, there are no others. Forgive me for losing you in the crowd. One moment you were there. The next I was fighting off a surprisingly amorous Portia. Where did you go?"

"Dancing."

"Dancing?" Boyish astonishment colored his voice, and she laughed. "An old lover, Mariel?"

"I have had no lover but you, Reverend," she retorted pertly. Her fingers curled around the back of his neck to tease the small hairs there. "And there is no other I want."

Not caring about the crowd around them, he paused in the middle of the pattern. As the others whirled to the light tune, he brought her lips beneath his. The music disappeared into the distance as she answered his passion with her own. Desperately, they grasped for the happiness they could share, not suspecting, in their dreams of happiness, the threat awaiting them.

Chapter Sixteen

Mariel rose late to find the others in Ian's house busy with their plans for the day. Phipps and Rosie had left earlier to visit some of the historical sights of London. Although the woman had spoken of the need for the child to learn of her country's great heritage, Mariel suspected Phipps was more interested than the little girl in seeing the castles and cathedrals.

Ian ate a quick luncheon with her, then excused himself. "I have to do some errands today. Mother is very capable of dealing with the solicitors, but she cannot tolerate the senior partners. Whenever she can, she has me meet with them."

"Of course, you must go."

"What will you do?"

She smiled as she took his hand. "I will enjoy a quiet day here. We have been so busy, and tomorrow is my appointment with the doctor. I think I deserve some peace."

Gently, he kissed her. "Don't worry about tomorrow, my love."

"Don't ask the impossible." She stroked his smoothly shaven face. "I cannot help being nervous." With a light laugh, she said, "Go! The quicker you deal with that business, the quicker you will be home to help me wait until tomorrow afternoon."

"I will hurry." He bent to whisper in her ear. Her eyes closed in silent delight as his arms enfolded her to

him. "I would be happy to do whatever you want to help
the time pass more quickly."

Tilting her face, he kissed her with the passion he
found impossible to hide. He drew her to her feet and
against him. The soft caress of her body against him
urged him to lead her upstairs. In the long weeks since
the few nights they had spent in paradise, he had been
suffused by the savage yearning to love her again.

"I love you, Mariel," he whispered.

Instead of stiffening, as she had each time he
approached her in Foxbridge, she answered as softly, "I
love you, too. I am sorry I have been so distant. Give me
time, Ian."

"All you want, my love." He could not help smiling
as he saw the invitation on her face. "I shan't be long.
Tonight, I think you and I have something to talk
about."

Bemused by the kisses he sprinkled on her face
amid his words, she nodded. When he released her, she
wanted to pull him back to her. She reminded herself
that he would be home soon. Then she would tell him
the truth about why she had refused to accept his
proposal in the past. If he wanted her when he knew the
risks, she knew she could pretend no longer. She wanted
to be his.

Those pleasant dreams were still with her when she
walked out of the house to sit on the bench in the small,
front garden. She enjoyed listening to the rattle of the
conveyances passing on the street. Accustomed to the
wide open spaces of the ocean, she found the city
claustrophobic. The late-afternoon sunshine on her face
and the aroma of the breeze through the last of the
summer blossoms eased that sensation.

They had two more days in London. Then they
would be returning to Foxbridge with the final prognosis.
If Ian spoke to her tonight about the subject she was
sure hid in his heart, there would be dissatisfaction
among his parishioners. Mrs. Rivers was only the most
verbal of her detractors. Others would be displeased to
see a match between Lady Mariel and the reverend.

Sunk deep in her thoughts, Mariel did not notice the
carriage, which slowed as it moved along the street. Only

when it pulled even with the house did she react. She
tensed on her seat by the doorway.

She heard its door opening. A man leapt out, his
boots loud on the cobbles. She asked, "Yes? Can I help
you, sir?"

He moved closer to her, and her brow threaded
with unease. That he did not speak disquieted her. Most
of the ones who called at this house knew she could not
see them. The guests made a point of speaking or
identifying themselves immediately to set her at ease. He
merely continued to walk toward her. As he stepped too
close, she involuntarily leaned backward. She bumped
into the wall of the house.

"Lady Mariel? How are you today?"

"Mr. Muir!" she gasped when his voice identified
him as the man who had taunted them at the ball the
previous night.

"Yes." He laughed, before saying in a condescend-
ing tone, "Very good, my lady."

She knew her startled reaction betrayed her. Cooly,
she said, "You must excuse me, Mr. Muir. If you wish
to apologize to Ian for your beastly behavior, you will
have to return later this evening. He is busy this afternoon." She stood. "If you will excuse me, sir. . ."

As she turned to enter the house, her nose bumped
into his silk waistcoat. Although she was sure he purposely had stepped in front of her, she started to pardon
herself. He put his hand onto her arm. Her fear escalated as she tried to tug away from him, and his grip
became a painful vise.

"What do you want?" she cried.

"It is a lovely day, Mariel," answered Muir as he
drew her along the short walk to the street. "I thought
you might enjoy a ride. That is all. My carriage is
waiting. Shall we go?"

"I don't think so. I have a very important appointment tomorrow, and I must prepare myself." She tried
to jerk her arm out of his grasp. "Good day, Mr. Muir."

He laughed. "A short ride through the park will not
take much of your time and will allow me to atone for
what you so graciously call my 'beastly behavior.'
Please."

She nodded, knowing she had to let him think he had her fooled. From his eager tone, she was sure he wanted only to cause her more trouble. As he turned her to walk toward the carriage, she went without protest.

He opened the carriage door. At the same time, she pretended to stumble. "My shoe button is loose. May I fix it?" she asked innocuously.

Grudgingly, he agreed. She bent, as if to check the shoe. When he released her, she paused only a moment. Then she exploded from her crouched position to race toward the house. She heard the shouts behind her, but she did not hesitate.

Arms caught her. A hand covered her mouth as she took a breath to scream. Her flailing legs were smothered by her gown while he kept her arms pinned to her sides. She was shoved into the carriage seconds before an order sent it careening down the street. As it rounded a corner, she was rocked from her knees to sit roughly on the floor. Feminine laughter brought her head up as she groped for the edge of the seat.

"Rupert, will you get her up? She is going to wrinkle my best visiting gown."

Wide hands grasped her waist and lifted her to a seat. She clung to the velvet upholstery as the vehicle continued at a breakneck speed along the streets. When she realized the driver must know these narrow avenues well, she relaxed. Turning to the man next to her, she demanded, "Is there any hope that you will give me an explanation for your continuing beastly behavior, Mr. Muir? Or you, Miss Muir?"

"Lady Mariel," drawled the woman in the same derogatory tone her brother had used with Ian the previous night, "we don't like you."

"Isn't that marvelous? We have something in common. I don't like you." She tucked her messed-up hair under her garden hat. Her fingers caught in the loosened veil, and she realized it was ripped. "Now why don't you take me back to the house?"

"Are you familiar with London, my lady?" asked Muir as he leaned back on the seat. "It is beautiful, indeed, with all the extravaganzas for the queen's diamond jubilee."

"I have heard that."

He twisted her face toward him. "Ah, I forget. These lovely eyes see nothing. It is a shame, isn't it, Portia? Yet, it seems so appropriate. How often we have been urged to pray for the halt and the blind! The Reverend Beckwith-Carter and Lady Mariel Wythe."

Her lips tightened as she pulled away from him. "I understand that remark garnered you a black eye at the ball. For a so-called cripple, Ian has a wonderful left hook. Don't you agree?"

When his hand impacted on her face, she almost fell to the floor. Clutching her reeling head in her hands, she leaned against the wall of the carriage and implored her stomach not to be ill. She listened through the rush of sound in her ears as Portia argued with her brother. That the woman would protest his treatment of her was a surprise.

Then she realized Portia was not complaining about him striking her. They were discussing what they would do to her. Her hand slid along the wall of the carriage as she edged across the seat. The carriage continued at its reckless pace, but it must slow when they reached the more well traveled streets. If she could find the door latch, she might have a chance to escape.

"It is two inches below your hand, my lady," offered Rupert with a laugh. His arm slipped around her waist and pulled her against the back of the seat.

When his other hand settled familiarly on her breast, she screamed and fought to avoid him. He simply laughed again as he captured her mouth beneath his. Her hands pressed against his chest as he pushed her inexorably into the hard boards she could feel beneath the upholstery.

He growled as he moved away from her suddenly. She backed into a corner of the seat, her arms wrapped around herself in a protective pose. Her breath was rapid from her fierce attempts to free herself. Struggling to control her fear, she listened as brother and sister continued to argue about her fate.

"Enough of that, Rupert."

"Why don't you just shut up?"

Her sneer was directed at Mariel as she stated, "I don't understand why you would want to touch her."

"You aren't blind, sister. Look at her. Even with her useless eyes, she is a beauty." He chortled maliciously. "You are jealous because your darling Ian wants her more than he ever wanted you."

"Jealous of that?" She sniffed inelegantly. "She probably is as mad as the rest of her family. Once Ian adjusts to her disappearance, he will be happy to have a normal woman to love."

Mariel could tolerate no more of their easy assumption that she would sit docilely through their insults. "Ian doesn't want you, Portia. He never will. He thinks you are ill-mannered and stupid."

When Muir laughed, his sister cried, "Will you allow her to say things like that to me?"

"I did, didn't I?" His voice darkened as he stated, "Why should I defend you when you refuse to let me treat her as I wish?"

"How long after Ian discovers her missing do you think it will be before he shows up on our doorstep? If you have her upstairs in your rooms, I think you will suffer more than a black eye." Portia snapped, "Find yourself another whore to take as your mistress! I want this woman out of my life for good."

Mariel listened as Rupert mumbled some sort of agreement. Fear more powerful than before surged through her. The Muirs intended to do more than simply threaten her. They planned to do her harm. Rage overwhelmed her fright. She would not meekly let them do as they wished. With her hands behind her back, she drew off the lovely ring she always wore. Her fingers pushed it down between the cushions. If something happened to her, and it appeared it would, the Muirs would be prime suspects. The police might find the ring if they searched for clues. It would signal she had ridden in the carriage.

From the street came the bilious stench of waste. It grew stronger as the carriage slowed. She could tell they were going through narrow alleys. The sunshine that warmed her face had disappeared. Voices of children followed the carriage. She could hear them begging for alms. Her terror returned as she realized the disgusting part of the city that lay around them.

A rap on the ceiling halted the vehicle. Portia reached past her to open the door. Her sickly sweet perfume was a nauseating contrast to the horrible reek of the streets. When Rupert took Mariel's hand and ordered her from the carriage, she knew resistance would be futile.

She lowered herself carefully onto the small metal step. Her foot was reaching tentatively for the ground when the carriage lurched into motion. A hand in the center of her back pushed her away from the deadly wheels, which churned through a puddle and sprayed her in the seconds before she fell into it herself.

Mariel lifted herself from the water at the edge of the street. As mud oozed around her, she hoped it was only rainwater she had fallen in. She felt fingers on her skirt and batted them away. A childish laugh warned her about the part of London in which she had been abandoned. Pickpockets started young.

Cautiously, she stepped up onto the curb. Using the senses she still possessed, she moved along the narrow, crowded street. It had been wide enough for the carriage to maneuver, so it was not one of the narrowest, most decadent alleys. The Muirs would not think of her again. They had had their enjoyment and had no expectations she would survive to escape this horror.

Her hand slid along the wall of a brick house. Steep stairs leading to its doorway were the only break in the hard surface. Before she had gone more than a few paces, she found herself surrounded by a dozen urchins. All of them pushed their hands beneath her nose.

"I have nothing to give you," she said sternly. She hoped her demeanor would urge them to leave her alone.

A growl met her words. One, tall enough so his face was level with hers, pushed close. She backed away from the reek of rum on his breath. When he spoke, she could hear his voice was deeper. She feared this older lad was the leader of this gang of young criminals. One of the boys called him "Cap'n. " That no one on the street had come to her aid warned her she could not expect any.

"Pretty lady, think again." The cold metal of a knife pressed close to her cheek.

Her hands trembled as they raised to her ears. He slapped them away as they were working to remove her jewel encrusted earbobs. With a vicious jerk, he pulled them off painfully. More patiently, he waited for her to undo the clasp at the back of her necklace. He crowed with delight as he accepted the sapphire and gold pendant, which had been in her family for countless generations.

"The rest!" he ordered.

"That is all the jewelry I am wearing. I have no money."

He lifted her hand and held it before her face. "There be a mark here. Ye be wearing a ring, pretty lady. Don't think ye can be playing Cap for a fool. I want it!"

"It's gone."

The knife moved to rest beneath her jawbone. One quick, upward motion would slice into her jugular vein. She froze. When he demanded the ring again, she whispered, "I told you the truth. I have no other jewelry. My—my lover took it back before he threw me in the street. He was so angry, he forgot to take the rest." She warmed to her tale as she felt the knife draw back from her. "The bastard!" she spat.

Laughter greeted her faked rage. The tall boy leaned forward and kissed her squarely on the lips. "Thanks, pretty lady. Next time you leave your rich lover, be sure to come this way again."

She closed her eyes as she sagged against the wall behind her. She wondered if the boys realized the value of the pieces they had stolen. Not likely. They would be cheated by whomever they sold them to. That person would find someone eager to buy such priceless jewelry at a low cost and with no questions about who once owned it.

Gathering up the shreds of her courage, she started again in the direction the carriage had been heading. She did not trust the Muirs to bring her directly here but she was sure they would seek the quickest way out of this slum.

No one said anything to her, except to growl in her direction. She heard the harsh accents of the area as food and stolen goods were hawked openly on the street. After once asking someone for directions and being told what it would cost her, she did not pause again. No one did anything without a reward. She was not yet desperate enough to trade herself for the promise of directions.

Her legs grew heavy as she tried to avoid the broken cobbles and the debris on the street. More than once, she stepped into reeking wetness. She wondered how anyone could live in this sickening place, but such thoughts vanished as she thought only of placing one foot in front of the other.

Music poured out of a place that stank of cheap rum. She hurried past. A woman alone in a place like that would be easy prey. She was in enough trouble already.

"Miss?"

The scratchy voice in front of her forced her to pause. Carefully, she asked, "Yes?"

"Be ye lost?"

"Yes. I need to find a hansom to take me home."

A deep but feminine chuckle met her words. "Ye'll not be finding the likes of that here at this time of the evening, dearie. They'll not be coming here after dark."

"After dark?" she gasped involuntarily. She had lost track of time and had no idea that the sun had set. In the caverns of the tenement houses, the sunset changed little.

"Ye cannot be staying on the street, dearie." A hand resembling the claws of a bird grasped her arm. "Who be ye?"

"Mariel Wythe," she said reluctantly.

Fingers grasped the material of her ruined skirt. "This be costly. I be thinking ye have a title."

"My uncle is Lord Foxbridge of Foxbridge Cloister on the western coast." She was sure this strange woman wanted the information to garner herself a grander reward for helping her find her way home. Exhausted,

Mariel would have promised her almost anything to repay her assistance.

"Lady Mariel Wythe ye be?" The woman chuckled again. "Well, well, 'tis seldom we be getting a fine lady here."

"Can you help me get home?"

"Not tonight." She put her face close to Mariel. The reek of perspiration-soaked wool and cabbage made Mariel's stomach churn uneasily. "Ye best come home with me. I'll find ye a bed among my girls."

"Girls?" She did not want to move when the nameless woman tugged on her arm, but her tired body could not resist. "Your family?"

"Nay, I be speaking of the girls who work in m'shop. They'll not deny Lady Mariel Wythe a bed tonight." Another jerk on her arm accented the command to follow.

As the woman led her along the street, she stumbled again and again. Exasperated, the woman demanded, "What be wrong with ye, dearie?"

"You are going too fast. My feet can't find the best route this way."

Suddenly the woman halted. "Feet? Look where ye be going."

"I can't," she whispered. She moved backward as she felt a hand flash before her face. Her unease increased as she heard the woman chuckle again.

"Can't see? Shame." Her satisfied tone did not match her sympathetic words. "Don't be worrying. Kitty'll take care of ye. Come, dearie."

Mariel wondered how much the woman truly longed to help her as she drew her up steps without bothering to let her know when they started and stopped. She nearly fell more than once on the uneven stairs. They went into a house filled with many female voices. From the sounds, she guessed there was a large room to the left and a staircase leading up on the right. She was drawn past both to the back of the house.

A heavy hand shoved her onto a bench. Before she could protest, someone pulled off her hat. Where they put it she could not hear as the room became crowded with chattering women. Cheap perfume and the rustle of well starched linen and lace could be heard in every direction.

She relaxed, guessing these girls were the ones who worked for Kitty. With the sound of so much lace, she decided this must be a dressmaker's shop. No wonder the woman laughed. A blind, titled lady would be of little use in such an establishment.

"Eat," urged Kitty when a dish was dropped in front of Mariel. Some of the food splashed onto the oilcloth on the tabletop, but no one bothered to clean it up. A spoon was pressed into her hand. The woman's hand fondled Mariel's hair. "Pretty, ye be, m'lady. Right pretty."

"I must send a message—"

Kitty interrupted her. "Not now. Eat, m'lady. Eat. Then I'll be taking ye to yer room." With a raspy chuckle, she wandered away.

She ate the tasteless mush with relish. The other women chattered eagerly, but she did not join the conversation. She wondered how they could have so much energy after the long hours they must spend working over the fine lace and materials their clients would demand.

Kitty returned. She did not urge Mariel to follow the others toward the large room at the front of the house. Instead, she took her up the kitchen stairs. Mariel's fingers moved along the filthy surface of the wall, as she automatically counted the number of steps and the doors along the hallway. Such skills no longer took any more thought than breathing.

A door opened with a squeal of protest. "Ye be using this room," she said. "The bowl's to yer left. See ye tomorrow." With another of her scratchy chuckles, she added, "Ain't what ye be used to, m'lady. Enjoy it tonight."

"Thank you."

She mumbled something and left. Mariel walked toward where she thought the bed would be. In only three steps she bumped into it. The room was far smaller than she had guessed. It did not take her long to explore it. Other than the bed, and a washbowl on a table with uneven legs, she discovered only the door and a window, which would not open.

Dirt met her fingertips whichever way she turned. She wondered how Kitty could allow such shoddy housekeeping in a place where fine fabrics would be stored. Telling herself this might simply be an unused room, dusty with time, she took off her shoes and reclined on the unyielding bed. She tried not to think about the bugs that might be sharing it with her.

Her foot touched the footboard, and it wobbled. She checked it carefully. The top board nearly fell off in her hands, but she thought it would last through the night. She doubted if she would sleep much.

Ian would not, that she knew. Tears filled her eyes, not for herself, but for the man she loved. If their situations were reversed, she would be mad with fear for him. He would be searching for her, unable to guess where she was. She wished she could reach out to him and Rosie to let them know she was safe. Although her situation was far from ideal, she did not have to worry about the worst element of the street tonight.

Tomorrow she would implore Kitty to find her a cab. Somehow, she would get back to Ian or his mother, even though she did not know the addresses of their houses. Cynthia lived in Kensington. That would help in her search. If she could not find those homes, she would have the driver find Dr. Gillette's office. She could send for them from there. She was not totally helpless. Somehow she would escape alive from the Muirs' plot to enable Portia to worm her way back into Ian's life.

Somehow.

Slapping at a bug determined to sample her, she rolled onto her side and put her hand beneath her cheek. It would be a long day tomorrow. She would be wise to sleep as much as she could tonight. That was easier to decide than to put into action. Her heart continued to beat rapidly while she imagined what she would say to the Muirs when they stood face-to-face again.

She had not been resting long when a sound came from the hall. In astonishment, she listened as the squeak signaled the door was opening. "Who is it?" she whispered when she heard the door close again. "Who is there?"

The sound of heavy footsteps neared, and she rose to crouch on the bed. Her heart beat so loudly in her ears she could barely hear the boots on the floor. When she felt a hand on her shoulder, she screamed in horror. The sound was halted by rubbery lips settling on hers. She was forced back onto the mattress. She heard the bed creak as whoever held her moved to pin her to the bed.

Fear gave her strength. She fought her way out of the stranger's grip and slid off the bed. "Get away!" she cried. "Get out of here, or I will call the police. How dare you touch me like that?"

He laughed. "She said ye be ladylike. Ye surely sound it, me lovely."

"She?"

The scratch of a match warned her the man was lighting a lantern. She raced for the door. Grasping the knob, she turned it and tugged. She cried in horror when it would not open. Her fingers moved along the wood. A splinter cut into her, but she paid it no attention as she sought a latch. She could not remember one. Her questing hand touched a steel-hard arm over her head, holding the door shut.

When the same moist lips settled on the back of her neck, she redoubled her efforts to rip the door open. A hand reached for the ribbon holding her skirts around her waist. She whirled to press her back against the door.

"Don't!" she moaned. "Please leave me alone. Please."

He laughed. "Enough of the ladylike, me lovely. Lie down and let me be having ye. Kitty did tell me ye would be a feisty gal, but I want ye now, me lovely."

Material ripped as she struggled away from him. Running to the washstand, she raised the china pitcher. With a crash against the edge of the table, she shattered it. She held a razor-sharp piece in front of her.

"Get out of here!" she cried. "If you don't leave now, I will. . ." She did not know what she would do if he pushed her further.

When the door creaked open, she turned expectantly. This must be aid. "What be the problem?" Mariel gasped when she realized Kitty spoke not to her, but to the man.

"She be too reluctant."

"New girl. I thought ye would like her."

He growled, "Not enough to risk her cutting into me."

In a conciliatory voice, Kitty murmured, "Go two doors down. Zola will take care of ye."

When the door closed behind the man, Kitty crossed the room and knocked the china from Mariel's hand. As viciously, she slapped her across the face. Ignoring the younger woman's cry of pain, she asked, "Why did ye turn that man away? Good man, he is. He would not be too rough with ye this first time."

"Why should I want to let that man touch me?"

Kitty chortled. "Ye may be a fine lady, but ye are a fool. What did you think this was? A boardinghouse? I don't look about the streets for girls to make hats." She grasped Mariel's arm as she tried to edge toward the door. Again the back of her hand impacted on the young woman's face. " 'Tain't sewing ye'll be doing for Kitty, my dearie."

"I won't—I won't do that!"

"Ye don't want to work for yer food? Then ye won't eat."

"I won't stay here!" asserted Mariel. "I won't act the whore for you. If you are smart, you will allow me to leave before my family comes to find me."

Kitty laughed humorlessly. "Ye think they'll find ye? In all the sewers of London, what makes ye think they'll look here?" She shoved Mariel back on the bed. "Ye ain't no lady no more, *Lady* Mariel Wythe. Ye be working for Kitty." Her heavy shoes crossed the floor. "Ye think on that, girl. I give ye one hour. If ye turn aside the next customer I send to ye, ye'll be sorry ye did."

Mariel flinched as she heard the door slam. The sliding of a bolt on the far side told her she had been locked in. One hour did not offer her much time, but she knew what she must do. With a screech to cover the sound of her actions, she pounded both feet against the loose board at the foot of the bed. It popped off with a crash.

Trying to avoid the pieces of the broken ewer, she sought the board. She walked to the window. She measured the distance from it to the board. Again she screamed as she rammed the wood through the window. She prayed Kitty and the other denizens of this house would think she was raging against her fate. If they heard her trying to find her way out, her hour's reprieve would vanish.

Night coolness flowed into the room, bringing with it all the disgusting smells of the neighborhood. She ignored the odors as she used the board to knock out every sliver of glass in the frame. Placing the board on the floor, she went to the other side of the bed and picked up several of the largest pieces of the broken crockery.

It was not easy to concentrate as she held one chunk out the window. At any moment, someone could come to investigate her screams, or worse. Pushing those thoughts from her mind, she thought only of the sound of the china as it dropped from her hand. She smiled as she heard it impact on a surface not far below her window.

She hastily tugged on the end of the bed until it sat beneath the window. Within seconds, she had climbed onto it and was squeezing through the narrow opening. Her clothes caught on the sharp edges. Scratches were etched into her arms as the fabric shredded. She thought only of the need for silence as she lowered herself feet first toward the roof below her window. When she had stretched as far as she could, her toes still did not reach the shingles.

Her fingers lost their grasp on the windowsill, and she tried to land quietly and without breaking a bone. She slammed into the wall closest to her and sat down harshly on the sloping roof. Tears of pain stung her eyes and ran along her cheeks, but she did not bother to wipe them away as she drew another piece of the shattered pitcher from her pocket.

Gently, she shoved it away from her. It rolled a short distance and stopped. Although she did not want to leave her perch, she moved in the direction of the broken china. Her hand swept the cracked tiles until she found it. Cautiously, she explored the area beyond it. A drainpipe had halted it.

Wrapping her arm around the pipe, she leaned forward and tapped the china lightly on the roof until she found its edge. She dropped the ceramic again. A smile crossed her dirty face as she heard it hit quickly. The ground was not far below her.

She slid forward until her feet hung over the eaves. Behind her, her skirts left a pattern of torn cloth to decorate the roof and offer material for the starlings to use in building their nests. Her tongue dampened her chapped lips as she rolled over onto her stomach. Again she went feet first, grateful for the years of climbing trees at the Cloister.

When her toes touched the top of a window molding, she drew them back hastily. She could not risk being seen. Kitty would delight in punishing her for ruining the room and daring to defy her orders. Neither could she stay here long. Her hour dwindled away too quickly.

Moving a few feet farther along the eaves, she tried again. This time she felt only the crumbling brick beneath her feet. She breathed a prayer as she released her hands from the protesting eaves.

Pain shot along her body as she fell onto the hard street. She could not move as she fought to regain the breath knocked from her. If someone had come to see what had caused the noise, she would not have been able to run away. She concentrated on breathing. As soon as she thought she could stand, she fought her way to her feet.

With her head against the wall, she listened. At first, all she could hear was the harsh sound of her own breathing and the clangor of her pulse in her head. Then she noted the scurrying sound of rats followed by the victorious meow of a cat. From a good distance, away on the left, came the sound of jovial voices and the clank of metal. Whether that was Kitty's house or another serving libations to the residents of this slum, she did not care. She knew she did not want to go that way.

Determined to escape from this place, if only to make the Muirs pay for this cruelty, she turned her back on the voices. She did not know where she was going. All she knew was that she must succeed. To fail would mean her death, or working for another woman no better than Kitty.

Chapter Seventeen

Mariel lurched along the deserted street, trying not to notice the searing pain in her right ankle. Again she longed for her cane. Although she had despised it when Ian first gave it to her, she had come to appreciate what it could show her. Leaning on the staff to ease her anguish would have been welcome.

When she reached the end of the street, she turned right only because that way she did not have to cross the road. The Muirs had made sure she could not guess where they had taken her. Their antics in the carriage had distracted her from keeping track of the turns of the vehicle. Even so, she was sure their driver must have had instructions to take a circuitous journey to where they intended to abandon her.

Although she knew it was insane to be out on these streets at night, Mariel thought how much worse it would be to stay at Kitty's house. She could not blame that debacle on her blindness. Only her blatant naivete had led her into that situation.

She moaned as the agony in her leg increased. Dropping to a set of stairs, she touched the aching ankle. Tears burst from her eyes again. It felt as if a million small fires burned within it. She began to fear she might have broken something. That would be tragically ironic. In the automobile accident, she had survived with minor injuries except for her blindness.

Here, in an insane race from a wicked woman determined to prostitute her, she had hurt herself this badly.

"Are you going to sit here in the cold all night?"

Her head jerked up at the male voice. She longed to flee, but she was too tired. Running through the labyrinth of streets would only send her into more trouble. She lowered her head to her arms, folded on her drawn-up knees.

"Answer me, girl!"

"Yes!" she snapped. "I am going to sit here as long as I please."

A jovial laugh washed over her, coming closer as the man bent down to put his face even with hers. "What are you doing here? Why don't you go home?"

"I don't know how to get there."

"So you intend to sit here until the sun shows you the way?"

She turned her face away from him. Her tangled hair dropped heavily along her arm. "I intend to sit here as long as I please."

Broad fingers, rough with work, twisted with age, caught her chin between them. Instinctively, she drew back as she felt a motion in front of her face. Sympathy entered the man's voice. "Poor child. Can't see, can you? And lost, too. You can't sleep out here, even though it isn't long until dawn. Let me take you to my home. It is just across the street. You can sleep there."

"No!" she stated emphatically when he tugged on her hand. "I have had enough of the hospitality of this part of London. I will stay here."

Quietly, he asked, "Whose?"

"A woman named Kitty."

His surprisingly cultured voice snapped a series of phrases she could not understand. She knew he must be speaking a language other than English, but she could not decipher any of the sounds to give her a clue to which one it might be. When he apologized, it confirmed her guess that they were curses.

"How did you convince Kitty to let you go?" Even in the dim light, he could see the young woman in her tattered dress was a beauty. If the madam trapped a girl like this in her house, she would not let her free until she sucked her dry of every bit of her self-respect. Then the girl would have no choice but to stay as one of Kitty's bedraggled whores.

"I didn't." Proudly, she stated, "I broke the window and crawled across the roofs until I could find my way to the ground. I hurt my ankle when I dropped to the street."

"Alone? Without seeing?" Admiration filled his aged voice. "You would make a damned good soldier. Excuse me, miss."

She shook her head tiredly, trying to decide whether she wanted to cry or laugh. "Don't think about it. Please, just leave me alone."

"No, miss. You can't stay here. I saw you reeling down the sidewalk from my window across the street. You must get some shelter. Kitty isn't the only one of her type on the streets. You might get robbed."

Now she laughed. "That happened, too. I don't have anything left to give the street thieves."

His gnarled hand reached under her elbow and brought her to her feet. When she moaned again as she inadvertently put weight on her foot, he drew her right arm over his shoulder. In this awkward position, he led her to the opposite side of the street and up a dank smelling set of creaking stairs to a second floor room. She was too exhausted to speak her gratitude when he told her they had reached the last step. If he had not, she might have fallen on her face amid the dirt she could hear crunching beneath her shoes.

Mariel did not speak as he seated her in a chair. When he pushed the ripped remains of her skirt aside, she gasped. His hands were gentle as he unbuttoned and drew off her right boot. His murmur of dismay urged her to ask, "Is it that bad?"

"Purple as a royal robe. I mean—"

"It's all right," she assured him. "I have been without my sight only a few months now. I know colors."

She heard the clank of metal, and he explained he was getting a small tub for her, so she could soak her injured ankle. When he told her to be careful, for the water was hot, she lowered her foot into it slowly. The warmth was perfect, and she sighed gratefully.

"Thank you, Mr.—?"

"Sassoon, miss. And you are?"

"Mariel Wythe."

He handed her a cup filled with tea. "Where do you live, Miss Wythe?"

"Foxbridge Cloister, in— Oh, you mean here. I don't know the street address. This is terrible. I am here to see an eye doctor and am staying at the house of a friend. His name is Ian Beckwith-Carter."

"London is a big city, Miss Wythe. It could take us weeks to find your friend."

"If we contact the police. . ."

"Hmm." He seemed to consider it as if it was a novel suggestion. "Mayhap they can help. There is a constable who wanders by here occasionally. I will see him in the morning."

She turned toward where he sat. "Thank you, Mr. Sassoon. I have interrupted your night and now ask you to run errands for me. That is so much to ask."

"Nonsense." His chair scraped the floor as he rose. "You sit there a minute while I find an extra blanket."

Mariel savored the consoling warmth of the tea. Through its rich aroma, she could smell the grease of the poorly cleaned kitchen. The building reeked of too many people and too many years. She listened to the man's footsteps as he wandered about the small room.

When he put his hand on her shoulder, she started. She had not realized she was nearly asleep. That he did not mention her skittishness added to her obligation to this kind stranger. He helped her towel off her foot. Determined to be brave, she bit her lip as he touched her tender ankle.

"Do you think you can stand?" His finger gently wiped away the involuntary tears rolling down her cheeks. "I am sorry to hurt you."

"I know you did not mean to hurt me," she gulped around the blockage in her throat. "I think I can stand."

She learned how optimistic her words were when she tried and fell back into her chair with a soft cry. Mr. Sassoon patiently consoled her. Again he placed her arm around his neck. This time, she realized he could not be much taller than she, for he did not bend forward far.

He sat her on a narrow bed and told her to have a pleasant night's sleep. Running her hand along the coarse wool cover, she said, "But, Mr. Sassoon, I can't take your bed."

His smile shone through his gentle reprimand. "Where I come from, and I suspect where you come from, Miss Wythe, a lady is given the best the house has to offer. Go to sleep. Tomorrow we will begin looking for your fellow. Good night, Miss Wythe."

"Good night, Mr. Sassoon." She knew it was useless to protest. Even if she could keep her eyes open, she did not want to argue any longer. She wanted to enjoy the relative luxury of this bed.

As she closed her eyes and drew the paper-thin blanket over her, she was unaware of the old man's gaze on her. It went from her to an age-dimmed photograph sitting on the sideboard. The beautiful woman in the picture shared Mariel's dark hair, although it was impossible to determine the color of her eyes. It did not matter to the old man. He held every facet of her face in his heart, although his wife had been dead for more than twenty years.

In his mind, he could hear her lyrical voice urging him to take good care of the lost lamb that had wandered into his life. He did not need to hear her on this matter. Too many he had seen destroyed by Kitty and her counterparts along these streets. This was one woman who would escape back to the world where once he was welcome.

Mariel woke to the aroma of fresh coffee and something frying. Grease snapped with the heat. Sitting up, she rubbed her eyes. As she stretched, she heard threads break. She ran her hands along her ruined blouse and was pleased to discover it continued to protect her modesty.

"Good afternoon, Miss Wythe."

"Afternoon?"

He chuckled, a sound like the distant boom of cannon. "You did not get to sleep until near dawn. I figured it would be best if you woke on your own."

From the jaunty tone of Mr. Sassoon's voice, she knew he had good news for her. She did not have to wait long to hear it. After he urged her to sit at the table, he checked her ankle for her with gentle, efficient fingers.

"Looks good," he pronounced with satisfaction. "Never did see a sprain a good soak didn't help." Like an elfin sprite, he jumped to his feet and sat in the other chair. "Saw the constable. He is going to see about finding your Mr. Beckwith-Carter."

"That is wonderful!" she cried. "Thank you, Mr. Sassoon."

"You're welcome and more, Miss Wythe."

"Mariel," she corrected gently.

He laughed. "Mariel, it shall be. Do not be expecting to hear from your fellow right away. Like everything else, the police department is overwhelmed by the activities for the queen's jubilee. Not that I am complaining. Our good Victoria has made this mighty Empire proud. She deserves this celebration." He leaned forward and placed his elbows on the table. "I wasn't here for the last one a decade ago, so I've been enjoying the pageantry. Of course, you don't remember the golden jubilee. You must have been not much more than a youngster then."

His easy acceptance of her made her comfortable enough to tell him about the small celebration she recalled in Foxbridge. Memories of bonfires along the cliffs and dancing on the village green eased the lines of worry from her face. He asked many questions about the western coast.

"Been all over this world, but I have never seen that part of the island." He chuckled. "Is it as wild as they say?"

"Not any longer. With the coming of the trains, we are much the same as the rest of England. I guess it was different years ago." She took a sip of the rich coffee. "At least, that is what I hear from the stories of my more adventuresome ancestors."

When they finished the late breakfast, Mr. Sassoon ordered her to soak her ankle again. He left her to that task as he went out to find food for their supper. She wondered how he could afford to feed an extra person. Her brief exploration of the room after he left showed her there was little of value here. A sideboard, the table, bed, and chairs nearly filled the room. On the shelves, she found several tins containing tobacco, coffee, tea and sugar. Nothing more.

Grease streaked as she touched the warmth of the cast-iron stove. He must use it both for cooking and for heat. She wondered how long it had been since it was properly cleaned. She moved her chair next to it. While she soaked her foot in the warm water, she used a rancid cloth to remove the most pungent filth. Although there was little she could do, she felt better offering something in exchange for the welcome her savior had given her.

Mr. Sassoon exclaimed over her work when he returned, and he urged her not to do more than she felt comfortable doing. He cooked a simple supper. While she set the table with the few dishes he owned, he shared the news he had heard on the street.

A knock on the door interrupted them just as they were about to sit down for their meal. With a grumble and creaking joints, he went to answer it. She heard him urge the caller to enter.

"Go ahead, boy," he commanded.

Mariel strained to discover what was happening as footsteps approached her. Someone lifted her hands, and she gasped as three objects were dropped into them. Instantly, she identified the uneven edges of stones and jewels as the jewelry stolen from her the previous day.

"Thank—thank you," she managed to say as she closed her fingers over the necklace and earrings.

"Boy!" Mr. Sassoon's voice was sterner than she had ever heard it.

In a drawling, superior tone she recognized as that of the "Cap'n" who led the band of hooligans, he stated, "Pretty lady, ye should have been telling me ye be a friend of Mr. Sassoon. We don't take from our friends. Only from snotty, uppity ladies and gents." He turned away to ask, "Is that good enough?"

"A bit of sincerity might be more in keeping with an apology," mused the older man. He looked directly at the scrawny boy, whose bones appeared ready to out-grow his skin. Fiercely stubborn spikes of black hair sprouted in every direction and nearly hid his intelligent eyes.

"Have you eaten, Cap?"

He started to answer with braggadocio, then hesitated. Having given back the fine pieces, he would not have coins to buy food until he could find his next wealthy victim. There was no guarantee if that would be tomorrow or next week. With a grin at the old man, who was unbent by the passage of years, he sat on the bed, held out his hands, and asked for a trencher.

"Wash your hands before you eat with us," ordered Mariel as she rehooked the necklace around her neck for safekeeping.

"Lordy. She may be pretty," complained the lad, "but she carps at me like a fishwife, Mr. Sassoon."

Their host chuckled, delighted by the spirit Mariel showed. He had been concerned in the early hours of the morning that she would be traumatized by her experiences with the roughest elements of the city. She clearly had rebounded. "You heard her, Cap. Bucket is in the hall. Come back with hands that don't stink of the sewers and alehouses."

With a grumble about such silly conventions, Cap rose and stomped out of the room. He left the door open behind him. They could hear his less than enthusiastic splashing in the bucket.

"Thank you, Mr. Sassoon," she said quietly.

"Cap is not a bad boy, Mariel." When her eyebrows arched in blatant disagreement, he said, "Don't judge what you haven't lived. He is doing the best he can in this hell. So far, he has been lucky. He has stolen enough to survive, but not enough to attract the attention of either the police or the more vicious criminals who stake claim to these streets." More gently, he added, "When you told me about who robbed you, I guessed it was Cap and his boys. I sent him a message to bring your jewelry here. He owes me a few favors for nights when he had no place else to go."

Mariel asked, "If he is so bright, why isn't he in school?"

"Tried it once. They couldn't teach me nothing." She turned as the lad reentered the room. His steps were so light, even her keen ears could not detect them.

"Don't you want to be more than a petty thief?"

"Naw." He took the saltcellar and spooned a generous serving on his food. Taking a large spoonful, he chewed enthusiastically. Around the food in his mouth, he demanded, "Why do I want to be a banker in a big house driving to work every day? Too much money, and a man worries about it. Too little money, and ye worry about other things, like food and where ye'll sleep at sundown."

"If that's the way you feel about it, Cap. . ." She gasped as she felt the edge of his knife against her nose.

"Didn't tell ye to call me by m'name, pretty lady."

"Cap," stated Mr. Sassoon in an exasperated tone, "put that away or you can leave with your empty stomach. We are all friends here. Mariel doesn't mean any insult to you."

He glared at her as she smoothed her skirt to hide her trembling hands. Slipping his knife back into its easily accessible sheath, he snapped, "Then tell her to stop ordering me about. I do what I want."

Mariel bit back her retort as she dipped her spoon in the stew. It tasted a bit dull. She reached for the salt cellar, but it was not where she had put it. Her fingers swept the portion of the table next to where it should be. When Mr. Sassoon placed it in her fingers, she heard Cap's choking gasp. He spoke, but not to her.

"She be blind?"

Mr. Sassoon answered quietly, "I thought you knew that."

"I don't rob no blind folk." His outrage showed his wounded pride. He shared the few morals of the street, and he clung to those tenaciously. His voice softened as he asked, "What ye really be doing here, pretty lady? Ye didn't get thrown out by no lover. Who tossed ye on the street?"

It did not take her long to tell the simple tale. He whistled in appreciation as she told of her escape from Kitty's house. When she finished, he laughed. "Kitty is raising hell up and down the street about her broken

window and busted furniture. Ye are not so bad, pretty
lady."

"My name is Mariel." She smiled. Being compli-
mented so sincerely by Cap she recognized as a great
honor. Already she was liking the brash young man. He
reminded her of the young people she worked with in
Foxbridge, although they would have been insulted by
the comparison.

He gulped down another spoonful. Pushing his too
long, dark hair away from his mouth, he wiped his lips
on his tattered sleeve. "So I heard. Lady Mariel Wythe
is the one Kitty is offering a reward to have brought
back to her. Did think Kitty was fooling us, but ye be a
lady."

"Lady?" Now it was Mr. Sassoon's turn to be
shocked. "You did not mention that, Mariel."

She shrugged. "It is not important."

The old man did not reply, but she sensed her title
did make a difference to him. If possible, he treated her
even more kindly as the evening passed. When she
yawned, he urged her to go to bed. She did not ask if
Cap was staying. Since she told of her escape from Kitty,
the lad seemed to give her the respect he grudgingly
granted to few.

Occasionally, over the next few days, as she became
accustomed to living in the small apartment, Cap would
stop in and chat with her. He told her he wanted to
keep an eye on her while Mr. Sassoon was out shopping,
but she suspected he was interested in having a noncom-
petitive friend close to his own age. When she confided
in him her need to find her way back to Ian, he was
surprised.

"Why didn't ye ask me if ye needed help? Constable is no good here. We pay him enough to keep him
in the pub while we be working the street." He leaned
back in the chair and put his feet on the table. When
she knocked them to the floor with a thump, he laughed.

"Pretty lady, tell me the name of yer lover."

"Lover?" she asked lightly as she wiped the now
shining top of the stove. When she ran her fingers along
its comforting warmth, she felt only the smoothness of
the metal. "What makes you think Ian is my lover?"

"Ye smile when ye talk about him. Sure sign of being besotted. Is he a peer?"

She shook her head. "He is not a peer. He is a minister."

"Like the prime minister?"

"No, a church minister."

"Ye have a lover who's a bloody parson?" He swallowed the oath he was about to say. Shaking his head in sorrow, he said, "Are ye sure ye want me to find the blighter?"

"Can you?"

He leaned forward and tugged on her patched skirt. "Try me, pretty lady."

Mariel dampened her lips. If she sweetened the challenge, he would be more likely to put his street intelligence to work in solving the puzzle. Like him, she had come to see that the constable would do nothing. Mr. Sassoon so enjoyed her company, he did not seem in any hurry to have her leave.

She drew the necklace from beneath her shirt, knowing Cap's eyes would rivet on it. "I say you can't find him. I am willing to wager this necklace you will not be able to find him in twenty-four hours."

"Earbobs, too?"

"All right. Twenty-four hours. You must have Ian here."

Suspiciously, he demanded, "And if I don't find the rotter? Of course, I will, but I want to know what ye expect from me."

"If you don't, you go back to school and stay for at least a year."

"That is no bloody deal! That is blackmail."

She smiled as she sat down in the other chair. "If you don't want to try, it is all right with me. I would just as soon keep my jewelry. It's very valuable, you know. More than three hundred years old, I believe."

As she expected, the lure of the jewelry was more than Cap could ignore. "All right. Twenty-four hours. I'll leave now. Yer minister bloke will be here by this time tomorrow. Give me a description."

He listened intently as she told him about Ian, about his home and his mother's home, even about the doctor she should have met days before. When he asked questions, she discovered he already was narrowing the search to certain sections of the city. With a laugh, he patted her on the shoulder.

"Should be simple, pretty lady. See ye before this time tomorrow."

"I hope so," she replied fervently. She realized he had not heard her as she heard the door slam shut. From beyond the portal, the sound of his footsteps racing away told her he intended to win what he once had stolen.

Mariel did not tell Mr. Sassoon about her bargain with Cap. The old man had been so kind to her. She did not want to hurt his feelings by showing that his assistance had been ineffectual.

That night, as she lay on the hard cot listening to Mr. Sassoon's snores, she wondered if she was putting too much credence into a cocksure lad's boasting. She drew the blanket over her and wished Ian would find her and take her back to her own world.

The morning dawned cold and damp. The stove sputtered and died. Finally Mr. Sassoon coaxed it into giving them heat. While he went to find some coal, Mariel started breakfast. The embers were fading as he returned. He placed the few pieces on the fire and puffed them into flame.

She glanced up when she heard a knock and the door opened again. Her hands remained poised over the table. Her breath froze in her chest. Some sense she could not name loosened the wooden spoons from her hand to clatter on the bowls. She leapt forward into welcoming arms.

Her whisper of Ian's name vanished into his lips as he pressed them against hers. A hunger she had quelled too long erupted forth to engulf her in longing. In the months since the accident, she had forced him away when she needed him most. The familiar comfort of his arms around her sent tears coursing along her cheeks.

"Mariel!" He repeated her name over and over as he examined her. Except for her ragged clothes, she seemed unharmed. His lips touched her damp cheeks, her eyelids, the delicious flavor of her mouth. So long he had waited to kiss her and feared he never would again. The days of waiting to find some clue to her sudden disappearance had left him with worry lines engraved in his face.

He pressed her head to his chest as he heard her sob. Looking over her head, he met the eyes of the man who had opened the door. This must be the old one who had offered her shelter. He noted the clean, though threadbare, clothes the old man wore. Well shaven cheeks glistened beneath his bald pate.

Quietly, he said, "I am Ian Beckwith-Carter."

Mr. Sassoon laughed, although his throat was thick with emotion. "I guessed that, pastor. She's been waiting for you, pining for you."

Ian nodded absently. He stroked Mariel's back and leaned his cheek against the top of her head. By her kiss, he had learned she was ready to face the future instead of wallowing in the past and what could have been.

"Thank you," he said. "Thank you, Mr.—?"

"Name is Sassoon. Take care of her, pastor. She is a special lady."

Ian smiled, unable to hide his love. "That she is." Keeping his arm around her, he withdrew his wallet from his pocket. "Mr. Sassoon, what I owe you I cannot repay, but you have been taking care of Mariel."

Taking his pipe from his mouth, the old man waved it. "Don't want your money, Reverend. Man of your persuasion saved my life in India. I see as this makes us even."

"India? You are retired army?"

"Regimental sergeant for her majesty. Forty years I spent in that hellish country. Got there just in time for the Sepoy Mutiny in '57."

Ian glanced around the bare room. "Forty years? Don't you get a pension, Sergeant?"

He shrugged. "Used to. It doesn't come any longer. I figure Victoria is too busy. What with her jubilee and all."

With a smile, Ian asked the man for his full name and former regiment. Storing the information in the

back of his head, he vowed to call on his good friend
Colonel Hoppe as soon as things were settled with
Mariel. The colonel still had many connections in the
cabinet. He would find someone to help this man.

He thanked Mr. Sassoon again. Turning Mariel
toward the door, he was not surprised when she pulled
from his arms and rushed across the narrow room. The
old man smiled as he embraced her.

"Can I come to visit you again?" she asked tearful-
ly. She tried to smile. "I promise I will not stay such a
long time, next time."

"Come as often as you wish, Mariel." He drew her
fingers to his face, allowing her to do what he had seen
her try with Cap. "Now you will recognize this ugly old
man."

"Thank you," she whispered as she hugged him
again. "If it had not been for you. . ."

"You would have survived," he finished. "As I said,
you would have made a damn good soldier."

Mariel went with Ian out of the bare room and
down the rickety stairs. When he handed her into the
carriage, she asked, "Do you think you can help him?"

"You were listening?"

"I can cry and listen at the same time," she retorted
with a bit of her normal acerbity.

Taking her hands, he drew her closer on the seat.
"That you can, my darling." He tilted her face so he
could kiss her. The lingering caress left them both
breathless. As he was bending to kiss her again, he
heard a rap on the door.

"Pretty lady?" came a familiar voice. Cocky pride
filled his voice as Cap stated, "I found him with more
than four hours to spare."

Ian watched as Mariel removed the fabulous pieces
of jewelry from her ears and neck and handed them to
the lad who balanced on the running board of the
carriage. She folded his fingers over it.

"Thank you, Cap. Will you accept a word of advice
with your winnings?"

"I know what ye be thinking, pretty lady."

"Listen anyhow. You are a smart boy. Too smart to
end up in prison, or dead from a rival's knife. Get

yourself apprenticed somewhere. If you sell that jewelry, you will have enough to convince someone in the trades to teach you a skill." She smiled. "With your brains, you will own the company within five years."

He opened the door and leaned forward to kiss her on the cheek. "Pardon me, parson." He tipped his cap and disappeared into the crowd, which had gathered to regard the strange sight of such a magnificent carriage on such a poor street.

Ian rapped on the roof to signal the coachman to drive them home. When Mariel sighed, he said, "He may listen to you."

"Probably not. Cap can make a living easily by robbery and extortion. He can't imagine why he should work harder to make less money and have to report to a boss." She smiled. "I should not have doubted he would find you when I offered him such a reward."

He stroked the delicate profile of her face as he asked, "Who was it?"

Mariel knew exactly what he meant. Her brief happiness faded. "The Muirs."

"Both of them?"

She nodded. "They took me from in front of the house where I was enjoying the sun. They threw me out about five or six blocks from here. I don't know exactly. I got confused. After I ran away from Kitty's house, I—"

"Kitty?"

With a shiver, she nestled against his strength. "Not now, Ian. Just let me be happy to be back with you."

"Happy? I don't think I have seen you truly happy in over a month."

She brought his face to look at hers and grinned idiotically. When he laughed, she joined him. "Is that happy enough for you?"

He squeezed her. Whatever the doctor might say during the appointment he had rescheduled daily in the hopes of finding her, he thought Mariel had come to accept her infirmity. He wondered if she knew how he had feared for her. He should have known that no matter where she landed, Mariel Wythe would emerge alive.

Most of the servants in his house met them at the door. Some of them were crying. Others just stood silently as their grins swelled across their faces. They watched while Rosie welcomed Mariel home.

After a hug, which nearly strangled Mariel, the child stated emphatically, "You stink!"

Mariel laughed. "Not as bad as some of the places I visited. Let me get clean, and I will tell you all about it, Rosie." She could entertain the child with the least depraved parts of her adventures.

Phipps pushed through the crowd to throw her arms around Mariel. "My lady, I feared you were gone forever."

"Never." Mariel laughed with unfettered joy to be back where she belonged. This was her world. To hold her daughter again. To be with the man she loved and share the things that made up his life.

She closed her eyes and took a deep breath. The aroma of freshly baked bread mingled with that of the oil used to clean the furniture. It was a homey smell and welcomed her. Overhead the prisms hanging from the gaslight tinkled in the breeze from the open door. She was home.

Phipps silenced the questions of the rest of the staff and swept Mariel up the stairs. Cooing over her as if she was a child, the older woman ordered water run in her lady's bath. She hushed Mariel's attempts to explain what had happened. "Later, my lady. First we must get you into clean things."

When the bath was ready, Phipps collected the ruined clothes and told her lady she would bring Rosie later to listen to the full tale of her adventures. The older woman scurried away to find salve for her lady's scratches and order a dinner tray for her.

Mariel sank into the tub with a happy sigh. She had not bathed in a week. Every inch of her body was covered with dirt. The warm water soaked away the filth of the slum. Ducking her head under the water, she soaped her hair. When she reached for the bucket, which had been drawn and left for her to rinse, she frowned.

"Is this what you want, honey?"

She gasped as the water cascaded over her head. Sputtering with laughter and wiping soapsuds from her face, she whispered, "Ian, you should not be here. Phipps will be back. Rosie will be with her."

"They can't get in when the door is locked."

"Locked?"

"Here." He took the soap and washcloth. Rubbing them together, he gently cleaned her back. "Hmm. You smell better."

Enjoying the soft stroke of his hand against her, she said dreamily, "I think so, too. I hated being so dirty."

His hands moved along her slick body as he murmured in her ear, "I never saw you looking more beautiful than when I saw you standing at that old man's table. I feared you were dead, Mariel. No one I contacted in the government or at Scotland Yard could find a trace of you."

She put her fingers over his. "Ian, you should leave."

"Not until I kiss every inch of you, my love." He drew her back against the slanted side of the tub. Leaning over her, he pressed his lips to hers.

Water ran along her arms as she lifted them to wrap around his neck. When he urged her to stand, she stepped from the tub to stand beside him. Only when he pulled her close to him did she realize he was as naked as she was.

She laughed. "You are very sure of yourself, Ian Beckwith-Carter!"

"You traded your family heirlooms to find your way back to me. I figure you have been yearning for me as desperately I have yearned for you."

His hands moved along her skin. He sighed into her soaked hair. He had forgotten how silken soft she felt. She leaned against him, savoring the sweetness of his touch. His strength revived hers and, at the same time, allowed her to yield to his love.

"This is insane." Her murmur vanished into a gasp of delight as his fingers found the sensitive surface of her breast. She became lost in the bewitchment of his intriguing touch.

Fiery kisses seared her neck as he bent to taste her skin, which glowed warm in the sunlight. "Is it insane to want you so much I would commit any crime to possess you?"

She laughed softly. "I think that is the definition of insanity, Ian."

When he drew her back into the bedroom, she did not hesitate. Reclining on the bed, she held out her arms to him. Her eyes closed in unspoken delight as his fingers moved along her, reawakening the loving response she could share only with him.

True to his promise, he attempted not to miss an inch of her. His tongue etched a trail of rapture along her body, pausing to drive her to the edge of madness as he tasted her most sensitive place. Her soft laughs became sighs as she struggled to contain the longing, which grew to swallow her in its ecstasy.

Seeing she could control her passion no longer, he drew her to him to share their love. With her arms locked around his neck, she felt his rapid breath on her face. All senses dimmed as they merged into the boundless crystal ocean. Even their silent vows never to part again vanished as they became one for an eternal second of perfection.

Chapter Eighteen

Portia Muir glanced up from her needlework as the butler announced guests. She put her full-lipped smile securely in place. Smoothing the scarlet satin of her morning gown, she tugged on the leg-of-mutton sleeves to make them fuller. She was sure they would emphasize her slender waist.

She rose to greet the men walking into the room. Immediately, she dismissed the second man as she seductively offered her hand to his companion. "Why, Ian, what a wonderful surprise. After what you said at—never mind. It is so charming of you to call."

"Is your brother in?" he asked, ignoring her outstretched hand.

She drew it back when he made it clear he did not intend to touch her. Dressed in his dark suit with the clerical collar bright at his neck, he did not seem like the Ian she longed to entice into her arms. In a cooler tone, she asked, "Aren't you going to introduce me to your handsome friend?"

Ian hid his disgust with her simpering as he turned to his companion. "Portia, this is Scott Nelson, a friend of mine here in London. Scott, Portia Muir." His brows drew a furrow across his forehead. "Where is your brother?"

"One moment." She tugged on an embroidered bellpull. When a maid peeked nervously into the elabor-

ately decorated drawing room, she ordered, "Fetch Mr.
Muir. He is in the library."

"Library?" asked Ian sarcastically. "I did not
imagine your brother as the type to spend a rainy
afternoon in quiet contemplation. I figured him to be the
type to waste his time harassing the household maids."

She said with cold hauteur, "Those are strange
words for a clergyman."

"We are talking about how your brother has never
changed from his adolescent pursuits. Not about me,
Portia."

Seeing she would not entice Ian easily this afternoon, she turned her attention to the silent man by his
side. "My dear Mr. Nelson, you must think me remiss as
a hostess. Please sit down."

"I'd just as soon stand, Miss Muir," he stated
gruffly.

Not accustomed to failing with two men in such
quick succession, she said only, "As you wish." When
she heard footsteps in the hallway, she smiled. Let her
brother deal with these cold men. "Here is Rupert."

"Portia, why did you—oh, Beckwith-Carter." A snide
expression oozed across his face. "To what do I owe this
unexpected pleasure?"

Ian smiled. "I heard about your black eye, and I
wanted to see for myself if it was as grand as the gossips
stated." He paused dramatically, then laughed. "As
green as it is now, it must have been at least that puffy
and dark."

Muir flushed, dimming the contusion on his face.
That a crippled preacher had bested him in fisticuffs
was something he would not be allowed to forget. He
recalled his revenge and knew that despite Beckwith-
Carter's tone, he must be suffering the loss of his blind
heiress.

"If that is why you came here, why don't you and
your buddy leave?"

His smile vanished as Ian said, "Not without you
telling me what you did with Mariel's ring."

"Ring?" he gasped. He had been prepared to deny
knowing anything about the woman. This question about

a ring was something else altogether. He did not know what to say.

"Yes. A small gold band with two emeralds and a diamond. She wears it on her right hand. Her mother's wedding ring, I believe."

"Grandmother's."

Portia and Rupert spun to see Lady Mariel Wythe standing in the arch framed by the wine portieres which matched her stylish gown. She held the arm of a man they did not recognize. Instantly, Muir whirled to snarl, "You can't blame us for her abduction."

"Abduction, Mr. Muir?" Nelson pounced on the words. "I am surprised to hear you use that term. No one else has mentioned it before now."

"Rupert, be quiet!" cried Portia when he started to retort. She glared at the men and the woman she despised. "If my brother speaks of that, he is only repeating the gossip we have heard. I suggest you leave immediately, or I shall be forced to summon the police."

Ian grinned triumphantly as he drew Mariel to stand next to him. "No need to do that, Portia. I must have failed to fully introduce Detective Nelson and his partner Detective Rohm. Scotland Yard."

With perfect aplomb, Detective Nelson tipped his head in their direction. "I assume we will have your total cooperation during the investigation of this heinous crime. We will, of course, wish to search your carriage, where Lady Mariel assures us she left her ring. Later we will go to the Yard for the interrogation."

"It was all her idea!" spat Muir, pointing to his sister. "She wanted to get rid of the Wythe woman so she could have her parson back."

"Shut up!" Portia's pale face was a caricature of its normal beauty. "You were the one who suggested leaving her in Southwark. I only wanted to scare her. You left her to be murdered."

Muir spun to race toward the door, but halted as the burly Detective Rohm blocked his way. The policeman said politely, "Please wait with your sister, sir."

Ian asked softly, "Scott, do you need us any longer? Mariel has an appointment within the hour for which she has already waited too long."

"Go ahead." He smiled. "I shall stop by later for a statement from you." He lifted Mariel's fingers to his lips.

"At tea," urged Mariel. She smiled at the police officer. "Thank you again, Detective Nelson." Her tone remained friendly as she added, "It has been a true pleasure to visit your lovely home, Miss Muir, Mr. Muir. I hope you enjoy your future one as much."

Portia stared at her, then her face fell as she realized what her jealousy would cost her. She waited for Ian to say something, but he turned to walk past her without speaking.

"Ian!" she cried.

"Good day," he replied. He did not look back at her. As they left the room, Mariel heard Detective Nelson say, "Now, Miss Muir, if you will tell me exactly..." His voice vanished as Ian shut the mahogany door to the street.

Mariel's hand held tightly to Ian's as they sat in the coach. Her reticule was twisted in her other hand. She stared straight ahead. When Ian spoke to her, she started, so deep had she been in her thoughts.

"Mariel, before we get to the doctor's house, there is something I want to ask you."

Hastily, she said, "I know the news may be less than what we hope. I understand that. It doesn't matter so much any more." She laughed tightly. "That is a lie. I would love to see again. I miss seeing the way your mouth quirks when you are irritated with me."

"That is not what I meant."

"Then what?"

He put his hand on her shoulder. "Look at me. I want to see your pretty face when I speak to you." Her fingers rose to relearn the lines of his face. "Mariel, I love you. I told you that for the first time months ago."

"Yes," she whispered. She remembered the night he first held her; she had thought her life would be perfect. So much had changed since then. One thing remained constant. The joy they could bring one another. Only her stubborn self-pity had kept them apart. "I love you, too, Ian."

"Then marry me. Don't marry me because you need me or because I understand the difficulties you face. Marry me because you love me and I love you. Tell me you will marry me before we hear what the doctor has to say."

"If it is bad news—"

"It doesn't matter," he finished for her. "Don't you understand, Mariel Wythe? I loved you as you were before the accident. I love you as you are now. Why? Because the part of you that calls out to my heart has not changed." He placed his hand in the center of her chest. "The part of you in here is the same."

Her hand covered his as his fingers moved along the gentle swell of her breast. The fire that had come to life again last night from the ashes of her sorrow burst forth once more. As her other hand stroked the breadth of his shoulders, she held up her lips for his kiss. He pressed her close as he tasted the luscious interior of her mouth.

He raised his lips slightly. "Mariel?"

"Yes, Ian," she whispered. "As soon as Uncle Wilford comes home, I will marry you."

With a joyous laugh, he drew her back into his arms. A shower of kisses delighted her until she was giggling as happily as Rosie did with a new toy. Only when the carriage rolled to a stop before an unprepossing door did he release her. He smiled as he told her they had arrived. This rapture would not end. They would spend their lives together savoring it.

Traffic was loud along the busy street as they emerged from the cab. Ian told the driver to return in an hour. Taking Mariel's hand, he walked with her to the door gilded with Dr. Gillette's name. Beyond they found a flight of stairs leading up into the musty darkness. A skylight lit up dancing motes of dust, which littered the air.

"Ready?" he asked, only half teasing.

"No," she whispered. "I don't think I can ever prepare myself for this. I have been waiting so long but. . ." Her voice strengthened. "Let's go."

A single door opened off the narrow landing. Ian felt Mariel's fingers tighten on his as they entered the room. A woman sat behind a desk. She rose and came forward to greet them. Her professional smile perfectly matched her understated blouse and black skirt.

"Good afternoon," she said clearly. "Lady Mariel - Wythe?"

"Yes."

"Come with me, my lady. The doctor has been anxious to see you."

Mariel smiled tremulously. "I have been anxious for this appointment as well." When the woman took her arm to lead her into an inner room, Mariel hesitated. "May Ian come, too?"

The secretary motioned for the man to join them. "Of course, Reverend, you may come in. Please make yourselves comfortable. The doctor will be with you in a moment."

The doctor's office smelled of camphor and rugs thick with ancient dust. They were seated on a horsehair sofa, which pricked through the fine silk of her gown. Her hands stroked the carved wood of the arm next to her. When she heard a door open, she glanced toward it expectantly.

Instead of speaking to Ian as she expected, Dr. Gillette bent down in front of her. "Lady Mariel Wythe?"

"Yes, sir."

"May I call you Mariel?"

She nodded. "Of course."

"And you may use your fingers to see me if you wish." He laughed. "One moment, while I remove my glasses. After one youngster nearly embedded them in the bridge of my nose, I decided I would let you use your imagination for that part."

With the technique she had learned through trial and error, she ran her fingers lightly over his skin, rough with bristly whiskers. A heavy beard attached to a mustache under his bulbous nose. Wide set eyes matched the fullness of his face. Lips, which tilted up with good humor, moved as she lifted her fingers from them.

"I am no beauty like you, Mariel, but I hope you will have pity on an old man."

"You aren't old!" she stated without thinking. "I mean—"

"Go ahead."

She hesitated, certain he was testing her in some way. Then her usual determination asserted itself. "There are no wrinkles along your skin. Your voice is not tremulous. You bent down here without the creak of bones tightened with arthritis. None of this may mean anything, but I would wager you are not much past thirty."

A chair scraped across the floor as he sat down in front of her. "Very good, Mariel. I see you have learned to use your other senses well. How long has it been?"

"Nearly two months."

Dr. Gillette looked at the man sitting next to the lovely woman. His keen eyes noted the way the gentleman wearing the clerical collar gazed at Mariel with a pride he could not hide. Holding out his hand, he said, "I am Dr. Lester Gillette. You are?"

"Ian Beckwith-Carter." His smile widened as he said, "Mariel is to be my wife."

"Good. I am glad you are here, Reverend. First I want to examine Mariel. Then I will talk with both of you about your options." He stood. "Mariel, my examination room is about five steps to your right. The door is closed. If you will go in there, you will find a chair another three steps in front of you. Please wait for me there."

This time she knew he was testing her. She simply said, "Of course, doctor." She wondered if she should tell him how she had bungled finding her way about the ballroom at the party. Then she remembered how she had managed on her own in the slums of London. She could find this chair.

His instructions were perfect, and she wondered how often he had given them to patients. When she felt the leather of the chair, she lowered herself into it gracefully. She leaned back against its headrest, deciding it must be like a barber's chair. She closed her eyes and wondered how she would deal with the prognosis, either good or bad. Her happiness pushed the dreary thoughts from her head.

Uncle Wilford should be home soon after they returned to Foxbridge. He would not protest her plans to marry Ian. Easygoing Uncle Wilford appreciated anyone who would make a decision for him. It had not been that way before Georgie was sent to the insane asylum. That was the last decision she could remember her uncle making, except for which strange corner of the world he wanted to visit next.

She looked forward to having him home again. Since Georgie's funeral a year ago, he had disappeared totally from Foxbridge Cloister. Perhaps she could convince him to stay. She adored her uncle. She smiled as she wondered what he would think of Rosie. Uncle Wilford had always loved children, and she was sure the little girl would worship him too.

Her thoughts were interrupted as she heard the door close. She turned her face toward the doctor. When she heard his rumble of laughter, she smiled. This test she had passed also.

"Open those pretty blue eyes, Mariel. While I look in them, I want you to tell me exactly what happened to you. Dr. Sawyer sent me his report, but I want to hear your version."

It was not easy to relive those terrifying moments when she discovered her automobile would not respond to her control. Her voice softened to near silence as she spoke of the horror of the impact and the flash of the explosion before pain and darkness overwhelmed her.

"I see," he murmured when she finished. "And the pain, is it gone?"

"Yes."

"Can you see any light?"

She nodded. "Sparkles sometimes in my left eye."

"Shadows or sunlight?"

"No."

"I see," he repeated.

As she had not in weeks, she wished she could look into a person's face and read their thoughts. Then she realized that hope was foolish. Even if she could see Dr.

Gillette's face, his professional demeanor would hide his opinion.

He took her hand and helped her out of the chair. When his hand shoved on her shoulder, she gasped and stepped backward to keep her balance. He mumbled something to himself, which she was sure he did not intend for her to understand. When he did the same to her other shoulder, she knew he had not intended to be unpleasant. He was checking her in some manner.

After he subjected her to a battery of equally incomprehensible tests, he told her to wait in the outer office. She wondered what he had been hoping to discover and how she had done. As she closed the door, she heard Ian's cane strike the floor, signaling he was rising.

"I am fine," she said quietly to his unasked question.

"You were in there so long. What did he say?"

She shook her head as she reached out for him. "Nothing. He told me only to come out here. He wants to talk to both of us." Her hands rose to caress his cheeks. "Ian, whatever he says, it is all right."

"Is it truly?"

"Yes, truly," she replied. "I was wrong to think you wanted to marry me only because you felt sorry for me."

Ian grinned and gave her loosened curls a tug. "And I thought you refused for the same reason."

Her reply was halted when they heard the doctor approach. Sitting on the settee, they waited impatiently. Ian held her hand as the doctor sat at his ornately carved oak desk. He doubted whether Dr. Gillette used it for other than times like this. Its top was clean, unlike the cluttered surfaces of the secretary's office.

"Let me read something to you," began the doctor. Opening a folder, he read aloud the report from Dr. Sawyer. It discussed the accident and its result before finishing with, "Lester, I would like you to check her. I do not have your expertise in ophthalmology, but I fear Mariel's eyes are irreparably damaged. The chances of her regaining her sight I feel are minuscule." He closed the folder and leaned forward. "Mariel, Reverend Beckwith-Carter, I am afraid I must concur with Dr.

Sawyer. There is nothing I can do to help you. I am sorry."

Mariel nodded numbly. As if she was outside herself, she heard herself say, "I understand, doctor. I expected this. Dr. Sawyer told me not to get my hopes up."

The doctor glanced at the man by her side as he said to her, "I suggest you have Dr. Sawyer check you regularly. If there is any change, any at all, I want to see you again." His gaze held Ian's as he added, "I do not expect there will be."

Looking from the doctor to Mariel, Ian knew Dr. Gillette was concerned by her lack of reaction to his pronouncement. It did not surprise him. He knew her well enough now to realize that she would not break down before strangers and show the sorrow in her heart. He stood and reached across the desk.

"Thank you, Dr. Gillette, for your time. We are pleased you are this honest with us." He took Mariel's hand and brought her to her feet.

"Yes," she echoed, "thank you, doctor." She offered her hand unerringly in his direction.

Dr. Gillette found himself the one unnerved as he felt her firm handshake. He had not read them the total of the report. In a private letter attached to it, his friend had told him some of Lady Mariel Wythe's past history. He wrote of her work for the downtrodden and for the children of her community. The tale of the free-spirited sprite who brightened each room she entered fit with this woman accepting the prognosis he had not wanted to make. As he shook her hand, he wished he could shout that he had been wrong and that she would regain her sight by some miracle.

When the two walked out of his private office, he rose to walk to the window. He watched when they emerged from the ground floor to go to the waiting carriage. The sound of their voices rose to him, but the meaning of their words was muted by the glass. A slow smile moved across his lips as he saw the woman throw her arms around her fiancé and kiss him most inappropriately on the public street. He turned away as they entered the carriage to ride back to their lives, far from his own.

"Mariel?"

"I am fine."

Ian drew her head back against his shoulder. Looking past her, he watched the fine houses on the streets they traveled. "I understand," he whispered into her hair.

"I know," she murmured. She did not want to refute what she had long since learned. Ian could sense what she was feeling, even when she tried to submerge it.

The rest of the ride passed in silence, but it was not uncomfortable. They thought of nothing—they simply stood poised between joy and grief. Although they had dreamed of a different ending today, they would find a way to deal with the truth.

As soon as they entered the house, Ian saw Phipps looking at him. Mariel bent to greet Rosie, and he shook his head sadly. The older woman pressed her handkerchief to her mouth to stop her sob of sorrow. For Phipps, acceptance of the whims of fate did not come easily.

Rosie chatted about the visit they had made to the Tower today. "And did you know they used to cut off people's heads there?" Her hand swept down on Mariel's arm. "Just like Mrs. Puhle has the boys cut the heads off the chickens."

"Amazing!" gasped Mariel with the right amount of astonishment. "Now, why don't you run off to the kitchen and order tea for three down here and for you and Phipps upstairs."

"Three?"

"Ian has a friend coming to call." She wrinkled her nose in faked distaste. "Business. Have tea with Phipps, and then you can dress up for dinner with us. All right?"

The sound of feet racing toward the back of the house gave her the child's answer. She straightened and brushed her skirt clean of invisible dirt. Taking a deep breath, she turned to Phipps. The smell of her companion's favorite bath powder always told her where the older woman was.

"It was not what we wanted to hear."

The sobs Phipps had tried to subjugate escaped. Mumbles of unintelligible words and a quick embrace overwhelmed Mariel before the woman went up the stairs almost as quickly as Rosie had run to the kitchen. Mariel wanted to shout after her. She did not want Phipps to feel so badly about something that could not be changed.

Ian took her hand and led her into the drawing room. "Phipps will be fine."

"And you?"

He bent to place his lips close to hers. "I, too, will be fine eventually. I do not like the idea of the woman I love suffering."

"I am not suffering," she retorted saucily. "I have a wedding to plan after I welcome my uncle home. That sounds wonderful to me."

"And to me."

His lips played a resounding melody across her mouth. The sensation of her slender body against him drove all other thoughts from his mind. He wanted only to feel her moving with the love they shared. As he tasted the fragrant moistness of her mouth, her hands clenched on his back.

The soft sound of a throat being cleared separated them. Ian met the embarrassed face of his butler. "Yes, Barbon?"

"Mister—er, Reverend, a friend has arrived to call on you and Lady Mariel. A detective from Scotland Yard, sir."

"Show him in."

Detective Nelson held his hat in his hand as he entered the room. He noted the fine wallcoverings accenting the stylish furniture. A large gilt mirror went from floor to ceiling between the two front windows. In it, he could see the reflection of the back of the lovely Lady Mariel. He found it difficult to believe that this beautiful lady had survived the adventures she had described. That all of them could be corroborated added to his admiration of her.

"Good afternoon," he said quietly. His quick eyes had noticed the soft expression on Lady Mariel's face and the way her fingers entwined with his friend's. That

Ian had a very strong emotional stake in the abducted woman Nelson had known from the moment Ian had stormed into the cluttered office at the Yard, where Nelson had been trying to finish up a report on his latest case.

Since their early years together in boarding school, the two men had been close friends. While the rest of their schoolmates went on to the more conventional pursuit of wealth, they had chosen these two divergent paths with the same goal of creating peace in the world. Those callings had brought them together again and again.

Mariel heard the distress in Detective Nelson's voice and said, "Please come in, sir. Ah, here is the tea tray right on time." She motioned for it to be placed near the settee. "Please sit and tell us what you must. The news will not become better by delaying."

Flashing Ian a sheepish grin, Nelson did as she ordered. The strict, though congenial, tone of her voice reminded him of a professor who expected continually better work. He admitted she was correct. The news must be told quickly.

It did not take him long to explain the details of the interrogation. Determined to save himself from criminal proceedings, Rupert Muir denounced his sister as the originator of the plan. He repeated again and again that he went along only to help Portia deal with the spirited Lady Mariel Wythe.

"Is that so?" demanded Mariel tightly. Her hands paused in midair as she was reaching for the teapot. "He is lying, sir."

Nelson nodded, then recalled she could not see him. "I suspected that. Are you prepared to testify to that?"

"Yes, if I must," she whispered. The idea of retelling that horrible series of events before the public was distasteful to her. Such titillating details would be the meat of headlines for reader-hungry newspapers.

"Good. Of course, it may not come to that point. Already the Muirs have contacted their father's barrister. He sent a message to expect a call from him first thing tomorrow. They will serve no time," finished the detective with regret. "With their father's influence in the present government, they will be released as soon as the senior Mr. Muir puts some pressure on the court. Thank you," he added as Mariel held out a cup of tea.

"Forgive what is splashed on the saucer," Mariel said lightly. "I am still as inept as a girl in the schoolroom when it comes to pouring tea."

"It is fine. Not a drop on the saucer."

She turned to Ian with a private smile, which made Nelson uncomfortable. He felt as if he was intruding on an intimate moment. Glancing down at his tea, he stirred it continuously until Ian spoke.

Breaking his mesmerism as he stared at her lips, which urged him to sample them again, Ian said, "You may not be able to keep them in prison, but I don't think they'll try the same trick again. Another woman might not have been as resourceful as Mariel."

"Or as lucky!" she interjected.

"Not just luck." Ian smiled with pride as he turned to his friend. "I don't know if I could have been brave enough to strike out across the trackless waste of London rooftops even being able to see in the moonlight."

Grimly, she said, "You would have when the only other choice was what awaited me at the end of an hour when Kitty brought back another of her clients. I had suffered enough groping by her heavy-handed patrons to know I did not want to share that disgusting room with one."

Embarrassed by the topic of which no lady should speak, Nelson adroitly changed the subject. Soon Mariel was listening as the two men shared reminiscences of their school years. She stored the tales away in the special part of her heart she reserved for Ian.

That was the last quiet moment she had during the remainder of their visit to London. Once the announcement was made that she would marry Ian, a round of callers came to offer their congratulations. That most were curious also about her adventures in Southwark they could not hide. She parried their questions by telling them she could not speak of such things while the case was being investigated.

Between those visits and the times they called at the Beckwith-Carter home in Kensington, it seemed as if she had no time to catch her breath. Only in the velvet hours of the night when she rested in Ian's arms did she have time to dream of the joy yet to come. He came in the hours after the rest of the household slept, and he slipped away before dawn. She did not like the necessity of him sneaking in and out of her room, but she knew once they returned to Foxbridge they would not be together like this until after their wedding.

Paddington Station was as busy as it had been when they arrived two weeks before. Rosie clung to Mariel's hand while she held a stuffed dog, a gift from her future grandmother, in her other hand. Phipps stood nearby, worriedly watching over her two charges. When the reverend came to collect them to board the train, she felt relieved. As much as she had anticipated this trip to London, Amanda Phipps was celebrating their return to Foxbridge. In their home, they would not have to worry about such madness as had occurred before.

Their compartment on the train was nearly identical to the one they had on the first trip, but their enthusiasm had dimmed to fatigue. Although no one mentioned it, they knew that within a few weeks they would be required to return for the trial. It would bring only more heartache as Mariel would be forced to discuss publicly the abuse she had suffered.

The train lurched into motion, and Mariel sighed happily. She was going home. Soon Uncle Wilford would be there as well, and the plans for the wedding could be put into motion. Then she could forget this trip, except for the parts she longed to remember . . . Ian's proposal and his heated kisses bringing her joy.

Suddenly the car halted, nearly throwing Mariel from her seat. She wanted to repeat Rosie's demand of "Why are we stopping?"

"Someone must have arrived late," said Ian with a chuckle. "Don't worry, Peony. We will be home before dark."

She leapt off her seat to tickle him. That Ian was joshing with her as he had before Mariel's accident seemed heavenly to the child. For what seemed an eternity to her, the household had been too serious. Although she understood that Mariel would be blind forever, she was delighted Mariel and Ian treated her with the joy she feared had been lost.

A knock on the compartment door halted her giggles. Ian put her on Mariel's lap as he rose to his feet. "Scott!" he gasped. "What is wrong?"

The detective did not attempt to smile. He said, "I wanted to catch you before you left, to tell you the news before you heard it secondhand. I thought it better to tell you in person than by letter."

"What is it?"

"I wanted to let you know the Muir case has been closed."

Mariel cried, "Closed? Why? Did—?"

His choked voice interrupted her. "The case has been closed because there is no one to prosecute."

"No one? Did Sir Darren recall his children to the Hills? I thought Scotland Yard could reach beyond the limits of London proper!" Rage burned in Ian's voice. He glared at his friend.

Nelson swallowed uneasily. "That is not the reason, Ian. Sir Darren Muir did not recall them." He looked uneasily from one anxious face to the next. He could not soften what he must tell them. Bluntly he stated, "Sometime during the night, Rupert and Portia Muir took an overdose of laudanum."

Mariel gasped into the shocked silence, "They killed themselves?"

"We suspect Miss Muir doctored her brother's drink, then swallowed her dose in wine." He gratefully sat when Miss Phipps motioned to the seat next to her. He sighed. "Now this must be investigated as well, to assure ourselves they were not actually murdered."

"If I am your prime suspect," said Ian quietly, "I can assure you the thought of revenge did cross my mind. Murder did not."

"Ian! This is no joking matter," scolded Mariel. Her voice shook with her distress.

"Ian," said Nelson calmly, "no one believes you did this, but questions must be answered. I trust you were home last night."

Before he could reply, Mariel stated, "Ian was with me all last night, Mr. Nelson. We had dinner with Phipps and Rosie. Then Ian and I—"

Nelson interrupted her hastily, his face as heated as the fire in the locomotive. "Lady Mariel, there is no need for such explanation. Ian is not under any suspicion. I am simply allowing you to understand the situation. Already my superiors have deemed it a murder and a suicide. There will be little more to say about it."

"Portia always tried to protect Rupert," Ian mused as if to himself. "She must have realized he would not elude prosecution this time. To see him in jail would be painful, so she granted him the only escape available. Death."

The conductor harrumphed in the hallway and looked at his pocket watch. The message was unmistakable. Nelson rose. "I will send you a copy of the final report when it is completed. I just wanted to let you know." For some reason he could not understand, he added, "I'm sorry."

"We are, too," replied Mariel. "Thank you for all you have done."

"I wanted to return this to you." He placed the emerald ring in her hand. "It was found exactly where you said it would be. We confronted the Muirs and their barrister with this yesterday." He sighed and added nothing else. There was no need. All of them guessed the Muirs must have felt they had a choice between jail and death.

"Sir. . . ?" came the impatient trainman's voice negating the chance for more comments.

With hurried farewells, the police officer left. Silence settled in his wake as the train began its interrupted journey anew. Mariel leaned the child against her as she placed her head on Ian's shoulder. With his arm around her, they gave each other what sparse comfort they could.

Mariel shivered when she heard Phipps's nearly inaudible comment of "They must have been mad." She wondered if insanity would discolor the rest of her life, as it had her childhood. She longed for the sanctuary of

the Cloister. Behind its solid walls, she could find the
haven she needed.

Chapter Nineteen

"Lady Mariel?"

The words echoed through the house. Mariel raised her fingers from the piano keyboard and listened. In the week since their arrival home from London, she had renewed her love of music. Although she had to have Ian read her the notes from the sheet when she started a new passage, she could enjoy memorized pieces as much as ever.

"Lady Mariel?" A flurry of footsteps skidded to a stop beyond the door of the drawing room, it opened with a crash. She turned on the piano stool.

"Lady Mariel?"

"Yes?" She smiled as she heard the breathlessness in the girl's voice. The maid must have been searching all through the Cloister for her.

"From the gate, my lady! From the gate!"

"Yes?" she repeated with a touch of impatience. She heard Ian rise. He had been rewriting his sermon while she practiced.

" 'Tis the lord, my lady. Lord Foxbridge is on his way home. He just passed through the gate."

The whirlwind of her skirts as she rose sent the pages of music flying through the air. She did not pause to worry about them as she hurried out of the room. Feeling the freshness of the autumn breeze on her face, she knew the front door was open. The crunch of

314

carriage wheels slowing on the dirt driveway told her the long wait for her uncle to return was over.

Heedlessly she ran down the stairs. Her outstretched hands were grasped, and she was twirled into a loving embrace against a coat covered with a layer of dust. For only the shortest second did her uncle hug her before he put his hands on her face and tilted it back.

"As lovely as I remembered you!" he murmured in a choked tone, which disguised his normally ringing voice. "Have I ever told you how envious I was of your father for discovering your mother before I did?"

"Once or twice," she replied lightly. Her fingers went automatically to touch his face. "Oh, Uncle Wilford, it is so wonderful to have you home again."

He did not respond to her teasing or to her welcome. His hands settled over hers as he asked, "How are you doing, Mariel? When Phipps wrote to me and told me about your accident, I thought my heart would break. My lovely Mariel blinded. It is too cruel. There must be something we can do."

"No, there is nothing," she whispered with sudden seriousness. "Do not feel that way, Uncle Wilford. I am alive. I know how lucky I am that I did not die in the accident. It doesn't matter anymore."

"Doesn't matter? Lamb, how can you say that?"

She heard the footsteps behind her and drew out of his arms. "Uncle Wilford, there is someone here I would like you to meet." Her smile lit the cloudy day as her hand unerringly reached for Ian's. "This is my fiancé, Ian Beckwith-Carter. Ian, my Uncle Wilford."

Ian stepped down from the last stair. He held out his hand to the startled man. He would have guessed immediately this was Lord Foxbridge after viewing the family portraits in the gallery by the solarium. Like the men in those paintings, Wilford Wythe's gray-tinted hair once must have been ebony. Clear brown eyes regarded him with the same lack of compromise as those stern ancestors of the Wythe family. For all his eccentric behavior, Mariel's uncle embodied the aura of power she had inherited in such large quantity.

"Lord Foxbridge, it is indeed an honor to meet you."

Wilford's eyes noted the clerical collar as he ignored the proffered hand. "Reverend Beckwith-Carter?"

"Yes, my lord."

"You plan to marry my Mariel?"

"Uncle Wilford—" she started, but he hushed her. Ian repeated, "Yes, my lord."

"Why?" When the younger man gazed at him in bafflement, Wilford continued, "Why do you want to marry her? Do you feel sorry for her? Do you see wedding her the act of a good man who will guarantee she is taken care of?"

Seeing the pain on Mariel's face, Ian reached for her hand and drew her into his arms. "You insult your niece, my lord, by insinuating that she is of less value since the automobile accident. I admit you do not know me and, therefore, cannot judge my motives for wanting to marry Mariel. You know her well, however. You should know that she would never accept pity as a recompense for love."

Expecting a fiery retort to his cold words, Ian stared openmouthed as the lord laughed. He glanced at Mariel and saw her lips twitching. When the peppery lord extended his hand, Ian put his in it and shook it.

"Do not look so confused, Reverend Beckwith-Carter," he stated in a much more jovial tone. "You have convinced me of your sincere devotion to Mariel. Only a man who loves a woman strongly would leap to her defense so quickly. I just wanted to be sure you were not taking advantage of her in order to gain your son a title."

"A title?" Instantly he wondered why he sounded so stupid. His hopes of making a good impression on Mariel's uncle were being undermined by his own idiotic statements.

"Mariel is my only living relative. She will inherit the Cloister to pass on to her children. If she has a son, he will gain the title. This is a proud peerage coming down through this family in an unbroken line from the time of the War of the Roses. You did not think of that, Reverend?"

"Stop it!" ordered Mariel with a laugh. "Uncle Wilford, you will be convincing Ian you are going to halt this wedding. Give us your blessing, Uncle."

He leaned forward and kissed her cheek. "You know you have it, my dear. Long overdue it is. Now, as you are the lady of this household, why don't you act as a good hostess and invite a cold man into the Cloister for a serving of brandy?"

Mariel slipped her hand into the crook of his arm and did the same with Ian. Walking between the two men she loved most, she listened as they spoke over her head. Once Ian became accustomed to Uncle Wilford's eccentric humor, he would feel more comfortable with him.

They stopped on the front steps while her uncle greeted Muffin, who adored the man nearly as much as Mariel did. In the foyer, she paused to give Dodsley a whispered message. He nodded automatically before remembering to answer her, also quietly. As he watched her hurry to catch up with the two men, who were discussing the lord's latest travels, he shook his head. So often he found himself forgetting Lady Mariel could not see. When she had been so desolate after the accident, he did not suspect she would recover so fully. Even as he was calling for a servant to send on this errand, he breathed a prayer of thanksgiving for the reverend and the love he brought to Lady Mariel.

Mariel's ears caught the furtive footsteps before the men noticed. With a smile, she rose and went to the stairs at the entrance to the solarium. When a trembling hand slipped into hers, she bent to kiss Rosie's cheek. The child's skin remained cool after her carriage ride from Foxbridge.

"Did Mr. Knowles mind you leaving early?" she whispered.

Rosie giggled. "You know he never minds me being gone."

"Come, darling. I have someone I want you to meet."

"I know."

The solemn words warned Mariel that Phipps had been giving the little girl a list of rules on how to behave when she met Lord Foxbridge. Not wanting to undermine her companion's lessons, but knowing the child had nothing to worry about, she decided the easiest thing would be to get this meeting over quickly.

Leading the child across the wide room, she gauged the location of the chairs by noting where the carpet began on the stone floor. She heard the men rise as she approached. She squeezed Rosie's hand to give her courage.

Softly, she said, "Uncle Wilford, this is Rosamunde Varney. The last name is temporary, however. Within a few weeks, it will be Wythe."

"Then Beckwith-Carter," the older man said with a chuckle. He leaned over to look at the little girl dressed in a red plaid school dress. White stockings covered her skinny legs. She wore heavy black shoes, and her two braids gleamed with brushing. "You are going to have many names, young lady."

"Yes, sir. I mean, my lord," she added hastily, remembering Miss Phipps's many admonishments. Her blue eyes regarded the smiling face before her. Lord Foxbridge was not the ogre she had expected. She had imagined someone as cold as the portraits in the gallery. The twinkle in his eyes reminded her more of the woman holding her hand.

"Why don't you call me Uncle Wilford, Rosamunde?"

"Rosie," she said quietly. Her eyes widened as she realized her impertinence in correcting a lord.

He grinned. "What a perfect name for you with your cheeks as pink as a rosebud! I am glad you are going to be a part of our family, Rosie."

When she smiled, revealing the wide gap where her top front teeth barely peeked into her mouth, he laughed. Holding out his hand, he suggested she come and sit next to him. She giggled when he teased her about being his escort while Ian stayed for supper and sat with his future wife.

Mariel smiled with joy as she heard her uncle joke with Rosie as he had with her when she was little. When all three children lived in the Cloister, he had divided his attention among all of them. After Lorraine's death and Georgie's incarceration in the insane asylum, Uncle Wilford had lavished his love on the only child left with the Wythe name.

An arm slipped around her shoulders. She leaned her head against Ian. "I told you everyone worried needlessly," she said softly. "Uncle Wilford will adore Rosie."

"And she him," he agreed.

Their light conversation lasted through dinner. Uncle Wilford kept them entertained with all he had seen in America. Time after time, he used his favorite description of "fascinating." He found Central America and its remnants of Indian culture fascinating. He thought the plains of the middle of the United States were fascinating. Even the stockyards of Chicago with their pungent odors and earsplitting noise were deemed fascinating.

As predicted, Rosie captured her great-uncle's attention. He roared with laughter when Ian continued to tease her with all the different flower names except her own. Mariel kept to herself her amusement with Phipps' changed behavior. Not once during the meal did she reprimand Rosie for being too boisterous. When Lord Foxbridge told the loudest jokes, she could hardly scold the child for laughing.

While Mariel went with Phipps to put the child to bed, Wilford took the time to draw Ian to one side of the solarium. Without preamble, Lord Foxbridge asked, "Is Mariel speaking the truth? There is nothing that can be done?"

"Nothing. We went to the best man in England. He said the damage is irreparable." Ian sighed into his glass of brandy. "She is far more accepting of it than the rest of us. Sometimes I think she has adjusted so well, she forgets the truth. We still find ourselves watching each word we say."

"After all she has suffered, it seems so unfair."

"I have noticed she speaks of the past so much more easily now. She talks about the good times she shared with Lorraine and Georgie."

The old man flinched. He lowered his glass to a table and walked to the long windows of the solarium. On the grass, moonlit sparkles of the fallen rain danced. He turned and said in a pleading voice, "Take care of her, Ian. I know she has always feared that the sickness that took Georgie from us would inflict her or her children. Other suitors could not understand why she would not let them court her. She has been afraid of marriage for this simple reason. Yet what she fears is impossible. Her cousin suffered from a horrible series of convulsions before she was born. Those unbalanced his mind."

"Doesn't she know that?"

"Here." He pointed to his head, then to the center of his chest. "In her mind, but not in her heart. She adored her cousin. None of us thought Georgie would harm the girls, although he could not hide his dislike for Lorraine. When Ambrose and Emma died in the epidemic shortly after the twins turned three, we saw nothing strange with their childlike cousin playing with them."

Ian put his hand consolingly on the man's arm. "I am sorry, Wilford. If it helps, I know Mariel mourns deeply for her cousin."

"As he did for her. The whole time he lived in that horrible place, he never once asked for me or anyone else in the Cloister. Only for Mariel. The staff told me that often in the reports they sent here. When he began to appear well, they urged me to bring her to visit him I could not take her to that place." His dark eyes showed the memories that haunted him. He recalled the rooms where the inmates were bound, to protect themselves and others. The scent of human waste and sickness could never be washed from his memory. Softly he said, "That was no place for a sensitive child like Mariel. Then the fire destroyed any chance of my son becoming normal again. I regret so much I did not let Georgie see her one final time."

"You never told me that, Uncle."

The two men glanced over their shoulders to see Mariel standing on the steps of the solarium. Deep in conversation, they had not heard her dainty footsteps or

the silent stones. She walked to her uncle and reached
for his hands. He put his much larger ones in hers.

"I'm sorry, Mariel. I should have known you were
strong enough to see the hell where your cousin lived
his last years."

Tears brightened her eyes. "For the past year, I
feared Georgie died hating me for what I said to him
that night when he lost control."

"What you said?"

She shook her head. "You would not understand,
for it was something only children can share. I did not
hate him, even that night. I hated what he could become, but I never stopped loving Georgie. I am glad to
know that he forgave me."

"If it comforts you, my dear, I am sure he did not
remember anything you said to him while he was in the
midst of his mental aberration. He listened only to the
'voices,' as he called them." In explanation for Ian, he
added, "Georgie was haunted by demons, which spoke
only to him. At first, when he was small, we thought he
was using those 'voices' as an excuse for childish mis-
deeds. Then we learned how wrong we were."

"Poor soul," murmured Ian. "I hope he has found
peace."

"I hope so, too." Wilford shook himself physically to
push aside the thoughts. "Enough dreary talk of the
past. I understand we will be having a wedding soon. Let
us talk about that instead."

Mariel smiled as they worked to forget the past that
haunted them. She listened to the men talk and added
her convivial comments. As she had guessed, everything
would be wonderful when her uncle came home. For the
first time in many years, she did not fear the future.

Mariel wanted to refuse the suggestion that Reverend Tanner marry them in the small church in the
village. No one mentioned that most previous Wythe
brides had been married in the chapel in the old Cloister. Now, only a pile of tumbled and scorched stones, it
would never be used for such services again.

"Ian, I do not want that old hypocrite reading our
wedding rite."

He laughed as he turned the carriage onto the well traveled road leading south. Reverend Tanner had retired to a small cottage overlooking the ocean which infected all who lived near it with a lifelong devotion. "What do you suggest, sweetheart? That I marry us?"

"You two aren't the only ministers in this area. There is Reverend Allen, and Reverend Eckert."

"Reverend Allen is busy with another wedding that day. Eckert is in Bristol on a well deserved vacation." He squeezed her fingers. "We could delay the date for a few weeks if you wish."

She leaned her head on his shoulder, savoring the comfort of his arm around her. With a soft chuckle, she whispered, "I don't want to wait as long as we must. It seems as if it has been forever since you have loved me, Ian. We have too many chaperones."

"You are Lady Mariel. Your behavior must be exemplary."

"Balderdash! None of the Wythes have ever cared what anyone else said about them." As her fingers roved along his face, she asked, "Did Sybill Wythe, the one in the painting in the drawing room, care when everyone accused her of taking at the height of the battle of the Spanish Armada, a Spanish sailor as her lover? If the stories I have heard are true, she cared little about anyone's opinion. She passed her child off as her husband's. The Wythes have fought duels and murdered enemies to protect the Cloister and gain our way."

His hand stroked her shoulder through her cape. "That was long ago, in a much more romantic era. Such things would not be sanctioned now."

She sighed. "I wish we were living then. I am tired of pretending. Each time I kiss you good night in the foyer, I wish it could be as it was when we slept side by side all night long."

The carriage came to a sudden stop as he pulled back on the reins. Sweeping her against him, Ian pressed his mouth over hers. His fingers sought beneath the concealment of the heavy cloak to find the soft roundness of her breast.

A rush of passion flowed through her. Her arm tightened around his broad shoulders. When he leaned her back onto the thick cushions of the buggy seat, she gasped and turned her face from his.

"Ian! If—"

"Didn't you just tell me that you did not care what anyone thought?" He laughed with a low rumble of eager desire. "No one can see us, my love. I have pulled the buggy behind a stand of trees. Your reputation is quite safe."

"Mine? I was thinking of yours."

Tasting the warmth of her skin beneath the collar of her cape, he murmured against her, "Even the church board has acceded to our betrothal. Do not think of that now, my love. Think of our love."

"I am," she breathed before her words dissolved into a gasp of delight.

When he slipped his hand along the lithe line of her legs, she shivered, but not with longing. With a laugh, she pushed his fingers from her and smoothed her skirt back over her ankles. "It is too cold."

"Funny," he whispered as he held her tight to him, "I do not feel the cold at all." He kissed her lightly once more before he retrieved the reins from the floor of the buggy. When he drove the vehicle back onto the road, he did not release her. The rest of the trip to Reverend Tanner's house, he kept her close to him.

The old man had not changed since he preached at the Foxbridge church. His officious manner irritated Mariel, before she had seated herself in his well-furnished parlor. While his housekeeper served the obligatory tea, they chatted inanely about the shire. She managed to maintain her composure until they discussed the wedding ceremony.

"No!" said Mariel suddenly.

"No?" repeated Reverend Tanner. He frowned as he looked at the bafflement on Ian's face. Lady Mariel's stubborn expression was one he knew too well.

She placed her cup back on the tray, ignoring the clatter as it struck the sugar bowl. "I will not promise to obey Ian."

"My lady, you must. That is part of the wedding vow. It is the duty of a woman to subjugate her will to that of her husband."

"No." She folded her hands in her lap and added nothing more.

The disconcerted clergyman turned to the other man. "Ian, perhaps if I left you alone with Lady Mariel for a few minutes, you could make her understand the reasons why this is in the service."

Ian stirred his tea with a reflective smile on his face. "Although I have not heard anyone protest as vehemently as Mariel, this is not the first instance of a bride deciding against this passage. What is that we preach over and over? That marriage is a partnership?"

Reverend Tanner slammed his book shut. In his sonorous voice, he stated, "Then I will not marry you. Never in all my many years on the pulpit have I been involved in an exchanging of vows when the bride did not promise to cherish, honor, and obey her husband. I do not plan to alter that precedent now."

He glared from one young face to the other. Lady Mariel's was set in those firm lines, which he knew from past experience meant she had no intention of doing as he commanded. He was less familiar with the man who had replaced him in Foxbridge, but his words had made it clear he was willing to do as Mariel wished.

"Very well," came a soft response to break the stilted silence in the study. Tanner's eyes returned to Mariel. "You can use the word in the service, Reverend Tanner."

"Mariel!"

She patted Ian's hand as she heard his astonishment. With a smile, she said, "Do not worry. It will change nothing of the love we share. I do not want to halt our plans for something so incidental."

"Good!" crowed Reverend Tanner. He had doubted he would ever triumph over Lady Mariel in a contest of wills, but it seemed when she wanted something as badly as she wanted to marry Reverend Beckwith-Carter, she would back down.

Over the days that followed, Ian tried more than once to discuss the offending word with Mariel. He did not want her to think she must obey him literally. She shoved aside his concerns, stating she was too busy with

the plans for the wedding. When, in the midst of everything, the news came from Mallory and Sons that
Rosie's adoption was completed, they celebrated with a
party at the Cloister.

Time flew past. Cynthia Beckwith-Carter came to
attend the wedding. Although Mariel invited her to stay
at the Cloister, she chose to sleep at the parsonage.
Most of the time she spent with Mariel making last-
minute preparations, but she was anxious to see the side
of her son foreign to her. As she saw him deal with the
needs of his parishioners, she could not hide her pride.

The morning of the wedding dawned with crisp
freshness. Dressing early, Mariel spent the morning
fussing with her hair, which refused to stay in the curls
she had wanted. Finally, she pinned it in a French twist
on the back of her head with several loose curls framing
her face.

Phipps fluttered about the room, assisting her dress
into the tarlatan wedding gown. The tightly fitting bodice
was accented with a wide swoop of thick lace dropping
from the leg of mutton sleeves across the front. Although plain in the front, the inverted pleats of the
habit-back skirt ended in a train extending ten feet
behind her. Pinned at the throat of the high collared
dress was the cameo her mother had posed for before
her own wedding day. Beaded satin slippers and a lace
mantilla decorated with orange blossoms completed her
outfit.

When she heard Phipps sobbing in happiness, she
knew she looked as lovely as she felt. She did not sit
while she listened to Rosie being dressed in her attendant's gown. The little girl did not want to stand still to
be hooked up. Finally, all was ready, just as they heard
Lord Foxbridge's bellow from the foyer.

Taking her train over one arm, Mariel took Rosie's
hand. A bounce in their steps showed their excitement.
With compliments on both their lovely gowns, Uncle
Wilford swept them out the front door. He was as
anxious as the bride to have this wedding begun.

"Thank you, Alistair," he said to the carriage driver
when he closed the door. "Drive carefully. I do not want
to arrive with a dusty bride."

"Alistair?" queried Mariel. "I thought Walter would be driving today."

"Who the—oh, the man you hired to take care of that blasted automobile. Haven't met the chap yet. Alistair told me he asked for some time off to visit family. He should be back at the end of the week."

She smiled. "You will like him, Uncle." She twisted her gloves in her hands and forgot everything but the wedding which would be starting within minutes.

The small white church was surrounded by buggies and wagons. Behind it, the leaves of the trees created a multi-hued backdrop. The fragrance of early fall cleansed the heat of summer from them. It was a perfect day and, many hoped, an omen of the good things to come for the newlyweds.

"Ready?" asked Wilford as he helped her from the carriage. "You look perfect, my dear. So like your mother did the day she married your father. I wish they could be here to see you this day."

She stood on tiptoe to kiss his cheek. "I am glad you are with me, Uncle Wilford. I could not imagine anyone else I would rather have escort me down the aisle." She did not add aloud that she had such nebulous memories of her parents that this man seemed the only father she ever had.

"Ready?" he repeated. His gruff voice showed his embarrassment with her effusive words.

"Yes." She ordered the tremors in her stomach to quiet. This is what she had wanted since the day she discovered she loved Ian. She should not be nervous, but she was. Trying to keep her voice steady, she turned to her left. "Are you ready, Rosie?"

The little girl chirped, "Yes!" She twirled, so her wide chiffon skirts billowed around her in a cloud of pink. Flowers to match her name were woven into her loosened curls. Rosebuds sewn to the bodice of her dress matched the brightness of her cheeks. For days she had been practicing her role as the flower girl. Today she would be able to reveal those skills for the guests.

A swell of organ music reached its crescendo as the door at the back of the church was opened to admi them. In the silence after the crash of sound, a rumble of murmurs announced that the guests had seen the bride awaiting the start of the processional. The heat of the many candles giving off their intoxicating scents throughout the small building combined with the lush aroma of hothouse blossoms.

Mariel sought for Ian with her heart. Although she knew he would be standing by the raised altar in the black frock coat he wore beneath his surplice on Sundays, she wanted to touch him with the love within her.

In her ear, Wilford whispered, "He is grinning like a child at a birthday party. I wonder if he will be able to wait until the music starts."

Her soft laugh was swallowed by the heavy chords of the beginning of the triumphant melody they had chosen for this wedding. With one hand on her uncle's arm and the other holding her bouquet, she waited nervously as Rosie stepped ahead of them to drop downy petals on the scarlet carpet. She heard the notes that signaled them to start. Her uncle patted her hand as they walked with forced slowness to the place where Ian waited.

Out of all the fragrances combatting her senses, she picked out his cologne. As it grew stronger, she held out her hand to him. A murmur of astonishment sounded behind them, and she knew many had feared the bride would trip on her long gown before she reached her groom. Perhaps if Ian had not insisted she become as independent as she had been before the accident, she would have been that pitiful creature they expected. He had inspired her to be more than she thought she could be.

The words of the wedding ceremony flowed over her. She answered when required and listened to Ian's deep voice repeating the vows to love her forever. When Reverend Tanner turned to her, she did the same carefully. She nearly laughed when Ian squeezed her fingers as she purposely omitted the promise to obey him. Although Reverend Tanner waited patiently for her to finish, she simply smiled.

"Lady Mariel?" whispered Reverend Tanner. "You promised to repeat the whole line after me."

"You misunderstood." Holding tightly to Ian's hand, she leaned forward to add as quietly, "I said only that the words could be in the service. I did not say I would repeat them. I love you, Ian, forever. I will cherish that love with all my heart and honor it every day of our lives."

"And I love you, Mariel." He glanced at the flustered minister as the guests moved uneasily in their seats at the delay. "Shall we continue?"

Recovering his composure, the elderly clergyman hurried on to finish the rite. Inside, he fumed. He should have suspected Lady Mariel's easy compliance was faked. This was not the time to argue about such duplicity. The ceremony must be completed without further disruptions.

He took a lighted candle from the candelabrum on the altar and handed it to Ian. The groom used it to light a candle on his right before offering the taper to Mariel. Her fingers found the table easily, and she put the flame to her candle. She handed the original to the minister before taking the one she had lit.

Ian's hand guided hers as they raised them toward a larger candle in the center of the altar. Together they said the words they did not need to rehearse, "Two hearts, one love." The wick burst into flame from the two touching it. He took her candle and inserted it in its holder. After doing the same with his, he put his hand around hers again.

When Reverend Tanner urged him to kiss his bride, Ian lifted the shimmering veil to see a smile matching his own. He leaned forward to taste her lips, knowing never again would he be parted from her. "My dear wife," he whispered.

"I love you, Ian."

Even before the eyes of the, she could not halt the leap of passion in her that overpowered all other sensations as he placed his mouth over hers. Her arms swept around his shoulders as he drew her closer.

The organ sounded with joy, and cheers from their guests filled the church. Reluctantly, Ian raised his mouth from hers. Later they would have the time they longed to have alone. It seemed too far away.

Taking Mariel's hand, he placed it on his arm. He offered his other hand to Rosie as they walked back down the aisle. They stepped out into the golden glow of the autumnal sun glittering on the colorful leaves and into the future they would share together.

Ian warmed his hands before the fireplace in Mariel's sitting room. The cool days of autumn would soon fade into winter. He smiled as he thought how luscious the winter nights would be with Mariel in his arms. Tomorrow, they would leave for their wedding trip to Paris, a gift from Wilford Wythe. Later, they must decide if they would stay all the time in the Cloister or spend part of each week at the rectory. He suspected he would use the parsonage as his office and open the rest of its rooms for church functions.

The reception that afternoon had been a joyous affair, attended by the members of his congregation and most of the population of the shire. At first, the guests had been unsure how they should tease a man of the cloth, but soon the barely veiled bawdy jokes were aired for all to enjoy. Mrs. Reed and the Foxbridge Cloister kitchen staff under Mrs. Puhle's autocratic eye, had created a magnificent meal to be devoured by the partygoers. Now, the last of the revelers had taken the party to the Three Georges in the village to continue until dawn. They left the bride and groom to their own celebrations of the nuptials.

"Ta-da!" came a laughing pronouncement to sever his thoughts of the day.

Ian turned to see his fantasy given life. A short velvet jacket of midnight blue clung to Mariel's body and accentuated her breasts. Her bare midriff led his eyes to the ruby gems forming a pattern across the sparse girdle. Sheer silk drawers floated in a gossamer cloud as she walked toward him. Caught at her ankles by a narrow, embroidered band, the trousers drooped over her golden slippers with their turned-up toes.

She whirled, and her hair, bound only by a jeweled ribbon around her forehead, flowed in a chocolate cascade behind her. When he put his arms around her waist and drew her close to nuzzle her neck, she giggled.

Stepping back, she placed her palms to her forehead and bowed.

"I am Fatima, princess of the desert, here to delight you, my sheikh."

He lifted off the veil obscuring the lower portion of her face. Caressing her soft cheek, his hand dropped to her shoulder to bring her back into his arms. "I beg to differ with you. You are not Fatima, princess of the desert. You are my beloved Mariel."

"Mariel Beckwith-Carter," she said as her eyes twinkled merrily. "How lovely that sounds!"

"How lovely you look, my love." He silenced her teasing with a heated kiss. As she softened against him, he released the band holding her hair back. It drifted over his arm.

She followed his lips as he stepped backward toward the bed she would use alone no longer. Compliantly, she climbed the step stool by the side of the high, old-fashioned tester. The mattress welcomed her as she held her arms out to him. When she embraced only empty air, she sat and asked in a confused voice, "Ian?"

"One moment."

Her head swiveled as she realized he stood behind her. Lost in the bemusement of his kisses, she had not known he had crossed to the other side of the room. Impatiently, she sat on the covers. Each movement she made brought the slick sound of silk to her ears.

Hands on her shoulders pressed her back into the mound of pillows. She gasped in unfettered longing as his tongue delved the shadows in the valley between her breasts. Her fingers curled around his head to hold him closer as she breathed in his musky scent. She smiled when her hands swept along his bare back.

The filmy trousers clung to her as he touched the firm length of her legs. Her breath accelerated when he found the sensitive skin along the embroidered girdle. With a laugh, he undid her slippers and tossed them to the floor. He reached for the hooks on the short jacket.

An involuntary gasp escaped his lips as he slid the sleeveless vest from her to see the beaded band outlining her breasts. She stroked his warm chest as he traced the pattern of the strange garment. Her eyes closed, and she clutched his arms as he caressed the curved surface of her skin. When he teased her with rapid kisses, she was sure her bones had melted in the fire of her yearning.

Suddenly, he gave a deep groan of impatience. His eager fingers rapidly drew the bits of material from her. As perfectly as she had brought his fantasy to life, he wanted to love the real woman beneath the harem costume. When he heard her sigh of satisfaction as he leaned her back into the bed once more, he felt a rocket bright flash spiraling through him.

Giving herself over to the passions ruling her, she swayed with their glory. Soon she was touching the many textures of his body. Then she became the heated moistness of her lips as he worshipped them with his mouth. Each bit of her he touched glowed to life with the power of a summer storm. The thunder of her rapid heartbeat in her ears accented the bursts of heat deep within her.

She closed her arms around him as they sought their pleasure together. Into her mouth came the sharp pulse of his breath, urging her to share this uncontainable rapture. It took her as its willing captive and imprisoned her in its unimaginable delights. Only when the power of the ecstasy became unbearably sweet did the walls collapse to cascade around them in the perfect harmony of love.

Chapter Twenty

Mariel's smile widened as Ian stepped into the bedroom of their hotel suite. She had been listening for the sound of his footsteps since he had left to check the departure time of their cross-Channel ship in the morning. Going to him, she put her arms around the trim body she had come to know so well. "Is everything all set, darling?"

Ian did not return her embrace. Instead, he said quietly, "The manager gave me this wire when I came through the lobby. It was addressed to Mariel Beckwith-Carter."

"I like the sound of that name." When he did not reply, she asked, "What is wrong, Ian? Is it bad news?" His silence forced her to think the telegram might contain more than wedding congratulations.

He held her fingers as he opened the page with his other hand. "'Lady Mariel,'" he read. "'Lord Foxbridge has had a carriage accident. Dr. Sawyer wants you to return immediately. Wire arrival time.'" It was signed with Miss Phipps's name.

"Oh, no, Ian!" she cried as her fingers clenched on his arm. "Can we get a train to Foxbridge from here today?"

He hesitated before he spoke. After rereading the wire, he asked, "Are you sure you want to take the train? We could rent a carriage."

"Whatever! Just get us home as soon as possible, Ian."

He pressed her to his chest. Her tears spotted his lawn shirt. As he comforted her, he cursed inwardly. Each time Mariel grasped for happiness, it was snatched away from her. She should not have to endure anything more.

"Let's go home, Mariel," he said in a subdued voice. "Pack for us while I go get tickets for the next train. If it is not until tomorrow, I will go to the livery and see about a carriage. Otherwise, the train will get us there more rapidly. I will let Miss Phipps know we are coming."

When he kissed her and went downstairs to make arrangements, Mariel opened the doors of the armoire to take out their clothes. Her fingers ran along the hangers as she visualized her uncle's loving face. To think of him suffering even a bit of the horror she had known during her accident made her blood freeze in her veins.

Mariel sat on the bed, holding her empty bag. Tears coursed along her face, and she longed to be with Uncle Wilford at that very moment. As long as she could remember, he had told her she would be his heir if anything happened to Georgie. While it was only a loving joke between them, she enjoyed it. Then her cousin had died, and now she feared the last of the Wythes would. She had no desire to accept the ownership of Foxbridge Cloister. Being Mrs. Beckwith-Carter was enough for her, especially when the alternative meant the death of her beloved uncle.

What awaited them at the Cloister? She hoped Uncle Wilford would survive the latest tragedy to befall their family.

"He must!" she whispered as she reached to take her clothes from the rack. Forcing her fears from her mind, she packed their things, so she would be ready when it was time to go to face the result of the disaster at Foxbridge Cloister.

Whatever it might be.

As Mariel stepped from the train to the platform, she took Ian's arm. Everything was wonderfully familiar. The station, the sound of the porters' voices, the odors of the locomotive. Everything was the same as when she left on her honeymoon, except for the deep fear in her stomach. The closer they had come to Foxbridge, the more she had dreaded the reality she tried to push from her mind. Uncle Wilford could not be dead.

Silently, she went with her husband down the steps. They found the carriage from Foxbridge Cloister. The carriage driver stepped forward as he saw them approaching.

"Hello, Lady Mariel, Reverend. Welcome back."

"Walter!" The welcome sound of someone from the Cloister increased her fright and comforted her at the same time. "How is my uncle?"

He glanced at the man by her side as he replied, "Lord Foxbridge is alive. He is hurt, but at least he is alive."

Ian caught Mariel as she swayed against him. He ordered the carriage door opened, then lifted her onto the green velvet cushion. Easily, he climbed in to sit next to her. Closing the door, he leaned out to say, "As quickly as possible, Walter."

"I understand." The gray-haired man regarded the weeping woman for a long moment before swinging himself up into the driver's seat. He slapped the reins on the back of the horses. A sad smile brightened his face. Lady Mariel was home where she belonged. Her presence would help the lord heal more quickly. Having Lady Mariel at the Cloister made Walter happy, too.

In the carriage, Ian tried to comfort her. He realized his words sounded foolish, but he repeated them over and over again. "Sweetheart, he is alive. You Wythes are not willing to give yourselves over to death. He will fight."

She did not reply as she fought to control the mixture of thanksgiving and rage within her. The miles did not pass quickly enough as she waited for the slow right-hand turn that would mean they were entering the gates of the Cloister.

As the carriage slowed, Ian opened the door. He could see Mariel's impatience displayed on her face. Lifting her to the ground, he took her hand to walk with her to the front door. Dodsley opened it to greet them quietly.

Mariel shook off her husband's hand as she raced up the stairs. Her gown threatened to trip her, but she ignored it, bunching it in her right hand as her left followed the wide surface of the banister.

At the doorway of the master suite, hands reached out to halt her pain-spurred flight. She recognized the touch instantly. "Phipps?"

"He is awake, Lady Mariel. He wants to see you, but you must be quiet. Do not upset him."

She nodded, willing to promise anything to gain entrance to her uncle's bedroom. The fear that he would die before she could arrive home did not lessen with Phipps's words. She no longer trusted her own intuition to know if people were speaking the truth or simply being kind.

The sitting chamber seemed a mile across as she walked to his door. When she heard someone walking toward her, she gasped, "Dr. Sawyer?"

"Lady Mariel, please come in."

"How is he?"

His smile permeated his tired voice. "I will let him tell you himself."

At his words, she forgot all promises to herself and others. She ran to her uncle's bed. Her fingers slid along the satin coverlet until she reached the turned down blanket. When a hand settled on hers, she smiled through the tears dripping along her face.

"Uncle Wilford?"

"My lamb, to think I ruined your honeymoon with my foolishness." His thready voice did not resemble his normal, boisterous tones. "Can you forgive a silly old man?"

Dr. Sawyer cleared his throat before saying, "Lady Mariel, before you ask I will tell you what I can about your uncle's condition and expected recovery. He has just roused from being senseless for almost a day. If he takes care of himself, he should be fine. The concussion he suffered will keep him in bed for a few days, but other than a sprained ankle, he is fine. You Wythes must have a guardian angel to protect you from your own inclination for self-destruction."

"Now, doctor," argued the obviously impatient lord, "I told you already, I was not driving that damn carriage too fast for the road. I am not sure what happened, but one of the wheels started wobbling. Then . . ."

"Hush, Uncle." She patted his hand. "It does not matter. All that matters is that you are going to be fine. I want you to rest while I tell Ian to come in and talk to you. He is as anxious as I am to see how you are doing. We are going to keep you company until you are up and about again."

"It will be soon."

"It will be when Dr. Sawyer says you are well, Uncle." She grinned impishly. "I had to listen to his orders. Now it will be your turn."

Dr. Sawyer added, "And if you are half as good a patient as Lady Mariel, my lord, you should be out of that bed by week's end."

"Then you can have your honeymoon, my dear." He patted her slim fingers and touched the plain band which announced her marriage.

"Don't worry about that. Just get well." She smiled. "Let me get Ian before he has to fret any longer."

The two men watched as she went confidently toward the antechamber. Low enough so she would not hear him, Wilford murmured, "What a good child she is! Thank God for her."

Ian straightened. Brushing his dusty hands on his tan trousers, he sighed. Wilford was correct. A wheel had loosened. That it had not come off had probably saved his life. Despite what Lord Foxbridge asserted to everyone, no one believed he had been driving at a sedate speed. If he had, it would have been the first time in anyone's memory.

A shadow moved in one corner of the barn. He smiled as it revealed itself as Walter Collins. The handyman was carrying a box of tools and seemed surprised to see the parson in the stable.

"Good day, Reverend," he said in his guttural voice. "I hear the lord is doing much better."

"Much."

"Having Lady Mariel home is helping?"

Ian nodded. "I think so. She refuses to be browbeaten by him. No one else could make him follow the doctor's orders as she has."

"Damn shame this had to happen to the lord." He dropped his toolbox to the floor. It clattered loudly on the uneven boards, but the noise did not seem to bother him. Turning his back on the other man, he knelt to inspect the wheel.

Watching Collins's competent hands for a moment, Ian concurred silently. He wandered out of the dusky stable into the bright autumn sunshine. The metal clang of tools faded as he crossed the courtyard to the Cloister. His eyes moved along the facade of the grand house before he turned to look at the empty shell of the ruined section.

It stood as it had the first day he came here. Empty windows revealed the blue sky beyond. It saddened him to see it destroyed. He could understand a bit of the love Mariel had for her home. The labor needed to dismantle the scorched stones would be too costly. So it would stand as a silent monument to the past until it fell into itself completely.

The Wythe family name had come to an end the day Mariel married him. Centuries of lords and ladies had paraded across these lawns and had lived out their days in the shadows of the gray walls. Unless the present Lord Foxbridge remarried and had another child, which he showed no inclination of doing, the proud name would be only a memory submerged beneath the name Mariel shared with him.

Mariel woke in the night with the feeling something was wrong. It was not Uncle Wilford. He had been out of bed for several days now and was back to terrorizing the household with his decision to write the memoirs of his travels. Something was wrong, but with someone else.

Careful not to disturb Ian, she flung her robe over her shoulders. A wry grin tilted her lips as she walked across the bedroom to the door. Once, she had stumbled through her room in the night. Now, the lack of candle-light made no difference to her.

Following her unease, she went to the next room where Rosie slept. She opened the door quietly. If she was wrong, she did not want to wake the child. She prayed she had made a mistake.

When she heard the strained breathing, she knew her nebulous fears were true. She placed her fingers on Rosie's forehead. Her groping touch did not bother the child lost in a delirium. Mariel gasped in horror as she felt the swell of heat there.

No longer caring who she woke, she reached for the bellpull. Tugging on it frantically, she ran to the door and back into her own room. She stubbed her toe as she flew to the bed, but she simply hopped in an uneven step on one foot.

"Ian! Ian, wake up!" she cried as she shook his shoulder.

He turned from her to reach toward where she should have been on the bed. She grasped his arm when she realized he could see little more than she could. "Here I am. I need your help."

Taking her by the shoulders, he swung his legs awkwardly over the edge of the bed. In the dim light, he could see her fear, so vivid on her face. "Mariel, what is it?"

"Rosie! She is ill!"

"Go to her, honey. I will wake Phipps and get whatever you need."

She spun to return to the sick child. Over her shoulder, she called, "Thank you."

He pulled his trousers on and reached for his dressing robe. He knew that if Mariel had heard the rumor circulating through Foxbridge, she would be even more upset. He had not told her, for he did not want her to fear needlessly. Now it seemed his worst expecta-tions would be given life.

Dr. Sawyer had confirmed that the sickness on one of the outlying farms was smallpox. Few in the shire had been vaccinated, resisting the modern idea, which was accepted elsewhere as a common practice. If this was what Rosie suffered, it must have been spread through the school. More would take ill.

The sound of retching greeted him when he entered the child's room after knocking on Phipps's door to waken her. He paused to turn up the gaslight. As slight as the noise of the switch was, Mariel turned from where she was holding the child's head over a basin.

"Turn that off! Too much light is dangerous. Hurry!"

Instantly he complied, berating himself for such foolishness. Everyone knew a patient with smallpox should be kept in a cool, unlit room. Mariel's words told him that she had heard the same rumors he had. He felt his way through the molasses-thick darkness.

"Ian," Mariel murmured as she placed the spent child back on her pillows, "I think we should send for the doctor."

"I told Phipps to do that. My love, have you been vaccinated?"

Fighting back her fear, she nodded. "Yes, two years ago. Uncle Wilford brought back some sort of sweating sickness from his visit to Africa. The doctor insisted everyone in the Cloister be vaccinated in case it was a variation of smallpox. And you?"

"Before I went to school, and again when I entered the seminary. I assume Rosie was not."

Her voice broke as she said, "I have been battling with the orphanage board to designate money for vaccinations. They have dragged their feet, citing other needs for the funds. I should have had Rosie vaccinated as soon as she came here. I did not think of it. Ian, if—"

"Enough!" he said sharply as her voice rose in panic. "Recriminations will not help Rosie now. Send for cool water to bathe her. That will keep the fever down. We will need some boric acid solution to protect her eyes. Also eucalyptol and petroleum jelly to keep the scars to a minimum."

He left the nursing in her hands as he dealt with the fear surging through the household. All of the staff loved the little girl and feared for her life. He allowed only

Phipps and the doctor into the room. When Wilford appeared in his nightshirt, Ian asked the lord to deal with the servants. He did not want Lord Foxbridge to overexert himself before he was fully recovered.

Dr. Sawyer examined the child quickly. He sighed as he put his stethoscope back in his bag. "The epidemic is spreading, Reverend. By the morning, there will be some families needing your services."

"Damn the shortsightedness of this shire!" cursed Ian. "This could have been prevented."

"As you know so well, you can preach only so long without anyone listening. My demands for vaccinations have been seconded by Lady Mariel. Few heeded our words." The doctor closed the bag with a snap. "I will be back tomorrow to check on Rosie. Lady Mariel?"

She forced her attention from the suffering child not yet covered with the red pustules. Her hand remained holding Rosie's as she turned to face the doctor. "She is so hot!"

"I know." He pressed a small bottle into her hand. "This is opium. It will ease the delirium of the fever. Use it sparingly. It is not without dangers of its own. If you can convince her to eat, try broth or eggnog. Oysters are especially good, if she will eat them."

Dampening her chapped lips, she whispered, "Is she going to die?"

Dr. Sawyer could not speak the truth. He could tell by the way the pustules were running together on his other patients that the shire had been afflicted with confluent smallpox, far more dangerous than the ordinary form. He knew that at least half of them would not survive.

When he looked up to answer her, he felt the minister's eyes on him. He said, "There is no reason to expect that, my lady. You are caring for her well. The prognosis is good."

He picked up his bag and met Ian's eyes squarely. The parson knew he was lying. Dr. Sawyer dared him silently to denounce him. For the first time since they had met, Reverend Beckwith-Carter lowered his eyes first. Like the doctor, he wanted to protect his wife from the truth for as long as possible.

Phipps and Ian soon became as unaware of the passing of night into day and light into shadow as Mariel was, while they struggled to save the child. He was called away more and more frequently to comfort the grieving families who were losing their loved ones to the epidemic.

Mariel did not leave Rosie. Hour after hour she stood by the bed, wringing out cool cloths to put on the child's head, or bathing her in the oils to ease the discomfort of the pustules breaking out all over her. With more patience than anyone ever suspected she had, she tried to convince the ill child to drink a bit of the broth she kept warm near the fireplace.

Days passed, then a week, and still she fought her enemy. An epidemic had taken her parents from her. She did not want to lose her child.

Wet cloth. . . wring cloth. . . remove cloth from Rosie's head. . . put on damp cloth. . . wet cloth. . . the routine was neverchanging and seemingly neverending.

Many days later, Rosie asked for something to eat. She wanted to shriek with happiness, for the child had been barely coherent during the illness. This was the first positive sign that Rosie would overcome the disease within her. Gratefully, Mariel sat on the edge of the bed and spooned the thin broth into the youngster's mouth.

When Rosie fell into a healing sleep, Phipps urged Mariel to rest as well. In a voice that brooked no disagreement, she ordered her to leave the sickroom. "Come back in several hours, my lady. Just go and rest for now."

"If—"

"I will call you if there is any change. Go!"

Mariel reeled to her room. Reaching a chair, she dropped into it. She could not remember the last time she had left Rosie's room. Tonight she could believe the child might survive the disease. The offensive odor of the dried pustules remained in her senses, but to her it was the sweetest scent. That Rosie had fought the smallpox to this point meant she had an increasingly strong chance of total recovery.

Others were not so lucky. Although Ian tried to hide from her the distress of his task of burying the victims

of the epidemic, she sensed his horror. To speak a
funeral service over even one youngster was a chore no
man wished to do. When the number of corpses increased each day, many of them being children, he
walked about the Cloister in a dull haze, trying to deal
with his pain.

Surging to her feet, Mariel wondered when she had
kissed her husband last. In the days of fighting for
Rosie's life, such little reminders of the love underlying
their struggle had been shunted aside. She realized how
much she needed his calm strength.

She had taken only a few steps when she bumped
into someone. Recognition was instantaneous. "Ian!" she
cried.

"Mariel, my love," he whispered as he brought her
into his embrace. He leaned her head against his
shoulder. Without moving or saying anything, he simply
held her as she had wanted so badly.

Tears of fatigue escaped her eyes, but she did not
wipe them away. She did not want to do anything to
disrupt this precious moment of silent communion.
When he started to step away, she gasped and tightened
her arms around him.

"I must go," he said regretfully. "The Lyndell family
sent a message for me."

She moaned, "Not Tip."

"This morning. I did not mention anything to you,
because I was afraid Rosie would overhear. How is
she?" He asked the question tentatively, for he feared
the answer.

"Better."

"Better?" he repeated, unable to believe such good
news. All he had seen in the last week was tragedy. It
seemed as if there could be nothing but death in the
shire. "Tell her I will come to see her as soon as I can."

"She understands. She knows you want to be with
her." She stroked his hand, which held her own. "Do
you think you could be home in time for supper?"

"Yes, but I will have to go out again afterward. I
will try to be home, my love." He paused as he was
leaving. He took her into his arms and kissed her
lingeringly. "I love you, Mariel. I know I haven't had

time to say it lately, but my love for you has only grown deeper with the passage of each day."

"I love you." She asked softly, "When was the last time you slept, Ian?"

"What day is it?" he asked with no humor.

"Wednesday."

"It's been three days, then." He tilted her chin to bring her lips near his. "Don't worry, my love. Once this is past, I will be sure to spend plenty of time in bed. . . with my beloved wife."

Her laughter sounded odd in her own ears. It had been so long since she had heard such amusement. She listened to his steps fading in the distance. As long as she had his love, she was sure nothing could be too horrible to survive.

Mariel hoped the button would be straight when she finished sewing it onto Rosie's dress. She listened to Phipps's comforting voice reading a fairy tale to the child propped among well-plumped pillows. The aroma of freshly squeezed orange juice wafted through the room, washing away the odors of sickness.

When she heard a jovial laugh by the door, and the answering giggle from the child, she knew Uncle Wilford was paying his daily call to the sickroom. He would have come more often if Mariel had allowed it. His antics to amuse Rosie tired her too quickly.

"Ten minutes, Uncle," she stated as she did each day.

His hand ruffled her tidy hair. "You are a dictator, lamb. It causes me to believe all the tales of your terrorizing the meetings of the school board for the past year."

"They are all true," she said with a wicked grin.

"I should not have doubted it. You are just like your grandmother. Mother never allowed anyone to tell her nay."

Mariel rose and stretched cramped muscles. "I am going to get some fresh air. Ten minutes, Uncle. Phipps has my orders to eject you if you do not cooperate."

He grinned at the slight woman holding the children's book. Phipps looked as if she could probably lift nothing heavier than the feather on the nightstand, but he knew she would be as exasperating as his niece on this issue. He had no intention of doing anything to endanger the child, but he let them enjoy giving him orders.

Mariel left the sounds of happy voices behind her as she walked to the front stairs. The lure of the world beyond the house led her outside. She shivered in the crisp air, but did not return to the house for a cloak. The tang of the sea breeze awoke and focused her senses, which had been drifting during the worst week of the disease.

Wandering aimlessly, she ran her fingers along the wall of the garden. It guided her toward the old Cloister. When she knew she stood opposite the once proud building, she crossed the path and reached for that wall. Remembering where she had tripped over fallen rocks in the past, she followed it carefully for a distance.

She smiled when she sat on the huge boulder, warmed by the sun. Drawing her feet up beneath her, she reveled in her joy. For days, she had been afraid to hope Rosie was getting well. Despite Dr. Sawyer's continually optimistic words, she had been aware how many had succumbed to the epidemic in the village.

"Thank you," she whispered into the heat of the sun. She knew the sky would be the startling blue seen only on the crispest days of the fall. The leaves crunching beneath her feet when she walked must be gold and russet and orange.

Leaning back against the wall, she did not add anything to her heartfelt gratitude. Her anger was gone. For so many years she had ranted against whatever powerful force had taken her parents from her before she could know them and had forced her to watch her beloved cousin slay her twin sister before her eyes. At some unknown time, the fury had died and the memories muted. It had dissolved so gradually, she could not remember when it had happened. She suspected Ian's love had enabled her to face the truth, which she had tried to hide in her heart to fester year after year.

The faint rustle of grass caught her attention. She sat up expectantly. "Ian?" she asked.

When she received no answer, she frowned. Everyone at the Cloister had learned to announce themselves when they came near. Again the sound came. She turned her face instinctively in the direction of the barely audible noise. Two rocks clicked against each other. She jumped in surprise.

"Hello? Who is it?" No answer enabled her to guess who skulked nearby. "Is there a problem? Hello?"

Her ears strained for the smallest noise, but there was nothing. Rising, she felt a sensation of eyes upon her. In the past few days, she had felt it too often. Her demand for the person to announce his or her identity had brought no response. She knew someone was close to her. Her ears caught the sound of steady breathing. Whoever watched her knew that she could not guess who was there if the spy remained silent.

Fear dripped like cold beads of ice water along her spine. The feeling of being invaded by something filthy urged her to flee back to the inhabited regions of the Cloister. Only her stubborn refusal to bow before the games of this sadist halted her.

How long the stalemate might have continued she would never know. From across the lawn, she heard her uncle's voice as he called to her.

"Here I am!" she answered. She was not surprised to hear the rabbit-quick scurrying of the person through the high screen of grass. The one who watched her did not want to be seen by anyone.

Her wool cloak was placed on her shoulders. Wilford said lightly, "You will note that you have been out here exactly ten minutes. Perhaps tomorrow you will allow me fifteen minutes with Rosie."

Putting her concerns about the silent spy from her mind, she smiled. "You love Rosie, don't you?"

He laughed. "How could I help it? She reminds me so much of you when you were that age. The only difference is she is blonde. I remember playing with you and . . ."

"Uncle Wilford, don't," she pleaded when his voice faded into sorrow. She placed loving fingers on his arm. "It was over so long ago. Don't be sad any longer."

He drew her hood over her head as he had when she was Rosie's size. With his arm around her shoulders, he steered her across the garden. The scouring sea breeze blew powerfully into their faces.

"I don't know if I can ever put it behind me, Mariel," he said with sudden seriousness. "Each time I return to Foxbridge Cloister, I see, as if it was happening again, the night when Georgie finally lost control."

"It was not your fault."

"No? If I had done as everyone suggested, he would have been in that asylum years before. Then Lorraine would be alive."

She sighed. "But he was not sick most of the time. Most of the time he was my dearest friend."

In surprise, he asked, "Dearer than your sister?"

"One should not speak ill of the dead," she said with a sad smile, "but Lorraine and I did not often see eye to eye. The fate of most siblings, I suppose."

"I suppose."

Stopping, she put her hands on his arms and turned him to face her. "Uncle Wilford, you should know that what happened that night was not totally Georgie's fault. Lorraine was cruel to him, so cruel sometimes it made me cry. Oh, I know she never acted that way when an adult was nearby, but she taunted Georgie horribly. She told me so often that he was a blight on the Wythes and should be destroyed like a mad dog. More than once, she said that when Georgie could overhear her." When she felt the quiver of his strong emotions through her sensitive fingers, she said, "I'm sorry, I should not have said that."

He bent and kissed her cheek. "Mariel, you love too well. For more than a decade, you have protected your dead sister from my wrath. And what is more, you guarded her demented cousin from the harsh world by welcoming him into your childish one. Thank you for telling me this. It is many years in the past, as you said, but it comforts me to know that my son was loved."

"Always."

She could not see the dampness on his cheeks as he turned her toward the house. They walked silently, lost in their remembrances of the past and disregarding the threat to their future, which stalked them as steadily as the sun moving in its exorable path across the sky.

Chapter Twenty-One

Slowly, the epidemic passed. Although many still suffered and died, fewer new cases appeared. Once Rosie was well enough to sit in the solarium to be entertained by her great-uncle, Mariel spent more time helping the others of the community. Each day she was driven out to the orphanage with supplies and medicine. She knew how desolate Mrs. Parnell was with the number of sick children there. Never did she mention why Dr. Sawyer submitted no bill to the board of directors. Only Mariel knew that Lord Foxbridge was paying for those services, to enable the orphans to receive the same care his darling Rosie had.

With her days so busy, Mariel had little time for relaxation. She tried to devote an hour to Rosie each morning and in the evening. The little girl was so accustomed to Mariel's full schedule, she did not complain. She simply delighted in the time they had together.

Ian was seldom able to spend any time with them. Occasionally his buggy passed Mariel's on the road to the Cloister. On more than one day, that was the only chance they had to speak before dropping wearily into bed. Several nights even those hours of sleeping in each other's arms were interrupted by an emergency call. He refused to consider his own health as he went to comfort one of his parishioners. Over and over, he told Mariel he would rest when the crisis was past.

The eerie feeling of being watched clandestinely continued to plague her. The feeling grew as each day passed. When she turned to catch the observer, no one answered her call.

She still did not mention her uneasiness to Ian as the fourth week anniversary of the smallpox epidemic passed without notice. That night, she sat in a bedroom chair, waiting for him to come home, exhausted. He started to refuse to eat, but she insisted on ordering a tray while he bathed.

Knocking on the door of the bathroom, she asked, "May I come in, Ian?"

"Of course, my love." His voice sounded fatigued.

She sat on the edge of the high tub and massaged his tired muscles while he relaxed. The slippery feeling of his wet skin beneath her fingers enticed her to lean forward and place teasing kisses on his ear.

"Mmm. . . that is wonderful." He turned so his mouth was directly below hers. "Do you want to join me, Mariel?"

With a laugh, she kissed him lightly. "Offer me that invitation some night when you want to do something other than sleep." She dipped her hand into the warm water and dribbled it over his head.

Wet hands gripped her arms and brought her to lean precariously over the edge of the tub. She squealed in shock. "Ian! Don't! I am fully dressed."

"I can see that. Why don't you take off those things, and I will show you exactly how much I want to do something other than sleep with you?" He laughed before he drew her closer to kiss her with the passion they had been able to share so seldom during the crisis.

"First, you take your bath. After you eat a good meal, we shall see if you feel the same." Standing, she straightened her clothes, marked with wet handprints. "If you fall asleep, as you have lately each night—"

"Wake me up with your kisses," he finished as he took her fingers and teased them with the tip of his tongue.

"You are impossible," she scolded with a chuckle.

"Do you want me to change?"

She shook her head. "Never. Oh, there is your tray. Hurry and rinse off. I ordered enough for two."

They continued with their light jesting while he ate. She nibbled on some carrot sticks and a slice of the luscious Smithfield ham they had had for dinner. When they were finished, she volunteered to take the tray back to the kitchen.

"Let me, Mariel," he said as he rose. "I have been away from the Cloister so much, I think I need to reacquaint myself with the hallways." He stroked her hair tenderly. "Why don't you get ready for bed?"

"My harem costume?" she teased.

Bending, he kissed her on the nose. "Keep that thought, my love. I will be back in just a moment."

Mariel curled up in the chair and leaned her head against its back while she listened to his footsteps, accented by the beat of his cane. Happiness. This must be happiness. A contentment so rich she could not imagine wanting more. Her loving husband, a sweet child, an adoring uncle, and the others around her who made her life important.

Rising, she went to the cupboard. She withdrew her favorite nightgown. The heavy lace at its deep neckline did not detract from the soft clinging of the material. What she enjoyed most about it was the sensuous caress of the fabric when Ian's hand moved in heated circles across it.

Without haste, she changed into it. Even if Ian hurried, it would take him five minutes to go to the kitchen and back. She was sure Mrs. Puhle would delay him by asking for the latest news.

She sat at her dressing table. Although the mirror in front of her was useless to her now, she never changed the habit of brushing her hair here each night. Suddenly, the feeling of the eyes piercing her back returned.

"Who is it?" she cried. A door creaked, and she knew it was not her imagination. Lifting her heavy silver hairbrush, she rose and stepped away from the table.

In the silent room, she could hear her fear-heightened heartbeat and the steady rhythm of the intruder's breath. A trinket dropped from a table behind her. She whirled, wondering if there was more than one stranger

n her room. A heavy arm went around her neck. She
tried to scream, but it was impossible. The arm squeezed until her clawing fingers dropped to her side.

Mariel moaned. She coughed as she put her hands
to her tender throat. Leaning against the damp stone
wall, she waited until the paroxysm passed. When she
could stand with wobbly knees, she slid her hand along
the wall to find a clue to tell her where she was. That
she had been imprisoned somewhere she did not doubt.
Her attacker had rendered her senseless with quick
precision. If he had wanted her dead, she would be.
Obviously, he had some other use for her.

Counting her steps, it did not take her long to
discover her prison was four paces long on two sides and
eight on the other two. Nothing interrupted her journey
along the stone wall. She discovered neither door nor
window. Her attempts to touch the ceiling proved futile.
There was a ceiling over her head, for the air moved
stagnantly in the room, but she could not reach it. The
floor beneath her sloped gently toward a metal grill
plate less than five inches square.

Although she knew the dimensions of her prison,
she had no idea where she was. As unpopulated as the
Cloister was, her abductor could have entered and left
with little difficulty.

Cold bit into her bare toes, and she shivered. She
was somewhere outside the Cloister. Exactly where, was
something she could not guess. If she had some idea of
how long she had been unconscious, she would be able
to narrow the list of possibilities to within a certain
radius from the Cloister.

Panic teased her to submit to it. Mariel knew how
easy it would be to allow the hysterical tears to fall, but
she feared they would never stop. Someone aimed to
hurt her, or one of those closest to her, by abducting
her. She feared the worst awaited her in the invisible
shadows of the future.

Trying to stay warm, she paced the narrow width of
her cell. Her feet ached with the cold. Her shoulders
cramped with the fear she refused to acknowledge. She
made and rejected several plans of escape. All of them

were useless until she learned where she was. She could
not guess who wanted her here.

A half-forgotten conversation blared in her memory
After the fire, Ian had asked her if she had any enemies
Jokingly, she had named the school board, for she could
think of no one who hated her enough to destroy her
home. They had not spoken of it again. As they had
become enraptured by the love they found, and caught
up in the events of their lives, the fire in the old Cloister
lost its importance.

She wondered if she had been foolish to push aside
what she considered only an accident. In her opinion
the fire had been started by two lovers trysting in the
Cloister. It had been a common practice. A candle left
burning could have ignited the building, and the culprit
would not have dared to come forth and admit to illicit
love and igniting the Cloister.

Perhaps she had been as wrong about that as she
was about having no enemies. Someone had taken her
from her rooms to bring her to this place. Over and
over, her mind demanded to know why. It was some
thing she could not answer.

Her thoughts were interrupted by a scratching
sound. She wrapped her arms around herself and backed
against the wall. Fear eclipsed all her thoughts as she
prepared to come face-to-face with the one who wanted
her here.

Straining, she fought to hear other sounds or to
discern clues that would allow her to know where her
captor stood. All she could hear were the reluctant
sounds of stone against stone. What it meant, she was
scared to speculate.

> "Mariel was a little lamb,
> Her hair as black as coal.
> Everywhere that Mariel went,
> Lorraine was sure to go."

The deep breathless voice repeated the rhyme again
and again. Mariel spun to face the direction where the
sound originated. She could not determine where it was
coming from until she tilted her head back. Fresh air

ourst over her face. Somehow, someone stood on the roof of her prison.

Cold, superstitious fear washed over her. Only three other persons could know the significance of that poem. Two of them were dead. When she heard maniacal male laughter resonating queerly through the small space, she struggled not to scream out her terror.

It could not be him!

It could not be!

He was dead!

Fiercely, she asserted her strong will to submerge the panic. Struggling to control her voice, she whispered, "Georgie? Georgie, is that you?"

"Mariel was a little lamb,
Her hair as black as coal.
Everywhere that Mariel went,
Lorraine was sure to go,"

was the only response.

A dull thud warned her that whoever had been on the roof had dropped to stand on the floor. He repeated the once harmless poem a final time as she fought the paralysis of fear.

Putting her hands on the slimy stones, she moved along the wall away from the speaker. "Georgie?"

Broad hands grasped her. "Lady Mariel."

This voice, so different from the husky whisper, she recognized instantly. "Thank heavens, Walter!" Sapped by her sense of relief, she stepped into his embrace and leaned against the coarse overalls he always wore. "Help me out of whatever this place is! Something is going crazy here. Someone is pretending to be my dead cousin."

When he bent to whisper in her ear, "Mariel was a little lamb," she pulled back in horror. His fingers tightened to hold her in the stone-strong prison of his arms.

"Georgie?" she whispered, in a fear that stripped her mind of all thought. She could not bring herself to ask how he could be here alive when she had seen him buried in the cemetery behind the Cloister.

"You were always the smartest one, Mariel." His voice held the same childish petulance she recalled although it was far deeper. "I thought you would guess Walter was Georgie."

"It has been so long since I saw you," she said cautiously. She did not know what to say, as he leapt from one persona to the other. If she spoke to Georgie, Walter might answer, or someone else entirely. "I was just a child when we played together."

"Smart Mariel." His heavy hand patted her head as he had so often. "Pretty and kind, even to your mad cousin Georgie."

"You—you were—you are my friend." She fell back on long-forgotten skills of dealing with the volatile man.

"Not like Lorraine."

"Not like Lorraine," she agreed quickly.

He snarled, "She said bad things about Georgie. She would do naughty things and tattle on Georgie. Then Georgie would be locked in his room. He would be tied to his bed. No one would talk to him, not even Mariel."

"They would not let me." She recalled that final year, before her twin was killed and Georgie banished to the asylum. More than once, he had tried to tell her what he was saying now. Like everyone else, she had not listened, for his distortions of the truth twisted all his words.

"She is gone." Pride resounded in his voice. She knew he had used his intelligence to fool his keepers at the asylum that he was recovering. He had no regret for the murder.

"Yes, Georgie, she is gone." Mariel moved slightly. His hands readjusted on her arms, but not so tightly. She kept her face from showing her hope. Georgie had been her friend. If she could help him remember that, she might be able to escape before his ungovernable rage erupted.

"She wanted to hurt my Mariel. She and the voices."

"They can't hurt me. Lorraine is gone, and I know you will keep the voices from me, Georgie."

Instantly, she realized she had said the wrong thing. His fingers bit into her arms. When he shoved her against the wall, she cried in involuntary pain.

"I tried, Mariel, but you fought me when I brought you to the attic to hide you from the voices. You screamed. You called the others. They hurt me. Then you said it."

She did not have to ask what he meant. As clearly as if it was happening now, she could see the scene from sixteen years before, when Georgie had lurched toward her across the attic floor. Her feet had been frozen to the floor, although Phipps tried to urge her to flee. Frightened, desperate to repay him for killing her sister before her eyes, she had taunted him with the childish poem Lorraine used.

"I'm sorry," she whispered. "I have always been sorry I said that. I was angry. You get angry, Georgie. You know how easy it is to say or do something you feel bad about later."

"No!" he screeched.

Cowering away from him, Mariel knew she could not guess how he would react to anything she said. One moment he adored her as he had when they played together as children, although he was physically nearly ten years older than her. The next moment he did not hide that he despised her.

When his hand settled on her cheek, she flinched. It slid to rest on the crook between her neck and shoulder. As his fingers spread out around her vulnerable throat, she froze against the wall. He had killed Lorraine by breaking her neck with his bare hands.

With a sob, he dropped his hands. He stepped back from her. "I don't want to kill my Mariel!" he cried. Listening to the voices torturing him, he shouted, "Not my Mariel! She always loved me." He fell to his knees before her and hid his face in her ripped nightgown. "Help me, Mariel!"

"Go away!" she ordered to the ones existing only in his head. "Leave Georgie alone. He is a good man. He does not want to do the things you say any longer." She placed her hands gently on his shoulders. "Tell them," she urged.

He shook his head. "No, Mariel. If I talk to them, they will make me do something horrible." He clamped his hands over his ears. "No! I will not listen to you."

"Georgie, Georgie," she crooned, knowing he did not speak to her. "Don't let them control you. You have done nothing horrid in all the time you have been home. You can best them."

When she heard the vicious sound of deranged laughter, she knew she had lost him again to the demons within him. He leapt to his feet to pin her to the wall. His voice had regained its taunting, strangely sane tone.

"Nothing? Nothing successful, you mean. All the years we were caged in that place, we thought about what we would do to the one who sent us there."

"Georgie, I—"

He paid no attention to her. "We pretended as they wanted us to. When we finally convinced them we were well, they did not watch us so closely. Setting fire to our prison was not hard. How we laughed when they sent another to be buried at the Cloister. They could not tell Lord Foxbridge they could not find his heir in the ashes. We watched. We hid. Then we came back to Foxbridge Cloister. It did not burn as well as our prison. It still stands."

While he continued with his tale, Mariel listened in growing horror. More than his use of the plural in talking about his actions, what he said nauseated her. Wrapped up in her busy life and her growing love for Ian, she had not suspected the kindly handyman of drugging the wine the day of their picnic. His hope that she would drown was stymied by the chance that she walked with Ian to the cave above the water level.

"No!" she screamed when he spoke of his second attempt to murder her. It had been so simple, and his involvement, in retrospect, was painfully obvious. That the brakes and the steering both failed simultaneously should have alerted them immediately to tampering. The electric car should not have exploded. Only his plot to kill her explained such improbable events.

"You did not die. We knew we had to try again, but you went away to London. We bided our time. We knew you would come back to the Cloister. Always so busy you were. Then you went away. We thought you were gone forever." His brow furrowed as he said reflectively, "Mariel cannot go away forever. We must make her pay.

for sending us to that prison. Arranging the accident for
Father hurt us, but we had to have you in the Cloister.
You had to come back. Now you have."

"Georgie, listen to me. Send the others away."

"No!" he cried. She did not know if it was to her or
the voices within him.

She moaned as he gripped her face tightly in his
long fingers. Muttering some incoherent threats, he
shoved her to the ground. Before she could scramble to
her feet, she heard him climbing out of whatever this
place was.

"Georgie!" she cried. "Don't leave me here, Georgie!"

His taunting voice repeated the rhyme she had
never forgotten.

"Georgie Porgie, Pudding and Pie
Kissed the girls and made them cry.
When the boys came out to play,
Georgie Porgie ran away."

His laughter surrounded her like a torturing curse.
"Cry, Mariel, cry. I will be back before the boys come
out to play."

"Georgie! Wait!"

The crash of some heavy article over her head told
her he had enclosed her in this unknown prison again.
She sagged against the wall. What he had planned, she
could not guess. In his madness he was capable of
anything.

Cradling her face in her scratched hands, she
moaned, "Ian, oh, Ian, I love you. Don't forget that.
Don't let Rosie forget me, please." She slid to the stone
floor to weep out the sorrow she could keep within her
no longer. Only a short time ago, she had been delighting in the joys of her life. Soon, those would be gone.

Again she struggled to escape from her fear. She
could not let it control her. She needed every bit of her
intelligence to best her cousin. That he was quick-witted
made him more dangerous. His complicated plot warned
her he had a diabolical death planned for her. She could
not wait meekly.

Calculating swiftly, she walked to the wall where she had heard him climbing from this hole. A smile creased her face as she felt the handholds in the wall. She had missed them earlier, for she had not been thinking to look for such. Foolishly, she had expected to find a door, hidden somewhere among the stones.

Carefully, she fit her toes and fingers into the lowest holes. They were spaced quite far apart, but she could manage. It surprised her how evenly placed they were. They were not there by chance.

Suddenly, she knew where Georgie must have put her. This must be one of the dry cisterns scattered around the property. All during her childhood, they were warned to stay away from them. That admonition made them only more determined to explore them. They had found five or six.

A curse escaped from her lips as she bumped her head against the ceiling. With caution, she explored the uneven surface of the stone. As she felt its breadth, she knew she could not shove it aside from this precarious perch. Hope drained from her, leaving her weak.

Slowly she lowered herself back to the floor. She had no choice but to wait for Georgie to return. He would. That she did not doubt. It was not part of his madness to leave her to starve in this well.

She needed a weapon. Sweeping the floor of the cistern, she sought something, anything, to use to help herself. When her fingers closed on a slab of the mortar which had dislodged from the wall, she smiled. It was nearly a foot long. She could use it to knock her cousin senseless without injuring him too badly. The thought of killing Georgie did not come into her calculations. She could not forget the bonds of love, forged from her earliest memories.

With her plan formed, all that she could do was wait. . . and wait . . . and wait. The minutes passed with accursed slowness. She had no idea if it had been hours she had been waiting or if fear simply slowed time.

When she heard a sound, she froze against the wall. Overhead, the rock moved reluctantly. Mariel remained poised in the shadows. She would have only one chance. As strong as Georgie was, he could kill her easily barehanded. She could not think of that now. She had to think solely of what she had to do.

A chill seared along her spine as she heard the cruel sound of the childish rhyme she once had loved. Uncle Wilford had invented it for her one night. Although he had forgotten it, the children had not. The poem gave Lorraine the idea of using another rhyme to torment Georgie.

Again she heard the thump of his feet as Georgie landed on the floor. "Where are you, Mariel? We want to see you."

His words warned her of his continued dementia and steeled her to do what she must. Hoping it was night, she slithered along the clammy wall. He kept talking, allowing her to narrow her search for him. She prayed for luck as she raised the slab.

The concussion of the blow raced along her arms. She dropped her weapon as she heard him fall to the floor. His moans of pain told her she had not succeeded in knocking him senseless. She must flee.

A hand grasped her ankle. Viciously, she stepped on his arm. Another screech ripped through the night. Although the sound of his suffering ached within her, she did not pause. Only by saving herself could she help her cousin.

Following the handholds up the wall, she left skin and bits of material in her wake. She did not pause to worry about such small pain. If she did not escape, Georgie would kill her.

She teetered on the edge of the hole. One attempt at shoving the monstrous stone over it told her how futile that was. She must find help. The sound of movement below her sent her running away from the hole.

Immediately, she tripped over an obstacle and crashed to the ground. Tears fell along her cheeks, but she ignored them as she rose on her ravaged knees. Pulling cinders from her palms, she realized where she was. Georgie had brought her only as far as the burned section of the old Cloister. Although she had feared the cistern was one beyond the stables, she should have guessed. This was his world. This was where he would do the bidding of his voices.

The scent of the dew swept over her. Dew unwarmed by the dawn meant darkness. It must still be night. Hope swelled in her. She might be able to elude him until the morning brought assistance from those who would be searching for her.

She scrambled over broken beams and walls, which had fallen when the roof tumbled into the fire. If only she knew where she was among the cells. They twisted in a serpentine path along the hillside. She had to find her way out and back to the main section of the house.

Forcing her groan of pain to remain unuttered, she backed away from whatever her shin had encountered. Georgie would be nearly as unable to see as she was. She tried to remember if anyone had said anything about the moon being bright last night. Nothing came into her reeling head.

Dust rose to clog her senses. Thick with ash, it reeked of the long-dead fire and the dampness which had soaked into it.

A wall halted her. She put her hands up to search among the rocks for a way out of this maze. Blood ran along her fingers as she desperately explored the stone. There must be another way. To go backward would mean her death. She could hear footsteps behind her, hesitant as they navigated the piles of stone.

When hands grabbed her, she screamed and cowered away in mindless terror. She was pulled against a night cooled shirt as arms went around her to comfort her in an aura of familiar cologne. Instantly, she raised her head as she whispered in disbelief, "Ian?"

"Mariel, what are you doing out here? We have been searching all over the Cloister for you." He kissed her lightly. "I thought you would be waiting for me when I came back to our room. Why did you leave for a walk now?"

"It wasn't my choice. Georgie abducted me from our room."

"Georgie?" Bafflement colored his voice, and she sensed his gaze roving over her to be sure she was unharmed. He was sure to see immediately the blood and rips on her ruined nightgown. "Why are you out in this dangerous area? Because of a dead man?"

"He's not dead! He is Walter Collins! He fixed the automobile to malfunction. He wants to kill me."

He shook her gently. "Honey, you are hysterical."

Viciously, she stated, "I have a right to be! Ian, if we don't—" She paused as she heard the soft crunch of two rocks against each other. "Ian, behind you!" she shrieked.

He whirled as a dark form leapt from the shadows. Ignoring Mariel's scream as he went down before his attacker, he twisted from beneath the man. He reached for his cane which had flown from his fingers. The other man jumped toward him again. With a victorious laugh, Georgie kicked the ivory-handled staff away. His other foot settled in the center of the auburn-haired man's stomach.

Ian gazed up into a face twisted by madness. In the moonlight, he could see the bloodshot eyes of the Cloister's mechanic. He did not move as he waited to see what Collins would do. Not Collins, he corrected himself mentally. Gregory "Georgie" Wythe, heir to the title of Lord Foxbridge.

"You hurt our Mariel," whined the man staring down at him. "Naughty man for hurting our Mariel."

"I have never hurt Mariel," he said carefully.

"We heard her. She said she hates you and never wants to see you again."

Ian did not dare to pull his eyes from Wythe's as he heard Mariel's gasp of horror. That loud disagreement had been months ago, during her recuperation, but this sick man had lost track of time. He remembered only what fit in with his distorted view of the world. He did not recall that since the argument, Mariel had announced her love for Ian before all the witnesses at their wedding.

Gauging the man's actions, Ian slowly lifted his hands. He held Wythe's eyes as he listened to his senseless ranting. With a sudden shout, he grasped the ankle of the boot in his stomach. Exerting all his strength, he twisted the leg at an impossible angle. Georgie went careening to the ground. Ian grasped the cane and clambered awkwardly to his feet. He did not curse his

leg as he raised the staff and brought it down on the
other man's head. Georgie moaned once and was silent.

Ian bent and placed his fingers against the man's
throat. The pulse was strong, but slow. He smiled with
satisfaction. Cousin Georgie would sleep until he could
be collected and returned to safekeeping.

When he heard Mariel cry, "Ian? Ian, are you
alive?" he walked away from the motionless man.

"I am fine," he murmured as he drew her into his
arms. Her tear-streaked face dampened his shirt. "A
few bruises and a ripped coat, but other than that, I am
fine. Let me take you back to the house. We can send
someone down here to take Georgie back where he
belongs."

She nodded, too fatigued to feel anything but relief.
Following Ian's instructions, she walked around the
many obstacles, which had daunted her on her flight
through the cells. She was surprised how quickly they
emerged from the burned structure to the fresh wetness
of the gardens. The cool night breeze evaporated the
tears on her face, leaving her skin tight.

Answering his questions, she felt his fingers tighten
on her shoulder. His anger at her cousin was lessened
only because of his pity for the man. When he paused
and turned her to look at him, she knew he was examining her for the signs of Georgie's abuse.

"I am fine, Ian," she whispered. "He did not want
to hurt me. That is what saved me. The part of him that
is still Georgie loves me."

He touched her bruised cheek. "The part of him
that is not certainly had no compunctions about hitting
you. Until we know he is secure, I think you should
leave the Cloister, Mariel."

"Leave? Where would I go?"

"Take Rosie to London. Stay with my mother.
Just—"

Caught up in listening to her husband, Mariel did
not notice the sound of sneaking footsteps immediately.
Then, with a screamed warning, she tried to flee. Ian
released her to face the madman again.

Mariel shrieked again as she heard Georgie's most insane voice rise in laughter. "Ian! Ian!" Putting out her hands, she ran to where her cousin chortled.

When she fell over something on the ground, she did not need to touch the motionless form to know it was Ian. She did not have time to check what Georgie had done to him before she was jerked mercilessly to her feet. Her head spun as she was shaken by strong hands.

"Georgie Porgie waited for the boys to come out to play," he crowed. "Georgie Porgie did not run away."

"No," she whispered. "Georgie did not run away. What did you do to him?"

"Our Mariel hates him. He hit Georgie. We hit him."

"With what?" She tried to keep her hysteria from her voice.

"Just a rock."

She moaned. Georgie's "just a rock" could have killed the man she loved. When she twisted to pull out of his arms, he surprisingly released her. As she dropped to her knees to search for Ian, she heard her cousin's most childish voice return.

"Mariel, are you angry with me?"

Salty tears burned in her eyes as she murmured, "Oh, Georgie, how could you do this?"

Fingers picked up hers and placed them on Ian. Her heart broke for her cousin who in his lucid moments loved her. As she sought along the unmoving man for where Georgie had struck him, she heard him beg her forgiveness.

"Do you love me, Mariel?"

Her hands found a damp stickiness on the back of Ian's head. Trembling fingers reached for the pulse in his neck. He must be alive. He could not die now.

"Do you love me, Mariel?"

Before she could answer, she heard a sharp detonation. In terror, she wondered if the whole world had gone mad. A heavy form dropped to pin her to Ian. She could not move or scream. For an eternity, she struggled to breathe. Then the body was pulled off her.

"Mariel, are you safe?"

"Ian? Uncle Wilford, is Ian alive?" She did not think of anything else as she reached again for the man she loved.

"Careful," came a soft warning in Ian's beloved voice. "I am alive, honey, but let me sit up. I don't need you poking those inquisitive fingers into my aching head."

She listened as her uncle helped him to his feet. Then Ian offered her his hand. "Georgie?" she asked.

"He's dead." Wilford Wythe whispered with the sorrow that had never faded, "At last that tortured soul has escaped the voices which have taunted him all his life."

Ian hushed Mariel as he watched Lord Foxbridge kneel by his son. The older man did not cry as he closed the wide eyes of the corpse.

"Take her to the house," the lord ordered.

"Uncle—"

"Now!"

Taking her by the shoulders, Ian turned her toward the Cloister. Behind them, they left the man and his son. The moonlight glinted off the rifle in Wilford's hand, the rifle he had used to kill his only child.

Epilogue

Screams echoed across the garden. Childish cries, exuding an excitement overwhelming in the summer sunshine. The noise drowned the tempo of the waves on the not distant shore.

Footsteps. Pounding feet struck dully on the soft ground beneath the luxurious carpet of grass. Coming closer. The shout changed into a shriek.

"Look out!"

Mariel ducked automatically as the whirr of a ball passed over her head. Reaching out a hand, she snared the child ready to run past to collect the toy.

"Isaac! You know you shouldn't be racing past this blanket. What if you stepped on your baby sister?"

Laughter sounded behind her. She smiled as she stated with mock anger, "Uncle Wilford, I will never teach these children any sense of responsibility if you continue to egg them on."

Bending, he picked up the ball and ruffled her neatly plaited hair. "We promise to be more careful, lamb. Come on, boy. Let me see if you can hit it farther than Rosie."

Another hand settled on her shoulder. She reached up hers to caress the strong fingers which brought her more happiness with each passing year. A rich voice stated, "He is incorrigible."

"Ian, I thought you were going to be busy all afternoon. A wedding."

"I decided not to stay for the reception." He looked down into her brilliant eyes, which rivaled the blue of the summer sky. Sitting beside her, he put his arm around her slender shoulders.

Silently, he watched the present Lord Foxbridge play cricket with his niece and the four-year-old heir to his title. His eyes dropped to the one-year-old, napping on the blanket while being guarded by faithful Muffin, whose snores were louder than the baby's soft breaths. Three children to complete their family circle.

He brought Mariel's head to rest against his shoulder. "I looked at the bride today, my love, and I thought of the day you walked along the aisle of that church to marry me. That day, I wondered if I could ever be as happy as I was when I saw you in your bridal gown. Now I know the answer."

"And?" she asked, running her hands along the front of his shirt. The firm muscles beneath her fingers had not changed with the passing of the years.

"I have learned that with you I am that happy every day. I love you, Mariel."

"Now?"

"Now?" he repeated with a laugh. "Always."

She rose and brushed grass from her light wool skirt. Holding out her hand to him, she asked, "No, I don't mean that. I mean, do you want to love me now?"

When he stood, he listened as she called to Phipps. The woman greeted him warmly, then picked up the baby in the basket. She took the child to the spot in the shade where she had been reading.

Ian took Mariel's hand as they walked toward the Cloister. The sun dappled the stones with light. As they stepped onto the heated surface of the terrace, he turned her in his arms. The kiss he pressed into her welcoming mouth was no less warm.

As if there had been no break in the conversation, he answered, "I want to love you now and forever, my love."

"As Fatima, princess of the desert?" she teased with the name that had become a private joke between them.

"As Mariel Beckwith-Carter, possessor of my heart."

They laughed as they hurried into the house and the privacy of their rooms. Behind them could be heard the joyous sounds of the cricket game being played with youthful exuberance. Wilford Wythe's shouts were as enthusiastic as the youngsters. Nowhere in the Cloister hung the shadows of one man's blind obsession to destroy a woman who wanted only to forgive him.